Copyright © 2021 Melissa Erin Jackson.

All rights reserved. This book or any portion thereof may not be reproduced or used in any manner whatsoever without the express written permission of the publisher except for the use of brief quotations in a book review.

This is a work of fiction. Names, characters, places, and incidents either are the products of the author's imagination or are used fictitiously. Any resemblance to actual persons, living or dead, businesses, companies, events, or locales is entirely coincidental.

Ebook ISBN: 978-1-7361866-2-6

Audiobook ISBN: 978-1-956335-07-1

Paperback ISBN: 978-1-956335-02-6

Front cover design by Danielle Fine at Design by Definition.

Sword and talisman drawings by Etheric Tales.

Luma map designed by Fictive Designs.

First published in 2021 by Ringtail Press.

www.melissajacksonbooks.com

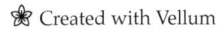

❦ Created with Vellum

DIABOLICAL SWORD

THE
CHARM
COLLECTOR

BOOK 1

MELISSA ERIN JACKSON

Ringtai
PRESS

City of Luma

Fae Lighting Design & Decor Warehouse

Industrial District

The Ghost Lily

LFL Factory

Trinity Park

Uptown

Downtown

Cabin

Tercla

WAREHOUSE DISTRICT

CALIFORNIA
Sacramento
San Francisco • Luma
Los Angeles
San Diego

Haskins's Warehouse

Kayda's Apartment

ARDMORE

Fae Clinic

Al's Burgers

Mathias's Building

MONTCLAIRE

Jo's Apothecary

Harlow's Apartment

NECROPOLIS

- Veil Obelisks
- Telepad Station
- Casino
- Visitor's Center
- Telepost Station
- Sorcerers' Collective Headquarters

CHAPTER ONE

Three buzzes sounded from the countertop. Quick, quick, slow. I snatched up Dad's pocket mirror and expectantly flipped open the lid. It would take a couple of moments for the message to form, so I grabbed the last piece of toast off my plate, nibbling on a corner of my meager dinner.

"C'mon," I muttered, my foot tapping a restless rhythm on the bottom rung of the stool I was perched on. "Give me something good ..."

Words finally materialized on the glass, like a fingertip carving letters out of steam.

WAREHOUSE DISTRICT. HASKINS. CODE 154.

I nearly choked on my toast.

I unceremoniously dumped the pocket mirror onto the counter, smooth convex bottom spinning on the faux marble, and scrambled off the stool so fast it clattered to the ground. Leaving it, I bolted across my tiny apartment to my bedroom. Off went the sweatpants and on went a rumpled—possibly dirty—pair of jeans. I swapped my pajama top for a probably clean T-shirt unearthed from under the bed. I pulled it on as I ran back into the dining room, searching for my boots. Yanking them on, I left them untied. No time for that.

A bulky, mostly empty backpack lay discarded by the door and I scooped that up, checking the front pockets to make sure I had my essentials—namely a couple of handheld fae lights, my wallet, and lock picks. Strapping it on, I darted out of my apartment, only to double back for the pocket mirror. I stuffed the remaining toast wedge in my mouth and slipped out into the hallway.

I pulled my necklace free from where it rested under my shirt and squeezed the small talisman at the end between finger and thumb. The inch-long metal pendant was flat on the back with an upraised top, like an egg cut in half. With my other hand, I pressed my thumb to the matching design on the metal where a lock would be on a mundane door. The talisman between my fingers and the mark under my thumb grew warm simultaneously. A mechanism inside the door clicked.

With the door locked, I stuffed my talisman back under my shirt and made sure Dad's mirror was tucked snugly into the pocket of my jeans. Then I was off. I ran down the dimly lit hallway before slamming the push bar on the door to the outdoor staircase that hugged the side of the ten-story complex. The summer air had a slight breeze to it, and the sky was dark save for the blue haze on the horizon. It was late, after ten, so the staircase was deserted, allowing me to take the steps two at a time and ensuring I didn't knock any unsuspecting neighbors on their asses. Again.

Being on the fourth floor meant I didn't have that far to go. My backpack flopped around, and my unbound curls whipped about my face as I went. When I reached the bottom floor, I pulled an elastic tie off my wrist and got my unruly mass of hair into a bun as I headed for the telepad station two blocks away. I needed my hair secured during transit—that was a lesson you only needed once. After it was out of my face, and my shoes were tied, I ran the rest of the way.

Even though my neighborhood of Montclaire was only a few miles outside Luma Proper, it was mostly dark and quiet around here at this hour. Luma Proper sat at the center of the city, made of uptown and downtown. Ringing Luma Proper were five districts. The Warehouse District to the north, the Industrial District to the west, the mostly residential neighborhoods of Ardmore and Montclaire to the east, and the Necropolis to the south. The five districts and Luma Proper made up the entirety of Luma as a city—all of it hidden behind a veil. Most of the lesser fae—like goblins and fauns—as well as a large population of humans lived in the neighborhood districts. Downtown and uptown swarmed with witches, shifters, draken, and griffels. Humans and lesser fae lived there, too, but in much smaller numbers.

I eyed the bluish hue that hung on the horizon again, just past the tops of high-rise brick apartment buildings. The ever-present glow of Luma Proper wasn't a welcome sight so much as a familiar one: the city that never slept, that kept its fae lights burning at all hours. The blue fae light—an even more reliable source of illumination than mundane electricity—was so bright in the heart of the city that it obscured the stars. I'd heard rumors that the mundane city of Los Angeles, about three hours south of Luma, glowed even brighter. I could neither confirm nor deny that; I'd never traveled outside of the city—never traveled outside of California.

The telepad station was the next block up. The steady stream of people heading in and out was the first sign of life I'd seen since leaving my apartment.

I pushed open the dingy glass doors of the station, the lobby bustling but the sound subdued. Fae lights were on at all hours of the day in here, unlike in the surrounding apartments and houses, but they were weak. The entire bank of lights on the leftmost side of the room was out, and a pair of maintenance witches were working on getting them back on. This station had three outgoing telepads and three incoming. An outbound one had been on the fritz for weeks. The station needed functioning telepads more than functioning lights, but the higher-ups paid the highly skilled maintenance witches and sorcerers handsomely if they lived in Luma Proper so they'd be more readily available. Folks like me, stuck on the edges of the city where things were slightly more affordable, got the short end of the stick. Better for the heart of Luma to look shiny and bright, even if the nonessential limbs where the blue-collar folks lived were starting to atrophy.

Welcome to Luma, where the lights are always on and you're always home, I muttered to myself in a robotic tone as I got into line.

On the right side of the station, where I stood, a row of people waited in front of either of the two functioning telepads. A pair of young women ahead of me wore skintight leather skirts and high heels, so they must have been out to party tonight. Everyone else was clad in uniforms, waiting for an available pad to take them to their graveyard shifts.

With a *whoosh*, the eight-foot-tall middle inbound cylinder suddenly held a weary worker, probably from a Luma restaurant, bar, casino, or club. He stood on the telepad's glowing blue base.

I slipped an arm out of one of the backpack straps and swung the bag around to my front. Rooting around in a side pocket, I found my wallet and pulled out my telepad card. The white plastic edges were rough from so much use. After getting my pack back on and giving the straps a couple of tightening tugs, I tapped the card idly on my open palm, hoping I had enough money on it to get me to the Warehouse District. There was plenty of money in my account, just not in my legal name. I didn't want to grant the Collective the ability to track my movements, thank you very much. If the telepad card had been tapped dry, I'd need either the fake ID and bank card with my false name on it, or cash—none of which were in my wallet.

"Next," the woman beside the telepad droned, waving me

forward without looking at me. All her attention was on the tablet she held in her hand. "Name."

"Deanna Kyle," I said, instead of my actual name: Harlow Fletcher.

"Where you going?"

"Warehouse District."

The woman looked up from her tablet to give me an appraising head-to-toe scan. Her nose twitched a fraction, then she tapped at her tablet. "Go ahead."

I approached the scanner, sent up a silent prayer, and swiped the card. I held my breath. A long moment later, I exhaled in a relieved rush when the light on the side of the box flipped to green.

"Have a nice trip," the woman said flatly.

I stepped into the cylinder, the air inside near freezing. There were outlines on the floor in the shape of feet, but each was twice the size of a normal human foot, just in case a draken in the area needed to use a telepad. Very few draken ever used telepads in the five smaller neighborhoods that ringed Luma Proper, as the cylinders were usually only seven to eight feet tall—their average height. The cylinders in Luma Proper were closer to fifteen feet. My best friend Kayda hated the telepads out here. They made her claustrophobic.

Even the smaller telepads were expensive, though, and needed constant maintenance from witches to reinforce the teleportation spells. Taking a ride in a pad anywhere was a risk, but even more so in the outer neighborhoods. I'd heard countless horror stories of telepads running out of fae power or the teleportation spell giving out while someone was mid-port—or both—and travelers ending up at their destination missing a limb or vital organ.

I tried not to read the details on the LAST SPELL REINFORCEMENT DATE card posted to the inside of the cylinder. If I was going to end up splattered across the streets of Luma, I'd rather be surprised.

The technician punched in the coordinates and the frigid air spun around the cylinder like a cyclone, the sound almost deafening. Just before the teleportation spell took hold, my feet felt as heavy as lead. It felt as if a giant had hold of my head, yanking it upward like it was trying to detach it from my body. For a split second, my spine was pulled so taut, I was sure my vertebrae had separated.

Just when the urge to scream bloody murder overtook me, I was somewhere else, all pain and unpleasantness gone as if they'd never existed. I blinked warily at my new surroundings beyond the telepad station. On foot, it would have taken me an hour to get from my apartment to the Warehouse District. With a telepad, it took seconds.

Though telepad travel could be dicey, it saved so much time. All forty-three magic-hub cities in the United States had telepads. I couldn't imagine how long it took to get around mundane cities. The humans there didn't know what they were missing, though. Hard for them to be jealous of our lightning-fast travel when they didn't know the hubs existed.

A pinched-faced man poked his head into the cylinder. "Move it, lady. A draken is coming through next. You wanna be squashed, or what?"

I scurried out of the pad.

The station here was three times the size of the one by my apartment—nine ports in, and nine out. The place reminded me of a massive airplane hangar: polished cement floor, impossibly high ceiling, and metal siding. Half of the ports here were as wide as they were tall—if not more—allowing large equipment like trucks and forklifts to be transported between locations in the blink of an eye. The sheer expanse of the place was intimidating, and as I headed for the imposing bay doors ahead of me, a little voice in the back of my head that sounded suspiciously like Kayda's said, *Are you sure this is a good idea?*

Good idea? Probably not. But the pay was good, and the thrill of the chase was even better.

"Get where you're headed quick, yeah?" the pinched-faced

man called after me. "Some weird shit's been going on around here lately."

I waved a hand in the air, acknowledging that I'd heard his warning. Steeling myself, I stepped out into the evening air of the Warehouse District, hoping the only weird shit I'd find was the kind I'd come looking for.

CHAPTER TWO

The Warehouse District was massive, and it was easy to get lost here—or worse. Situated on the north end of Luma, it was a confusing amalgamation of wealth and poverty, luxury and industry. Every morning, people who provided the labor that kept Luma running twenty-four-seven—like construction workers, telepad engineers, and fae light repairers and installers—piled into the same telepad station with people whose accessories cost more than the laborers' monthly salaries.

If you knew where to go, you could also find a legendary underground nightclub here—which pulled in a whole other swath of various people. The location rotated, as did the illusionary spell cast on the outside. One day it might look like an abandoned warehouse and the next like an empty lot. Even if you were sent an invite, and could find the place with the aid of a very specific talisman, you had to have the right password to get in, and it changed every few hours.

I'd only been there once with Kayda—her on the right side of buzzed, and me on the wrong one—though she hadn't realized that until later. When she'd wandered off for a minute to talk to a fellow draken giving her the sexy lizard eye, I'd stupidly accepted a drink from a stupidly hot elf. That was my only defense. I knew better than to take drinks from elves—they were the race most notorious for slipping questionable substances to humans. But, honestly, he'd been the most beautiful man I'd ever seen—aside from Felix. But I hated Felix with every fiber of my being, so he didn't count.

The drink had been laced with some elfin nonsense that made me believe I was capable of flight thanks to the nonexistent wings sprouting from my back. The elf promised me a night of pleasure I wouldn't forget, but he wanted to see my wings in action first. I was determined to prove to my beautiful elf companion that I was worthy of whatever world-rocking he was capable of, so I marched off looking for a good place to scale the wall so I could launch myself from the rafters. Kayda—being seven feet tall, strong as an ox, and smarter than me by a mile—had, thankfully, realized what was going on. Abandoning her hot lizard friend, she'd plucked me off the wall, thrown me over her shoulder, and carried me out. She told me later that I'd sobbed the whole way home, ineffectually pounding my fists on her back as I told her in no uncertain terms that she'd ruined my chance to be ravished by the most gorgeous being in existence and I would never know pleasure ever again.

Kayda let me carry on, got me home and into bed, and somehow was still my best friend. She was a saint.

Despite being nearly blackout magic-drunk, I could still picture the smug little smile on the elf's face. Elves were essentially cats in a human-like body: they possessed an utter disdain for every creature in existence and enjoyed torturing them for entertainment, yet had no actual plans for world domination since they'd rather take a nap. They were even more cat-like than the Collective's werecat guards.

A car horn blared, and I jumped. I glanced up the street where a line of taxis always waited and watched as a woman in precariously high heels slammed her fists on the yellow hood of the cab in the middle of the road. She shouted something unintelligible, her speech slurred. She'd likely just come from the club—either that or she'd done too much pre-gaming and was now drunk and lost. Something about her was off, though, and not because of the obvious. Unease tingled in the back of my skull.

"You almost hit me, you sonofabitch!" she screamed, slamming her fists on the hood again.

Stay in your car, I thought to the cabbie. *Don't provoke her.*

The cab driver, a faun from the look of him, tossed open his door and shouted at her for getting her grubby hands all over his taxi. The drunk woman insulted his hooves, while he insulted the woman's breath. She accused him of having fleas. He accused her of having crabs. On and on it went. I shook my head and pulled out my pocket mirror again. A new message was on the reflective surface now.

HASKINS APPREHENDED. BOUNTY TO FT97.

Damn, that was quick. Was that some kind of record?

It worked just fine for me, though. That meant the bounty hunters would be gone by the time I got over there. The criminal, Haskins, who had triggered Code 154 was in the custody of hunter FT97. Code 154 meant ownership of contraband.

Illegal items were my favorite kind, and they were why I was here.

I pocketed the mirror and jogged for the cab at the back of the line. I yanked open the back door and slid in. My backpack's straps bunched up by my ears since I hadn't bothered to take the bag off. The driver flinched at my arrival, startled; her attention had been focused out the window where the drunken woman and the cab driver were still in a screaming match. My bets were on the drunk lady.

"Where you headed?" the cab driver asked me, and then her dark eyes flicked to the rearview mirror. I sucked in an involuntary breath. Her eyes weren't dark as in brown irises. They were dark as in wall-to-wall black. A vampire. There weren't many of them in Luma. Before the Glitch happened around the turn of the century, vampires had already existed on Earth, dating back to the 1600s. They'd dined on the blood of humans, but they'd done so sparingly, rarely outright killing their victims.

The fae had opened the portals to Earth on purpose for years. They'd been as interested in exploration as humans here were. Humans had trekked across great stretches of land, traveled across expansive oceans, and would eventually go to the moon. The fae opened doors to other worlds. "Fae" had become a blanket term for anyone magic-touched or able to wield magic—from vampire to sorcerer to goblin—and everything in between. Perhaps the fae had wanted to observe life on a planet nearly devoid of magic.

The Glitch happened when the portal magic had gone wonky on the fae side—it had to have been their glitch, seeing as the humans here couldn't open portals. Some gateways stayed open for forty-eight hours, some for only a few, and others popped into existence long enough to let some unsuspecting fae into this world before the door closed behind it a moment later. That was how a handful of dragons had ended up on Earth: portals had opened in the sky, below the oceans, and on land. Werewolves and witches had existed on Earth before the Glitch, too. They all experienced mutations after magic unexpectedly swept across the planet.

Forty-eight hours after the event started, every portal slammed shut, marooning hundreds of fae on Earth and probably just as many humans on the fae world. The portals hadn't opened since. The fae brought magic with them, and an alternative source of warm blood for vampires. But the blood of the fae didn't sustain vampires as human blood did. The high they got off fae blood was apparently ten times as good as anything they experienced with humans. The fae blood warped the vamps, turning many into highly intelligent, feral animals.

When feral vampire attacks had gotten out of control fifty or so years ago, a pact had been made between the leaders of the magical hubs on Earth and the still-sane vampires that all humans in the hubs were protected, but humans outside were fair game. If a vampire wanted to live in Luma—or any hub, really—they had to go through an extensive vetting process to even get into the city, as the magical veils that kept unsuspecting humans out also kept out vampires.

For this cabbie to be working in Luma, it meant she'd been a feral animal who was now spayed and domesticated. She got her food out of a bag, her weekly rations supplied to her from a government-sanctioned blood bank.

"Where you headed?" she tried again.

I coughed, trying to look relaxed. How long had I been gaping? "763 Bower Street."

She punched a button on the box on her dash, numbers lighting up red. Her sleeves were rolled to her elbows, revealing a pale arm lined with two vertical lines of tattooed runes. I wondered how long it had taken the spells and words of power inked onto her skin by a sorcerer to curb her appetite. What had happened to her to make her decide to live this life instead of being surrounded by others of her kind?

Her driver's-side window was down with her bent elbow poking out into the night air. Runes decorated that arm, too. Sounds of the argument floated into the car as she pulled out onto the road and then made a U-turn. A crowd had gathered around the screaming pair.

"That's not going to end well," I muttered, turning in my seat to look out the back window.

"She's probably drunk on elfin wine. Humans get so *stupid* on elfin wine," the vampire said, her voice younger and smoother than I expected.

I tried not to be offended, mostly because she was right. "I don't think she's human—not fully, anyway."

The cabbie huffed, unconvinced. "I'm here every night picking up humans from that club. Trust me. Humans always get into trouble down here."

My attention was still on the argument happening in the middle of the street. Even though the pair grew smaller and smaller by the second as we drove away, the uneasy feeling I had continued to grow.

Just then, a burst of orange and yellow flames shot into the air behind us—as did the other cab. It gave an almighty crash as it collided with the pavement. The vibration of the blast lightly rocked me in my seat. I gave the air an instinctive sniff as if I'd be able to detect a hint of burnt goat hair. Hopefully the faun was just maimed, and not dead.

"Told you," I said, facing forward again.

It was never a good idea to piss off an elemental witch, and when you did, doubling down on your insults usually got you blown up or drowned or impaled on a building's chimney. Emotion fueled their magic. The faun had to have known that.

"How'd you know she wasn't full-blooded human?" the vampire asked, her black eyes finding mine in the rearview mirror.

I shrugged. "A hunch."

The vampire huffed again. "You humans are usually clueless. Many of you wander into the Warehouse District looking for a good time and don't come back out because you're not paying attention."

I didn't reply. It wasn't a good idea to get too caught up in a conversation with a vampire, either. From what I'd heard, though the runes covering a vamp's body tamed them, the desire for warm human blood was impossible to completely quell. All someone had to do, though, was report a vampire to the authorities, and the Collective would exile the bloodsucker. Violating the Pact was a one-way ticket out of Luma, no questions asked. It was nearly impossible for a vamp to get away with an attack, let alone a murder—the evidence was too clear-cut. Even so, if a vampire was a new arrival to Luma, their bloodlust might be impossible to ignore given the right opportunity. Their seductive charms could get them a quick intoxicating sip while giving the human a little zap of euphoria. Not even casual small talk with a newly tamed vamp was safe; if they turned on the charm, a conversation about the weather could drive a human insane with want. Then, the next thing a human knew, she was waking up in a dingy alley with a sore neck and the worst hangover of her life.

I was absolutely not speaking from experience. Nope.

I stared out the window as we drove down the stretch of road lined by high-end luxury residential buildings. It was where the high-paid workers lived—people like magical code inspectors and spell regulators. Witches, mostly. A smattering of draken lived out here too but most preferred the bustle of Luma Proper.

Within ten minutes, I was outside 763 Bower Street and my cabbie had driven off. The address was for one of the many warehouses that had given the district its name. The warehouses here either held legitimate businesses—like mechanic shops and telepad part manufacturing—or they housed legit-looking businesses that were a front for things like chop shops, off-regulation talisman crafting, and way stations for contraband goods. Haskins's proclivities wedged him into the gray area in the middle.

I knew the address because I'd dealt with Haskins before. Though he owned this warehouse and the business within, he'd started a side venture about a year ago trying to make a name for himself in the black-market scene. He was squirrelly and too aggressive, so he mostly made potential buyers nervous. What he had, though, was an eye for interesting items. Last month I heard he'd sold a griffin's egg. I had no idea where he'd gotten something that rare, assuming it wasn't a bullshit rumor he'd started himself, but if there was a chance it *was* true and that he had more, I wanted to get my hands on it.

The warehouses on Bower Street were smaller units than the ones used by the telepad and fae lighting mega-companies, but Haskins's warehouse still boasted eighty thousand square feet. On the surface, it was a legit restoration company that refurbished old slot machines and then sold them to local casinos for a nice chunk of change. I just happened to know that Haskins had *other* hobbies and that he kept his stash of illegal goods in the basement of his office.

The same night that I'd gotten drunk on elfin wine and had tried to fly, I'd bumped into Haskins. We'd been running in the same circles for long enough by then to recognize each other. I may or may not have flirted with him to get information about his source. He was a round, sweaty man with bulbous eyes, so he didn't have the best luck with human women. He'd been stoked about the attention, but since I'd been on the wrong side of buzzed even before the elfin wine, my common sense had already fled the scene. I'd only gotten the hiding place of said items out of him before I'd laid eyes on the gorgeous elf behind him. To get to the pointy-eared troublemaker, I'm pretty sure I shoved past Haskins hard enough that he'd glanced off a wall and spilled his drink. Haskins had *not* been amused.

In the months afterward, I'd swung by his warehouse to try to sweet-talk my way into his office, but he was hip to my ways and sent me packing every time. That, or he'd sic his draken bodyguards on me, who would effectively throw me out the door on my ass.

I eyed the warehouse now. The front had two metal roll-up doors in the middle, a bank of small windows that ran along the top of the building twenty feet up, and an eight-foot-tall mundane wooden door on the left side with an equally mundane lock. Pulling the picks out of my bag, I made quick work of the lock and let myself in. I held my breath as I pushed the door open.

Silence.

Haskins typically wasn't here at night, but he'd gotten his human hands on some decent protection and alarm wards for the building. I knew this because I'd set them off once. Okay, twice.

I was banking on the wards being down now, since bounty hunter FT97 wouldn't have reset them after carting Haskins off, even if FT97 knew how. And seeing how the Collective's elite team of hunters were all human, FT97 probably didn't have the skill set to know which specific wards had been used. Plus, the next step in the Code 154 protocol was to get the Collective's guards over here ASAP to collect the contraband that had gotten poor sweaty Haskins arrested.

Which meant time wasn't on my side. I had to get in and out of here before the Collective's guards found me and hauled me in, too.

I closed the door behind me. Haskins's office was straight ahead, but the path was littered with bits and pieces of slot machines, which I more or less navigated successfully in the dark. The door to the office was ajar. This door was only six feet tall, rather than the much taller one in the warehouse entrance—a subtle message from Haskins that his draken goons were welcome in the warehouse, but less so in his private office.

The room wasn't anything special: a desk in the middle, a couple of potted plants in the corners, a filing cabinet, and a bookshelf full of boring manuals. What I wanted was below the desk. I rounded the side of it and eyed the rug underneath.

I shoved the desk a few inches, grunting with the effort, and flipped back the musty-smelling rug. A trapdoor. Grinning, I grabbed hold of the embedded circular handle and pulled. I held my breath again as the door lightly creaked open. Bounty hunter FT97 would have used his or her ward-breaking talismans on the building itself, but if FT97 didn't know about the treasure trove under the warehouse, the wards might still be up here.

No flashing lights or piercing alarms tore through the still evening, and I relaxed a fraction.

The outline of a ladder materialized in the darkness as my vision adjusted. It was made of dark metal and was bolted to the side of the cement wall.

I cast a glance out the office door, waiting for any sign that someone else might be outside—another charm collector, the cops, or members of Haskins's goon squad. It was as quiet as a courier mouse.

I half slipped off my backpack and poked around in one of the front pockets. I produced one of the handheld fae lights and touched a finger to the rune on the side. A beam of weak blue light shot out. Wedging the light between my teeth, I pulled my bag back on and climbed onto the ladder, then crept below the floor.

CHAPTER THREE

After fifteen steps into the unknown, my booted foot hit cement rather than another blasted rung. Once on solid ground, I plucked the fae light from between my teeth and swung the weak blue beam to the left; cement walls surrounded me on the other three sides. The beam swept over the toes of my boots and the slight drop-off just ahead of them. As I stepped down half a foot, motion-sensor fae lights flicked on. I turned off my light and pocketed it, cautiously walking farther into the room. Thankfully, the space below Haskins's floor was not as massive as the warehouse; it was the same size as the office above me. Walking to the middle of the cement floor, I turned in a slow circle, letting out a little whistle of appreciation.

I hadn't given Haskins enough credit. Not only was his collection impressive, but he clearly appreciated his goods. More often than not when I conducted my raids, I spent too much time sifting through the criminal's belongings, trying to find items of value. Often, it seemed like these idiots didn't even know what they had. Once, I'd found a golden goblin-made crossbow bolt with fletching made of phoenix feathers ... being used as a letter opener! I'd found it sticking out of a gaudy faux-ceramic mug with "Luma City Casino" printed on it, alongside pencils, pens, and a cheap fae light, also imprinted with the casino's logo. Bits of dried adhesive had been stuck to the expertly crafted bolt's tip. I would have taken the bolt anyway, but I'd wanted to free it from its location solely out of irritation at the lowlife who hadn't treated the item with respect.

I sold it to the perfect buyer—a goblin who appreciated the item so much, he practically broke down and wept at my feet once it was in his small gray hands. Mathias had thanked me profusely for bringing a piece of his lost homeland back to him and tearfully told me, *"If you ever need anything, anything at all, please don't hesitate to ask. You're family now."* He even assured me that he'd mount it in a glass case and hang it over his mantel. His intense gratitude had lessened the sting of how poorly the previous owner had treated the item.

Haskins, much like the goblin, knew the value of what he had. As I slipped my backpack off my shoulders and dropped into a crouch on the smooth cement floor, I almost felt bad about looting the guy. But the guards would be here any minute now and they wouldn't feel a shred of guilt about cleaning Haskins out. They'd round all this up and cart it off to the Collective's supposed megavault of contraband magical items—like a teacher's drawer at school full of confiscated invisibility charms and heightened-sight talismans.

From my three years on the job and sharing intel with "colleagues," it was a so-far-unsubstantiated theory that the Sorcerers Collective took charmed items from low-level criminals so they could then turn around and sell them to high-level criminals—or allies in other magical hubs—at three times the going street rate.

I unzipped my bag on the floor and triple-checked that my charmed bags, carrying cases, and ties were still in there. They ensured I'd be able to properly wrap up the pointy bits on the weapons so they wouldn't slice through my bag and fall out during my escape. I had a witch friend downtown who maintained protective and magic-dampening spells on my bags and carrying cases in exchange for my giving her first dibs on any interesting items she might like.

Everything was in order, so I stood to full height, scanning the walls. I decided then that I was doing Haskins a favor by re-homing some of this stuff. Better with me than with the Collective, right?

Haskins's collection was well organized, all of it mounted carefully and hung from hooks wedged into pegboards. Straight ahead, hanging from chains, string, or ribbons, were talismans and other charmed trinkets, like the locking charm that hung around my neck. There were dozens of them, and even if I had all the time in the world, I wouldn't have known which spells they were infused with. Detecting specific types of magic wasn't a skill my boring ol' human self had been blessed with.

To the right and left of me were small weapons fit for goblins, pixies, and brownies—maces, flails, scourges, spears, and crossbows with their bolts. I wanted to take a few of the spears if only because they were cute. Several of them weren't any longer than my hand, from the base of my palm to the end of my middle finger. Such weapons were less cute when enchanted with magic and in the hands—albeit small ones—of a creature who knew how to use them. The idea of a gang of pixies armed with any of these things made me shudder.

Turning around, I found the larger weapons: longswords, battle-axes, cutlasses, and scimitars. These were the ones that sold the best, as they were usually infused, inlaid, and decorated with things they shouldn't be—bits of ground-up unicorn horns, the ivory of troll tusks, feathers and beaks of griffins, the spikes off a chimera's tail. It wasn't just that all these magical beasts were extremely endangered or outright extinct now—at least on Earth—but because weapons crafted with the parts of these animals tended to take on the magic of the beasts. It was little wonder that crossbow bolts with phoenix feather fletching were outlawed when, after they hit their mark, they burst into flame and incinerated whatever they hit. There had been a report from Oregon's hub that a large stretch of forest had burned down last year because one such bolt had been shot into a tree by a pair of reckless, pixie-hunting kids with terrible aim.

I went through the space methodically, snatching items off the walls based on my knowledge of the market, my best buyers' tastes—and the pretty, shiny things that called to me the most. One particularly pretty sword tugged at me, but I vowed to ignore it. When the light hit it just right, I spotted iridescent blue, purple, and green on the cutlass's hilt. My gut told me they were dragon scales. It was an exquisite piece, and I wanted it if only because it was so shiny, but not even I was stupid enough to grab a dragon sword. If Haskins ever got out of prison—and after seeing his collection, I wasn't sure that would be any time soon—I would buy him a beer and make him tell me where he got all this stuff. I'd doubted that he'd gotten his meaty paws on a griffin's egg, but now I didn't doubt it at all.

My bag was full in a minute flat. I had just strapped my awkwardly bulging pack onto my back and was heading for the exit when that familiar buzz thrummed in the base of my skull. It wasn't identical to what I'd felt when I'd spotted the drunk elemental witch earlier, but it was close. I call it my sixth sense. Just like a deer could be munching calmly on leaves one minute, and then freeze, body taut and wide ears flicking the next when it senses danger, humans on Earth had quickly adapted to detect magic after the Glitch. Dormant survival instincts had resurfaced once we were no longer at the top of the food chain.

Life was relatively safe in Luma now, but I refused to let that instinct go back into hibernation. Instead, I called on it often, strengthening it like a muscle. This sense had rarely led me astray. In fact, it had saved my ass on countless occasions. I doubled back to the large-weapon wall and eyed the selection.

My sense nudged me in the cutlass's direction. The hilt was a standard black now, not the beauty it had displayed earlier. Then suddenly, it was something more again. I eyed the colorful hilt. My fingers instinctively twitched, eager to grab it. I balled my hands into fists at my sides. *No.* No dragon swords. Weapons infused with even the smallest amount of dragon magic were the rarest and the most dangerous. The things were rumored to have minds of their own. It would be an exceedingly bad idea to take it with me, no matter what my sixth sense said. Besides, there was no room for it, *and* I didn't have a magic-dampening sheath that would fit it. A dragon sword most definitely needed to be dampened.

I turned to leave.

But I hesitated.

Was the hilt ... glowing? I squinted at it, then gazed up, eyeing the bank of fae lights above me, wondering if they were flickering like the glitchy ones in the telepad station by my apartment. No flicker.

I returned my attention to the maybe-glowing sword and I chewed on my bottom lip, gaze darting from exit to pretty sword and back again. Those stories couldn't be true, could they? Dragon swords were so rare, it was hard to believe that any of the tales were based on actual facts. I reached up and touched tentative fingers to the iridescent hilt. A lady could like something solely because it was pretty. Even if said pretty thing was potentially dangerous and better to leave behind for the shady Sorcerers Collective to deal with.

Yet, I knew just the buyer who would love the sword. Grayson would lose his mind when I told him about it.

"Please don't murder me," I muttered to the cutlass, then snatched it off the wall. The hum at the base of my skull instantly disappeared.

Shrugging, I wedged the blade into a slot between my belt and jeans, and then took off for the exit. Just as I stepped onto the small landing, the motion-powered fae lights in the room winked out, plunging me into darkness. Pulling my fae light out of my pocket, I touched the rune on the side. After a couple of sputtering flashes of weak blue light, the thing died. Of course. Shoving the dead light back into my pocket, I muttered curses to myself as I groped around in the near-total blackness. The only light came from above, where moonlight shone in through one of the small windows at the top of Haskins's office. I went as fast as I could because now my sixth sense was telling me I needed to get out of here—and fast.

My hand finally made contact with a metal rung of the ladder, and within a few seconds, I was slowly making my way up. If my boots on the ladder sounded too loud, the occasional *twang* of the cutlass smacking into the rungs as I went was deafening. I might as well have been banging a pair of pots together. *"Hey, guys! I'm down here!"* I briefly considered yanking the sword free from its spot on my hip and letting it clatter to the cement.

"Shh!" I told the sword, as if it made a racket on purpose.

I almost slipped off the ladder when the twangs stopped, even though the blade still made occasional contact with the ladder. Unease solidified in my gut like a stone. *You just snatched a sentient sword, Harlow!* said a voice in my head—a voice that sounded suspiciously like Kayda's again. It said a lot about me that my inner voice of reason was someone *else's* voice.

As I hastened my ascent, I tried not to recall the stories I'd heard about dragon swords. Apparently, one had gotten loose in a farmer's market once and had just started ... murdering people. It flew around on its own, lopping people's heads off. Werecat guards had needed to throw a metal net made of a silver and iron alloy over the thing just to get it contained. The alloy had been the material humans used in substantial quantities to aid them in killing off the dragons, so I supposed it made sense the alloy had also been used to quell the wild antics of a sword powered by dragon magic.

How did a sword get loose in a farmer's market, one might ask? Hell if I knew. That was what made it a good story, right? A heavy dose of fiction?

When I popped my head out of the hole in Haskins's floor like a thieving gopher, I peered around, listening for any sounds of the guards. My gaze flicked left and right. I hoped my senses would tell me if trouble lurked nearby. Still silent.

I scrambled the rest of the way out of the hole, closed the trapdoor, flipped the rug back over the top of it, and ran around to the front of the desk. I used my backside to press the desk back into place. With any luck, the guards wouldn't find the hiding spot and I could come back later.

I darted for the main warehouse, the dark shapes of broken-down slot machines reminiscent of sleeping ancient beasts. I'd only taken a few steps toward the door when blue fae light flashed along the bottom of one of the roll-up doors. A muffled voice accompanied it, followed by another sweep of a fae light near the base of the second roll-up door. I came up short. There were at least two people out there with handheld lights.

One of the metal doors rattled, while someone else went to the door I'd come in earlier—and hadn't locked behind me.

Shit.

By the time the door swung open and the guy had called to his buddy, I had darted off to the left—away from the door and my escape route—and had ducked behind a hulking slot machine at least five feet tall and a couple of feet wide. As I crouched there, I scanned the length of the warehouse, searching for another way out. On the far end were a couple of windows, but crates were stacked in front of them. I could probably shove the stuff aside and dramatically heave myself through the glass if things got really dire. The only other windows were the row that lined the top of the wall, a good twenty feet above me. The roll-up doors were padlocked shut from the other side. That door the men had just come through was the most viable exit.

"You think the Collective guards already been here? Or maybe the mundane police?" a gruff voice asked. "Haskins is gonna be so pissed if someone got here before us …"

I was too scared to peer around the machine to see who'd come in. There were a couple of fellow charm collectors I was on good terms with, but while these voices were vaguely familiar, recognition didn't kick in.

"Nah," a guy said. "The guards aren't here yet and the police are still dealing with that crazy witch outside the telepad station. There were at least seven cabs on fire."

I winced, hoping again that the faun cabbie—and his colleagues—had been taken to the hospital to treat their wounds and not zipped into body bags.

The first guy asked, "So who left the door unlocked? Bounty hunters—especially 97—never leave places unlocked."

A brief pause. Then two sets of feet pounded toward Haskins's small office. *Large* feet, from the sound of it. Heart hammering hard, I readjusted the straps of my bag, my back sweaty beneath my shirt and the weight of the pack. The two guys had left the door to the warehouse ajar, even though they'd just been fretting about it being unlocked. Moonlight spilled into the space, painting the dark floor with a swipe of light gray.

When I heard the desk being pushed aside and the soft creak of the trapdoor being lifted, I beelined for the door. My eyes had mostly adjusted to the dark while I'd been hiding, so I was able to navigate the maze of parts and workstations littering my path toward the door. I'd almost made it, my booted feet and stolen goods somehow making nary a sound, but a shouted "Hey!" made me stumble. My hip clipped the corner of a workstation, knocking me wildly off course. Spots swam in my vision from the pain. I abruptly halted, biting back a cry. The gray light of freedom was still a good twelve feet away.

Giving the workstation a quick look-over, I swiped a wrench off the surface. Despite having a bag full of weapons, I wasn't the fighting type. Even if I couldn't properly use the sword hanging from my belt, I could throw a wrench.

I glanced toward the office door to see a seven-foot-tall draken man hunched in the doorway. He was bodybuilder buff, but while dressed casually in jeans and a T-shirt, he looked human enough—

except for his orange eyes, glowing in the dark like embers, that is. I gripped the wrench a little tighter. I'd need ten wrenches to fight this guy off if he decided not to let me out of here. Even from this distance, I noted that his gaze darted to the lopsided bag on my back.

He took a step forward, ducking under the doorjamb. "What you got there, girlie?"

A lie spilled out. "My dad works here. He forgot some of his tools." I took a step forward as well. Draken, despite their size, were wicked fast. Now that he'd seen me, if I made a break for it, he'd catch me before I reached the door.

"Oh yeah?" he asked. "What's his name?"

I took another step forward and walked into a weak beam of moonlight shining in from one of the warehouse's upper windows.

The draken's orange eyes narrowed. "Hey … you're that chick who keeps trying to get into Haskins's office. Fletch, yeah? Or *the Charm Collector*?" He scoffed, but then his gaze slid to my pack again. "My boss is gonna want whatever you got, girlie. Give it all back and I won't tear your limbs off."

"What a lovely offer," I said, taking another step. "But I don't think Haskins is gonna need this stuff, and I got rent to pay."

The second draken appeared in the office's doorway. This one was so tall, the top of the doorjamb reached his chin, his eyes and nose blocked by the wall. "Yo, Pratt. There's a buncha stuff missing down there." He ducked and peered out. His orange gaze fixated on me. "Oh … what we got here?"

I gulped like a nervous cartoon character. With their superior draken hearing, the goons had probably heard it. I couldn't outrun them. Even if I got out of the building, it would take me at least half an hour on foot to get back to the telepad station. I didn't keep a cell phone on me because I was paranoid, so I couldn't call for a cab. The draken had excellent night vision and speed on their side, too. If I took off, they'd find me eventually.

"This is that little thief who keeps trying to sweet-talk Haskins out of his merchandise," the first guy, Pratt, said.

I chucked the wrench and hightailed it for the door at a record-breaking speed.

Precious inches from that sliver of moonlight on the floor, something grabbed hold of me by the waist and yanked. I yelped, hands flung forward in a desperate attempt to grab the doorjamb. A second later, the pressure on my waist disappeared. Confused, I whirled around, only to find the draken mere feet from me, frozen in place. My chest heaved. Their chests heaved. Their eyes were wide and staring, but they weren't focused on me. They were focused on the dragon sword hovering in the air between me and them.

The sword jutted forward an inch toward the draken men. It was their turn to yelp and they stumbled back. Then the sword lurched forward another inch.

"What'd you do to activate the sword, girlie? Is that why you're always trying to get in here? You were here for the demon blade?" Pratt asked, followed by a high-pitched yip as the sword jerked toward them once more. "Call it off!"

I was equal parts confused and scared. I couldn't think straight. I'd been so sure that the pressure on my waist had been from the grabby hands of the draken who'd threatened to rip off a limb or three, not that it was the sword yanking itself free from the confines of my belt. I wouldn't say my life flashed before my eyes, but I was convinced my snooping and stealing had finally caught up with me.

Even though I'd tried not to recall stories of dragon swords earlier, now I begged my panicked mind to pull up everything it could. The only thing in my head, though, was the horrifying image of a sword run amok in a busy farmer's market. So much screaming. So many caftans, straw hats, and Birkenstocks covered in blood. I didn't want to stick around if the thing planned to start lopping draken heads off, especially since my head could be next.

The sword lunged. The draken cursed.

"Call it off!" Pratt tried again.

"I don't know how!" I called back, not sure if I should have admitted that. "Bye!"

I ran for the door.

I'd just made it outside when the draken men screamed bloody murder. Goose bumps sprang up on my arms and I skidded to a stop. I stood just outside the warehouse, my back to the open door, my pulse pounding out a frantic rhythm in my temples. Those guys had planned to tear my limbs off, so I shouldn't care that a possibly possessed sword might decapitate them, right? A sword I might have inadvertently activated.

The draken wailed again.

Dammit.

I headed back inside and immediately came up short in the doorway, finding the draken men collapsed just inside the office across from me. Pratt was somehow underneath the larger one. As far as I could tell from twenty feet away in the near dark, they still had their heads attached to their bodies, but the sword was several feet above them now and angled up as if preparing for a killing blow.

"Please!" Pratt cried, though his voice was muffled, squished as he was under the larger draken's body. That one was still screaming and had his large hands covering his entire face.

"We're sorry!" the big guy said through his fingers. "Make it stop. We won't tell no one we saw you here!"

Hoping these two knew more than I did about what was going on here, I said, "Sword!" as if I were calling to a dog. If the sword didn't respond, I was out of here.

The sword swiveled in my direction. I nearly choked on my tongue. Now the tip of the blade was facing me instead of the ceiling. I swallowed hard. If I ran, would the sword chase me? I imagined my decapitated head rolling down the pavement, catching sight of sky, asphalt, sky, asphalt before everything went black.

Yeah, yeah, I wouldn't see *anything* once my head was severed from my spinal column, but panicked thoughts weren't logical.

"Please!" Pratt begged, though it was hard to make out his words over the wailing of the other one.

In a tone that I hoped sounded confident and not wobbly, I said, "Sword, come."

Miraculously, the sword started to float my way. What in the *hell*? I was grateful it was floating and not careening.

"Get off me, you oaf!" Pratt muttered from the office. "Igor! Stop. Screaming!"

Igor shut up. I looked away from the slowly floating sword long enough to see that Igor had parted his large fingers on his face so he could peer through the spaces. Once he clocked that the sword was moving away, he sat up. "Get that unholy thing out of here!"

The sword whirled back around and zipped for Igor's face, stopping what looked like a hair's breadth from his nose. Igor appeared to be so scared now that he couldn't even get a scream out.

Holy *hell*, that thing was fast.

"Do something!" Pratt whimpered from his awkward position behind Igor, peering around Igor as if he were a tree.

"Sword …" I said carefully. "Leave Igor alone."

The sword didn't move.

"Come!" I said.

It hovered there for a few more tense seconds, then backed up, turned around, and floated toward me. I glanced down at myself, aware for the first time that my belt had been cut clean in half when the sword flew away from me to, what … *protect* me? Pulling the two belt pieces loose from their loops, I debated what to do with the sword now. I stuffed the belt pieces into my bag. There was no room for the sword in the backpack and with my belt ruined, I had nowhere to hang it from my person either. Couldn't exactly have it floating along behind me like an obedient, murderous duckling. Weapons like this weren't supposed to exist, and if I showed up at the telepad station with an obviously magical sword, the police who were still caught up in the mess with the drunken elemental witch would arrest me on the spot—unless the werecat guards, who were no doubt on their way, caught me first. Whether they showed up on two feet or four, I needed to be out of here before the guards showed up.

When the sword was a foot away, it stopped; it was hovering in the space in front of the threshold, with me just behind it. I'd instinctively stepped back outside again. I willed my heart rate to slow. The sword probably wouldn't lop my head off, right? Unless it was mad that I'd stopped it from decapitating Igor and Pratt. No. I was getting caught up in the stories about these weapons. The sword couldn't *think*. It didn't have *feelings*. This was just a matter of very complicated magic doing things a mere full-blooded human like me couldn't understand. Maybe a spell infused into one of the stolen talismans in my bag was messing with the sword's magic. Pratt had asked what I'd done to activate the sword. As a magic-less human, I obviously had done nothing. I quickly went back over the events of the last few minutes.

The sword had hung innocuously on the pegboard in the basement and hadn't tried anything fishy when I'd first grabbed it. It hadn't gone berserk until I was almost outside the warehouse, when it had ripped itself loose from my belt. A fae light went off in my head. It hadn't been protecting *me*; it was warded to stay on the premises! Haskins must have put some kind of protection ward on the sword to keep people from stealing it. Maybe if I got the thing back into the basement, it would go back to sleep and the guards could deal with it when they raided this place later. If it decapitated *them*, that wouldn't be *my* fault.

Swallowing, I said, "Uhh ... Mr. Sword? I'm sorry I took you out of your ... uhh ... home? I can make Igor and Pratt leave and then put you back in the base—"

Thwack! The sword flung itself into the still-open door.

I recoiled. Igor and Pratt shrieked.

The blade had sunk two inches into the wood, moonlight winking off its iridescent hilt. With a few yanks from a phantom hand, the sword pulled itself free and then resumed hovering before me.

"I think it wants to go home with you," Pratt called out. "Keep it! It never did nothing like this with Haskins. We won't tell no one you were here if you promise to take it."

"I can't!" I said, peering around the sword to address the men across the warehouse, who were too scared to venture out of the office. "I don't have any way to get it home without someone seeing it. Maybe I should leave it here for the—"

Slam!

The sword forcibly embedded itself into the door again. I would have said "Fuck it!" and bolted, but I was worried that would piss the sword off even more—and the next place it slammed its blade into would be my retreating back.

A moment later, a gift from Pratt and Igor landed on the floor and slid toward me. It looked like a small duffel bag.

"For you!" one of them added—the bow on a present I didn't want.

Sighing, I carefully squatted to pick it up, the sword still stuck in the door. I cautiously waved a hand behind the sword's hilt, wondering if an invisible sword handler was responsible for the thing's movements. My hand met no resistance. Standing, I unzipped the bag and held it open by its handles. Feeling ten kinds of foolish, I said, "If you want to come with me, get in the bag."

The sword pulled itself free, then floated into the bag and settled inside with little fuss. I offered Pratt and Igor an exasperated look of confusion.

Before they could react, a crackle of what sounded like a walkie-talkie sounded to my left. My head whipped in that direction. Beams of handheld fae lights bounced along the ground a few feet away. Someone was walking between this warehouse and the one next door.

"You hear that thud?" a woman asked. "Sounded like it was

coming from Haskins's place. Maybe we waited long enough that we'll catch a couple of looters this time, too."

The guards had finally arrived.

I slung the bag over my shoulder, hoping the sword didn't get testy about the bumpy ride, and offered a salute to Igor and Pratt, who stood crouched in the office's doorway. "Good luck, fellas!"

Turning in the opposite direction of where the guards came from, I ran.

CHAPTER FOUR

I sprinted through the dark streets for a solid ten minutes. I had always been light on my feet, but even when my pounding footsteps moved from asphalt to gravel and back again as I traversed the district, ducking between warehouses and darting down alleys, I never made a sound. My overexerted brain idly wondered if this was the sword's doing, as if it were as invested in our escape as I was.

But no. That was silly. This sword wasn't really ... alive.

It wasn't so much that I refused to believe such a thing was possible. It was more that I *needed* it to be impossible. I was in a world of trouble otherwise. I was possibly in a world of trouble, regardless.

I eventually slowed to a jog when my lungs felt like they were on the verge of collapsing. The extra weight from the pilfered items in my bag—many of them made of metal—slowed me down. And, when it was clear that I wasn't being followed, the adrenaline from the whole wacky situation began to ebb, too.

Over the next half hour, the buildings shifted from warehouses to small, dilapidated homes to large houses surrounded by elegant fences and elaborate wards meant to keep out the riffraff, to sprawling condominium complexes with even more elaborate wards. The level of magic used on a place or object wasn't always easy for humans to detect. The fact that I could often see and almost always *feel* the magical energy crackling off the ritzy buildings told me the power behind the protections wasn't something to mess with. The grids of energy humming like invisible electrified fences didn't give off the same haunting glow that hung on Luma's horizon, but the faint auras of purples, reds, and blues were eerie in their own right.

By the time I was walking alongside the massive brick wall of the Warehouse District Terrace Condos on the main road out of the district, exhaustion had set in. This stretch of sidewalk led directly to the telepad station. The station was only a few blocks away, and I easily saw my destination from here—not because of the station's light spilling onto the street, but because of the flaming cabs. Three of them still burned bright. Elemental witch fire was a pain to put out, and the gas in the cabs' tanks had no doubt made the situation even worse.

An ambulance drove out of the bay doors of the telepad station, closely followed by a small fire truck. They had probably just materialized in the massive teleportation cylinders seconds before—empty one moment, and full of multi-ton vehicles the next.

When I was a block away, I crossed the street to the sidewalk on the other side. I tucked my duffel bag with the illegal-as-hell sword in it closer to my hip, and rolled my shoulders back. I willed myself to look nonchalant and innocent. Silently, I begged the sword to behave itself.

The undulating orange flames of the fires pulsed in time with the flashing lights of the emergency vehicles. Unnervingly in time. Elemental witch fires weren't a pain to put out because they were impervious to water or anything like that—it was that, like the sword clutched to my side, they eventually took on strange characteristics if the witch who created said fires didn't call off the flames—whether willingly or under duress. Currently, the flames slid away from the firefighters' hoses, as if the fire were made of slick oil. The flames didn't attempt to jump off the burning cabs, which meant the witch probably didn't mean harm; she just wanted to give the firefighters a hard time. Maybe she'd been drunk *and* bored, which for an elemental witch was a terrible combination.

At least the witch had been apprehended. She was currently handcuffed and two officers escorted her toward the telepad station, which meant she'd been giving the emergency response teams hell for at least an hour. The cops on either side of her didn't look remotely amused, especially the one who had a wealth of burn holes in his blue uniform.

I had just reached one end of the wide bay doors of the telepad station when the witch and her escorts reached the other. Goose bumps sprang up on my arms when she made direct eye contact with me across the couple-hundred-yard space. A moment later, the witch threw her head back and got out a spell before either of the officers could clamp a hand over her mouth. I halted, convinced she'd set *me* on fire, too, just for kicks. The cops bodily yanked her inside the station. When flames didn't lick up my clothes, my attention shifted to the flames the firefighters were still trying to put out.

A round of curses went up from the first responders, and suddenly four cops were running my way. My first instinct was to bolt in the other direction, but I quickly realized they were chasing a dozen one-foot-tall imp-like creatures, made entirely of flames: the witch's final "fuck you" to all in assembly. The fire imps ran past me at incredible speed, then banked right, running down a side street. They cackled as they went, their laughter like wood popping in a fireplace. The officers ran after them, two of them struggling to run with full buckets. Water sloshed out of the containers as they rounded the corner after their fellow first responders. Poor human cops stuck with the dangerous grunt work of dealing with the antics of a drunken witch.

The imps would dissolve on their own if they got too far from their creator—especially once she was shoved into a telepad cylinder—but the cops couldn't risk the imps deciding it would be more fun to set things on fire than to keep tormenting their pursuers.

I sent up a silent thanks for the chaotic scene to whoever was listening and ducked into the telepad station, no one paying me any mind. As I approached one of the smaller outgoing cylinders, the two officers and the drunken witch standing on a glowing blue circle whooshed out of view, no doubt already reappearing in the Luma City Jail's lobby. The same telepad monitor who had talked to me earlier still manned the inbound cylinders on the opposite side of the room. He swiveled his wide-eyed expression toward me, the only departing visitor in the whole place who wasn't involved with the madness outside.

"You weren't lying about the weird shit!" I called out to him.

He sputtered a laugh. "My shift isn't over for another four hours. I hope it doesn't get weirder."

I was about to say, "How could it?" but then I remembered the cackling fire imps, as well as Haskins's basement probably swarming with guards. For all I knew, the sword at my side wasn't even the weirdest thing in there. "I hope your night ends on a more boring note!"

The lady in charge of outbound teleportation punched my destination into her tablet. I swiped my card, and then I stepped inside. I turned around in the cylinder, my feet placed in the middle of the too-large foot outlines on the ground. I couldn't see much of the commotion outside from where I stood, but I could hear it—for a few seconds anyway. The cyclone of frigid air whipped around me. As my spine was pulled taut, two slow-moving cops with what appeared to be empty buckets walked into view. Hopefully, the imps had been taken care of.

An eye blink later, I appeared in a cylinder in my neighborhood telepad station. The bank of fae lights above me was still dark, and the workers were gone. I stepped out, disoriented for a moment. The familiarity of the run-down station was so comforting, I half wanted to drop to my knees and kiss the filthy ground.

Instead, I walked out of the station, giving the duffel bag a soft pat as I went. Partly to assure the sword was still there, and partly in hopes the thing had been ripped apart in the teleportation process and I could go to bed in peace without worrying about having a demon sword—as Igor had called it—in my apartment. But the damn thing was still there.

Once inside my place, I eased the duffel bag off my shoulder and gently placed it on the kitchen island, as if it were a bomb that would detonate if jostled too much. My backpack came off next, which I set beside the duffel. The contents clanged and clacked.

I stared at the duffel bag for a long time, chewing on a thumbnail as I waited for ... something.

Nothing happened.

The sword didn't stir in the bag. It was possible, of course, that the wards in Haskins's warehouse hadn't been as completely dismantled by bounty hunter FT97 as I'd originally thought, and the sword's weird behavior had been a product of that. Which would mean said behavior would stop as soon as I got it out of the warehouse. Yeah. That had to be it. Now it was just a pretty sword, and I'd make an even prettier penny on it.

I pulled off my boots. I was a sweaty mess from all that running, so I headed for my bathroom, yanking the elastic free from my hair as I went. My curls flopped around my shoulders and I gave my sweaty scalp a scratch before peeling off my shirt.

By the time I emerged from my bathroom, a towel around my body and a second one used to dry my hair, I felt much better. The heat had loosened my tense muscles, and the steam had helped clear my head. All I needed to do was contact Grayson—my favorite wannabe pirate—in the morning and I'd be rid of the sword in a few days, tops.

I got dressed, braided my hair into a single plait, and then padded back into my kitchen to do a bit of reconnaissance on my haul. Rounding the kitchen island where the new items were, I grabbed a bottle of water from the fridge. I guzzled it down as I stared at the bags, my bare feet on the little stretch of tile that covered the floor between the main kitchen counter and the center island. Once I finished, I walked to the other side of the kitchen island.

I went through the backpack first, laying out two short swords, a set of six daggers that had all come with their own scabbards, three throwing stars, and a mace. One by one I examined them, hoping that their magic wouldn't somehow set off the dragon sword's own.

The short swords had ivory hilts, and I guessed they were made from unicorn horn, or tusks from a water beast. Weak magic, but they were beautiful. The daggers all looked mundane, but as I pulled each one free from its scabbard, my fingertips buzzed as I touched them in turn to each blade. All of them were imbued with spells. Even though I couldn't detect specifics, the feel of magic usually told me which level of magic objects held.

Magic levels were determined by the Food, Drug, and Magic Association, with 1 being the lowest, and 8 the highest. It was a scale humans worried about most since even the lower levels could affect us. But high levels could be detrimental even to a witch or sorcerer, especially since a good number of sorcerers were full-blooded humans. Sorcery could be taught, but it was such an arduous process to become a practitioner of the art, with years of intense study, that most people, human or not, dropped out.

If the magic in an item or consumable good was below a 4 on the FDMA's safe list, a full-blooded human could eat, drink, or use it without worrying about getting maimed, killed, or worse. Coffee shots with Level 2 mental acuity tonic sprinkled in could help you get through a rough day of training at work. A Level 4 tonic would turn you into a savant for roughly thirty seconds before you passed out as your brain shut down. A Level 5 would probably make your brain explode in your skull and ooze out your nose.

The illegal stuff—like the kind that tripped the Code 154 alarm—was usually Level 4 and up. Anything above it buzzed like the wards around the ritzy buildings in the Warehouse District, so I knew to keep my skin away from those.

I touched my finger to the last dagger—and was zapped with enough force that I pitched right off my stool and just narrowly avoided whacking my head on the floor. Black spots swam in my vision. My tailbone hit the wood floor and my stomach gave a little heave.

"Sonofa*bitch*," I muttered when the nausea had passed and the spots faded. I winced as I got back to my feet and glared at the offending dagger lying innocently on the counter. Lightning spell. My whole body felt fizzy, and my head throbbed. My sixth sense had failed me on that one. How had a spell that strong not given off any indications that it lingered in the danger zone? Ugh. Maybe I was too tired for recon.

Or maybe I was just too old for this nonsense. I was *two years* away from thirty. When my mom was my age, she was married, had a career, and was pregnant with me. But, given my parents' professions, they were no doubt getting their asses zapped by too-potent magic on the regular well into their forties.

As I righted the stool, grumbling to myself all the while, the vampire cabbie's words echoed in my head. *"Trust me. Humans always get into trouble down here."* I sat back on the stool, giving myself a slight shake.

Even though the dagger's magic would take a few minutes to recharge, I didn't want to get my ass flattened again, so I gingerly slipped it back into its protective scabbard. The throwing stars were in a magic-dampening pouch, and when I pulled the bag open, the metal inside the dark bag glowed red. They hadn't been doing *that* before. I pulled the cord taut. Definitely not touching those. I eyed the mace. A protective leather cover had already been fastened over the spiky head when it was on Haskins's wall, like a falcon with a hood over its eyes. I wasn't going to uncover that one either. One zap a night was more than enough, thanks.

The last of the items were the smaller ones—talismans on chains, leather thongs, and ribbons. They all gave off faint traces of magic, probably nothing higher than a Level 2 or 3. My locking charm was a 2.

There were large egg-shaped ones, half-domed ones, and some that looked like mundane lockets. Given that they'd been part of Haskins's collection, I knew they were far from mundane. I would take all the talismans to Josephine in the morning so she could tell me what I'd found.

Last of all, I had the dragon sword to contend with. Also like a hooded falcon, I worried that if I unzipped the bag, the sword would come flying out, searching for prey.

Hopping off the stool, I went to the five-shelf metal bookcase in the corner of my living-slash-dining room. I winced the whole way there. Stupid lightning spell.

The bookshelf was stacked not with books, but with charmed items I'd collected and still needed to sell. Larger weapons took up the bottom two shelves; the middle two were lined with pouches, carrying cases, and small boxes; and the top had three plastic tubs. I pulled one down and rummaged around in it until I found a scabbard for the dragon sword. I had at least two scabbards that would fit a sword of this length. Because of the cutlass's shape, I chose the scabbard that was narrower at the top and wider at the bottom. The blade of the cutlass was about thirty inches long and swooped in a wide curve at the end. Sliding a blade like that directly into a scabbard would slice the thing in half. Snaps lined the side of the leather scabbard so that it could be opened like a book. And, like all my scabbards from Josephine, it was imbued with a magic-dampening spell, assuring that the sword couldn't get bored in the night and cause havoc while I slept.

Walking the scabbard back over to the counter, I unsnapped the sides and laid it beside the duffel. All I had to do was unzip the duffel, grab the sword, place it in the scabbard, and then snap it into its magical straitjacket. Easy peasy.

"Please don't kill me," I repeated, then quickly got the sword out of the bag and into the scabbard.

Aha! The sword was subdued, and I still had my head attached to my body. Success.

I stifled a yawn, exhaustion really taking hold now. Leaving my new items on the counter, I double-checked that the door was locked, slid the security chain into place for a little added mundane safety, turned off the lights, and headed for bed. My apartment never got totally dark, thanks to the glow from Luma Proper to the west, but I pretended it was moonlight that filtered in through my windows and not the shining eye of Big Brother.

As I made my way to my bedroom, I smiled to myself. With this haul, rent would be secured for several more months, with enough left over that I could finally buy that new fae-powered bike I'd been coveting. "Your loss is my gain, Haskins."

I had just crossed the threshold of my bedroom when a *whoomp!* sounded behind me. I whirled just as a bright orange light flared on the counter. My mind screamed *fire!* But, just as it did, the flames were out again. I hurried back to the kitchen and stared in dismay at the dragon sword—and the bits of blackened leather surrounding it. Three charred metal snaps lay on the counter, blackened and curled like the husks of dead beetles.

Slowly, the sword lifted itself from the counter and gave itself a shake, knocking loose any remaining bits of ash and fried leather. The looming blue light from Luma Proper winked dully off the sword's iridescent hilt. Then, ever so slowly, the sword turned to face me.

"Oh shit."

CHAPTER FIVE

With my hands out in a placating gesture, I took a step back. "Nice sword … you're a nice sword."

The sword didn't move. It just … hovered there.

I flicked a glance to my right, toward my front door. When it came to fight or flight, I was a flight kind of girl. I needed to get out of here. I knew the sword could follow me, but if I got the heavy metal front door between the sword and myself, it would buy me some time. Some time for what? I didn't know.

I took the merest of steps toward my door and the sword flew across the room at such speed, my head spun. I squeezed my eyes shut and prayed the sweet release of death was quick and painless. And that there wouldn't be too much blood. And that Kayda didn't come looking for me after I'd gone MIA for a few days so that she didn't have to be the one to discover my mangled body.

SLAM!

I screamed bloody murder. I screamed and screamed and screamed.

But I didn't feel any pain.

Eyes flying open and mouth snapping shut, I patted my body. When I didn't find a thirty-inch sword sticking out of it, I shot a glance at the door. The crazy sword had embedded itself into the metal.

Okay.

Okay, think.

The sword didn't want me going anywhere.

I considered scurrying into my bedroom and locking the door, but the sword would eventually slash its way through that.

It wasn't like I expected to get much of my security deposit back on this apartment, but I had a better chance of getting *something* if there weren't massive holes in all the doors.

"Uh … sword?" I squeaked out. Clearing my throat, I said, "Mr. Sword. Are you going to kill me? My nerves are shot and if there's no chance of escape, I'd like to know. I could polish off the last of the vodka in my freezer so I won't feel it when you slaughter me."

The sword gave itself several yanks and pulled itself free from the door. It left a rather sizeable slice in a *metal* door, which said a lot about how sharp the damn thing was. Weak fae light winked off its steel blade as it slowly floated back to me. It hadn't damaged itself whatsoever from all the times it had slammed itself into things. Probably thanks to being a dragon sword.

A dragon sword! In my apartment!

I was such an idiot.

"Hey!"

I almost fainted. Could the sword *talk* now?

"Hey, what's going on in there?"

My gaze and the sword swiveled toward my door. A neighbor clearly had heard the commotion and had come to investigate. Ugh. My heart raced. The last thing I needed was a nosy neighbor to call the cops on me. I could hide the sword if the cops showed up, but who the hell knew if the thing would *stay* hidden? Getting caught with a dragon sword would land me in front of the Collective, who would then feed me their legendary truth serum. I would be forced to tell them about my charm collecting habits over the last few years. For every magical item I'd sold—knowing full-well that it was a banned item—I'd be awarded a minimum of one year in jail. I'd sold dozens of weapons at this point. They could also decide that my infractions were too numerous, and I'd be exiled. Not just from Luma, but from all hubs. Blacklisted. Forced to live in the "normal" world populated almost exclusively by humans with no knowledge of the worlds hidden behind veils.

I held up a hand to the sword, hoping the universal sign for "don't move!" applied to sentient objects, and then made my way to the door. I opened it, security chain in place. My pinched-faced neighbor stood on the other side of the door, hands on hips. She was full-blooded human, pushing eighty, and unfortunately had excellent hearing. Though, I suppose my bloody-murder screams could have woken the dead.

"Hi, Ms. Rawls," I said, peering through the gap. "Sorry for the noise. I was watching a scary movie and had the volume up too high."

Ms. Rawls was just a hair over five feet, yet still got up on her tiptoes to try to see over my head. I prayed the sword stayed out of sight. "Sounded like more than a scary movie …"

"I'll keep the volume down. Actually, I'll just stop watching it altogether. Too scary for me to watch all by myself." I offered her the cheesiest smile I could muster. "Thank you for being concerned about me."

Ms. Rawls stared a moment longer, then waved a hand dismissively. "Bah. Keep it down. I'm trying to sleep. You cause a racket again, I'm calling the cops." She tottered away.

"Got it," I said, waving at her retreating back even though she couldn't see it. "Have a good night!"

When she was out of view, I closed and locked the door. I stalked farther into my apartment where the sword hovered at eye height near the kitchen.

"You almost got me in trouble!" I whisper-hissed, then winced, unsure if it would retaliate.

The sword didn't react. The longer it went without any of the aggressive behavior it had shown the draken men—without any behavior at all—the more the tension in my shoulders subsided.

"Okay, so you're ... not going to kill me ..."

It didn't move.

The thing could clearly sense and understand me, but could it see me somehow? I raised a finger in front of my face and slowly moved it away. The sword's tip followed it. I brought my finger back toward my face, and the sword mirrored it as if I were pulling it along with a magnet. Well, that was freaky.

I dropped my arm back to my side. The sword resumed hovering.

Where in the hell had Haskins gotten it? When I'd asked the sword if it wanted to be returned to the basement below the office, it had thrown itself into a door. So far, that seemed to be one of its very few means of expressing itself. Either hovering like a silent, creepy death drone, or dramatically slamming into things to show displeasure. And, well, incinerating things.

"Were you stolen?" I asked. "Do you want to be returned to your original owner?"

The sword quivered in the air, like it was vibrating. Was that excitement? Like a dog wagging its tail? But then the blade turned from shiny gray to rose to crimson to cherry hot, like a piece of charcoal turning molten. This reaction was potentially way worse than colliding with doors.

"Whoa, whoa, whoa," I said, hands up. "Chill."

I meant that both literally and figuratively.

When the blade slowly returned to its normal color of cool steel, I heaved a little breath of relief.

"All right, sword, we need to figure out a better way to chat. You seem to have an anger management problem, which, let me tell you, is not working for my anxiety."

The sword quivered. The surrounding air is what quivered, really, but it was easier to think of the whole thing vibrating.

Giving the sword a wide berth, I stepped around it and walked to the kitchen island where the other pilfered items—as well as the charred remains of the leather straitjacket—still lay. I frowned at the mess. That cutlass scabbard had been expensive.

As I cleared away some space on the opposite side of the ring of ash, the sword came into view in my peripheral vision. I couldn't shake the feeling that it was watching me with interest. Which didn't make sense, because it didn't have *eyes*.

"Okay, I'll try to keep things simple for now," I said. "Yes and no answers. One tap for yes, two for no." I knocked my knuckles on the counter's surface in demonstration.

The sword quivered.

Okay then. "Did Haskins steal you?"

Turning itself so it hovered perpendicular to the counter—the hilt facing down—the sword gave the counter two quick taps of its hilt. I had my first answer: no. The sword remained floating upright, waiting for my next question.

"Did Haskins have you made as a commissioned piece?"

For a brief moment, the blade blazed red. Tap-tap.

No, and it was offended by the question, apparently.

"Did Haskins buy you?"

Tap.

"At auction?"

Tap.

I worried at the inside of my cheek with my teeth as I thought. Every month or so, one could find a black-market auction if one knew where to look. I'd been to a couple myself, but not in at least a year. The Collective's werecat guards managed to show up to half of them, arresting anyone who didn't flee the scene in time. Dad's pocket mirror was a safer way to find contraband goods. It allowed me to steal already untraceable items.

The artifacts up for purchase at auctions were usually items exactly like this sword: highly dangerous, illegal-as-shit weaponry. One guy in particular ran them more often than anyone else. For years, people wondered where the man got his seemingly endless supply of contraband weapons. By now, it was a poorly kept secret that the guy was a rogue sorcerer. He'd gone through the rigorous program to become a member of the leading body of the Sorcerers Collective—whether in Luma, or one of the other magical hubs scattered across the country—and instead had chosen a life of crime, like a doctor who turned into an angel of death, using his power for evil instead of good. The rumors about him had been circulating for years, especially during the last two. He was our Banksy.

The guy was also a trained blacksmith and hadn't just been collecting illegal weapons, but creating them in his lair of doom. Which, from what anyone could parse out, was a mansion in the hills somewhere because, the guy was richer than God. There had to be a lair of doom in the basement, though. I refused to picture anything else.

He created Frankenweapons that were crafted with bits and pieces of magical beasts he'd gathered over the years, and then melded it all together with off-regulation spellwork. Fae and witches could handle the weapons well enough, but humans typically bought them—humans who had no business being around magic that strong. Humans who tended to use the weapons, and either lost control of them or immediately got killed by them. That was how I knew about the Frankenweapons ... when you're a human living in a magical city, rumors about terrifying human-killing items spread quickly, no matter your walk of life.

Had this sword come from one of *those* auctions? A dragon sword was bad enough, but a Franken-dragon sword? I'd need to move. Perhaps to a different planet.

"Were you made by Caspian Blackthorn?" I asked, noting, as I always did, that Caspian's name had to be made up. It screamed villain.

Tap-tap.

Phew!

Auctions were led by others often enough that this information did little to narrow down where my new friend had come from.

"Do you want to be returned to your owner?"

The blade blazed red, but I got no taps in reply. It didn't like this question.

I cocked my head. "So it's the 'owner' thing that's got you into a tizzy? You don't belong to no man? You're your own person ... uh ... sword?"

Kayda's voice of reason flitted through my head. *You probably shouldn't antagonize the murder sword, Harlow.*

The sword quivered a moment, then offered a tap-tap.

So, no, it didn't have an owner. Not only was this a dragon sword, but a dragon sword going through an identity crisis. Great.

I thought some more. Given the sword's ability to burn through magical charms—Josephine's were nothing to sneeze at—and its ability to seemingly make its own decisions, why had it placidly stayed in Haskins's basement for this long—however "this long" had been? It could have escaped whenever it wanted to, couldn't it? But these questions were too complicated to ask when our communication system was currently limited to taps, slamming into doors, and going molten.

"Do you want to ... uh ... live here?" I asked. "With me, I mean?"

The sword seemed to hesitate before it slowly tapped once, and then after a long pause, a second time. Was that like a maybe? I sighed.

"Do you need my help with something?"

A quick tap.

Help with *what*? We established it didn't want to be returned to Haskins's basement. It didn't "belong" to anyone, so it presumably didn't want to go back to its literal maker. I was out of ideas about what the whims of a sword might be. The only lead I had was that it had come from an auction.

"Did the auction take place locally?"

Tap.

"Are *you* from here? The greater Luma area, anyway?"

Tap ... tap.

Another maybe?

"You don't know?"

Tap.

I squinted an eye. Yes, it didn't know if it was from here? Or no, it didn't know? My head hurt.

"Well, I'm going into Luma Proper tomorrow to get some information on the other items I took. I can ask around about you, too. Try to find out where you came from."

Tap.

It was a start.

What I really needed was to talk to Kayda. She'd know what to do. She'd yell at me for a long time first, but then she'd help me figure this out. I debated whether to wait until morning to contact her. She had a landline, but I didn't. I could walk a few blocks to the telepad office and magic a message to her, which she'd find in her personal telepad tube in the morning. I buzzed with nervous energy, and talking to her now felt imperative. That was my impulsive side talking. But I also had a freaking dragon sword in my apartment and I needed to talk to someone who was both sane and had vocal cords.

I rounded the kitchen island and padded across the tile floor to a drawer next to the fridge. I opened it and stared at the one item inside. A cell phone. Depending on which magical hub you lived in, cell phones were either abundant or scarce. Even though Luma was removed from the outside world via the veil, we were only a little behind the times here. Our TVs played mundane shows, movies graced the screens of our theaters, and we had all the same technology that they did beyond the veils. We just got everything a month or two after everyone else.

Everyone knew technology could be used to track a person's whereabouts, and that listening devices were easily planted, given means and opportunity. But when magic was added to the mix? The possibilities were endless. A phone call could look and sound like it had come from a friend, but glamour spells could change a person's perception of any number of things. If a person in Luma was even remotely associated with hobbies or a career that crossed the line of legality, cell phones weren't used. Period.

My career most definitely crossed the line. More than crossed it. I would have thrown the thing out entirely if it weren't for Kayda.

And maybe Felix. And Mom.

Had those thoughts been in my voice or Kayda's that time?

"What if there's an emergency!" she would say, as if there weren't dozens of other forms of communication possible in a place like Luma—the charmed pocket mirror I used to get information about Haskins's apprehension being a perfect example. Bounty hunters couldn't risk having their communications intercepted by the very people they were trying to catch, so they needed a way to stay in contact that couldn't be hacked. Hence, a closed-circuit communication system that was *mostly* government-issued and powered by very specific spells placed on a very specific piece of silvered glass that all the mirrors had been cut from. The mirrors were easy and relatively inexpensive to make, and since no one but a person with insider information knew what the codes were, bounty hunters weren't that concerned about keeping track of them. Plus, they fell out of pockets and bags so often, smashing into pieces during jobs, that cataloging them was a fruitless effort.

The only reason I had one was because my father's hadn't been on him when he was killed. I'd found it after the fact. I knew the codes, because up until the day the job got Dad killed, I'd been in the bounty-hunting program alongside Felix, who had been pulled in by his own parents. When my dad was killed, I dropped out, and Felix did too shortly afterward. The job was too dangerous; I didn't want to lose him to it the way I'd lost my dad. Of course, I ended up losing him, too, just in a different way.

Mom's mirror was gone—but so was she. She'd skipped town after Dad died. Hadn't even said goodbye. She and Felix had a lot in common that way.

I clenched my jaw, willing myself not to go too far down Memory Lane. There only lay alcohol-fueled pity parties.

I still stared down at the cell phone lying in the drawer. I wasn't sure why I'd held onto it for so many years. I had the same number, just in case. Yet, the phone was always off. It was one of the few things I'd kept from that time, though. It felt like a lifeline to the past, but I knew deep down that made little sense. Heartbreak and grief didn't result in the most logical of actions.

Grunting, I picked the cell up, popped the battery back in, and powered it on. The blue glow from the screen had just washed across my face when something whizzed past my head. I jumped back, heart in my throat.

Slam!

I clapped a hand over my chest, my heart rocketing beneath it.

The damned sword had skewered my phone to the wall!

"What the hell!" Without thinking, I grabbed hold of the hilt and yanked. I gave the sword a shake to dislodge the mangled phone from its blade and then tossed the sword away from me. Bits of black plastic and cracked glass littered the countertop. "You better hope Ms. Rawls is asleep!" I added.

I gingerly picked up the tiny pieces, but the phone was well and truly destroyed. I whirled on the sword, tears in my eyes for reasons unknown. It hovered to my right and had the decency to dart back a couple of feet when I aimed my furious expression at it.

"*What* is wrong with you!" I snapped. "I was contacting someone to help *you*."

The sword quickly inverted itself and tapped twice on the counter.

"No? What, you think I'm lying?" I asked, quickly swiping away tears.

Tap-tap.

I locked my jaw. "Like I said. Anger management problem. You can't just destroy things that upset you."

Tap.

I tossed my hands into the air in frustration. "Are you worried I was going to tell someone you're here?"

Tap-tap.

What was its problem then? "I know phones can be dangerous—"

Tap.

"It was only going to be on for a second!"

The blade burned red. Tap-tap.

"Ugh!"

I stalked to my bedroom. I'd have to figure out in the morning how to contact Kayda. I would also have to figure out how to get into Luma Proper—an area teeming with magic, magical people, and magical beings—and not get caught with a sword that had a hard time with impulse control.

I flopped onto my bed and stared up at the dark ceiling. "Don't get into trouble while I'm sleeping," I grumbled out loud, not sure where the sword was now. I didn't care either.

After a few minutes of deafening silence, I curled up on my side, scowling at the gauzy curtains that covered the one small window of my bedroom which overlooked the edge of the rusting fire escape ladder that was accessible from my living room. Luma Proper's glow hung on the horizon.

I couldn't tell who I was more pissed off at—the sword for destroying something I shouldn't have been holding onto this long, or at myself for being this gutted by its loss.

Maybe the stupid sword would bust out of here on its own by morning, choosing someone else to torment. I wouldn't miss it. My life was enough of a mess without it.

Yet, when I awoke the next morning to soft sunlight cascading across my face, I found the sword lying on the foot of my bed, like a cat.

Dammit.

CHAPTER SIX

The sword and I had a literally heated "discussion" about how to get it into Luma. I argued that a magic-dampening scabbard would be best, not to impinge on its freedom and individuality or whatever the hell it was worried about, but because it would keep magic-sensing people and creatures from detecting it on me. I had thought we were on the same page, but after I'd snapped it into my last cutlass-sized scabbard, the bastard incinerated it.

The only way it would agree to be carried was in the duffel bag. I tossed the other magical items—just the talismans and the daggers for now—on top of it out of spite, realizing later that that was a fantastic way to get my future rent payments to go up in smoke, but the bag remained dormant and in one piece even after I zipped it closed.

By the time I was packed and dressed, it was just after 7:30 in the morning. Kayda would be going into work at 9, so I planned to swing by her place first, and Josephine's shop after.

I took my time getting to the telepad station this time, dread slowing me down rather than excitement urging me on. I needed to make a stop a block away first, and a line snaked out the door of the telepad station. Commuter traffic was always terrible in the morning.

I eyed the splatters of black and blue ink that decorated the inside of the telepost office door as I pushed it open. It wasn't nearly as crowded as the telepad station, at least.

At the back of the room, three chipper telepost employees stood behind a counter. Each employee had a line of at least four people waiting before them, and they happily asked questions of their patrons about the contents of their parcels and where they were headed. Message-sending was a self-run affair, but packages had to be cleared by telepost workers first, who were the only ones with access to the larger teleportation tubes in the back. The public at large had lost their self-service package delivery privileges almost immediately when people started shipping explosives. Explosives and teleportation spells do not mix. Or they mixed too well, depending on your perspective.

In the self-run section of the office, it was impossible to send anything other than telepost-approved stationery and envelopes. Delivery of mail in the hubs was highly regulated, as it was a steady income stream for the sorcerer-led government, but it also offered a relatively safe way for humans to communicate with each other with a lower chance of magical interception. Every piece of approved stationery was spelled by a government-employee witch, and any piece of paper without accurate, up-to-date magical watermarks infused into it would burst into flame the second it was slipped into a telepost tube. The watermarks also had a time limit embedded into their magic. If the stock wasn't used in three days, it disintegrated on its own. A new batch of paper was delivered every three days with new watermarks.

Although written mail was one of the safest ways to communicate in Luma, it was still a largely outdated system. Only humans —usually old ones— along with low-level criminals, people being unfaithful to their partners, and paranoid folks like yours truly still used it. Criminals and cheating spouses liked it because one could choose how the missive was delivered, and what would happen to it upon arrival.

There were intake tubes with labels like "disintegrate in a week," "disintegrate in three days," and "disintegrate five minutes after pickup." Problems arose on the other end, depending on where the message ended up. If the message arrived in an outbox in another public telepost office, any number of things could happen to it: if a telepost courier didn't deliver the message in time, it disintegrated before it was delivered. Urgent delivery couriers were easy to spot—they were the ones pedaling at high speeds on their bikes while sweating bullets.

As I walked to the letter station on the right side of the room directly opposite the package counter, a door straight ahead opened and out walked a man with a parcel under his arm. I caught sight of several banks of private boxes inside the room before the door swung shut again.

A line of windows ran along the length of the letter-writing counter and I peered out the dingy glass at people streaming toward the telepad station. I sighed to myself. I'd be in line for ages. Gingerly, I took off my duffel bag and laid it carefully on the counter. The contents made an unnecessary clatter, as if I'd just dropped a bucket of spoons on the floor. I glared at the bag. A woman nearby, who was busily working on a letter of her own, flinched so violently that she scratched a line of black ink across her page.

She glared at me, then turned her body away and used her forearm to shield her letter from view as she went back to scribbling her lengthy missive. Sending handwritten love letters by telepost was a quaint dating ritual. I fought an eye roll. As if I cared about her love life! I barely cared about my own.

In cubbyholes and boxes along the back edge of the writing counter were sheets of paper and envelopes of varying sizes. I grabbed one of the smaller ones and a pen that was filled with ink spelled to show up only on telepost paper. If one tried to abscond with a telepost pen, it exploded very dramatically as soon as you walked out the door—hence the splotches of black and blue on the door to the lobby.

K,
I found a thing. Don't be mad. I'll be at your place before 8:30.

H.

I folded the note and stuffed it into one of the offered envelopes, then wrote Kayda's address and personal telepost box number on the outside. As I reached to place the pen back in its holder, I paused.

When I'd first seen the sword, Grayson's face had popped into my head. Grayson Ipram was a wannabe pirate, more so in spirit than in action. Living in Luma didn't give one much of a chance for swashbuckling. He came from a long line of actual pirates, and had spent a good deal of his twenties out on the open oceans. He'd worked on crabbing ships, but as a water elemental, he used his abilities to search for the fae-enchanted island said to have been the last refuge for the now-extinct ancient fae beasts. Legend had it that untold riches were still on the island, left behind by the beasts and shielded by a veil similar to the ones that surrounded each hub city. The island apparently also changed location—in the Pacific Ocean one month, and in the Indian Ocean the next. Grayson's many-great grandfather, an infamous pirate in his day, was said to have found the island and possess a map of all the locations where the island showed up most frequently. Naturally, the man's ship capsized, taking the supposed map with him to his watery grave. Grayson had told me on numerous occasions that it was his destiny to find the island someday.

It sounded like a magical version of the lost city of Atlantis to me.

The summer before he'd moved here, he landed a gig giving tours on a pirate ship on the East Coast. He thought the experience would scratch his pirate itch, or somehow give him insight into his past, but being surrounded by humans who cared less about history and more about taking selfies had driven him to such sullen moods that he'd single-handedly caused a Category 2 hurricane in Florida. That was when he relocated to Luma. He needed a change of pace and a way to exercise his magic in a safer place.

Currently, he worked in one of the fae light mega-companies, using his water magic to aid in the manufacturing of tubing which housed the fae light for the ever-glowing signs of Luma. The tubing was made of mostly mundane materials, but was strengthened by spellwork. What would his pirate ancestors think about him working for a corporation?

He made bank at his job and had grown a bit soft due to the comforts Luma offered, but he was still restless. He was always happy to look at anything I found, sure that one day I'd stumble across something that would set him on his path to fulfilling his pirate dreams. When a sunken pirate ship had been found off the coast of Washington last year, Grayson nearly came unglued.

"Our time has arrived!" he'd written in a telepost note. *"If any bounty from that ship crosses your path, come to me first. I'll pay top dollar!"*

The guy was a nutter, but he was a nutter with cash, so I liked him just fine. If the sword was tied to that sunken ship found a year ago, how long had it been in Luma? It was wild to think the sword possibly had hung from the belt of a pirate—perhaps one who had been a water elemental, like Grayson.

I grabbed another piece of paper out of a cubbyhole and penned a second message.

Gray,

I found something that'll blow your mind. Meet me in the usual place around 10 this morning?

MELISSA ERIN JACKSON

Fletch

I wrote his address and telepost number on a second envelope and stuffed the note inside.

In a side pouch of the duffel bag I found my wallet. The slight jostling of the bag caused another one-million-spoons-falling-off-a-mountain rattling clang, and the woman beside me screeched again as her pen jumped across the page unexpectedly once more.

She sneered, but I did my best to ignore her. It wasn't like I could explain myself, anyway. I pulled my telepost card out of the wallet, the card a dark blue plastic as opposed to the white telepad's. Leaning close to my bag as if I were examining something on it, I harshly whispered, "Kindly knock it off, or I'll stuff you into a box and ship you off to Tercla so you can have vampires for company instead!"

The bag vibrated softly under my hand, but the fabric didn't warm, nor did any other raucous sound spill forth.

Satisfied, I stood to full height, draped the bag over my shoulder, and cheerily said, "Have a nice day!" to the still-fuming woman. Given the stack of turned-over pages next to her, I guessed she was on at least page five of her epic love letter.

I made my way to the intake tubes. The sound of transported letters was like a gentle whisper compared to the constant *whoosh* in the telepad station. Even though similar magic was used in both places, it took a lot less energy to send a letter than a living being.

The intake tubes were lined up next to each other along the wall, and a payment box the size of a cell phone was embedded into the wall beside each one. The tubes snaked up into the ceiling. I found the "disintegrate in an hour" tube and got in line behind two patrons.

When it was my turn, I tapped the address on the payment screen, swiped my telepost card, and the light on the box flipped from red to green—the money automatically taken out of my account with the fake name. A little door in the tube opened, large enough for a hand to slip inside. Cool air tingled against my fingers as I stuck the letter and my hand into the space, placing the letter on the glowing blue circle at the bottom. When I pulled my hand free, the little door snapped closed. A muted whirl sounded, the corners of the envelope flapping in the vibrating air inside the tube, and a blink later, the envelope was gone.

I repeated the process for Grayson's note.

Once his was sent, I headed back across the lobby. As I pushed open the ink-splattered door, I figured there was little chance Kayda would heed my warning not to be mad.

"A *dragon* sword?" Kayda said. "What the *hell* were you thinking?"

"I was thinking it was pretty!"

"Stop making decisions based on how pretty something is!"

"I'm a simple woman!"

Kayda almost, almost smiled at that. "Don't be funny."

"I'm sorry," I said, fighting a grin.

We moved to stand side by side in front of her dining room table and stared at the sword. The top of my head barely reached her shoulder. At five-eight I was relatively tall for a human woman, but next to Kayda, I always felt tiny.

She grumbled to herself as she crossed her massive arms over her chest. "These dragon sword stories can't be real, right? I mean, I get that it's communicating with you, but they aren't actually murder machines, are they?" She cocked her head. "It hasn't moved at all."

She sounded vaguely disappointed.

"It's probably biding its time," I said.

"How ominous."

The sword was out of the duffel bag and lying on the worn

wooden surface of the table near Kayda's unfinished breakfast of toast and eggs. The iridescent scales lining the hilt shimmered, as if they were pebbles below gently lapping water. It really was a gorgeous sword … when it wasn't being a jerk.

I stared at Kayda's profile. Though she was a descendant of dragons, she looked mostly human—a human on growth hormones. She was wide across the shoulders but slender in a crazy-fit kind of way. The tight black T-shirt she wore made her appear even slimmer. The shirt was tucked into black cargo pants cinched with a black leather belt. "Intimidating" wasn't a strong enough word to describe her.

Kayda idly ran a hand back and forth over the back of her head, where the short white hairs were the softest. Draken had next to no body hair. When she'd hit puberty, she sprouted short hair on the top of her head—as excited as the human boys in our class about sprouting hair below their noses and belts. All these years later, her white hair was only a few inches long. Kayda would kill to be able to wear her hair in a ponytail, but not even the beauty witches could do anything to help her. Many draken women wore wigs since it was so hard for them to grow hair, but Kayda was proud of what little she had and refused to cover it up. She said it made her feel feminine: when you were seven feet tall, built like a tank, and worked as a security guard-slash-bouncer, femininity was hard to come by. She was currently employed at a casino and mostly just stood around looking menacing, occasionally tossing out drunk idiots when they caused too much trouble.

"What do you think I should do with it?" I finally asked her.

"I don't know." She wasn't looking at me; she only had eyes for the sword—a sword inlaid with scales from a long-ago ancestor.

Heat tinged her light brown cheeks, making the faint hints of green in her skin darken. Aside from superior strength, speed, and eyesight, draken had also retained hints of what color scales their dragon ancestors once had. Before humans had driven dragons into extinction on Earth, green had been the most common, followed closely by brown, black, and gray. Depending on how close a draken was to her ancestry, generationally speaking, skin color could be extreme—forest green, shale gray, sunset orange, blood red. Kayda was so many generations away from her dragon ancestors that the flecks of green in her skin only came out when she was emotional or intoxicated.

I knew it bothered her that she knew very little about her dragon heritage, so seeing artifacts made with the literal pieces of noble beasts whom she'd never know riled her up. She pursed her thin lips.

"Do you have any draken contacts who wouldn't immediately call the werecat guards on me if they found out I had this?" I tried.

She wrinkled her nose, finally turning her yellow eyes to me. That was a dragon-descendant thing that remained a dominant trait, no matter how far removed a draken was from her lineage. Usually it was yellow eyes for the ladies and orange ones for the men. "Most of the draken I know work at the casinos. None of us make much money. Turning in a human with a contraband weapon for the finder's fee would probably be a month's worth of rent, if not more. It would be too enticing for them *not* to turn you in, even if I said you were a friend."

I figured as much.

"Have you considered just ... getting rid of it?" she whispered, a massive hand shielding her mouth. "It's behaving now, but who knows what makes them do what they do. Do you want to deal with the fallout if the thing goes berserk and goes on a murder spree?"

"I haven't tried yet. Mostly I just run away, but that seems to tick it off." I dramatically shook my fist in the air, and in an equally dramatic tone said, "How dare you run from me, puny human!"

"You're weird, you know that?" Kayda asked. She looked from the sword to her third-floor window, and back to the sword. Saying nothing, she grabbed the sword by the hilt, stomped to her window, pushed it open, and tossed the sword out as if it were a frisbee. After shutting the window, she slapped her hands together in an "all done!" gesture and strolled back to me. "Piece of cake."

My mouth was still hanging open several long seconds later.

"Stop gaping at me," she said, hands on hips.

"What if it impaled someone on the way down!"

"It's an alley," Kayda said. "If someone is creeping around out there, they deserve to get skewered." Cocking a hairless brow, she said, "In case you've forgotten, the correct words here are 'thank yo—'"

We both shrieked at the sound of shattering glass. I hit the ground, hands and arms clasped over my head, and Kayda, startled, tripped over her own large boot-clad feet before pitching over the side of her sofa. Her yip of surprise was so out of character that I would have laughed had I not been this rattled.

"What in the ..."

I unshielded my head to find Kayda standing in front of the sofa, her wide yellow eyes locked on something not visible from my vantage point on the floor. But I already had a damn good guess what it was.

When I stood to full height, I groaned. The sword hovered above the dining room table, its blade blood red. This time, the blade itself really *was* vibrating. The air around it rippled. Though there were a couple of pieces of furniture between them, the sword's tip was pointed at Kayda's heart. Kayda with her draken abilities was fast, but I had no doubt the possessed sword was faster.

"Yo! Calm down!" I said, scurrying to stand between it and my best friend, hands out.

Kayda offered words of concern, but I kept my back to her.

The sword angled down a fraction as if acknowledging me. I *felt* the heat coming off it now. The vibration hadn't slowed.

"Don't be mad at her. She's my friend. She's trying to protect me."

Somehow, the blade glowed brighter.

"You can't be offended by that!"

The sword inverted itself and tapped its hilt once on the table. *Yes*, the tap said.

"Hey!" Kayda snapped from behind me. "Don't do that, Stabby. That's an expensive table. You're going to damage it."

Quick as a snake, the sword flipped itself 180 degrees and slammed its blade directly into the wood, pulled itself free, and then slammed into the wood a second time.

I slapped a hand to my forehead.

"Oh my Goddess!" Kayda said. I didn't have to look over my shoulder to know she'd just vaulted over the couch. "Stop it!"

The sword yanked itself out of the wood, hovered there for a brief moment, and then slowly turned itself so the tip of its curved edge kissed the wood. Then it dragged itself across it, like keying a car.

Kayda lunged for it, but the sword was too quick. It zipped to the other end of the table and then drew another long, deliberate line on the wood.

"No!" Kayda screamed, swiping for it and missing.

"Sword, stop it!" I tried.

The sword flew back the other way, where Kayda's unfinished breakfast still sat on a white porcelain plate. It hovered, tip first, a hair's breadth from the pile of scrambled eggs.

"Don't you dare!" Kayda said, pointing a finger at it from the other end of the table.

"I think you have to apologize for throwing it out the window!" I blurted.

The sword hummed.

Well, that was new.

"I'm supposed to apologize to *that*?" Kayda snapped. "I'm not going to say sorry to something that needs to be melted down and turned into something useful—like mundane cutlery."

The blade blazed, then lifted itself so it was parallel to the breakfast plate.

Oh hell.

I took several steps back.

SMASH!

The sword crashed, curved edge first, smack into the plate. It cut through eggs and porcelain and into wood. Porcelain shards scattered across the table and clinked to the floor. The sword yanked free and then swung wildly to the right, shearing off a chunk of a dining room chair. My mouth dropped open, my feet rooted to the ground, while I watched in horror. Kayda darted around the table at incredible speed, but the sword shot into the air above her head before she could grab it.

The sword could easily slice Kayda's hands off, but it was toying with her. Could it be enjoying this game of keep-away? It hovered near the nine-foot-tall ceiling. Kayda jumped, her fingers grasping frantically, but the sword stayed out of reach.

"Help me!" Kayda said.

"I did! You have to apologize!"

Kayda grabbed a non-mangled chair and stepped onto it, but the moment she did, the sword harpooned toward the kitchen, slicing through the curved neck of her faucet as if it were made of butter. The severed metal clanked into the sink below. The sword pivoted and flew toward a cabinet.

"I'M SORRY I THREW YOU OUT A WINDOW!" Kayda bellowed, her voice more hysterical than I'd ever heard it.

The sword stopped in midair, tip barely touching the cabinet door. It turned to face Kayda.

She glared at it, her chest heaving. My gaze darted between the sword and my best friend. The only sounds were our ragged breaths.

As the silence stretched, the blade slowly went molten.

"I think it wants you to be specific in your apology," I whisper-hissed.

Kayda sent me a long-suffering look. Of all the shit we'd been through, and the crazy crap I'd gotten myself involved in, a dragon sword slicing up her apartment might be the thing that finally broke her. Then she swiveled a look of disgust at the sword. "I'm sorry I said you should be melted down," she said through gritted teeth.

The sword grew even hotter, vibrating.

Kayda groaned. "And for suggesting you'd be more useful as kitchenware."

The blade instantly went back to a cool steel, and the sword floated itself into the open duffel bag. Kayda and I sagged in relief.

Wincing, I spun to take in the damage to her apartment. "I'm so sorry, Kay. I'll pay for all of this."

"The table is a family heirloom," Kayda said, stalking past me and into the kitchen. She touched a large fingertip to the hacked-off edge of the faucet, lost in thought.

I wrung my hands while I waited, worried she'd tell me to get out and never come back.

Finally, she turned to face me, her massive arms folded across her chest again, her upper thigh resting against the counter. In her usual matter-of-fact tone, she said, "You have to get rid of this thing, Harlow. I take back what I said about the dragon sword stories …" She motioned to her ruined table. "It was holding back. Think about what kind of destruction this thing could do if it really put its mind to it."

I eyed the bag warily and then hurried into the kitchen with her, grabbing her by the sleeve of her shirt as I went, and depositing us both by the front door. I lowered my voice. The sense of privacy, even if it wasn't real, made me feel better. "It wants me to help it. I think that's the only way to get rid of it. It doesn't want to stay with me, but it needs me to solve whatever its problem is."

"Why you?" Kayda asked, her tone curious but not unkind.

"No idea," I said. "Haskins's goons said the sword had never done anything like this. Why was the sword dormant until I stole it? I don't even know how long Haskins had it. All I know was that he bought it from a black-market auction—"

Kayda's yellow eyes went wide.

"Not one of Caspian's," I added quickly, and Kayda relaxed. "I need to figure out where it came from, though. Once I know that, then maybe I can figure out what to do with it next."

Kayda sighed heavily. "After that last one, I hoped I'd never have to go to one of those auctions ever again. But if you need to crash another one, just tell me when and where."

The last one hadn't been that bad, honestly. Though, to be fair to Kayda, during our escape, she'd torn her dress and broken a heel off her very expensive custom-made shoes.

"If we go to another one, you could put those new shoes to good use," I sing-songed. "Especially since dumbass Henri is still too scared to ask you out."

Kayda wrinkled her nose. "I think one of the guards at work is Pratt's cousin. His name is familiar. I'll see if he knows anything about recent auctions."

Luma might have been large, but the draken community was tight-knit.

My shoulders slumped. "I really am sorry about your apartment."

"I know," she said, sighing.

The first time Kayda visited my new apartment after the whole Felix fiasco, I'd been a puffy mess and she'd come over to both cheer me up and bring me a housewarming present. She hadn't known how to comfort blubbering-mess me, as blubbering wasn't wired into draken DNA. The last time she'd seen me that much of a mess had been after I'd just found out my dad had been killed in a drug-bust gone bad, and my mom had skipped town.

I'd been more angry than sad at first, and she, Felix, and I had gone out drinking at an ax-throwing bar. Throwing shit to make myself feel better had made sense to Kayda. The sobbing on the couch for a week after Felix dumped me had not.

Kayda's declarations of "you're better off without him" and "I never liked him anyway" and "he wasn't that hot, was he?" had done nothing but make me cry harder. In a fit of frustration,

Kayda had plopped her seven-foot frame on my coffee table, determined to be eye level with me when she gave her tough-love pep talk. The table had collapsed underneath her, the wood splintering, and she'd tipped backward, tumbling into my flimsy TV stand and knocking the TV off the surface and directly onto her rock-hard head. The TV had shattered much the same way the coffee table had, with knocked Kayda out cold.

The whole thing had been such a shock, it snapped me out of my crying jag. Aside from the couch I'd been sobbing on all week, Kayda had destroyed all my remaining furniture in a matter of seconds. But I'd been more concerned that Kayda might have irreparably harmed herself. When she finally came to, we both laughed so hard we cried.

The sword slicing up Kayda's place today was way worse, though.

Kayda said, "I have an idea. The upper floors had that pixie infestation last month, remember? They stole jewelry, chewed through wires, pooped all over the place. The landlord is terrible about actually getting rid of the things. I'll blame pixies first and see if he'll replace the faucet for me. Maybe he'll give me some extra cash to shut me up. He's already being sued by a former tenant, so he's not going to want more trouble. But if that fails …"

"I gotta replace a priceless family heirloom."

"And scrub this place top to bottom once a week for a month," Kayda added.

I grunted. "Fine."

Kayda cast a wary glance to the other end of her apartment. "I know it's too late to say this, but be careful, Harlow. Just *being* in Luma Proper with a sword like that is dangerous. And the scary thing is, I'm not even worried about you being arrested or someone sensing the sword and kicking the shit out of you to get it."

"Gee, thanks."

Ignoring me, Kayda said, "It's chosen you for some reason. So

I'm not worried about *you*. I'm worried about anyone stupid enough to try to *take* it from you."

I sighed.

"We'll figure it out," she said. "We always do. Check in with me later, okay? Let me know how the meeting with Grayson goes." She lowered her voice, casting a conspiratorial glance toward the sword's last known location before saying, "If Grayson takes the sword, you can finally get that finder's fee he's been dangling in front of you for a year, and you can stop looking for sunken pirate treasure. Win-win."

After collecting my stuff and hugging her goodbye, I walked down the hallway of her apartment complex, reminiscing about the last time I'd gotten myself into trouble over Grayson Ipram's whims …

CHAPTER SEVEN

One year ago

It was a minor miracle that I stepped out of the telepad without rolling an ankle or face-planting. It was also a minor miracle that I didn't pull off one of my stiletto heels to jam it in the eye socket of the guy who'd whistled as I headed for the exit. He was a burly guy who had shifter written all over him. Possibly a werecat, but given the overall bulk of the guy, I was leaning toward bear. A *recently* shifted bear, since the feel of his magic hung about him like a cloying fog. I kept moving.

As I walked out into the cool evening, I gave the plunging neckline of my little black dress a quick check to make sure the telepad ride hadn't caused an involuntary wardrobe malfunction. Spaghetti straps rarely held up in transit, so I'd gone for a halter dress tonight. Everything was where it should be.

I pulled out the hair tie that had kept my curls in place during teleportation, and let them flop around my shoulders again. I gave them a few sprucing shakes with my hand, then slipped the tie into my clutch purse.

I found Kayda standing on the sidewalk a door down from the telepad station. The woman was seven feet tall, yet still insisted on high heels for this evening's event. She'd had the shoes custom made a while ago and was excited to finally have an excuse to wear them. Her cherry red dress was skintight with a slit that hit her mid-thigh. She leaned against the wall, her focus on her phone, so she didn't see the draken man walking past her who gawked so hard he walked into a pole.

The *clang* of his giant head thwacking into the "No Parking" sign, and the groan of the pole being partially ripped from the cement, made Kayda look up. The draken man gasped when she made eye contact with him, his pale cheeks turning a dark purple in his embarrassment, and then he sprinted for the telepad station.

"What the hell was that?"

"Further proof Henri is an idiot for not asking you out," I said.

Kayda whimpered pitifully. The two had been dancing around each other for over a year now. I was half tempted to lure them both into a dark closet, barricade the door, and leave them in there for a couple of hours.

"I need to give up on Henri," she said, rubbing a hand across her short, soft white hair. "I got dressed at work and walked out of the bathroom like this," she said, first gesturing to the leg slit, and then giving a modeling twirl. "I timed it all perfectly so he'd see this rocking dress. His jaw damn near hit the floor. Then he ran away from me even faster than that guy." She shot a thumb toward the telepad station.

"I keep telling you: *you* have to ask *him*," I said, and jerked my head to the side, indicating that we should start walking.

She fell into step next to me. "If it was anyone else, I'd just go for it," she said, head bowed as we walked, her focus on the shiny red polish on her nails. "I just don't want to scare him away. He's such a gentle, kind guy, you know?"

I didn't. All draken were huge and intimidated the crap out of me, even if they happened to wear glasses and had a mild anxiety-induced stutter. "Yeah."

She gusted a long, weary sigh. "Anyway … what's the guy's name who we're meeting again? Is this a client thing?"

"His name is Fabian and yes, he's a client," I said. "When he sent the invite, he said it was to help me make more connections. But then he also said he couldn't wait to see me 'all glammed up.' So maybe he was hitting on me? I don't know." I coughed awkwardly and scratched at my neck.

Kayda's eyes bored holes into the top of my head. I refused to look at her. "What aren't you saying?"

"First and foremost, you need to know that he's crazy hot …"

Kayda groaned.

"He's also a … badger shifter."

She came up short. "Girl. You have *got* to be kidding me. They're batshit. Every last one of them."

"*Yeah*," I said, drawing the word out. "Did I mention crazy hot?" The glare she angled my way told me she did not care one iota about how attractive he was. "I figured this little outing would be up your alley because you like dressing like a fancy lady, but you also like to hit things. If badger boy misbehaves, you have my full permission to drop him to the ground."

Kayda pursed her thin lips, then looked down at herself. "The leg slit lets me kick ass even while looking like a ten."

"This is what I'm saying," I said, walking backward to encourage her to keep moving.

She followed me, a small smile tugging at her mouth even though she tried to tamp it down. "And you're sure this isn't a Caspian Blackthorn auction?"

"Positive," I said, turning to walk forward again. "Fabian said even if he could snag an invite to one of those, there's like a five grand door cover charge or something ludicrous. Caspian Blackthorn's auctions are for the super-elite. We are not super-elite."

"Yet … those super-elite weapons keep getting sold to humans who then blow their faces off," Kayda said.

"At least we can say Luma has its very own supervillain. A rogue sorcerer who takes gobs of money from the rich to fund his magical, off-regulation experiments that he tests out on humans like they're guinea pigs. Except the guinea pigs always die."

Kayda frowned. "I don't get why the Collective lets him do it. I mean, at this point, he's a household name. All of them are powerful sorcerers, and they hire and recruit some of the best magic users in the country. There's no reason they couldn't find him, right?"

"Unless Caspian is even stronger than they are. He could have cloaking spells strong enough that not even the Collective can detect him. He could be a master glamourer, too, or have someone in his entourage who is," I said.

Kayda shook her head. "Something about it doesn't add up."

I agreed with her, but we'd also had this conversation half a dozen times and I had no new insights—just as I hadn't a couple of months ago when the rogue sorcerer came up in conversation after that human had died in the very weird fire—weird, as in elemental-fire-weird. There had been rumors for years about a guy who sold Frankenweapons in high-end auctions. But just like the legendary club in the Warehouse District that changed locations, news of the latest Caspian Blackthorn auction only made the rounds well after the event was already over. The guest list was exclusive, the items one-of-a-kind, and the host elusive.

I'd heard about a gun, purchased by a human, that had "accidentally" gone off and killed the buyer. This particular story had made the rounds in record time because guns were banned in Luma, as they were in most hubs. Magic and firearms didn't mix, and when magic-enhanced parts were added to one, things usually went south very quickly not for the person in front of the barrel, but the one behind it. Spells had been layered into the city's veil to keep guns out.

This gun had exploded in the guy's hand, incinerated him instantly, and set his apartment on fire. It was clear it was no ordinary fire, though, because no smoke reached neighboring units. The fire didn't move into the hallway or even the walls outside the windows that had been blown out from the heat of the flames.

And in the middle of the room, on an unmarred patch of dingy carpet, lay the gun. The barrel had been peeled back like a banana, the metal melted.

It wasn't long before Caspian Blackthorn's name found its way into the whispered stories about strange human deaths.

If Caspian was believed to be a threat to Luma at large—mostly to the full-blooded human population—the Collective was clearly in no hurry to track him down and send him to a prison hub. Citizens of Luma were apprehended by the Collective's werecat guards, put on trial, and exiled for a lot less. It made a lady wonder if the Collective just didn't care enough about humans to intervene, or if Caspian was so powerful, they left him alone out of fear of retribution. Neither option sat well with me.

"Is there something specific at this auction you're looking for?" Kayda asked, thankfully changing the topic.

"Grayson gave me permission to bid up to three grand on anything that might be remotely sunken-pirate-ship related," I said, then patted the side of my clutch purse, where a pre-loaded payment card was taking up residence.

"What do you think the odds are that we'll ever know what was on that ship?" she asked.

"Slim to none. But he's promising a very high finder's fee, so I'll keep searching as long as he wants me to."

Grayson never came to these things himself. Witch elementals tended to avoid recreational venues where emotions could run high—casinos, sporting events, auctions. If a bidding war got too intense, things got ... dicey. Flooding an auction hall because you were upset about losing a bid was a surefire way to get yourself on the blacklist. Not to mention that the idea of Caspian Blackthorn loomed large in auction-goers' minds. No one truly knew who he was, so no one wanted to cause a scene and possibly anger the rogue sorcerer who could be hiding in the crowd, like a high-level talent agent lurking in the audience of a play. If Caspian was powerful enough to either evade the Collective for this long, or spook the Collective into looking the other way when it came to his blatant transgressions, none of us peons wanted to get on the supervillain's bad side.

After three more blocks, we took a left. A few doors down, twinkling fae lights ringed the roof and second-story balcony of a repurposed theater. A stretch limo pulled up out front and an elegant couple stepped out, the human-looking woman's arm looped around the bent arm of her elfin companion—if the tall, unnaturally lithe form was any indication. Men and women in their finery strolled toward the entrance in their shiny black shoes and towering heels. My feet were already killing me.

This event was black-tie optional, but everyone dressed up—that was half the fun. And no one here cared what brand name graced your labels. Events like this could make a girl feel like a million bucks … even if her dress had come off the clearance rack.

A male troll stood at the door, checking invitations while a female faun with a clipboard double-checked the list of approved attendees. The troll looked miserable, as did the buttons on his black vest, which were trying their best to stay fastened across the troll's barrel chest. He was my height, but twice as wide. My guess was he'd been roped into manning the door as a deterrent to any funny business. Maybe he'd cheer up if someone without an invitation tried to sneak past him, and then he could toss them against a brick wall.

Once the faun confirmed we were on the list, she pulled two black paddles out of a box by her hoofed feet and handed us each one. "Good luck!" she said, then waved us inside with a flourish.

Kayda had been quiet for most of the walk, but as we stepped into the lobby, she let loose a little gasp.

The area that had once held a ticket booth and concession stand had been transformed into a woodland paradise. The short tile entryway gave way to a floor covered in spongy moss and grasses. I took a tentative step onto the loamy ground, worried my stilettos would pierce the soft earth. Instead, it felt as if I were walking on a cloud in bare feet. A giant oak tree had sprung up at the back of the lobby, the trunk fused to the wall behind it. Leaf-covered branches stretched several feet into the room, squirrels and birds scurrying and chirping among the foliage. Curling vines snaked up the walls, their woody branches dotted with colorful flowers the size of my head.

At the base of the tree was an elaborate, tiny village. Houses were made of pebbles, their windows crafted from twigs, and their roofs topped with wide, sturdy leaves. Even more houses, these ones made of wood, hung from the branches of the tree like Christmas ornaments. Fae lights twinkled in tiny windows, while pixies, brownies, and other small winged fae walked down curving roads and flitted among the houses. They all wore finery, too. Small gems glittered on bodices and hems, and dotted their hair. They were all hired actors, I knew, meant to play roles, like humans in period dress giving tours of ghost towns. But I liked to think that this was what the fae world looked like. Did the hired pixies feel a connection to their lost home, or was this a kitschy, sugar-coated version of what they'd had? I hoped it was the former.

A few feet from the tiny fae neighborhood, a trio of goblins worked under a white pop-up canopy, its edges hung with twinkling lights. The interior of the canopy had been fashioned to resemble the inside of a goblin home. These three were in character, too, speaking in Goblish as they went about their tasks. A male goblin manned a cauldron, where something frothy bubbled menacingly—probably a soup. A woman and a young male goblin sat opposite each other at a table, the woman darning a shirt, while the boy painted a clay pot.

Woodland creatures scampered around the feet of a pair of elves who walked through the scene, bows strapped to their backs. Speaking in Elfin, they moved around Kayda and me as if we weren't there. In a far corner, a pair of draken women demonstrated their ax-throwing abilities—small hatchets whizzing through the air before *thunk*ing into a mounted circular cutout of a tree.

The air was perfumed with the heady scents of rich earth,

blooming flowers, and the threat of a warm rain. Even the ceiling was hung with twisting vines and vibrant flowers. I glanced at Kayda and smiled softly at the childlike twinkle in her eye.

"We are about to begin!" piped a voice through hidden speakers, breaking the illusion that a portal had opened and was giving us a glimpse of the world that had been closed to Earth for a century. "Please find your seats."

Reluctantly, Kayda and I followed other auction patrons out of the lobby, where the actors had resumed their roles after the brief announcement, and into the main auditorium. We had seats in the seventh row in the orchestra section, courtesy of Fabian. Normally, where you sat during an auction didn't matter as long as the auctioneer could see your paddle. But in Luma, auctions were a spectacle. On the wide stage, there were already acrobats and fire elementals putting on a pre-show. Kayda and I hustled to our seats so we wouldn't miss anything.

Fabian was already seated in our row, hard-core flirting with a woman in the row ahead of him. When we were halfway down the aisle, he glanced over and his mouth dropped open. He abruptly abandoned the woman he'd been talking to and jumped to his feet. He wore dark-gray slacks, a button-down white shirt, and his jacket had been tossed over the back of his chair. The sleeves of his shirt had been rolled up to his elbows, and the shirt unbuttoned to his navel, revealing smooth, tanned skin. His dark brown hair was almost shoulder length and shot through with lighter natural highlights. It wasn't a length most men could pull off. He swiped a hand through the already mussed curls, disheveling them into an even more random arrangement sexier than it had been before. He scanned me from head to toe and back again, his gaze lingering on my chest for a few long seconds before sliding back up. A slow, infectious smile inched up his face, his golden eyes vibrant.

Behind me, Kayda wrapped a hand around my elbow. "Holy. Shit," she muttered.

I know! I wanted to say, but my mouth had gone dry.

"Harlow!" he said, arms out.

I slipped into them, taking in his warm, spicy scent. Cinnamon, maybe? His chest was firm, his arms strong.

In my ear, he sensually purred, "You look gorgeous. I wish I could tear off your skin and wear it—to be inside you like you were a meat coat." He pulled back, holding me by the arms, and clacked his teeth three times. *Clack, clack, clack.*

Was I aroused or terrified for my life? Who could say?

He peered around me and gave Kayda and her leg slit an appraising scan. He licked his top lip, then let one of my arms go so he could give one of his exposed nipples a flick. Good grief.

This was exactly why I only interacted with this loopy man in public. I vowed that if we saw Fabian try to leave with the now-grumpy woman in front of us, we'd save her from herself, the same way Kayda had saved me from the elf. Fabian was radiating peak badger energy tonight.

As people made their way to their seats, concession vendors with sturdy trays resting at lap height and held aloft by thick straps that hung around their necks called out, "Soda! Beer! Cocktails!"

Many of the servers were wind elementals, so once an item was paid for, beverages and snacks magically floated to any waiting patrons seated in the middle sections of long rows. The air of the auditorium in the ten minutes before the start of the show was filled with shouts for refreshments and traveling cups.

When the lights dropped, the servers whisked back up the center aisles and cheers filled the space, especially from those in the second-floor balcony seats, which usually filled up first. If you had little interest in the items for sale but wanted relatively cheap drinks and a magic show, that was the place to be.

I idly tapped the edge of my auction paddle on my knee. Bidding with someone else's cash always made me nervous.

After a performance reminiscent of a mundane circus act—though all the animals were shifters—the emcee of the evening strolled onto the stage to great fanfare. He was one of the better performers, what with his ringmaster presence and wry sense of humor.

A group of goblins wheeled two tall boxes covered in billowing black sheets onto the stage while the emcee explained the rules of the auction for any novice attendees. Both boxes were a good six feet tall and positioned on either side of his lectern. When the emcee finished with his introductions, he said, "And without further ado, these are your items for the evening!"

The four remaining goblins whipped the sheets off the boxes with a great flourish, then scurried offstage as the audience collectively leaned forward. As the emcee explained what was up for sale, I deflated little by little. There was nothing here Grayson would want, so his money would go unspent tonight. However, the shield the size of a hubcap made from the hide of a chimera tickled my fancy. I had a human buyer uptown who was obsessed with chimeras. She'd given me a two grand finder's fee for a pair of hideous car dice I'd found at an estate sale last month. Well, the full-blooded human owner had *thought* they were car dice, and his father had used them as such for years, but they'd actually been made out of dried chimera tail tips. The magic in them had buzzed under my fingertips when I touched them. They'd reminded me of the spiky balls that fell off sweet gum trees. Little did the owner know that if one were to activate the dormant strength spells, a tiny ball that was no larger than a child's palm had devastatingly destructive capabilities. When attached to the end of a rope or chain, and with a powerful enough swing, one could punch holes through walls, fell trees, or destroy the limbs of an enemy.

After three auction items sold and two more performance interludes, the shield went up for sale. Throughout the auction, as the auctioneer called out the details of an item and the starting bid, the item in question was held aloft by a beautiful fae who walked up and down aisles and across the stage. It seemed that bids went up in direct proportion to the audience's increasing inebriation—and how attractive the fae participating in the display was.

A striking man with rust-colored hair strolled onto the stage from the wings, then plucked the shield off the rack and secured it to one of his toned arms. He wore only loose joggers—no shoes, no shirt. As the emcee went into detail about the shield, a second man walked onto the stage and grabbed a short sword off the other rack. While the first man moved with the grace of a dancer, this second man moved like a fighter. They both *looked* human, but either one could have been a shifter. My sixth sense did me little good in places like this, with magic pinging off every wall and corner.

The fighter twirled the sword a few times, then both men lowered into fighting stances. The fighter lunged for the dancer, fire sparking along the blade. When the flaming sword crashed down on the chimera shield, which the dancer crouched behind, the sword and the fighter were flung backward several feet, while the dancer didn't move a centimeter.

"Starting bid is $200!"

My paddle shot into the air.

In record time, the bid had jumped to $1,500, and I was locked in a bidding war with a guy in the back. Sometimes the price tags on these things skyrocketed solely due to pride. I knew Vanessa would match anything I paid, but anything over $2,500 pushed the limits of what I had readily available.

When I raised my paddle, raising the price to $1,700, Fabian leaned in close and whispered, "What do you say you and me get out of here, huh? I'll get us some Bliss and I'll pay *you* $1,700 to paddle my ass until I pass out."

He was now drunk on top of being … him. Which meant I couldn't explain to him—again—that while Bliss would make his crazy fae self feel incredible, it would probably kill *me*. And my dad would rise from the dead solely to slap me if I even considered it.

Something crashed in the back of the room, followed by a

scream. There was a collective shift of bodies in fabric-lined seats. A door that had been closed when the auction started had been thrown open—possibly *kicked* open. In the doorway stood a wide-shouldered man backlit by the fae lights still burning bright in the lobby.

"In the name of the Sorcerers Collective—" the man started, but was cut off by a woman who shot to her feet in the middle of the room.

"Werecat guard!"

And then everyone was on their feet and scrambling for the exits. This was a raid. Anyone in the building could be arrested simply for attending. Paddles couldn't be abandoned on the ground, because they could be examined with fingerprint analysis or the guards could use the scent left behind on the items to track the owner down.

I glanced over my shoulder, watching in horror as guards poured through the doors leading into the auditorium. Some came in as humans, some already in their giant feline forms, and others shifting from human to cat in mid-run.

Fabian led the way out of the packed row, but when that took too long, he shot an apologetic look over his shoulder, shifted into a badger, and took off under the seats. Streams of smaller animals barreled for the now-open doors on either side of the room. Goblins swarmed the stage, helping the emcee wheel the contraband items back into the wings. Screams filled the auditorium, blending with the cacophony of general panic as werecat guards poured into the room, pinning auction attendees to the ground with their massive paws. Once one was in magical shackles, a guard would pounce on someone else.

After Kayda and I made it into the aisle, I turned to the right, where the path sloped upward toward the four possible exits. But those paths were all clogged with werecats and fleeing patrons. I grabbed Kayda's wrist and pulled her to the left, where there were two exits. One led to the wings, then a back hallway, and eventually the back parking lot. There were doubtless tons of werecats waiting out there for attendees to spill out the back, so I pulled Kayda to the other door, which led to the second floor. Bodies shoved their way toward us, trying to get to the ground floor, so we had to push against the tide. When we hit the landing, I yanked off my shoes, grabbed them by the straps, and made a quick left.

My parents had conducted a raid of their own here once, and Felix and I had tagged along while they chased a pair of goblins up here who had successfully robbed four banks in as many months. They were short, gray-skinned Bonnie and Clyde knock-offs. Mom had said there'd been rumors circulating that the goblins were holed up on the top floor of the theater, in the old dance studio, which had been closed off for renovations. As I came up short at the padlocked door at the end of the hall, it was clear the renovations were still on hold.

I pulled my lock picks out of my clutch and got to work on the padlock. Kayda leaned against the wall next to me and groaned. I still heard an endless stream of feet pounding down the steps in the stairwell just behind the wall where Kayda stood. No one had come running down this hallway—after all, when one is being chased in a scary movie, going *up* the stairs was a quick way to get cornered, and then dead.

"This is awful," Kayda moaned miserably, and I glanced over my shoulder, an apology on my tongue for dragging her out here, but she wasn't looking at me. She had one of her fancy shoes in her hand, and the other idly flicked at the broken heel, barely holding on by a scrap of red fabric.

"Aw, damn," I said, returning my attention to the padlock. "I'm sorry, Kay."

"This is stupid Henri's fault," she muttered, then sniffed.

If she was going to blame him instead of me, I wouldn't stop her.

"Got it!" I said, triumphant, and the padlock popped open.

I pulled the chains free from the handles, yanked open the door, and darted through. Kayda ran after me, in bare feet now, too. The floor was dusty and littered with the debris of a half-finished renovation. Windows surrounded the room, but it was high up enough that no one could see in unless they were on the roof of the building opposite.

"This way!" I said, heading for the swinging doors of a balcony. This one faced a back alley. The Clyde half of the bank-robbing goblin pair had tried to go out this way, but Dad had caught him before he could get over the side.

I pushed open the doors and ran to the edge of the wrought iron balcony. A stone-wall-enclosed patio was directly below us.

Kayda joined me, looked down, and then sighed. "Up and over?"

"Up and over."

She and I had scaled walls, jumped fences, and dropped off enough balconies in our youth that the height didn't bother either of us. Doing it all while clad in skintight dresses was new, though.

A minute later, neither one of us any worse for wear—though a tear marred one side of Kayda's dress; she thankfully hadn't noticed yet—we walked barefoot up the alley, our shoes dangling from our fingertips. We stopped at the mouth of the alley and peered around the corner to gauge the situation. It would probably be a good idea to avoid the telepad station for at least another hour.

We jumped back when a rust-colored caracal sprinted past us, a black panther in hot pursuit. Thankfully, the panther was focused intently on the other cat and didn't even glance our way. We stood straight again.

"Being friends with you is an experience, you know that?" Kayda asked. "I get into a lot less trouble when I stay home."

"True, but girl's nights out with me are more fun."

She frowned at that, giving her broken heel another tentative flick. It flopped like a broken, lolling neck.

I knew she wasn't upset with me. She was still bummed about Henri—and her shoes. I wanted to cheer her up. Peering across the street, I spotted the glowing sign of one of my favorite restaurants on this side of town.

Peering up, I asked, "Ramen?"

"You paying?"

"Yep." I held out my bent arm to her, eyebrows raised expectantly.

A small smile graced her face, and she slipped her arm through mine. We darted across the street, the sound of distant sirens wailing behind us.

CHAPTER EIGHT

Present Day

I stood on the sidewalk outside Kayda's place and permitted myself to take a breather before I made my next move. Kayda lived just outside Luma Proper, in the Ardmore neighborhood, which was north of mine. It ended up being the perfect location for her when she landed the casino job; it was a ten-minute walk. If I peered between the two buildings across from me, I could see the casino from here, the golden walls of the massive structure glinting in the morning sun.

Kayla's neighborhood was still far enough away from downtown Luma that buildings were squat and more widely spaced here. Across the street was a block of one- and two-story office buildings intermixed with coffee shops, cafés, and, farther down the street, the only telepad station for several miles. People in business casual streamed out onto the sidewalk from the station. Personal vehicles were more common on this side of town, but there still weren't many of them on the streets here. Cars were usually of the older, mundane variety—with actual engines instead of computerized machines. Those were too easily tampered with—both by technology and magic. I, and most of Luma's residents, preferred to get around by foot or bicycle when a telepad ride wasn't an option. In the heart of downtown Luma, it was all taxis, delivery vehicles, and buses transporting large swaths of tourists and heavy drinkers between casinos and events.

People occasionally road-tripped between magical hubs, needing a travel talisman to get them through the veil and into the city. But why drive for hours when you could teleport yourself in a few seconds? Teleporting longer distances exponentially increased your chances of being reduced to a pile of meat, but what was life without a little risk?

The morning sun already felt relentless and sweat pooled at the small of my back. I knew I wasn't sweating just from the heat. Kayda's warning rang in my head.

Since no one was currently in earshot, I pulled the duffel off my shoulder and held the bag in front of my face. In an authoritative tone, I whispered, "I need you to be on your best behavior. If you have some kind of cloaking magic, use it now. Most dragons had that, so hopefully you do, too. The last thing either of us needs is someone detecting you."

I got a single muted metallic tap in response.

That was the best I was going to get. I stuck my arm back through the handles and rested them on my shoulder.

"Uh … hi? Hello?"

I turned at the sound of a male voice and found a decidedly human guy stumbling toward me. He was neither intoxicated nor injured, but his wide eyes told me he was in distress all the same.

"Yeah?"

He stopped in front of me, then bent forward, hands on his knees. After taking in a couple of gulps of air, he stood to full height, wincing dramatically. "Aw, man. I'm so glad to finally find a normal person."

He clearly hadn't seen me giving my bag a pep talk a second

earlier. I tucked the duffel a little closer to my side. He just stared, heaving.

"Can I help you with something?" I asked. "Are you lost?"

The man laughed, but it was semi-hysterical, as if it was the most ludicrous question he'd ever been asked. "You have no idea. Or, I don't know, maybe you do, since you're here."

I cocked a brow.

"So, uh, my car unexpectedly and spectacularly broke down on the highway. And my cell phone died right after that, so I couldn't call a tow truck. I was walking toward what I thought was a mechanic shop, but it was like a mirage or something because the shop never got any closer no matter how far I walked," he said, talking faster and faster with each word. His face was flushed and perspiration dotted his hairline. "Then I turned back to my car, thinking I should wait there in case a cop drove by or something, you know? I get there and this *weird*-looking guy is sitting on the hood of my car. Like *on* the hood. Cross-legged. He looked like he was straight out of *Lord of the Rings* or some shit and I was thinking maybe I was farther south than I realized and a comic book convention was happening. Those are in summer, right? But if I'm in San Diego now when I swear I was in Central California like an hour ago, I have bigger problems than I realized. But why else would a guy be dressed like *that* when it's 100 degrees out? And he had pointed ears!"

Ah, another human who had gotten himself into trouble because of an elf. "Did he give you anything to eat or drink?"

The guy sputtered and stopped mid-ramble. "I … uhh … yeah? He gave me a bottle of water 'cause it's hot as hell and he said if I walked this way for a few minutes, I'd find a gas station on the edge of a new residential development. He said it wasn't on maps yet."

I stifled a groan. Elves were the worst!

Whatever the elf had laced the water with had probably included something that would keep the guy from feeling the full effects of the veil surrounding the city when he passed through it.

The elf was also likely responsible for the broken-down car and dead cell phone. To a full-blooded human, touching the veil would feel like touching a cattle prod, and would fill a person with such intense fear that they'd sprint away from the location, vowing never to return.

I glanced around now, looking for the elf who had lured this unsuspecting human in here. Humans ended up here one of three ways: recruitment from the Collective because of their perceived usefulness, like my parents; or they were born here, like me; or they were closely associated with fae on the outside, and the fae made arrangements to get their human friend/lover/bandmate past the veil.

I stalked down the sidewalk, the lost human calling after me while staying close on my heels. I didn't expect to see the elf. More than likely, he was still on the other side of the veil, waiting for another human to bestow with roadside grief. The elf would care little about what happened to the traumatized human who stumbled into a hidden magical city. Telling him this "residential development" wasn't on maps was the hugest understatement possible for this poor guy. The elf was probably still cackling over his successful prank.

For a minute or two, I scanned the area, willing myself to detect something. The guy had stopped rambling and was just wringing his hands now, his wide gaze darting this way and that. Nothing.

"All right," I said, "follow me." I headed the other way.

He quickly made an about-face and hurried to walk alongside me. He started to say something, but he snapped his mouth shut when a woman up ahead on the sidewalk thrust her hands out toward a building, water spraying from her palms and dousing the windows of a bakery. A small geyser of water shot up below her feet, lifting her into the air so she could give the windows on the second floor a quick rinse, too. Elemental witch turned window washer. The man next to me gaped.

"What *is* this place?" he asked, voice soft. "Where the hell am

I? Did that weird guy give me drugged water? Is that why you asked if he gave me anything to eat or drink? Am I high on PCP? Is the pointy-eared guy going to put me in a bathtub full of ice so he can steal my organs?"

"Movie studio," I said calmly, hoping my chill vibe would take his cracked-out one down a notch. It was a common lie Luma residents told lost humans when they found the place by accident. "A lot of high-level stunt work happens here. We test out stuff for superhero movies. Got to keep pushing the envelope, right?"

The guy's expression said he only half-believed me.

I led him to a building nestled between the telepad station and an office. The sign outside the plain brick building said, "Visitors Services," but inside were government employees who could get the guy home safely, with all memory of this place scrubbed from his short-circuiting brain. Centers like this were stationed along the outer edge of Luma, where there had been enough instances of humans slipping past the veil that instead of treating the source—bored elves, in this case—they treated the symptom. Visitors centers were like deer crossing signs on the highway.

"Ugh," a woman behind the counter said softly as we walked in, hurrying over. She had bright green eyes and moved in a quick, graceful way. As she peered at the man with wide, unblinking eyes, her head cocked to one side, and then quickly to the other. Bird-like. Probably griffel—a griffin descendant. More to herself than to either of us, she said, "Another one? This is the third one in a week."

"Someone gave him a bottle of water," I told the woman, then tapped the top of my ear to indicate I meant an elf.

She pursed her lips. "Thanks. We've been wondering. I'll call it in."

The man hardly paid attention to our conversation, too busy looking around the room as if he expected someone to pop up and yell "Gotcha!" But then he gave the woman who had just gently taken him by the arm a thorough once-over. She guided him toward a couch in the lobby. "Your eyes are so green. Are they contacts?"

She laughed, a melodious sound reminiscent of bird song.

The guy seemed charmed, at least, and I offered the woman a quick wave before I ducked back out onto the street. I got in line at the telepad station next door.

"Just being in Luma Proper with a sword like that is dangerous," Kayda's voice repeated in my head as I joined the line curled and bent in on itself three times. It would take at least ten minutes for me to reach the front. Ten minutes for my nerves and wild thoughts to have a free-for-all.

Luma Proper was roughly circular, and at the dead center stood the Sorcerers Collective headquarters, housed in an obelisk-shaped tower. Uptown and downtown made up Luma Proper, cut horizontally across the middle by a figurative line, rather than a literal one. The werecat guards' stronghold took up the ground floor of the tower, the bounty hunters headquartered on the floor above that, and the Collective sorcerers themselves resided on the third floor. It was easily the safest location in the entire city. The top half of the tower was covered in runes that matched the ones etched on smaller obelisks which ringed Luma as a whole. The main obelisk fed magic into the smaller ones, and the smaller ones kept the veil in place. They were like fence posts that surrounded the city, connected by the invisible veil magic that kept the hub city hidden.

The sorcerers-in-charge maintained the runes on the obelisks, and the magic was touched up and reinforced depending on how much activity a section of the veil got. Official entrances to the city saw daily traffic from tourists and supply vehicles, so the rune magic had to be strengthened every few days. The sections of the veil that got less activity, like the stretches on the side of a highway, were touched up less. Once in Luma Proper, you either lived "above" the Collective's tower in uptown, or "below" the tower in downtown Luma. Josephine lived and worked downtown.

Magic would surround me there. I pulled the elastic out of my ponytail, letting the curls tumble around my shoulders, then got the wild mass back into a tighter hold. Mostly, I needed to keep my hands busy. I hoped like hell that the sword was doing what it could to shield itself from detection. No one in the station seemed to notice anything out of the ordinary. It wasn't like I expected a mob of people to tackle me to the ground, driven mad by sword lust. But anyone with any semblance of a sixth sense would be able to detect that I was nothing but a full-blooded human, and yet had an object on me with more magic than someone like me should be carrying—which would mark me either as a bounty hunter or a charm collector. The average Luma citizen wouldn't want to deal with either: the former would be working for the Collective, and the latter purposefully bypassing its laws.

"Next!"

I stepped up to the telepad attendant and told him where I was headed. After he keyed in the information and I'd paid my fee, I was about to walk inside the cylinder when a piercing wail sounded in the station.

Oh no! They found me! They know I have the sword!

I whirled around, sure I'd see a pack of werecat guards barreling toward me on massive paws. But everyone's attention was focused to my right. Glancing that way, pulse pounding in my ears, a man stumbled out of the cylinder at the end of the room, then collapsed. Just straight-up face-planted on the tile. His face—probably his nose—landed with a meaty *thunk*.

Three triage nurses burst out of a room in the corner with a stretcher, loaded the elderly man onto it, then took off with him back the way they'd come, the door slamming shut behind them. I flinched.

Over the loudspeaker came a calm, female voice. "A telepad passenger without the proper health clearance suffered cardiac arrest while in transit. He is being treated now by highly trained professionals. This is a reminder to get your six-month checkup. Telepad travel is safe and effective, but should only be used with express permission from your physician. Travel may now resume. Thank you for traveling with us."

I just stood there dumbly, staring at the door where the unconscious man had been taken. Was this a sign? Maybe I could drop the sword down a sewer drain. It would take it a while to find me again, right? Especially if I took a telepad ride to Alaska right afterward.

"You change your mind?"

I jumped. The telepad attendant stared expectantly.

"Nope." Then I stepped into the cylinder.

CHAPTER NINE

A second later I stepped out into the utterly gigantic Luma Central Station. My nerves were shot. I walked the six feet from the telepad to the throng of people and slipped into the fray. Voices filled the cavernous space, the sound echoing off the high ceilings. I tipped my head back as I walked, searching for pixies. They were always in here, as common a sight as the cooing pigeons in the rafters. Several pixies crouched atop kiosks, watching travelers. A draken ahead of me walked past an eight-foot-tall kiosk, eye level with him, and causally swatted away the gathered pixies with the wave of a giant hand. The tiny winged pests took to the air en masse, hissing, spitting, and calling obscenities from a safe distance above the draken's head.

In most transit stations, one had to mind their purse and/or wallet, as goblins, imps, and human children, being no more than four feet tall, were the prime height for snatching people's valuables without notice. But in places like Luma Central, one had to watch for threats from above, too. I'd once had a swarm of pixies fly at my face like a swarm of bees, and while I was busy swatting them away, a couple of others had sawed through my purse strap with their little needle teeth, and then the gang had made off with my bag. I'd almost lost everything—a wallet full of cash, a set of unicorn-ivory daggers, and a pouch of two dragon scales—but a pair of air elemental teenagers had seen the commotion and not only knocked the thieving pixies out of the air, but returned my bag to me with nothing missing.

That had been a few years ago. The pixies hadn't stopped harassing travelers since then, but they'd gotten smarter about it. Now, when pixies robbed you blind, you wouldn't know it until you were already outside, trying to pay for a taxi.

Draken, shifters, witches, goblins, less common fae like fauns, and humans were all here. There were beings as tall as nine feet and as short as just one. Skin colors ranged from the palest white to the darkest black and everything in between. The *whoosh, whoosh, whoosh* of beings popping in and out of existence was like a heartbeat, the pulse of the station. Voices, shouts, and laughter filtered through the air among the watching pixies. Courier birds zipped to and fro—ravens, owls, and falcons. At night, courier bats dipped and wove through the rays of moonlight pouring in through the windows that lined either side of the wide, peaked roof.

There was a constant flow of travel at all hours in here. I let the swell of movement carry me toward the exit and kept my bag held tight to my side. Like Kayda had said—I wasn't worried about myself so much as the idiot who tried to take the sword from me. I imagined the sword playing possum while a gang of pixies ran off with it, cackling madly at finding such a rare sword. Tiny screams would echo across the station soon after, followed by charred leaf shoes, flower-petal clothes, and shredded gossamer wings raining down like black snow on horrified patrons.

Shaking the image loose, I stepped out into the sweltering summer heat. I stopped beside one of the columns holding up the stone pediment that stood above the dozen propped-open doors of the station. A line of taxis idled at the curb, with dozens more waiting around the corner for an open spot.

Across the wide street, clogged with bicycles, delivery vehicles, and taxis, was downtown Luma. People swarmed every inch of the sidewalks, where restaurants and shops lined the road facing the station. The prime real estate location meant the prices for food and goods in most of them were out of my price range. It was a fun place to window-shop, though. Towering office buildings and hotels rose in the distance, sunlight winking off shiny windows and gilded accents. Banners and signs advertising casinos, renowned magicians' shows, and happy hours hung from lampposts, sat atop taxis, and flashed from the tops of buildings.

Blowing out a steadying breath, I stepped back into the throng of beings making their way on foot across the street, weaving around the taxis pulling up to and leaving the curb. Horns blared, hooves clopped, massive feet stomped, tiny wings fluttered. I'd been to downtown Luma countless times, and yet there was always something overwhelming about it during the first few minutes, as if I needed to recalibrate my breathing and heartbeat to match the frenetic energy of the place.

As I stood on the corner clustered with hundreds of people waiting to cross Central Avenue, a thick line of bicyclists rode by. I spotted a few sweaty-faced blue-shirt-wearing telepost couriers and hoped they'd make it to their destinations in time.

The pole of the traffic signal was plastered with posters and flyers, wrapped round and round with tape. They'd be removed in a few days, only to be replaced overnight by others: restaurants advertising lunch specials, missing pet flyers, a photo of a guy with a white rodent of some kind on his shoulder, and a headline above his picture that said, "Are you looking for love? Look no further! Must love ferrets." There were pull tabs cut into the bottom of the flyer, several of which had been torn free.

There were several missing person photos, too. *"Have you seen this girl?"* I spotted the smiling mouth of an elfin girl and the shy eyes of a goblin teenager. Luma might have been shielded from the outside world, but it wasn't as if it were free from the same crimes and tragedies that befell every large city, magical or not.

The light changed and we all moved as a unit across Central and toward Farrow. Once the group hit the curb, people streamed left, right, and forward, up the inclining Tabbert Road. That was where I was headed. During the warmer months, between six in the morning and eleven in the evening, the weaving, meandering streets of this area of downtown didn't allow any vehicles other than bicycles. People freely walked up the middle of the road without fear of being mowed down by a delivery driver. Street food vendors shouted from behind their carts, offering everything from burgers to goblin delicacies—which were usually comprised of all the scraps of things most people, of all races, threw away. I'd tried corn-husk-and-cactus soup once when a particularly persuasive goblin had convinced me I hadn't truly been living until I had his signature dish. What I got was a severe case of food poisoning that left me bedridden for three days. Goblins were the goats of the fae world; they could eat literally anything.

This was one of the busiest intersections in downtown Luma, and offered five directions, each one lined with restaurants, shops, hotels, and the occasional high-rise residential building. People were everywhere.

A contingent of the Vampire Hunters of America was here too, shouting at passersby that the end times were nigh and that we had to arm ourselves if we had any hopes of survival. Fifteen men and women of all human races and ages, including a couple of teenage girls, milled about. Everyone wore head-to-toe black, and they'd also coated the entirety of their necks with red paint to signify their biggest vulnerability. The ringleader stood atop an overturned trash can, yelling into a megaphone while his followers crowded around him, holding homemade signs and handing out pamphlets.

They were the religious fanatics and doomsday preppers of hub cities. Just like with the mundane world's fanatics and preppers, it wasn't always the message that was the problem, but its presentation. It was difficult to get behind someone's deeply believed philosophy when they were aggressively shouting it in your face. Clothes dirty and ripped, they looked like they'd just stumbled here from a battle with vampires—and had barely made it out alive.

They were known for getting into scuffles with the werecat guards, as both sets prowled the veil perimeter at night. The werecats were out there on assignment from the Collective, making sure no one from other hubs was attempting to sneak through the veil without going through proper channels first. Travel talismans —regulation and off-regulation—could be purchased in every hub, but they could get pricey depending on the kind you got. Even the off-regulation one-ways that could get a human through the veil without scrambling their brain only worked to get someone *into* a hub. Once inside, you had to find another talisman to get you back out; the magic needed to keep said brain from scrambling required too much juice, so most of them fritzed out after one use. The Collective had enough systems in place that if you snuck into Luma, establishing any kind of legit life here would be damn hard.

The Vampire Hunters of America ran their own nightly patrols, searching for any signs that feral vampires were trying to breach the veil.

Across the street from the hunters was a rival group, though it was much smaller. There were usually never more than two to three people setting up shop wherever the vampire hunters were, actively working to debunk the hunters' claims. Each one wore white, calmly sat in a lounge chair, and instead of screaming into megaphones, had a wide-screen laptop set up on top of a large boxy subwoofer. Additional speakers sat on the ground on either side of the seated pair, blasting a news clip that had become a viral sensation over the past couple of months. The vampire hunters on the other side of the street were doing what they could to be heard over the voice of Frank Leslie piping out of the speakers. Sadly for the hunters, the debunkers had a larger audience.

On-screen, Frank Leslie was being interviewed about his claim that a vampire had snatched his wife out of their bed in the middle of the night. He did a walkthrough of his house, showing the reporter the thick trail of blood that led from their bed, down the hall, out the back door, across the yard, and down the driveway. The blood trail had stopped abruptly at the end of the driveway, as if someone had picked up the bleeding body and run off with it.

"He flung her over his shoulder like she weighed nothing!" Frank wailed, his eyes dry. "See this ..." He held out his arm, showing a pair of puncture marks on his wrist. "The vampire bit me first to get me all doped up on its poisoned saliva, and then it attacked my wife. I watched it drag her out. I stumbled out the door even though my legs weren't working right, slamming into walls and almost slipping in her blood—so much blood. I could barely walk but I still chased that vampire out here. I stood right here as that beast ran off with her."

The reporter, despite the man's hysterics and how soaked in blood he was, didn't seem at all moved by the man's story. "You're a member of the Vampire Hunters of America, right?" she'd asked him.

The small, assembled crowd around the laptop booed at the name of the organization. The hunter atop the trash can shouted a little louder into his megaphone.

Frank Leslie stood straighter on-screen. "Yes, ma'am. I'm doing God's work, helping to save Luma from these monsters when the Collective won't lift a finger to help us."

"Do you think this was retaliation from the vampires for your ... work against them?" the reporter asked.

A light seemed to go off in Frank's head. "That's gotta be it! They targeted me." He turned his blood-streaked face to the camera, pleading with his audience. "This is what I'm sacrificing for you people. Wake up! The vampires are out there and your family might be next!"

Just last month, though, good ol' Frank Leslie really became a household name when overwhelming proof had been collected by the mundane police that Frank had been the one who'd brutally murdered his wife. He suspected she'd been having an affair with another vampire hunter—which *also* turned out to be false. After killing her, he'd dragged her body out of their house, thrown her in the back of his SUV, and driven to a secluded rural road before setting the car on fire. One neighbor had witnessed Frank driving away in the middle of the night, while another had seen Frank return to his house on foot, covered in blood and soot. Footage of Frank's arrest and arraignment were played next on the propped-up laptop.

As if the Vampire Hunters of America needed any help to look like an unhinged band of loons. My attention swiveled back toward the hunters.

"The veil doesn't keep you safe!" the ringleader shouted into the megaphone. "The veil keeps us trapped, makes us lose touch with our instincts. The vampires are out there, man! They're out there preparing. They grow strong while we grow weak. The veil isn't a cage that keeps *them out*, it's a cage that keeps *us in*!"

A teenage girl noted that I'd gone from watching the Frank Leslie footage to watching her illustrious leader, and that apparently bolstered her confidence to dart over to me with a pamphlet. She was pale, with hair so blonde it was almost white. She couldn't have been older than seventeen.

"You're a fighter," she said in a small but firm voice as I took the pamphlet from her. "We can help make you even stronger. We're going to need all the fighters we can get."

Before I could think of a response, she hurried back across the street to join her group. She flushed a deep red, almost matching the red paint coating her long, thin neck, as she was welcomed back into the fold with pats on the back and shoulders from her fellow hunters. Good job, they were saying. We'll win this war one recruit at a time.

I stared down at the pamphlet in my hand, the black, trifolded glossy paper. All the text and images were in stark white or blood red. Their logo was of a set of teeth, the canines elongated, enclosed in a circle that had a slash through it. The words "Vampire Hunters of America" curved over the top in the shape of a horseshoe. It wasn't the most creative of logos, but it got the point across.

I skimmed the words briefly, finding the same information their ringleader had already shouted at the uninterested crowd. I slipped the pamphlet into my bag and offered the teen girl a slight smile as I headed off. Mostly I didn't want to kill her high by having her see me toss the pamphlet in the trash. I'd toss it later.

I harbored some sympathy for the group, since my parents had met because of it. Just as I had a sixth sense that tipped me off when something magic-related was nearby or about to throw a wrench into my plans, my parents had both grown up with an ability to sense supernatural beings. Having seen and experienced enough decidedly not-human things in their young lives, they'd joined a vigilante vampire-hunting group in their hometown. Most of the members, they said, had a screw loose, but the two of them had connected instantly, going on to create their own small monster-hunting company. It was that work that got them on the radar of the Collective's recruitment team.

If fringe groups like the Vampire Hunters of America didn't exist, I might not exist either. Though I liked to believe that my parents' connection had been strong enough that if it hadn't been the vigilante group in their hometown of Sacramento that brought them together, something else would have.

The man's voice on the megaphone battled against the looping video of Frank Leslie behind me as I walked away. I lightly shook my head. The Vampire Hunters of America needed a cause where their organizational skills, dedication, and passion could make a difference in Luma. It was like people on the West Coast being deathly afraid of being bitten by recluse spiders when recluse spiders didn't live here.

My stomach rumbled, derailing my thoughts of vampires. I ducked into a small draken café to grab a breakfast sandwich smothered in cheese. I had devoured half of it by the time I got back outside, then continued up Tabbert Road.

Ahead of me, a pair of performers were getting ready to start their circus street show. Observers formed a wide oval around the two men. Even though I had places to be, I stopped to watch and finish my sandwich.

"I am Enrique, an elemental fire witch," one of the buskers said, clad in a white bodysuit with red-and-orange simulated flames licking up his right leg. He raised a toned brown arm in the air and gave his audience a debonair smirk.

"I am Carlo," said the second man, walking around the outside edge of the circle of people, winking at ladies as he sauntered by. He was dressed in an outfit identical to Enrique's. With an even more dramatic flair of his arm, he added, "And I am human."

A few murmurs flitted about the group. I threw the wrapper in a trash can and slipped my hands in my pockets.

"Magic is not everything," Enrique said as he walked to the end of the circle opposite Carlo and, with a flourish, formed a perfect O of fire that had the diameter of a hula hoop. He lifted it in the air so the hollow center faced Carlo on the other side of the circle. "Magic is a skill to be honed like any other." With elaborate hand motions, the ring of fire changed shapes. A heart, a diamond, a swarm of fire butterflies that winged across the circle and fluttered over the heads of children, just out of reach. Then he reformed the perfect O. "It is not I who you should watch, but Carlo."

Heads swiveled toward the human on the opposite side of the elongated oval. Carlo stomped his feet—left, right, left, right. He theatrically looked around those assembled while he stomped, then raised his hands in the air several times, palms up, urging the crowd to join in.

The observers stomped their feet—left, right, left, right. Thump, thump, thump, thump. Once the crowd had the rhythm, Carlo stilled, took a deep breath, and then ran toward the ring of fire. A moment later, he thrust out his hands and completed a complicated series of tumbling passes, hands and then feet touching the hard asphalt for only a breath before he was tumbling again. Spinning and flipping, head over feet.

Thump, thump, thump, thump.

"It's getting smaller!" a little voice cried out, worried Carlo wouldn't reach the circle in time.

Heads swiveled back the other way. With every second that passed, the width of the fire ring shrunk. The smaller the circle got, the more tense the crowd became, and the quicker they stomped their feet, as if they'd decided as one that if they picked up the pace, the human would too.

Thumpthumpthumpthump.

Carlo twisted himself in midair before he landed his next flip, and now was flipping and spinning backward. I'd seen this routine dozens of times, yet my heart was still in my throat, worried Carlo wouldn't get to the ring of fire and slip through it in time.

"He's not going to make it!" someone yelped.

Just as the tips of Carlo's perfectly pointed feet passed through the rapidly closing circle, the ring snapped closed, leaving only a spot of black smoke wafting in the air. The human landed perfectly on his ballet-slippered feet. His pristine white costume was unmarred by scorch marks, holes, or soot. He thrust a hand into the air. The crowd cheered.

Smiling, I kept moving up the inclined sidewalk. Two more blocks and a right turn put me outside Josephine's shop. The sidewalks and streets were no less busy here. Across from her shop, an elemental air witch dressed like a clown made balloon animals for a gaggle of excited kids. But these were no ordinary balloon animals. These galloped around in the air and dipped and swooped like living creatures.

I pushed my way into Jo's Apothecary.

Josephine's shop was a cramped maze of a store, crammed full of everything a witch could ever want. The inside was warm and smelled earthy. Even though the wooden floors creaked under my feet, I always half expected the ground to be layered in soft rich soil, with moss growing on the walls. Most witches were students of nature, pulling their magic from the world around them. Josephine had waxed poetic to me enough times for it to sink in that witches believed magic was in everything. Elemental witches were rarer and could only tap into one of the four major elements. They were flashier, and often sought dynamic careers, partly because they needed to use their magic often or it affected their moods. They were temperamental, connected to the wildest, most extreme parts of nature. They were often the celebrities of the witch community, not unlike Enrique outside.

But the average witch was more like Josephine: happy to use their magic in practical ways, always aware of maintaining the balance of nature, and never abusing their connection to it. The wares in her shop reflected that, offering potions and talismans that never tipped past a 3 on the magic scale.

I was sure that the dagger I'd taken from Haskins's basement, and that had zapped me straight off my stool last night, had a Level 4 lightning spell in it.

I scanned the shop, searching for Josephine. Patrons wove between the freestanding shelves and old wine barrels, wooden crates, and baskets scattered around the room filled with goods. Floors creaked underfoot every few seconds, making me think of an old woman complaining about her aching bones. Josephine must have been in the bowels of the shop somewhere helping a customer. She wasn't behind the counter, but her young apprentice was. He was a nice guy, but he always watched me warily. I couldn't tell if I made him shy because he was attracted to me, or if I made him nervous because I gave off an unsettling vibe. I had my bets on the latter.

A display of homemade soaps caught my eye and I perused the selection while I waited. The clear, rectangular bodies of the soaps had dried flowers dotting their insides. Little cards detailing the soaps' ingredients, as well as the spells infused into them, were held in place by bows tied around the bars with burlap string. I picked up the Summer Swoon bar, flecked with sunflower petals. The associated spell was supposed to encourage a shy admirer to approach you if he or she inhaled the scent wafting from your skin. Maybe if this bar of soap got Kayda a date with Henri, she'd let me off the hook and I wouldn't have to scrub her bathroom for the next four Saturdays.

"Is that you, Fletch?"

I smiled as I looked up, instantly recognizing Jo's voice. I put the bar of soap back. "Hey."

Jo was in her fifties, with deep brown skin, and long black hair that fell past her back in gentle waves. She was slender, soft-spoken, and, even in warm weather, dressed in long flowing dresses that fell to her ankles. Where Kayda was terrifying at first glance, Jo was easy to dismiss as a spacey weirdo. But all one needed to do was make eye contact with her and the intelligence staring back would make a person rethink their assessment of her.

When she reached me, that alert gaze locked on the duffel bag tucked against my side. Then she cocked a dark brow. "What in the world have you gotten yourself into now, Fletch?" Her tone was somehow both light and cutting.

I winced. "I was hoping you could tell me."

She ticked her head toward the back of the shop. I followed. She opened a door in the corner that led to her work-slash-storage room. When I pulled the door shut behind me, Jo waved a hand in the air, not even looking over her shoulder. The mechanism in the door clicked, locking us in. The sides of the narrow hallway were stacked so high with books and boxes that they touched the low ceiling. There was only enough room for one person to make their way down the hallway at a time. While her shop had a rich earthy scent, her workroom had a faint aroma of damp towel. There were no windows to speak of; she usually kept this part of the shop locked up tight.

Jo turned left into a small space even more cramped than the store beyond the door. A desk was pushed against the wall, a wooden arch lined with small cubbyholes sitting on top. Every cubby was stuffed with odds and ends—small glass vials, bundled dried herbs, spools of twine. The other two walls of the little alcove were as stacked with books and boxes as the hallway. The main surface of the desk was cleared away though, and Jo gestured for me to place the bag on it.

I did so, then slowly unzipped the bag. "Behave," I said, then took a step back as the sword floated out of the duffel.

Jo gasped, a hand to her mouth. Her eyes were wide as she took in the details of the sword, which turned this way and that to help her get a good look at it, like a peacock showing off his colorful feathers. Why the sword took an immediate shine to Jo was anyone's guess.

She listened intently as I told her about how I came to have the sword in my possession. Jo might have operated solely on the right side of the law when crafting her goods, but she was no stranger to how I made a living, so she was unfazed by the thievery part of my tale.

"It has imprinted on you," Jo said once I'd finally stopped talking, her assessment confident.

"Imprinted?"

"Yes," Jo said, taking a step toward the sword. Perhaps the thing appreciated how awed Jo was, showing it the proper reverence or whatever its ego craved. "When a dragon chose a mate, it was said that they were imprinted on each other."

The sword hummed, the blade glowing a faint red.

I stared at Jo, aghast. "My love life is terrible, but things aren't so bad that I'm going to start mating with a *sword*."

Jo snickered. "It's not a term only for romantic entanglements. Dragons chose their inner circle with great care, marking those who they trusted most. It wasn't like a brand or anything like that. It was more like granting permission, but in a magical sense."

My brows furrowed.

"Like, oh, I don't know, giving a close friend a key to your house," Jo said. "It gave the marked pair a way to share a closer bond. Sometimes that meant granting permission for telepathic communication. For others, it meant that when they were in proximity, they could share their magic or strength. It doesn't mean the sword wants to mate with you. It means it trusts you."

I flicked a gaze at the sword. The blade had cooled once more and when it realized I was looking at it, inverted itself to tap its hilt once, gently, on the wood. I asked, "So you didn't trust Haskins?"

Tap-tap.

"Remarkable!" Jo said, clapping her hands once. "You've found a way to communicate."

"Sort of." Turning toward her, I asked, "Have you heard about any auctions lately that a sword like this might have come from?"

She still gazed at the sword in wonder. After a few long seconds, she finally addressed me. "There was one a couple of months ago. You heard about that sunken pirate ship found off the coast last year, right? When they finally got the thing ashore, it was supposedly full of lost treasure. It certainly looks like it might be a pirate sword, doesn't it?"

It did. Cutlasses had been a common choice for pirates.

"The ship was off the coast of Washington state, though, not here," I said.

Jo nodded. "That's right."

Had Haskins gone out to Washington to attend a black-market auction, or had the auction pieces ended up here where Haskins had then bought them? The ship had been found by human divers. It made the mundane news because the ship hadn't been built the way the average human would expect. When a vessel was going to have air and water elementals onboard, it was crafted to withstand magical gales. The local media had been flooded with theories about the ship's origins. The Sorcerers Collective in Kensey, the magic hub in Washington, had to do some serious intervention to make sure the discovery didn't hit national news, as well as get the ship and all its contents back into magical hands. Cleanup crews—Visitors Center employees on steroids—had been flown in from magical hub locations all over the world to help scrub all information about the ship from mundane media and memory. It had been a huge undertaking.

Information on what had been found on the ship had never been released, as far as I knew. And I'd looked, since Grayson had hounded me for months. The fact that Sorcerers Collectives from dozens of hubs had worked together so thoroughly, in addition to the lack of published details available to the public, had sent the rumor mill into a tizzy. Everyone assumed it had to be highly dangerous stuff. Naturally, all of us black-market aficionados wanted our hands on whatever had been uncovered.

I was even more impressed with sweaty old Haskins now. Perhaps his arrest had more to do with him being associated with this auction than the dragon sword. Wouldn't apprehending this sword have been as important as apprehending Haskins himself? Which might mean the local Collective and their bounty hunters hadn't even known what Haskins kept in that basement.

If the dragon sword *had* come from that haul, had there been even scarier things aboard the ship?

A rustle of paper snapped me out of my thoughts, and I found Jo rummaging around in a drawer on her desk. She trundled the drawer closed, bent a little further, and opened a lower one. It was by no means a filing cabinet; there were no folders or tabs of any kind. It was a wonder Jo could find anything in this place.

"Ah, here we are," Jo said, pulling out a folded newspaper clipping from the middle of the stack. She handed the paper to me.

As I unfolded it, the sword moved to hover above my shoulder, as if it were reading it too.

"Can it ... see?" Jo asked softly.

"I honestly have no idea," I said, not looking up. "Nothing about the sword makes a lick of sense so I try not to think about it too hard."

The sword hummed by my ear. Humming seemed to mean

any number of things, so I ignored it. The article had been written nearly a year ago and had come from a Washington-based newspaper.

World Sorcerers Collective Remains Silent About Ship's Cargo

It has been three weeks since the World Sorcerers Collective's cleanup crew scrubbed the minds of all humans associated with the ship's discovery, as well as any humans who reported on it and those who viewed the story. Witches, alchemists, and sorcerers not needed for veil maintenance were recruited in droves to implement the largest-scale memory wipe in recent history. But why? We still don't have answers. What was on that ship that was so threatening to the magical community that the independently run magical hubs across the country banded together to quash all knowledge of the cargo?

I looked up at Jo. "I didn't realize witches, alchemists, *and* sorcerers had been called in."

Jo nodded, arms folded tight across her chest as if she'd just gotten chills. "A few members of my coven live in Kensey and were recruited for the project. That's how I got this clipping."

My brows arched toward my hairline. "What happened out there? Did they see what was on the ship?"

Jo shook her head. "They all signed Soul NDAs."

"*Shit*. The Collective wasn't playing around."

Jo nodded. "I watched a friend struggle to talk to me about what she'd seen. When she hit a topic she was soul-bound not to speak about, her eyes glazed over, as if the words she'd been about to say had been plucked right out of her head."

"If she somehow found a way past that spell, the Soul NDA would kick in and kill her, right?" I asked.

With another nod, Jo said, "No one believes the secrets they're forced to live with are worth dying for. So they all keep it to themselves."

"How voluntary was this assignment?" I asked.

Jo pursed her lips.

Ah. Voluntary insofar as refusal meant you'd have your throat ripped out by a werecat. Or your loved ones' throats were threatened. If a werecat showed up at your door to request your services, it was best to agree to whatever it was. Luma had one of the largest contingents of werecat guards in the nation. I'd managed to avoid run-ins with them during my charm collecting escapades, and I hoped that lasted for many years to come.

I scanned the rest of the article, but it was mostly theories on what the writer thought were the reasons for all the secrecy. I handed the clipping back to Jo, who folded it and stuffed it back into the drawer.

Needing a change of subject, I took out the remainder of my goods for Jo, letting her examine the talismans and magic-infused daggers. The sword floated nearby, quietly observing.

Jo confirmed that the lightning spell on the dagger was a Level 4. Most of the stuff I pilfered from criminals was in the 2-to-3 level range. But lately, it seemed like more and more of the stuff in Luma was higher level, and not just because of Caspian and his Frankenweapons. If these items were both illegal and rare, why were their numbers increasing? And why were they getting stronger? The mythic beasts that humans had driven into extinction had been gone for hundreds of years. Sure, a dragon was huge and had countless scales that could be utilized, but they were a limited resource. Unless someone had been stockpiling artifacts all this time, and had just started making weapons with them recently—but why now?

Crime in magical hubs was like in any other big city in the country—robberies, assaults, murders. But we had the Sorcerers Collective who dictated the laws; and the werecat guards, mundane police force, and bounty hunters to enforce said laws. Most people here were law-abiding, if only because the punishment dealt out by the Collective could be swift and severe. The worst of the worst were exiled to a hub in Antarctica.

I skirted the lines of legality, sure, but I wasn't a high-level threat. I mostly supplied humans in rough areas with weapons that would keep them safer, and sold artifacts to magical beings who wanted a taste of their fae heritage, since every year that passed convinced more and more of them that the Glitch had permanently damaged the portals, and there was no going back to their home world. I moved merchandise that was already here.

My thoughts drifted back to Caspian Blackthorn. It seemed unlikely that the Collective was completely unaware of what he was doing. Maybe he got a pass for being a fellow sorcerer. He, unlike me, was adding *new* merchandise to the mix, and had done so more in the last couple of years. Were his Frankenweapons related to all this, or was it happening independently?

"This talisman here …" Jo said, redirecting my thoughts. She held a crescent-shaped talisman in her palm while running a dark finger along the smooth surface of the charm. "It's imbued with a calming spell. If worn for too long, it can make a person so calm, they fall asleep. If one falls asleep wearing it, they might not wake until it's no longer touching skin. But its magic is gentle enough, a Level 2, that it would be helpful to wear in a stressful situation to keep you levelheaded."

Sounded like a muscle relaxer in necklace form.

Jo went through the other five, selecting two for herself: a locking talisman, like the one I already wore, and a mystery talisman which she said held Level 4 magic that was hidden behind an incantation or word of power. She had guesses as to who had spelled the talisman, since the magic on it was familiar to her—I hadn't felt a thing when I touched it—and would do some digging to uncover its secrets. Her eyes were alight at the thought of solving the mystery of the talisman's uses. I gave them both to her for no charge. Our relationship was a bartering one. I came to her with trinkets, and she supplied me with information when I needed it. Jo's Apothecary was the go-to shop for most witches in downtown Luma, and she had business contacts with a wide range of fae. Even if Jo didn't have answers for me right away, she knew enough people that she could usually track them down for me.

Knowing Kayda would want to kick me in the shins for my

next question, I asked, "Can you find out when Caspian's next auction is?"

Jo had just placed her two new talismans in a small wooden box on the desk's surface, and upon hearing my question, slapped the lid closed with more force than necessary. She whirled to me. "It's not a good idea to attend one of those, Fletch. You're a very capable human, but you're still a human. The level of magic in those items could kill someone like you just by being around them for too long. Humans have lived away from ancient magic for long enough now that any tolerance they once had is long gone."

I knew all this already. "I'm not saying I would attend. But if I knew when his next one was, it would give me a chance to observe things from afar. See what kind of people attend these things."

Jo squinted.

"I don't have a lot of options, Jo," I said. "I need to figure out what the sword needs. As you said, it imprinted on me. The only person who knows where this sword came from is Haskins, and he's locked up indefinitely."

"What about his associates?"

I thought of Pratt and Igor and wrinkled my nose. I didn't know enough about Haskins to know who else was in his inner circle. When I saw him, he was usually alone. If only I'd stayed to flirt with him in that bar instead of getting lured away by the pretty-faced elf. Stupid elves.

"Perhaps you could try the sorcery university. Caspian offers introductory sorcery classes occasionally," Jo said, eyeing the sword behind me.

"Occasionally" was more like once a year, depending on whether or not Mercury was in retrograde. The classes themselves were offered nearly year-round. Kayda and I had taken one such class at the local college after we got out of high school, mostly out of curiosity. We lasted two weeks before we dropped the class. A whole week had been devoted to the theory of so-and-so and how the angle of the wrist while drawing runes could change how much power a spell had. I'd silently fake-cried through the entirety of one lecture, eventually sending Kayda into a bout of uncontrolled cackling, and we'd had to run out of there. Three others followed us though, one guy declaring, "I know if I see this through till the end, it means I get to use magic, but I'll be dead of boredom before I get there!"

Introductory sorcery classes were offered so often mostly because the veil maintenance job was as vital as it was excruciatingly dull. It was hard to get anyone to sign up for the profession when it was almost guaranteed that at the end of your grueling years of schooling, you only had one career path available: becoming a very well-paid maintenance worker. Attendance at the university had been in a constant decline for years. The college even offered several full scholarships a year to anyone who showed an aptitude for sorcery. I was pretty sure half the people who attended the classes hoped they'd lay eyes on the infamous Caspian Blackthorn.

Jo still gazed at the sword. "I can feel the magic wafting off it. I can even sense that the sword is holding back. It's humming from how much it's restraining itself."

The sword hummed louder in response. I felt the vibration in my chest, like standing near a base at a concert. I figured that the humming meant agreement.

"Though, I suppose the humming could be from pent-up emotion that needs an outlet," Jo said, cocking her head. "The sword is sentient, that much is clear. But is it sentient because of the magic, or something else?"

Completely baffled by her question, I merely stared at her. How else would a sword be sentient other than by magic?

"Sorcerers are trained not just about runes and how to draw them, but to take deep dives into the history of magic itself, as young as it is here on Earth. They study ancient beasts in great detail. A sorcerer could probably look at the scales on that hilt and tell you which dragon family they came from, and what their magical properties are." A light twinkled in her eyes that mirrored the delight she felt at the prospect of unlocking the mysteries of the talisman I'd given her earlier. No one loved a magical puzzle more than Jo. "A sorcerer would be an unparalleled source of information on the magical properties of the ancients, a branch of study that grows less popular by the year."

"Not an option, Jo. There's no sorcerer in this city who wouldn't turn me over to the Collective if they knew about the sword. Well, the rogue probably wouldn't turn me in, what with him being a rogue and all, but it's not like I can just pop over to his mansion with a tray of cupcakes and ask him to tell me everything he knows about the sword. His place is going to be warded to high heaven, so my ass would get zapped into next Tuesday just for walking up to his front gate. Plus, if I showed him this"—I gestured to the sword still hovering behind me—"I have no doubt he'd just take it from me. I'd be no match for him."

I felt the heat of the sword, knowing without looking at it that it didn't like this idea either.

"How curious …" Jo said, taking a step toward me. "Sword, if I may presume to ask, could you move a little closer?"

I tensed, but the sword gently floated past me and toward Jo, hovering between us.

"Can you heat up again?" Jo asked.

The sword obliged.

"Ah! I was right," Jo said, leaning so close to the sword that her eyes crossed. "Have you noticed these markings on the blade, Fletch? They're quite small, but along the curved center groove in the metal are runes. There are spells here. Spells that can be unlocked with incantations, words of power, possibly even potions."

I stepped closer, my face a few inches from the red-hot blade. The heat of it felt like it was evaporating the moisture in my eyes. But one had to be that close to see the runes. Jo was right.

"This is very complicated spellwork," Jo said. "Whoever made this was a master crafter."

I took a step back when the heat got to be too much. Jo leaned away as well. The sword cooled, the metal returning to its usual shiny steel. When cool, the runes disappeared.

I sighed, head buzzing with even more questions now than when I got here. "You're quite the enigma, sword."

It hummed in agreement.

CHAPTER TEN

A knock sounded on the door and Jo and I peered down the box-and-book-lined hallway.

"Lady Josephine?" came a muffled male voice.

"I'll be out in just a minute, Erik," Jo said in a volume fit only for present company, then used her magic to carry the message on an air current and under the door to ensure he'd hear her.

"As you please, Lady Josephine," came the reply.

I cocked a brow. Erik had started with Jo a year or so ago, but the "Lady Josephine" thing was new.

"I told him to call me Jo and he refuses," Jo said, shaking her head. "He said the informal name doesn't suit my status, and—I quote—a lady as distinguished as myself demands respect."

"Oh my," I said, fanning my face. "Sounds like someone has a crush on Lady Josephine."

Jo grumbled. "He's a fetus."

I snorted. "Ain't nothing wrong with it as long as that fetus is legal. Hmm. That didn't come out the way I meant. I just mean … it's okay to be a non-werecat cougar."

Jo stared blankly.

The sword offered no commentary, just floated itself back into the duffel bag, which I supposed was comment enough. I put the daggers and remaining talismans inside too and zipped the bag up before strapping it onto my shoulder.

"I'll find out what I can about recent auctions," Jo said. "And any that might be associated with Caspian," she added reluctantly.

"Thanks. Let me know if you find out what that other talisman does."

Her eyes lit up again. "Will do."

She led us down the narrow hallway and we stepped out into the bustling shop. She closed and locked the door behind us. Before I could make a move to leave, Jo took my hands in hers, her skin cool and dry. "Be careful, Fletch. I mean it."

"I will," I said, smiling in a way that I hoped eased some of her concerns.

The way she looked down at my bag for a long moment told me my smile had not affected her in the slightest. With a pat on the back of one of my hands, she walked away.

I strode for the exit, offering Erik behind the counter a wave as I went. He had a stack of books in his hands and when we made eye contact, he gasped, tripped over his own feet and I immediately lost sight of him. His startled little scream was punctuated by the thud of the books crashing to the floor.

I shook my head and kept moving. I had no clue why Erik was always such a mess around me, but I didn't have time to figure it out.

I had a pirate to meet.

Grayson's work was in the Industrial District, a neighborhood that took up most of the western side of the hub outside of Luma Proper. It was one of the rougher areas of the hub. It would be a twenty-minute walk from the telepad station, and it meant I had to go *back* to the downtown station first. That, or take a bus for forty-five minutes, if not longer, depending on traffic.

By the time I was trudging up the street toward Luma Fae Lights, I was too tired to feel much of anything. This sword better appreciate all the work I was doing. Granted, the sword was unaware that I hoped it and Grayson would hit it off. If it imprinted on Grayson, I could leave the sword with him and go home to take a nap.

The usual meeting spot for Grayson and me was a park a block away from the looming LFL building—a massive cement thing that took up half a city block. LFL was the biggest manufacturer of fae light receptacles on the West Coast. Grayson's particular branch made the glass tubing for billboards, business signs, and slot machines. He'd been recruited specifically for his water magic, and they paid him very well because of it. The last time I talked to Grayson about his work, he'd mentioned that LFL was getting into the actual production of fae essence, too. Some complicated combination of using a phosphorescent byproduct of a fae's magical use—along the lines of "fairy dust" from mundane fairytales—and alchemical potions. I hardly understood what he'd been talking about, but I'd done my best to listen because that was what a successful businesswoman did when her clients wanted to talk her face off about things she couldn't have cared less about.

All I knew was that fae essence powered Luma and kept it on at all hours of the day and night, making it one of the wealthiest magical hubs on the planet. Wealthy people had expensive and weird tastes. Expensive and weird were my bread and butter. I didn't care how the sausage was made as long as the city was full of people willing to pay me to find charmed items.

The trek across the damp grass of Trinity Park only took a minute or two. As my boots squelched in a few muddy puddles, I suspected the sprinklers had given the area a good soak shortly before my arrival. I plopped onto a bench near the back to wait for Grayson. A wooden fence ran around three sides of the rectangular-shaped park, giving the place a sense of privacy. Directly across the street was a run-down, humans-only apartment complex. Most of the residents worked for LFL but did grunt-work jobs the magic users and fae didn't want, largely because despite being work that was vital to keeping a company of that size going, it didn't pay very well.

I glanced around the park. I'd sold several weapons here, mostly to single women who needed protection from the orc who had purchased the building across the street and had set himself up as the on-site landlord to have down-on-their-luck human women at his disposal for lord knew what.

More benches sat on the opposite end of the park. It wasn't uncommon to see a drug dealer or two posted up there. The pushers tended to be witches, alchemists, or elves, selling substances to humans with the promise of magical abilities or heightened senses to see into the fae world—or simply promising a good time. The dealers knew the kind of people who lived across the street. People who had little and saw daily what having magical abilities could get them—high salaries, cool powers, and job opportunities they'd never get, no matter how impressive their résumé. The dealers took those desperate people's money in exchange for lies laced with more magic than they could handle. It almost always resulted in dead humans.

The drug with the most staying power was called Bliss—and it was also the most deadly to humans. I'd tried none of the street drugs myself because my parents had seen too much, and they'd done all they could to put the fear of a gruesome death in me. As the name suggested, it gave the user an intense feeling of euphoria—I'd heard it compared to an intoxicating blend of ecstasy and heroin. There was a twenty-five percent chance one tab of Bliss would kill a human, and it shot to seventy-five percent after consuming two. No thanks. In fae, it wasn't deadly but extremely habit-forming. A whole drug empire had sprung up around it, according to my parents.

I kept a hand on the duffel bag beside me and crossed my feet at the ankles. I had no way of knowing if Grayson had received my telepost message; I'd give him half an hour before I had to get moving again. It wasn't the kind of park to hang out in for too long, even during the day.

While I waited, I fished my dad's pocket mirror out of the side compartment of the bag and flipped open the lid, pretending to give my reflection a once-over, when I was really checking it for any new bounties. I hadn't checked it since yesterday. The glass was blank.

Which meant the last message had been, **Haskins apprehended. Bounty to FT97.**

As I snapped the mirror closed and stuffed it back in my bag, I wondered how much a bounty for someone like Haskins was. My parents had made a rather comfortable living off bounties, so I was sure it was a decent chunk. Felix and I had almost been a second-generation, bounty-hunting power couple.

We'd met through our parents, both sets of them transplants from cities outside California working as private detectives and monster hunters, tangling with magical beings who were getting up to no good outside the veils. When it was clear that both the Turners and the Fletchers could handle run-ins with the magical, even though none of them were magical themselves, the Collective's bounty hunter department had recruited them out of the mundane world and introduced them to the secret world of the hubs, giving them places on the Collective's elite team. In the hubs, human bounty hunters took care of human and lower fae criminals—the goblins, fauns, and other beings without a lot of magic—while the rest were assigned to the werecat guards.

Felix had been a teenager when his parents had relocated to Luma. I'd been born here, so we hadn't met until high school, when Felix was the sullen new kid. I'd been assigned as his school liaison for the day, and by the end of it, Kayda and I had ushered him into our little circle. I'd fallen head over heels for him shortly after that.

When we turned eighteen, we entered the rigorous program to join the Collective's bounty-hunting team. We were taken on ride-alongs—sometimes my parents taking Felix, and sometimes me tagging along with the Turners. We were top of our classes. But three years into the four-year program, my dad had been killed and my mom skipped town. I dropped out the next day. Felix and I fought constantly about me wanting him to drop out, too. I went through therapy to try to work through my anxiety of losing Felix to a job that had imploded my family. I knew that if I lost Felix, I wouldn't recover.

Felix dropped out a month before the final exam, telling me it wasn't worth making me sick with worry for the rest of our lives. I bounced between jobs while Felix became head of security at a casino—his training in the bounty-hunting program making him a perfect fit for the job. In the years after the breakup, I often wondered if Felix was still a security guard there. I wasn't a huge fan of casinos anyway, but I'd actively avoided his old haunt for the past five years. It was a little incredible that I'd never run into him in all this time. He could have left Luma, for all I knew. I'd probably never know.

"There's my favorite lady!"

My head snapped up, and I grinned at Grayson as he approached. He was in his forties, fair-skinned, and six feet tall. He always kept his long brown hair in a low ponytail, and he walked with a casual loping gait, like he was never in a rush to get where he was going. He looked more like a lost member of the Grateful Dead than an aspiring pirate.

I hugged very few of my clients, but I gave Grayson a quick one when he reached me.

He stuffed his hands back into his oversized leather jacket and jutted a scruffy chin at the duffel bag lying on the bench. "The thing that's gonna blow my mind is in there, eh?"

"Yep." I unzipped the bag and then stepped back a few feet, so I was beside Grayson again. I wasn't planning to yell "Tada!" when the sword rose from the bag or anything, but I was a little disappointed when nothing happened.

"We waiting for something?" Grayson said after a moment.

"Uhh ... one sec," I said, and bent over the bag, holding the sides open. "What, you shy now?" I whispered.

The sword hummed.

Oh, this was ridiculous.

I grabbed the sword by the hilt and lifted, only to slip a little in the damp grass when the sword wouldn't move. Suddenly the thing I'd been carrying in a bag on my shoulder all day with little discomfort felt like it weighed a million pounds. I yanked so hard, I nearly threw my back out, but the sword didn't budge. The bag itself slipped off the end of the bench, and a pouch that held one of the talismans tumbled into the grass, but the sword itself didn't move. What the hell?

Grayson's face came into view in my peripheral vision. He reached out to open the bag further to get a better few. A bright blue substance dotted the cuff of his white work shirt. Fae essence. It was similar to neon, but was an abundant resource and had properties that proved to be more versatile than the noble gas, while also having none of the negative effects that neon could if it were inhaled.

"Can I try?" he asked.

I shrugged. "Sure." Maybe the chance of it imprinting on Grayson would increase if he touched it. Shared energies or whatever.

Grayson wrapped his hand around the hilt and gave a few tugs of his own. He put his back into it, the heels of his shoes sliding in the muddy grass. He eventually gave up and let go. "So weird. You know that means I want it, right?"

He wants it! "Get out of there, you wacko sword," I muttered, and tried to pull it out of the bag again.

A second later, the weight of the sword vanished, and I tumbled backward into Grayson. We both went down, me on top of him. He let out an *oof* of air as my backside landed squarely on his stomach.

Stupid sword!

I scrambled off Grayson, doing my best not to slice him to

ribbons—because now, instead of being a million pounds, the hilt seemed to be super-glued to my hand. I opened my hand wide and shook it, trying to dislodge it, but it wouldn't let go.

"Ho. Lee. Shit."

I whirled around.

Grayson had his hands pressed to his temples. "I didn't get the best look at it when it was in the bag. And, like, wasn't the hilt black before? Now it's ... it's like *glowing*. Is it ... oh shit. Is this a ... Fletch, my beautiful friend. Did it finally happen? Is this from the, you know, *ship*? Is it a ...?" He looked behind us and scanned the area, as if he expected someone to be standing behind one of the nearby trees. He spun back to me and dramatically whispered, "A *dragon sword*?"

"Sure is," I said, grunting, still trying to get it off my palm. I grabbed it with my other hand, and got my original hand free, but now it was stuck in my left, nondominant hand. I groaned and dropped my arm, the sword's tip pointing toward the grass. My arms ached. "But—"

My arm shot straight up of its own volition, the tip pointed at Grayson's chest.

Grayson's eyes widened as much as mine did. He put his hands up, palms toward me. "Whoa, Fletch. Watch where you point that thing."

The sword lunged forward a few inches, dragging me with it. Grayson visibly swallowed, then took a step back. The sword lunged again. It was just like back at the warehouse, but this time, instead of the sword acting on its own as it threatened Pratt and Igor, I looked like I was the one brandishing the weapon.

The sword jumped. I lurched forward a step, even while using all my weight to lean backward. Grayson stumbled away, almost tripping over a fallen branch.

"Sword! Stop it!" I said, still leaning back. It felt like trying to control a kite in a windstorm.

When the sword didn't heed my demand and jerked us forward again, I clapped my free hand over the other, as if that would help somehow. It was the weirdest game of tug-of-war I'd ever played. "I don't know what the hell is going on, Grayson, but you have to get out of here!"

Movement caught my eye, and I spotted a pair of men watching us from behind the jungle gym. They whispered and pointed, but they made no move to come any closer. I couldn't imagine how crazy this looked. One of the guys looked vaguely familiar. I'd been in this park enough times, making sales, that I might have seen him here before. Maybe he knew enough about me to know it was safer to keep his distance if one of my wares went apeshit.

Kayda's voice floated into my head. *"It was holding back. Think about what kind of destruction this thing could do if it really put its mind to it."*

I gulped.

"Knock it off," I hissed at the sword, squeezing my hands tight against the hilt, hoping it would feel it and listen to me. When the sword had been pissed at Kayda, it was over a perceived slight. Grayson hadn't even been given a chance to insult the crazy thing. It hadn't reacted like this at all to Jo. "Grayson is a friend," I tried, my arms aching even more now.

The blade blazed red. What, did dragons instinctively hate water witches or something? The dragon scales under my palms pulsed with power in time with my thudding heart.

The sword slowly inched toward Grayson, who still had his hands out, wild gaze flitting from me to the sword and back again. I couldn't tell if my actively working against the sword slowed it down, or if it was stalking Grayson like prey. I dug my heels in, the force of the sword so strong that I left twin trails of muddy soil and ripped-up grass in my wake.

The blade burned brighter. The scales pulsed faster. I needed something to distract the sword—something to give Grayson a window of time to get out of here without being maimed.

"Grayson! Hurl water at us!"

"What!"

"Use water to blast us back, then run!"

I yelped when the sword jerked us forward again.

"Shit. Okay. Sorry!" Grayson said, then thrust his hands out. A gush of water flew at us from the palms of his hands. That's an oversimplified explanation of how water magic works—it wasn't like he shot it out of holes in his hands or anything—but it *looked* like it came from his hands. Water materializing out of nowhere.

Water hissed into steam as it hit the red-hot blade, but otherwise had no effect. I tried to use my shoulder to wipe the water out of my eyes. It didn't work. Now I was just half-blind.

The blade grew crimson again. The scales thrummed. Now it was *really* mad.

"Grayson! What kind of weak-ass shit was that?"

Grayson's jaw clenched. Good. A pissed-off elemental was a more powerful one.

"How are you going to *fulfill your destiny*," I said in a purposefully mocking tone, "when your stream is as powerful as a kid's water gun with a leak?"

The guys across the park squatted low, hands gripping the bars of the jungle gym as if that would keep them from washing away should Grayson turn the hose on them next. Or maybe, they just knew what kind of force could be behind an elemental witch when provoked.

I braced myself, but nothing could have prepared me for what came next. Water slammed into us as if Grayson had just opened the valve to a fire hydrant. The sword and I shot backward. I tumbled, flipping end over end with much less grace than Carlo the gymnast. The blast had severed my super-glue bond to the sword's hilt, so at least I didn't impale myself as I was flung back like a piece of debris. I rolled to a stop, drenched and peppered with blades of grass and streaked with mud.

I coughed, water leaking out of my nose. My hair tie had come loose during the deluge, and tight, spiraled curls hung in my face, water dripping off the ends. I blew my nose into my hand and more water shot out. I coughed, tasting mud. Staggering to my feet, I spotted Grayson hauling ass across the park and then around the corner, back toward the LFL building.

"What the hell was that, sword?" I asked, spinning in a wide circle, water droplets flung free from my hair.

I didn't see the sword in my immediate vicinity.

Brow furrowed, I glanced toward the corner Grayson had just vanished around. I didn't see the sword hurtling through the air behind him.

The two men still cowered behind the jungle gym.

"Did you see it go past there?" I called out, pointing.

They stared, mouths hanging open.

I stalked toward them and they scrambled to their feet, the crisscrossed bars of the jungle gym between us. I glared through one of the pentagon-shaped spaces. "The sword," I said slowly. "Did you see it fly past you? Did it go after the guy with the ponytail?"

One guy frantically shook his head.

The other licked his lips several times, like his mouth was parched. Maybe it was a nervous tick. "You're that Charm Collector chick, yeah?"

The first guy elbowed him hard in the side.

Now that I was closer, I guessed the guys were teenagers. Sixteen or seventeen. "Yeah."

"Told you," the second guy said, hand to his side where his friend had elbowed him. "People are saying you got a dragon sword now. Is that what that thing was?"

It had only been twenty-four hours! How had someone heard that already? "Which people are saying that?"

"My dad works at Haskins's place and Pratt told him the Charm Collector stole a bunch of Haskins's stuff and sicced her dragon sword on them," the kid said, licking his lips a few times. "He said the sword was going to kill him and Igor, and you called it off like a trained dog."

I frowned. Pratt had a big fucking mouth.

DIABOLICAL SWORD

"Doesn't look like the sword is that trained to me," the first kid muttered, and now he got an elbow jammed into his side.

"You didn't see where it went?" I asked.

They shook their heads in unison.

Then a light went off in the head of the first kid. "Aw, shit." He whirled this way and that. "That means the thing is on the loose?"

With that, the kids took off at a sprint through the park, across the street, and into the apartment complex.

I groaned and returned to the scene of the crime. I kicked at clumps of grass and overturned earth. I dug my fingers into mud puddles. I scanned the park bench where the duffel bag still lay, though soaked through now. No sword. No sword under the bench, behind it, or near the fence a few feet away.

I heard no screams of horror in the distance, so it probably hadn't gone on a murder spree.

It had just ... disappeared.

I knew I needed to get the hell out of here. If those kids were to tell adults what they'd seen, someone was sure to call it in. If authorities believed the kids that a dragon sword was "on the loose," the Collective would send out werecats to assess the situation and scour the area. If the sword was still here and went on a rampage, I didn't want to be here when it happened. Not to mention that the sooner I left, the faster my scent would fade. I couldn't give the authorities more opportunities to find me. Any of the items in my bag right now would get me in trouble. Most of them would tie me to Haskins—and who knew what kind of trouble *that* guy was in? Most importantly, the pocket mirror would be confiscated if they found it.

After a few more minutes of searching, I grabbed my sopping wet bag and began my twenty-minute trek back to the teleport station, feeling an unexpected pang of loss now that the diabolical sword was gone.

CHAPTER ELEVEN

When I got back to my apartment complex, I considered curling up on the first level of the outdoor staircase to sleep. The aches and pains of having my body hurled twenty feet, on top of all the walking, had caught up with me. That blast of water had been so strong, it was a wonder nothing had broken on impact. With a whimper, I started up the four flights of stairs.

By the time I reached my floor, I was almost weeping. I pulled open the door to the hallway and shuffled down it. My hip felt like it was on fire. I just had to get inside.

One foot in front of the other.

I was only two apartments away when a door to my right opened and my neighbor stepped out. He came up short. He was my age, and cute in a nerdy kind of way. He was fair-skinned, had tousled brown hair, and hipster glasses. My gaze traveled lower to his plaid shirt, and then lower still to his hairy legs. Hairy goat legs, to be precise. It was like he wore Hammer pants made out of fluffy brown fur. His hoofed feet tapped a little nervously. He'd been my neighbor for several months now, and I knew he was interested.

I've been told that the ... uhh ... nether regions of a faun are comparable enough to those of a human male that if a human lady fancied herself a goat lover, they could have a relatively normal time of creating their version of the perfect nuclear family. I wasn't really into the whole faun thing, though, so I always cut off conversations with him before he could ask me out. Too much chest hair on a man was often a dealbreaker, let alone on half of his bodily real estate. If a faun was shorn like a sheep, what would one find under all that fur?

"What the heck happened to you?" he asked.

I forced my gaze back up to his face, and I was grateful that my dark skin masked the blush that surely had risen in my cheeks thanks to my brain's wild tangent.

He had a reusable bag on his shoulder, and I figured he was heading for the grocery store a few blocks away. "You okay?"

I wanted to say something like "you should see the other guy!" but I didn't have the energy. "Yeah, fine. New workout regimen."

"Oh …" he said as he watched me walk by, clearly not believing me.

"Have a good day," I said, waving one hand without looking back.

When I finally got inside my apartment, it was just after eleven in the morning. That was it! Eleven. I felt like I'd been awake for a century and it wasn't even noon yet.

I peered over at the island counter, half expecting the sword to be lying there like, "Where have *you* been?"

But it wasn't here.

I slid the security chain into place, then tossed my wet duffel bag into the corner.

I took a hot shower, washing the dirt and grime out of my hair and checking my body for bruises. One already bloomed on my hip, the deep purple still managing to stand out on my dark skin. I suspected another one colored my tailbone. I hissed when soap hit my right elbow, the skin scraped raw. Grayson might have looked like a laid-back stoner dad, but that guy could still pack a wallop with his water power. Wherever that damned sword had gone, I hoped it had been in the opposite direction from Grayson.

I slapped a large Band-Aid on my elbow, and I rinsed my filthy clothes out in the sink before draping them over the curtain rod. Now that my muscles had loosened from the hot water, I was zapped. No way was I hauling laundry up and down two flights of stairs right now.

Instead, I flopped facedown on my bed and passed out.

When I awoke, it was with a start, as if a nightmare had yanked me from sleep. I pushed myself up on my forearms and blinked several times in rapid succession, disoriented. My scraped elbow ached below the bandage. The too-bright orange of sunset streamed through my curtains. How long had I slept?

Thud, thud, thud.

I winced, rolling onto my side to peer out my open bedroom door. My hip screamed in protest at the sudden movement.

Thud, thud, thud.

That was what had woken me up.

"Miss Harlow Fletcher?" someone called out in a voice with such authority, it made my heart lurch into my throat.

I gingerly swung my legs off the bed. The bun on my head flopped as I moved. My curls were probably still damp. Sleeping with wet curls was never a good idea—I'd just been too tired to care for them properly. I idly scratched the edges of the bandage, the skin around the cut tight and hot. The details of what had happened today—assuming it still *was* today—started to come back.

Thud, thud, thud.

"Miss Harlow Fletcher! This is the police!"

Shit. *Shit.*

I tried to walk with confidence to the door even though I felt like I'd just been hit by a train. I opened the door, keeping the security chain in place. My head throbbed. I willed my voice to stay steady. They could be here for any number of reasons. "Hi, officers. Sorry to keep you waiting, but I was asleep."

It was a pair of human-looking cops, one male, one female. Granted, werecats when they weren't in their animal form looked human, too. My sixth sense flared to life as I watched them, the tingle at the base of my skull mingling with the pounding in my temples.

I didn't want to let two shifters into my apartment. Run-of-the-mill werecat guards who kept an eye on things at telepad stations were mostly okay. They were like the mall cops and security guards of the mundane world. But the werecats who answered directly to the Collective were another matter.

The female one was closest to the door, peering into the gap. After a moment, she leaned back, and a piece of paper filled the space instead. "We have a warrant to search your apartment, Miss Fletcher."

I swallowed hard. "W-warrant?" I cursed my voice for cracking. "Search for what?"

"A murder weapon."

I slammed the door in her face, unlatched the security chain, and wrenched the door back open. "Excuse me, *what*?"

"I'm not repeating myself," the female said, muscling her way inside and shoving the warrant in my face. I instinctively grabbed it, staring down at the words but not registering what any of them meant. They swam around, reminding me of the shimmering scales on the sword's hilt, like pebbles viewed from above gentle waves.

The sword!

... *Grayson*.

"If you're innocent of the crime, there's nothing to worry about," the male officer said, slowly sidestepping me as he made his way into the apartment. He offered me a small smile, loitering just inside the entrance. His voice was calm and even, almost gentle. "We're just covering our bases. We'll be out of your hair soon."

Maybe they were playing good cop, bad cop. A thud sounded from inside my room and I assumed Bad Cop was pulling drawers free from their runners.

"Who ... who was murdered?" I asked him.

He eyed me. It wasn't fear I saw there, but curiosity. He wasn't sure if my wide-eyed panic was real or if I was putting on airs to appear less guilty. I had to imagine that I truly looked like I'd just woken up from a nap—or, rather, a very hard sleep. I swiped at the corner of my mouth and dislodged something flaky. Had I been drooling?

Without answering my question or taking his eyes off me, he addressed his partner. "I'll check the kitchen and living room."

Something hit the floor in response.

I followed the man, who strolled toward my living room, leaving the front door open. Didn't want the officers to get the wrong idea that they were welcome here. I stood in the middle of my apartment, allowing me to look into my bedroom to the left, the kitchen to the right, and the living room-slash-dining room straight ahead, where Good Cop was currently flinging my couch cushions to the floor and poking his fingers into revealed crevices. He hadn't whipped out a pocketknife to slash through the fabric, but I didn't doubt it was a possibility. He opened the two drawers on the coffee table next, pulling everything out in one fell swoop of practiced destruction.

He sent me a Good Cop smile and had clearly been intending to walk to the kitchen next when he caught sight of my bookshelf in the corner. The bookshelf I'd forgotten about in my fog of pain and confusion. The bookshelf lined with weapons, talismans, and other charmed goods I most certainly shouldn't have.

"Well, this is interesting ..." he said. "Harrison! You're going to want to see this."

Bad Cop came sauntering out of my bedroom. Not a cocky human saunter, but the saunter of a cocky shifter trapped in a human body. Their confidence, their systematic destruction of my stuff, and the ever-present tingle at the back of my skull all told me they worked directly for the Collective. They played by different rules.

Looked like I'd end up in whatever hellhole Haskins was in after all.

Bad Cop pointed at me as she walked by. "Don't move."

When her back was turned, I eyed my still-open door, debating my odds of outrunning them. The answer was slim to none, even when I wasn't exhausted and beaten up.

The shifter cops put their human paws all over my collection of stolen items, standing close together as they discussed what they'd found. What was there to talk about? Any trained cop would know a contraband weapon on sight. I wasn't supposed to have them. End of story.

But then I remembered they were here for a murder weapon.

"Tell me, Miss Fletcher," Bad Cop said, taking a few steps in my direction with her hands tucked behind her back. "Do you know a Norbert Haskins?"

I willed myself not to react. His name was *Norbert*? "Sure, I know him. Is *he* who was murdered?"

Bad Cop smiled briefly—a flash of sharp, pearly white canines. "You tell me."

Warrants and arrests in Luma weren't the same as they were in the mundane world. The ideas were similar, but the processes were different. I could try to lawyer up until I was blue in the face, but it wouldn't change anything. I wouldn't get one, not right away. And it didn't matter what I said to these cops now, or in an interrogation later, that might incriminate me. Once the Sorcerers Collective had me on their radar, I had little recourse. Whenever I was called before the Collective, I'd be given a truth serum made by a government-trained alchemist, so I'd spill all my secrets then. Incriminating myself now would save everyone some time.

"I know Haskins because we share similar hobbies," I said, having no intention of saving either of them even a moment.

"You two were close?" Bad Cop asked.

"Nope. I know *of* him. We talked a few times."

"See ..." she said, taking a few more steps toward me, arms still tucked behind her. "It seems strange that if you don't know him that well, that you'd know exactly when he was being arrested. Within minutes of him being brought in for questioning, you show up at his warehouse and make off with some of his ... what did you call them? Hobbies?"

"Are you here because you think I'm a thief or a murderer?" I asked.

"I don't see why you can't be both," Bad Cop said with a purr that sounded far more feline than I liked.

She could shift at any time and torture me into answering her questions if she thought it necessary. Good Cop would back her up without question, claiming I'd been uncooperative, and that drastic measures had been required. It wouldn't matter that they were powerful shifters and I was a lowly, magic-less human.

"Despite your abhorrence for cell phones," Good Cop said, palm-sized tablet in hand as he came to stand next to his partner, his eyes downcast as he tapped away at the screen. "We have a trail of everywhere you've been today. We can still monitor you, you know. No one can truly stay hidden in Luma."

I pursed my lips.

"Let's see here ... at 7:53 this morning you sent two letters at the telepost office, both sent with one-hour disintegration. Isn't that curious, Harrison?"

"Quite," Bad Cop said without inflection and without taking her eyes off me.

"At 8:03," Good Cop continued, "you took a telepad into the Ardmore neighborhood. At 9, you took a telepad to downtown Luma. You were there for roughly 45 minutes, then went back to the downtown station before heading to the Industrial District." He glanced up then, offering me a smile even toothier than the one his partner had angled my way earlier. "The Industrial District. I wonder if that's where your second telepost went, hmm?" He returned his gaze to his tablet. "You were there just shy of an hour, and then you took a telepad home. Your neighbor said he saw you stumbling down the hallway around 11 this morning, looking quite worse for wear. What happened?"

"Like I told him ... new workout regimen. Really kicked my ass."

Bad Cop narrowed her otherworldly green eyes. "What were you doing between 11 this morning and our arrival?"

A glance at my microwave clock told me it was eight in the evening. "You're the one with my itinerary."

"Cash payments could get you all over Luma and there would be no trace of it," Bad Cop said.

"Sure, but I was asleep the whole time. You two banging on my door woke me up."

"Exhausted from your workout," Bad Cop deadpanned.

"Exactly."

Good Cop tapped the screen of his device a few more times, nudged Bad Cop with his elbow, and jerked his head toward the bookshelf. After telling me, again, to stay put, the two walked to my charm collection to have another hushed chat.

These looping conversations and line of questions had revealed one thing to me: they suspected I was involved in a murder, yet they couldn't place me at the scene of the crime. The Sorcerers Collective might have less than ethical ways of getting the truth out of people, but they still acted based on facts. Planting evidence, falsely imprisoning people ... not their brand of corruption. Because even though they wouldn't make it easy for me to lawyer up, I would be granted one once their truth serum revealed that I hadn't committed homicide. The Collective didn't want this to turn into a public stink any more than I did. My current problem was, even though they couldn't pin a murder on me, they had enough evidence staring them in the face about my "hobbies" that a sentence of "intent to sell contraband magical artifacts" was most assuredly in my future. I didn't think that would get me shipped off to Antarctica, but could it get me exiled from Luma? The only person I knew outside of Luma was my fugitive mother—and I didn't even know if she was still alive, let alone how to find her.

I wondered what Haskins had revealed during his truth-serum confession. Had he brought up my name, or had it been Pratt or Igor who ratted me out? Pratt had already been running his mouth enough that the kids who lived across from Trinity Park had heard about me and my living dragon sword.

Where had that damn thing gone?

Glancing wistfully out my open apartment door, something black snagged in my peripheral vision. My still-wet duffel bag! I'd tossed it inside when I got home. A jacket had fallen off the nearby coat rack and mostly obscured it from view.

If Haskins had given the Collective an itemized list of all the illegal items in his basement, they'd be able to figure out which of those items were missing—including the dragon sword. The sword wasn't here, of course, but several other items were. Dad's pocket mirror would be a bonus. I had to keep the shifters away from that bag without calling attention to it at the same time. If they couldn't find anything to tie me to Haskins or that sword, they might leave to find more evidence.

I planned to calmly wait this out. They had nothing on me, and my faun neighbor had backed up my story. I owed that guy a beer. I knew he'd prefer a date, but not even providing me an alibi could get me past the fur thing. I was appreciative, but not *that* appreciative.

After five agonizing minutes, Bad Cop glanced over, checking that I hadn't run off or was doing anything weird. I smiled warmly from my spot in the middle of my apartment, my back to the open door to show that even though I had an escape route, I wasn't taking it. If I was cooperative, they'd go away, and I'd figure out what to do once they skedaddled. She squinted menacingly, then resumed her conversation with Good Cop.

Something dripped onto my shoulder. My brows creased, and I idly wiped at the damp spot. A smear of red decorated my palm.

Rusty water? The ceiling in the old place leaked all the time when it rained, but it was always in the corners, not in the middle of the apartment. And it was summer. In the desert. Maybe a pipe had burst upstairs?

Another drip.

I looked up.

The bloody sword was back. Literally.

CHAPTER TWELVE

I stumbled back, sudden horror dawning on me that some probably murdered person's blood was dripping on my skin. Good and Bad Cop looked to see what the problem was, and then everything happened very quickly. One second I was on my feet, staring in shock at the hovering, blood-covered sword, and the next I was on my back, a warm, heavy panther paw on either of my shoulders, pinning me in place.

The panther shifter was nose to snout with me, and it hissed softly, pearly white canines gleaming. I figured this was Bad Cop. My heart was about to rocket out of my chest. For about ten seconds, panic seized every cell in my body so thoroughly, black spots flooded my vision. Was this werecat going to rip my throat out? Was I going to bleed out on my floor, only to have my faun neighbor find my destroyed body and then need therapy for the rest of his life?

Just as quickly, the panic shut off like a switch. My system had been so overloaded that it glitched out and gave up. No time to panic now. I had to survive. I could be freaked the hell out later.

Good Cop hadn't shifted yet, as it sounded like booted footfalls on the other side of the room, not padded paws. I couldn't see anything past Bad Cop's massive panther body, though. She

DIABOLICAL SWORD

was twice the size of a standard panther and had to weigh at least eight hundred pounds. I silently thanked her for keeping the pressure on my shoulders relatively light, because she could easily crush me to death just by sitting on me. My hip and tailbone screamed at her, though. I'd hit the floor so fast, I didn't remember it happening, but now the pain was kicking in.

The man shouted and Bad Cop whipped her massive panther head to look over her shoulder. She snarled. I tried to squirm out from under her now that she was distracted, but she didn't budge. I was rewarded with another flare of pain in my hip for my efforts.

When I heard Good Cop's voice, it was clear he was making a phone call. Given the staccato burst of his words, I guessed he was trying to talk and avoid a murderous sword at the same time. "This is ... O'Neill. Code 154. Dragon sword ... located. Need a ... containment team ... ASAP."

Containment team?

My mind flashed back to the story of the rogue sword in the farmer's market. Werecat guards—the containment team—had needed to throw a silver-iron-alloy blanket over the sword to catch it. The alloy wouldn't rid the sword of its power, but it would be like stunning it.

I couldn't explain what I did next. All I knew was that as much as this sword had brought me nothing but grief, I didn't want it to be captured by the Collective. "Sword! Get out of here!"

Bad Cop pressed down, hard, on my shoulders. I gasped.

"Harrison! Watch out!" called out Good Cop, O'Neill, and a second later, the panther pinning me to the ground roared and scrambled away. Her paw stamped down on my arm, and the uneven surface made her stumble. The sudden sharp pain stole my breath. As the werecat tried to gain better footing, I got trampled. A paw slammed into my side, a whip-like tail whacked me in the face, and an impossibly heavy haunch landed in the same spot on my arm. I heard something crack—possibly shatter.

I screamed.

I clutched my arm, curling into the fetal position even though my hip throbbed in protest. The sound of heavy, padded footfalls and twin roars told me O'Neill had shifted now, too. I heard claws tear into the wooden floor and across fabric. My mind conjured up the images to go with the sounds because my eyes were screwed shut.

What was the extent of the sword's power? Would it be outmatched by two government-trained shifters?

When one of the cats roared, followed by the sound of splintering wood and a reverberating thud that vibrated the ground beneath me, a delirious laugh bubbled out. Just last night I'd been worried about holes in the doors. After this, the walls might not be left standing.

When a gurgling cry tore through the room, instinct made me sit bolt upright. Through my tear-filled eyes, I found the panther shifter on her side in my living room, smashed coffee table under her large body, just as the sword yanked itself free from her gut. Blood gushed out of the wound, down her black fur, and onto the floor below. My stomach roiled. I watched the light in her otherworldly green eyes go out.

Oh, holy shit.

The other cat, an orange-and-black striped tiger with a gash across one eye, blood matting its fur, bolted for me on massive paws. I squeezed my eyes shut again, unable to move, convinced the tiger would maul me in retribution for his fallen partner even though I hadn't been the one to kill her. But I felt the heat of O'Neill's giant body as he sailed over my head and landed with a thud behind me, darting out the door into the hallway. On hands and knees, mangled arm still clutched to my side, I twisted to watch the tiger go. It shot a glance over his shoulder as he sprinted down the hall. The look in his good eye was all wild animal panic. The instinct to live, to fight another day, had taken over. Perhaps guilt too for leaving a fallen comrade behind.

I scrambled to my feet long enough to kick the door closed,

then used my good hand to lock the door from the inside with the security chain.

Steeling myself, I turned around. The apartment was even more wrecked than I expected. The couch had been gutted, cottony stuffing scattered about like fistfuls of giant popcorn. Every piece of wooden furniture was little more than a pile of splinters. The bookshelf of magical items had been tipped over, the weapons and talismans strewn across the floor. The TV had been split clear down the middle—I didn't know how that one had happened.

And, of course, the dead werecat in the middle of it all. A werecat sent by the Collective itself. If I had been in trouble before, I was royally screwed now. O'Neill knew it had been the sword that had done the killing, not me. But that didn't mean my ass wasn't grass. I hadn't been controlling the thing, but the sword had returned to me—and it was covered in blood. At the very least, it would look like the sword and I had formed an alliance. At worst, it would appear that the sword was willingly doing my bidding.

When I said the Collective believed in the truth above all else, I meant it. Their werecat guards, even though they answered to the Collective, didn't necessarily believe in the cause. What trumped all else was taking care of their own. The Collective maintained the veils, and wrote and decided the laws that governed the hubs, but the werecats were the ones with paws on the ground. Since the sorcerers-in-charge were rarely seen, the werecats were the authority most Luma citizens didn't want to tick off. Now that one of their own had been killed in my apartment, I would be on the werecat shit list—truth, protocol, and laws be damned.

I whirled toward the sword that hovered somewhere in the vicinity of the kitchen, fresh blood dripping onto the counter. "We have to get out of here. We'll discuss later how mad I am at you."

The blade burned red.

"I don't want to hear it!" I said, waving my non-mangled arm toward my apartment at large. "There's a fucking dead panther shifter bleeding all over my living room!"

The blade cooled.

I darted into my bedroom and pulled my sheets free. "Sword! I need your help."

It zipped inside.

"Can you cut this into a couple of long strips? I need to make a sling." I held the sheet up.

The sword wiped itself clean on my bedspread before slowly slicing its way through the sheet. Working together quickly, I got the fabric into a sling and got my ruined arm into it. I've needed to pre-treat broken arms before, and had gotten good at using my teeth in a pinch to tie knots.

My arm still hurt like a sonofabitch, and every once in a while, I stopped in my frantic rushing around to lean against a wall until the world stopped spinning and my stomach stopped churning. Adrenaline took care of the rest. I stuffed my backpack with clothes. I moved my wallet and pocket mirror into it, too. Harrison either hadn't found the wad of emergency cash I kept stuffed in a sock, or she hadn't found a justification for taking it. I threw that in the backpack. I grabbed the still-wet duffel out from underneath the jacket in the front room, and picked through the fallen charmed weapons on the floor by the bookshelf, selecting as many as would fit.

After stuffing my feet into boots, which I had to leave untied, I slung my backpack over my good shoulder and grabbed the handles of the duffel. I skidded to a stop at my front door, my chest heaving, debating about the best way to get out of here. Could I flirt my way into my neighbor's apartment and hide there until I heard the werecats busting down my door?

Would the werecats storm the building knowing the sword was up here, or would they take their time to devise a plan? O'Neill had seen what it could do. The two werecats had been no match for the sword, but maybe five would be. Ten? And who knew what was in the arsenal of the "containment team." If the plan was to throw in smoke bombs that expelled liquefied dragon-subduing alloy or something, I would be dead in seconds. I knew I would be collateral damage at this point and the Collective would shed no tears, assuming they even asked about my demise. But if the werecats thought I was in cahoots with the sword, maybe they'd try to negotiate with me first to help minimize damage and casualties. The cats probably wouldn't care what happened to me, but the other residents of the building didn't deserve to have their homes destroyed.

Right?

I slowly eased the door open, the chain still in place. The hallway was deserted. Had O'Neill's team arrived yet? Were they on the ground floor?

A moment later, the soles of my boots vibrated, the ground thrumming. A door opened down the hall and the faun stuck his head out.

"Do you feel that?" he called, his eyes wide as saucers.

Creaking sounded next. Footfalls. The vibration grew stronger by the second. It took a second for me to realize it was the sound of metal creaking. Groaning, really. Under the weight of massive bodies. The werecats were coming up the staircase—they had no choice; the building didn't have an elevator. Arriving in cat form ruled out negotiations as a possibility.

"Get back inside, lock your door, and get under something sturdy!" I called to the faun through the small gap made by my chained door.

"What?" he shrieked. "What's going on? Harlow?"

"I'm sorry!" I slammed the door again, pulled my locking talisman from under my shirt, and activated the magical lock. It wouldn't stop a werecat from eventually knocking the door off its hinges, but it would slow it down. I spun and stared at the sword hovering behind me. "Plan B!"

I had no fucking idea what Plan B was. Hell, I wasn't even sure what Plan A had been.

The sword zipped away from me long enough to hover over the counter. It inverted itself and tapped once.

Yes? Yes *what*?

Before I could ask that out loud, the sword went molten and harpooned toward a pile of splintered wood. I realized what it was doing a second before the pile caught flame.

Oh, good. The diabolical sword's Plan B was to burn the whole goddamn building down. With us still in it. Brilliant.

At speeds hardly trackable with my eyes, the sword lit four more localized fires, then stabbed its way through the window that led to the old-as-hell fire escape. I flinched at the sound of shattering glass. The sword disappeared out the broken window, leaving me standing in horror in a room slowly engulfing in flames. The sword flew back through the hole a second later and knocked its blade against the windowsill.

I didn't budge—eyes stuck open, too shocked to move.

Something slammed so hard into my front door that my teeth rattled in my skull. Right. The band of revenge-thirsty werecats had arrived.

Cursing, I bolted for the window. I slid it open since I didn't want to get myself shredded to ribbons by broken glass on top of everything else. The fire escape creaked dangerously once my full weight was on it, and I was convinced the rusty bolts would give way any second. I stood with my back to the open window and stared through the mesh of the platform to the long, long way to the ground. The sword zipped around behind me and shoved its hilt into my back.

"Okay, okay!"

I ran across the short platform and down the stairs. I swear bits of rust flaked off as I clomped my way down fifteen steps. Just as I reached the next platform, I looked up. A wall of flame shot up from the windowsill outside my place. The sword had ignited the wood there, too. It beelined for me. I took two long strides to cross the platform, and then was running down the next flight of stairs. My whole body was in such excruciating pain at this point that I didn't feel anything but the all-consuming need to not die.

The sword, once it was convinced I would keep up the pace, shot straight down toward the ground and out of view.

I had two more flights of stairs and then I would be on the ground. Just two more. I made it to the third platform. One more flight.

The whole staircase jolted and I screamed, listing to the side. My thankfully unbruised hip collided with the rough metal. Shooting a wild-eyed look up, I recognized the shape of a werecat, this one a puma, on the fourth-floor platform. I was right about the fire escape being one heavy body away from collapsing.

The puma snarled and then cleared the first fifteen steps in one graceful leap.

"*Oh*, fuck."

I was only halfway down the last staircase when a thud jostled the staircase again. This time, my bruised hip hit the railing, and I bit down on my bottom lip to keep myself from screaming.

The puma had just cleared the next set of steps, landing on the second-floor platform, the one just above me.

Pop! Pop! Pop!

Three of the bolts holding the staircase in place pulled free from the brick.

I practically leaped the rest of the way down but came to an abrupt halt on the last step. A dead tiger—not O'Neill—lay there. The sword hovered just above it, coated in blood again.

Thud.

The puma had landed on the platform just behind me.

The fire escape gave a great, groaning creak. The puma roared.

I leaped over the dead tiger just as the sword flew past my head going the other way. I made a sharp turn around the base of the staircase and ran hard down the alley.

The yip from the puma told me the sword had taken down another werecat. That put us at three. Three dead government werecats!

I didn't stop running for ten blocks. Sometime after the third one, I heard an almighty crash in the distance that sent goose bumps skittering down my arms. I knew it was the fire escape ladder—at least part of it—breaking free from the building to the ground below. Sirens wailed. I hoped the faun, and all the residents of my building, were okay.

I wasn't sure I was.

The sword was behind me, I knew, but I didn't dare look back.

I had been running blindly at first, focused solely on escape. But once it was clear that the werecats hadn't found me yet, I knew I needed to figure out a place to lie low for a while. Using my telepad card was out of the question because they'd track me that way. I'd have to start paying in cash.

I neared the border of the Montclaire neighborhood—my neighborhood—and Ardmore. Going to Kayda's was out of the question, too. Not to mention that her apartment was still at least a half hour away and I needed to get off the street before then. I knew this area well because I had quite a few fae clients here. When I hit Winter Grove Lane, I got an idea.

Two more blocks, a sharp right, and down the narrow steps of a recessed alcove. I banged my fist on the metal door at the bottom. Half a minute later, a rectangular hole—about the size of a mundane mail slot—halfway down the door slid open and a pair of brown eyes stared out.

"Hi, Mathias."

"Fletch?" came a small, squeaky voice.

"Yeah," I ground out. "Remember when you said if I ever needed anything, all I had to do was ask?"

A pause. "Yes?"

"I'm asking."

The sound of sirens grew louder.

"I can't afford any trouble," he said.

"Then you better open the door if you don't want a living room full of werecats," I said, and winced, my head spinning from the pain emanating from … everywhere now that I'd stopped running. My vision grew fuzzy at the edges and I listed to the side, the shoulder of my bad arm hitting the brick wall beside me. I stifled a groan.

For a few agonizing seconds, I was sure Mathias wouldn't open the door and that I'd pass out on his doorstep. When the sound of locks springing free reached my ears, I almost burst into tears. The door swung open.

"Get inside," Mathias hissed.

I stumbled into the foyer of his hideaway apartment, taking in the aroma of a pine-scented candle, the sight of the posh leather couch in the living room, and the golden bolt encased in glass above his mantel—and then promptly fainted dead away on his pristine tile floor.

CHAPTER THIRTEEN

When I opened my eyes, a wide-faced, bulbous-nosed creature was hovering over me. I flinched and immediately regretted it. Pain lanced my body, and I bit down on my tongue to keep from crying out.

"She's awake, Mathias," the tiny woman called out.

A moment later, a second bulbous-nosed creature swam into my vision.

"Hi, Mathias," I croaked.

He harrumphed. "This wasn't exactly the kind of favor I meant, Fletch."

"I know. I'm sorry," I said, slowly pushing myself into a seated position. Goblins averaged four feet tall, so their furniture wasn't miniature, per se, but what worked as a couch for them was more like a love seat to me. My still-booted feet hung over an armrest. I wondered if they'd had to drain their magic just to get my dead-weight body off the floor. My arm had also been splinted and was in a better, sturdier sling. "Thank you," I said, knowing it wasn't enough.

I cast a quick look about the room—what I could see of it from my position—looking for the sword. Had it gone off on its own to murder more werecats? The goblins didn't look terrified out of

DIABOLICAL SWORD

their gourds; hopefully that meant that if the sword *was* in here, it hadn't threatened our hosts.

I'd come here not only because Mathias lived nearby and had once offered to help me, but because he and his wife Geraldine worked in the only fae clinic on this side of town. They were both sought-after podiatrists, of all things. It was a specialization always in demand since fae like goblins never wore shoes. Going shoeless when one lived in a forest made a heck of a lot more sense than when living in a city, but it was a cultural thing most of them didn't want to give up. Being barefoot made the fae feel closer to nature. Even if that nature had been paved over with concrete.

Mathias had contacted me six months ago because he'd been missing his homeland. He'd been feeling homesick in a way that made little sense even to him, as he was sixth generation earthbound. But he'd felt homesick, nevertheless. Even then, he'd struck me as a straight-laced kind of goblin. An honest guy doing honest work. Contacting a known charm collector had seemed out of character for him, like the whole thing made him nervous. He wasn't my usual type of client, but I'd been happy to find a piece of home for him.

The golden bolt hung over his mantel could be dangerous in the wrong hands, but I'd known it would be safe with the Stones. Mathias had wept softly when he finally held the bolt in his hands. Overwhelmed with emotion, he'd said, *"You don't know how much I will treasure this, Fletch. Now I have a piece of my homeland here in this home. I will think of you every time I look at it, and I hope you'll sense my gratitude. If you ever need anything, anything at all, please don't hesitate to ask. You're family now."*

In a cool, distant tone that snapped me out of my thoughts, Geraldine said, "You'll need to get to a proper hospital and get your arm into a cast."

Now that she knew I wouldn't die on her couch, she had taken several steps back and had her short arms crossed over her chest. She was four feet tall, while Mathias was only half a foot taller.

They both had sickly gray skin and straight black hair they tied back in matching low ponytails at the napes of their necks. They had pointed ears, much like elves.

"Or track down a healer," Mathias added, in a gentler tone. "Given the hubbub happening up there, I'm guessing they'll be watching the hospitals. If you have a fae healer for a client, that'll be your best bet. They'll be less inclined to turn you in, as the Sorcerers Collective would no doubt use all means necessary to find out the details of how said client was associated with you in the first place." He shot a quick look at the bolt.

"I'm sorry for the position I've put you in. I had nowhere else to go on such short notice," I said, lifting my broken arm a fraction. "I knew your skills would be the best I'd find outside of Luma Proper."

Geraldine's tense shoulders relaxed slightly at the apology and the compliment. "I have a few healing tonics I can give you now to tide you over. They won't mend the bones completely, but it will buy you at least a week should you need to lie low until you can get someone to tend to your injuries better. You can stay until morning."

"Thank you," I said again.

The clinic where they worked was fae-only—that was all I knew about it. I wasn't even sure where it was. The few times I'd asked Mathias details about the place, just trying to make friendly chitchat, he'd changed the subject, so I'd given up.

The tonic Geraldine brought me came in a two-inch-tall vial and tasted like burnt cherries. I choked it down. The Stones offered me leftover soup, too. My stomach had grumbled at the idea of food—I hadn't eaten anything since that breakfast sandwich this morning. Geraldine added that she'd made "a traditional goblin dish" and though I didn't recognize the goblin word for the meal, she mentioned banana peels among the ingredients. I politely declined, claiming my stomach was too messed up from nerves to eat. I mostly didn't want to insult their hospitality by vomiting up whatever hell-chowder they'd made.

Geraldine went to bed first, heading for the master bedroom somewhere in the back of the apartment. Mathias lingered to give me a rough idea of where everything was. Since I was too worn out for a proper tour, I stayed on the couch while he pointed the rooms out to me and mentioned any idiosyncrasies. The bathroom was the first door on the left, and I needed to flip the flusher back up after I used the toilet or the tank would run all night. The kitchen was on the right, and the soup Geraldine made was in a green-lidded plastic container in the fridge. I was not to open the one with the yellow lid under any circumstances.

I vowed to stay out of the kitchen entirely.

He finally bid me goodnight and turned to leave, only he hesitated in the doorway of the living room. "Can I ask you a question, Fletch?"

I adjusted myself on the couch, my face involuntarily twinging when the movement caused a flare of pain in my arm. It felt like the *inside* of my arm itched. Could bones itch? I guessed it was the magic in the tonic Geraldine had given me, speeding up the healing process. "Sure."

Mathias came back to stand in front of me. With him standing and me sitting on his low couch, we were almost at eye level. He wrung his gray hands. "Do you live in Montclaire Oaks?"

"Yeah ..."

"Ah, well, you see, a friend of mine ... a fellow goblin ... lives in the apartment complex that shares an alley with yours."

I didn't like where this was going.

"She lives on the third floor and she said she watched as a woman matching your description ran down a fire escape while flames shot out of a fourth-story window," Mathias said, scrutinizing my face. "She said this woman was chased by at least one werecat, and that while the woman herself didn't seem to do anything other than run for her life, a sword with her killed at least two of the werecats. A sword held by an invisible person or that acted on its own. She watched the sword follow this woman out of sight."

I hadn't even thought about witnesses. I'd only been thinking of escape. Of course someone had been watching! Several some-ones, probably. We'd made one hell of a racket. How many of them had called it in? How many in my complex or the one next door knew who I was and offered up my name?

"Don't tell me anything," Mathias said, holding up his small gray palms. "If I don't know details, I won't be lying if I get questioned. Truth serums only work if the truth is in my head for them to extract."

I nodded, not trusting my mouth. My eyes felt itchy with unshed tears.

"Keep it together," he said firmly, but he smiled as he said it. "You are strong and resourceful and you'll figure out what to do. You're just in shock and pain right now. What I suggest is that in the morning, you find a glamourer. Glamours don't hold on full-blooded humans as long, but there are many options for magic-created disguises. Potions, color-changing hair accessories, talismans, rune-activated tattoos. With the right glamour, you can get treated at one of the underground clinics. They won't ask questions."

Underground clinics?

"Do you know of a glamourer I can trust on this side of town?" I asked. "The witch I trust the most is in downtown Luma, and until I can get a single-use telepad card—they're probably watching the stations too—it would take me at least an hour to get there. Any glamour I got here would probably wear off by the time I got downtown."

"And even if it held, the telepad ride would knock it loose," Mathias said.

Right. I knew that. I squeezed my eyes shut for a moment until the throbbing in my head subsided. I needed sleep. Sleep would help clear the panicked fog in my brain, but my anxiety would prevent me from relaxing enough to doze off.

"I'll contact Zander Welsh first thing in the morning," Mathias said. "He's a witch who specializes in glamours and illusions."

My brows shot up at the name. "And fake IDs."

"You know him?"

"Sort of. A friend and I wanted fake IDs in high school. My friend had to pick them up alone though, since Welsh refused to deal with full-blooded humans directly. His hatred of us is legendary. Has that changed?"

Mathias grimaced. "Uhh ... well, no. But he'll do it as a favor to me. He's the guy you go to if you want to disappear—whether that means a new identity here in Luma with a new face and name, or creating a new life outside Luma, or even leaving the magical world entirely."

I knew that, because his name kept coming up during the two years I tried to find my mother after Dad died. When she'd left Luma, all traces of her had vanished. Had she managed this on her own, or did she have help? I'd had to communicate with Welsh through Kayda, which involved a lot of telepost messages sent to private boxes, clandestine meetings in dark alleys, and ridiculously high "consultation fees." Only for Welsh to tell Kayda that he'd never met my mother and had no idea where she was—because he didn't trouble himself with the activities of full-blooded humans.

"He won't rat you out," Mathias said. "His hands are too dirty. He won't want the Collective *or* their werecats on his doorstep. Assuming they can find his doorstep, since it changes so often ..."

"How do *you* know him?" I asked, unable to help myself. It was like finding out the class nerd with his pocket protector and too-big glasses was an assassin for the mob.

Part of why I'd felt terrible about throwing all of this on Mathias was because his request for a contraband goblin-made item was probably the most law-breaking he'd done in his whole life. He'd wrung his hands when we first discussed making him a client, looking over his shoulder several times as if he expected a werecat to pounce on him at any moment. And he'd been wringing his hands all night tonight.

I flashed back to what he'd said when I first got here, broken and wild-eyed. *"I can't afford any trouble."*

"I don't want trouble" would have been a normal, law-abiding thing to say. Couldn't afford trouble meant something else. Did his worries stretch further than the possibility of being caught with an illegal crossbow bolt?

"Mathias?" I asked cautiously. "How do you know Welsh?"

He sighed. "Did I ever tell you that Geraldine and I came here from a hub in Georgia?"

I shook my head.

"My younger sister, Nyla, was living here for a time. She and her best friend visited Luma, wanting to experience the city that never sleeps. They fell in love with the place and decided to stay. She was working at a club for a while as a server. About a year ago, she … disappeared. No calls, no telepost messages. Geraldine and I took a telepad here to try to track her down. We went to the club she talked about and asked around there. The friend had disappeared, too. The other servers at the Ghost Lily assumed they'd gone back to Georgia."

I'd been to the Ghost Lily a few times, though not in years. It was in the northwestern corner of Ardmore, near the Warehouse and Industrial Districts. It was a popular location for the blue-collar crowd. Kayda had worked there once but she'd bailed after a few months because it could get too rough there, even for her.

"Did you report it?" I asked.

Mathias nodded. "We had two humans assigned to the case. That was our first sign that no one cared about my sister. No offense to humans, but a human cop would never get the same information from witnesses as a goblin cop would have. Human cops get the fae cases that are considered low priority. After a few months, the police told us they'd concluded their search and had ample evidence to suggest the girls left Luma."

"What kind of evidence?"

"They wouldn't give us specifics," Mathias said, wringing his hands. "We asked about getting a goblin cop on the case, or appealing directly to the Collective. We're still caught in a paperwork nightmare a year later. When we asked if we could hire an independent investigator, they said we were welcome to do so, but it was our money to burn because they had unlimited resources and were unable to find the girls, therefore the girls didn't want to be found. They implied the girls had help disappearing."

"Which led you to Welsh?" I asked.

"Yeah. The more we asked around, the more Welsh's name came up. We went to see him, hoping if we showed him a picture of Nyla, he would recognize her."

"Would Welsh admit it if he had?" I asked. "If he's in the business of helping people disappear, it's probably not a great idea to share his clients' secrets."

"He told me that around here, young fae go missing all the time. The Collective, so he says, either is the reason they go missing, or their police force—of all species—are instructed to make sure trails go cold so no one panics about a widespread problem. Can't do anything to tarnish Luma's reputation …"

I frowned at the bitter sarcasm. That wasn't Mathias's way, either. "What do you think happened to Nyla?"

His breath hitched at the sound of his sister's name. I wasn't sure how old Mathias was. Goblins didn't age the way humans did. His black hair was robust, with no hints of gray. What might seem like mid-forties to me might be closer to twenty. Had Nyla been a mere teenager in goblin years?

"The cops insinuated that Nyla got into drugs. Mostly that Bliss stuff," Mathias said, shaking his head. "There's no way, though. Not Nyla. I suspect foul play. She was a free spirit, going off on her own at a young age to see the world, but she always called home. Always. She was the type to check in on others when she hadn't heard from *them* in a few days. She wouldn't just vanish on us without saying anything. If she'd gotten herself into some kind of trouble, she would have found a way to at least tell someone. And Vian disappearing at the same time?" He shook his head.

This was all making me think of my friend Naomi. She'd been human, though, and after only being missing a week, she'd been found—though not alive.

Could elves be behind the disappearances? I immediately dismissed the idea. Elves were mischievous. They caused havoc because it amused them—like making that human cross the veil, knowing he'd lose his marbles when he laid eyes on the hidden city. Making young fae disappear without a trace wasn't flashy enough to be an elfin prank.

But I also couldn't understand why the Sorcerers Collective wouldn't only cover up that young fae were disappearing, but discourage a grieving family from investigating the matter. Why shove the case to the bottom of the priority totem pole?

"Did you and Geraldine settle here because of Nyla?" I asked.

Mathias nodded. "We wanted to be here if she ever came back. It's also easier to search for her when I'm in the city where she went missing."

"There's been no sign of her?" I asked.

His shoulders drooped. "Nothing."

"I'm sorry," I said, knowing it was inadequate this time too, but also not knowing what else to say.

He nodded once, his lips pursed, telling me it was both okay and not at the same time. "I'll send Welsh a telepost in the morning," he told me again. "After months of searching for Nyla, I know that if she *did* have help to get out for good, she would have gone to him. He's very good at what he does. Despite hating humans, you pissing off the Collective's werecats will please him. He'll help you. I'm sure of it."

I watched Mathias shuffle off to his bedroom. He offered me a small, sad wave as he rounded the bend in the hallway before disappearing.

I lay in the dark, staring up at the Stones' low ceiling. My mind drifted from Nyla, who vanished without a trace, to my most vivid memory of Naomi ...

"Hey, girl! Wait up!"

I spun around to find Naomi run-walking toward me down the sidewalk. I grinned. "I wasn't sure you were going to make it."

She wheezed a laugh, grabbing at the stitch in her side. "I'm still not sure. I had a blast last night with you guys, but it's embarrassing how much of a lightweight I am when I work at a *bar*."

Chuckling, I kept heading for the front door of the Blind Mongoose, Naomi beside me now. "I'm glad you had fun. Felix and Kayda can be ... competitive ... and it can scare off newcomers."

"I know Monopoly can bring out the capitalistic monster in us all, but the way they banded together at the end was ... ruthless," Naomi said, shaking her head.

"Yep. That's the right word for it."

After we got our stuff put away in the back room, I waited for her to pop one more pain reliever before we clocked in. The night was a whirlwind, as usual, and I checked in on Naomi periodically to make sure she wasn't going to pass out on me. Working this place on a weekend while nursing a hangover was the literal worst, and I knew from experience.

At the end of the night, after counting up our tips, we clocked out and pulled on our coats as we headed for the door. We both lived within five blocks of the Mongoose, so we walked most nights. The area could get a little sketchy, but it felt safe enough with two of us. Before Naomi had swooped into my life four months ago, I'd catch a ride home with one of the other girls, or Felix would come pick me up. I always felt terrible about making him get up at two in the morning to get me, especially during the weeks when he got stuck with the dreaded morning-to-afternoon shifts at the casino. Dealing with day-drunk middle-aged ladies was Felix's nightmare, if only because day-drunk middle-aged ladies were drawn to Felix like flies to honey. I smiled to myself just thinking about it.

"How long have you and Felix been together?" she asked, as if reading my thoughts—or maybe she'd just recognized the goofy grin for what it was.

"Going on ten years."

Naomi whistled. "What, you were like fourteen when you started going out?"

I flushed. "More or less. Been best friends for ages. My rock. All that mushy crap." A little pang hollowed out my gut when I thought about how my rock didn't feel as solid lately. But I wouldn't admit that out loud to Naomi. I liked her a lot, but she and I weren't there yet. Only Kayda got to hear all the gory details of my doubts and fears.

"It's good you had him when all that stuff happened with your parents."

I looked sharply at her, but then a memory of last night bubbled to the surface—Felix and I drunkenly regaling Naomi, her boyfriend, Kayda, and the draken guy she'd been seeing about some of the wild things we'd seen during our bounty-hunting runs with both sets of our parents. When Naomi had innocently asked if I was still close with my parents, I'd shut down. Felix and Kayda had to tell Naomi and the other two guys in attendance the very condensed version of the fate that had befallen Nelson and Camila Fletcher.

Naomi wasn't prying.

"Yeah, I don't know if I would have gotten through it without him," I said. "Him and Kayda."

"Your found family," Naomi said softly, and I nodded. We walked silently for a block before Naomi spoke again. "Did you ever hear from your mom again?"

I sighed. "Nope. When she left, she left for good. I don't even know if she's still alive."

"I hope she is," Naomi said, a little hitch in her voice.

I wrapped an arm around my new friend's shoulder, touched by how much sympathy she had for me. I was glad I'd met her and that she'd fit perfectly into our little circle. I didn't expand my pod often.

Three blocks later, we'd reached the intersection where she and I parted ways. My apartment building was just around the corner. If I craned my head just right, I could see the hallway light Felix left on for me. Naomi's place was a duplex on a block to the left. We hugged goodbye, as we always did, but I held onto her for longer than usual when I spotted a figure across the street loitering under a tree. My gut told me it was a man, and that he was watching us. His features were a blur at this distance, but I saw the glowing red tip of his cigarette.

"What's wrong?" Naomi asked.

I let her go. "Do you know that guy? That doesn't look like Jeremy."

She glanced over her shoulder. The man had stepped out of the shadows now and while I noted he had short dark hair and a light complexion, I couldn't tell much else. He took a final drag on his cigarette and then tossed it onto the curb, snuffing out the end with the heel of his shoe.

Naomi's expression was cheerful when she turned back to me, but strained. "Yeah. That's my stepbrother. He's staying with me this week. Family trouble."

Somehow I knew she was lying, but I wasn't sure about which part. "You'll be okay?"

"Sure. Nothing I can't handle."

I watched as she crossed the street, meeting up with the guy. They fell into step together. Naomi looked back just as they rounded the corner. She waved, one hand in the air in farewell.

I never saw her again.

Whatever had happened to Naomi wasn't the same as what had happened to Nyla and Vian. Naomi had been found, possibly killed by the man she'd met up with that night. I hadn't gotten a good enough look at him to describe him. The lead had gone cold almost instantly. All records—at least the ones the police told me about—showed that Naomi didn't have a brother, step or otherwise. I hadn't thought about Naomi in years …

All that was in the past, anyway. What I needed to focus on was the present—which was currently an absolute shitshow. This had started because of the dragon sword, and I currently didn't even know where it was. My apartment was ruined beyond repair. The werecats had probably pissed on the fire to put it out. I hoped feline urine hadn't leaked through the floor and into the apartment below mine.

It hit me then that I was homeless. Homeless and alone.

Contacting Jo or Kayda wasn't viable until I had more secure methods of communication at my disposal. Day passes for the telepad were how most people low on funds got around. They were paid for in cash and couldn't be tracked. I didn't buy that the werecats had tracked my telepad card, though, since the account linked to it was under a fake name. I'd gone through a human with the tech skills needed to create a false digital footprint for me. That guy hadn't recognized my mother's picture either.

My guess was, the Collective pulled up security footage at every telepad station they could find and had tracked my movements that way. Still, it made me feel less paranoid about my anti-cell phone policy.

I was grateful to have a plan for the morning, even if it meant contending with the likes of the human-hating Zander Welsh. With his glamour magic, I could travel around the city without being detected. Making it to Welsh without getting arrested along the way would be its own special challenge.

A series of buzzes sounded. Quick, quick, slow. I froze at the sound. A Pavlovian reaction stirred in me: it was impossible to ignore the impulse to check the message on the mirror when I heard that sound.

I scanned the room for my bag and found it slouched against a short bookshelf. Groaning, I got to my feet, trying not to jostle my arm too much. Squatting before my backpack, I worked open a side zipper with one hand and rooted around inside, searching for the familiar disc.

When my hand finally closed around the smooth, round surface of the pocket mirror, I flipped open the lid with my thumb. While I wasn't surprised by what I saw, it was upsetting all the same.

At large. Armed and dangerous. Fletcher. Multiple Code 158 violations.

The Collective had officially put out a bounty on me.

CHAPTER FOURTEEN

I actually slept for a couple of hours. Perhaps the added stress of having a bounty out on me had sent me over the edge. Too much worry and pain piled on at once and my body gave up the ghost and shut down. Sleep was fitful, though and I woke with a start, gasping for breath because a pair of giant werecat paws were on my chest, pressing the air out of my lungs. I tried to get out from under the weight before the beast crushed my lungs like Harrison had crushed my arm.

But when I opened my eyes, I saw no pearly white canines or piercing yellow eyes. My skin felt slick, and I itched under my skin, a reminder that the healing tonic Geraldine had given me was still fast at work. My hip was sore, but it wasn't as excruciating as it had been. Same with my tailbone. A moment later, I realized the pressure on my chest was from the dragon sword lying on my sternum, the tip of the blade facing my chin, and the hilt pointing to my feet that hung over the armrest. Was it … sleeping? If the thing had snored, I wouldn't have been shocked.

I placed a hand on the hilt, whether to convince myself it was here, or to let it know I was acknowledging it, I wasn't sure. It wasn't currently covered in blood, but that didn't mean anything in particular. I imagined it swiping itself clean on a patch of wet grass before finding me here. I gently took it by the hilt, climbed off the couch, and slipped the sword into my duffel bag, telling it to stay out of sight for now. It didn't protest.

How had the sword gotten in here? I crept to the edge of the living room, craning my neck to peer into the short entrance hall. The rectangular slot in the door looked intact, but could the sword have used its tip to pry it open so it could get in? Had the Stones left a window open? Maybe they'd find a hole in one of their walls tomorrow where the sword had forced its way in, chipping through brick, cement, and drywall to get back to me.

In the sitting room, next to the crossbow bolt on the mantel, was an analog clock, the numbers marked in golden Roman numerals. The second hand spun slowly around the face, not making a sound. It was just after midnight. This was turning out to be the longest night of my life. I settled back on the couch, staring at the ceiling.

Despite Pratt's claims, I hadn't activated the sword. I didn't for a second believe the sword was reacting to some hidden magical ability in me. A long-lost dragon princess, I was not. Yet, it kept returning to my side. It had decided to trust me, but for the life of me, I had no idea why.

When I next awoke on the Stones' couch, it wasn't a bulbous-nosed goblin who stared down at me, but a long-faced man who had the deadest eyes I'd ever seen. His hair was shoulder length, dirty blond, and greasy, like maybe he'd never washed it in his entire life. He parted his mouth in some semblance of a smile, revealing brown, jagged teeth. For a moment, I was convinced I'd died and woken on the zombie home world. Did a zombie home world exist? No fucking clue. But if you'd seen this guy, you would have wondered too.

I yipped and scooted back, willing the couch cushions to suck me into their depths, preventing the zombie lord from smashing my head in with a rock and eating my brains.

"Humans," he muttered, somehow sounding deeply bored and completely disgusted at the same time. "Am I to believe that you're the reason the sorcerers' werecats have their collective hackles up? Supposedly, you murdered three of them." His gaze scanned me from head to foot. It was a disturbingly slow scan, as if he were committing every inch of me to memory.

"Stop it, Zander," came a female voice from somewhere behind the dead-eyed guy. She sounded a touch amused. I assumed it was Geraldine, but couldn't discount the possibility that it was Zander Welsh's zombie wife. "You're scaring her. You promised Mathias you'd help her."

"I didn't realize you made house calls," I managed.

"He usually doesn't," came Mathias's voice. I couldn't see him either from where I was smashed into the couch. "When he figured out who you were, he wanted to come see you right away."

"I'm flattered."

"Don't be," Welsh said, head cocked. "I don't understand how you, a mere human, killed three government-trained hell-cats all by yourself and your only injuries are a broken arm and a few cuts and bruises. I was deeply curious before I saw you, and now I'm utterly baffled. It's not possible. You're so ... puny."

Puny was not a word I'd use to describe myself, but it wasn't an argument I wanted to get into with Captain Creepshow. How widespread were the dragon sword rumors? Even if Mathias said Welsh wouldn't rat me out to the werecats, and as much as I needed his help, no part of me trusted him. I swallowed down my fear and said, "I need a way to get around without being recognized. A glamour strong enough to get me in and out of Luma Proper if you can manage it. But I'll take whatever I can get at this point. I have cash."

He grinned, a faint hint of genuine humor seeping through. Swiping a lock of greasy hair out of his face, he said, "You are an interesting one, aren't you? You speak with confidence, yet you look terrified."

"Dude. You look like the offspring of an animated skeleton and a vampire who went on a meth bender," I blurted.

Someone nearby gasped. Maybe Geraldine worried I'd die on this couch after all, once the pissed-off witch knifed me in the heart.

Welsh threw his greasy head back and laughed. A deep, hearty sound. At least he thought I was amusing.

When he refocused on me, his lips moved rapidly, though no sound came out. Was he casting a spell? I scooted back a little further. What if he was calling on his undead horde to tear me apart?

My mouth fell open as greasy blond hair shrunk up to soft brown locks, a perfect little curl resting on his forehead. His fair skin was no longer sickly, and his dead eyes lightened to a striking green. His sunken cheeks filled out, cheekbones and jawline becoming more pronounced by the second. A smattering of brown stubble sprung up along his jaw like sprouting grass. When he smiled, his entire face lit up and a single dimple appeared in his right cheek. My face heated involuntarily. He went from king of the undead to the lead singer of a boy band in less than a minute.

"Do you prefer this?" he asked, his voice a deep rumbling purr.

I swallowed, dumbstruck, and fought the urge to reach out and gently swipe that curl out of his face.

Welsh rolled his new eyes. "Humans. So easily cowed by an attractive face."

If Kayda were here, she'd elbow me for once again going stupid over something pretty. Giving myself a little shake, I asked, "Which face is your real one?"

"Both," Welsh said. "Neither."

Now it was my turn to roll my eyes.

Welsh was all business after that, settling on a tone somewhere in the middle of utter disdain and sultry. He kept the pretty face, which was a little distracting.

"Humans can't keep a complex glamour on for long, since there's no magic in your nervous system to keep it going," he said. "Glamour magic, though, when done right, isn't immediately detectable. If we keep the glamour to something simple—hair and eye color change, for example—that will give you more time. Given the ruckus you caused, simple won't be enough to get you around town without being noticed. You also need a healer. I will create two glamours for you. The first will be a goblin, and the second will be a human male."

Changing me into a goblin was some heavy-duty magic. "Why goblin?"

Geraldine spoke up. "Mathias and I had a long talk this morning. If you look fae, you'll be granted access to the clinic where we work. All fae are allowed there, but goblins are treated the most often. I already sent them a message that Mathias's cousin would be coming by."

"Thank you," I said, knowing that when this was all over, I would need to send the Stones a gift basket of goblin-made items to make up for the imposition.

Welsh said, "I also brought a set of accessories with me that alter one characteristic at a time. You can wear up to three before the magic starts glitching. You can try those out and select three you like best while I craft the tonics for you."

I swallowed and nodded, wondering what this would cost me. His "consultation fees" that resulted in no information whatsoever about my mother's whereabouts had been exorbitant.

Welsh reached down and picked up a small black case that had been resting by his feet. It was a two-foot-by-two-foot square with a latch on the front and a handle on top. He placed it on the cushion beside my thigh. "To get started, I'll need a lock of your hair, a couple of fingernail clippings, and a small vial of blood."

After he had all three, he followed Geraldine into the kitchen. Grabbing the case with the hand not attached to a slinged arm, I got up and shuffled into the Stones' small bathroom. Mathias made sure I was okay before he joined Geraldine and Welsh in the kitchen.

The bathroom was small—only a toilet and sink. From the doorway, I eyed the mirror above the sink warily. Many mirrors were made with silver nitrate, which, it turned out, was very magically conductive. The mirrors used by the bounty hunters had a high silver concentration. Silver tarnished easily if exposed to the elements, which was why they were in pocket mirror form. As long as the lid was closed most of the time, the mirror stayed shiny and conductive. Copper and aluminum were common in mirror production too, but their conductivity was less consistent.

A few decades ago, a sorcerer discovered mirrors were essentially viewing portals into people's homes. Mirrors in hubs across the globe were "hacked." There hadn't been any reason for the hack other than curiosity. If a sorcerer, witch, or alchemist knew your name and where you lived, they could figure out how to spy on you. Most Luma residents weren't as untrusting as I was, so while everyone knew the potential danger of having mirrors in their homes, most figured it was no big deal if you had nothing to hide. It wasn't unlike mundanes knowing cameras could be hacked, yet allowing cameras into countless facets of their lives, unwittingly opening themselves up to the possibility of the devices being commandeered by a stranger behind a computer screen.

Personally, I had lots of things to hide. Including my whole person. As anxious as the bathroom mirror's presence made me, I knew I'd need it to get my glamour right. If the Collective or their cats thought I was here, they'd break the door down, not wait for me to use the bathroom. When I'd used it last night, I'd employed a scoot-and-shuffle method on my back to get to the toilet, and then wiggled out the same way, all to keep out of direct range of the mirror. I'd washed my hands in the kitchen.

I stepped inside now and deposited the case on the corner of the small sink before flipping open the latch and folding back the lid. An attached tray inside moved with the lid, revealing a space below. In the small tray were little square-shaped partitions lined in black felt. There were earrings, cufflinks, rings, and clip-on hoops of various sizes that might have been earrings as well, but I wasn't sure. They all looked normal enough, and when I swept my fingertips over them, I felt no tingles of magic. In the bottom of the case were dozens of white pouches. I pulled one out and peered inside. A lock of hair rested there. Mildly disconcerted, I held the pouch with one hand and reached in with finger and thumb with the other. When I pulled the red lock free, I yelped as it morphed into a long wig. I wasn't sure how I was supposed to try on wigs when I only had one good arm.

With little grace, I flung it onto my head with one hand, intending to just check out the color against my skin tone. It sat awkwardly on my wild mess of curls. Yet, the second the wig touched my hair, the long red locks *became* my hair. The soft red waves fell around my shoulders. I peered at my bewildered reflection, turning my head this way and that, not seeing any hint of my real hair. I reached up and gently pulled the red hair away from my scalp and saw no hint of a wig's seam against my hairline. The little hairs at my temples were red, too.

The color was such a vibrant contrast to my dark skin that I would stand out when I walked down the street. The color screamed "Notice me!" I needed the opposite of that.

Now, how to get the damn thing off?

I tugged gently at my temple, then a little harder when the hair stayed firmly in place. I pulled at the hair on the back and top of my head. I twisted the long locks around my fist and gave a hard pull that did nothing other than give me a headache. When I released the hair, a chunk of it swung up and whacked me in the face, like it was mad at me for the rough treatment.

"Ugh! It's not like you came with an instruction manual," I said, spitting a strand out of my mouth. "Relax, wig."

What little curl the wig had smoothed out, and now the red mane was stick-straight. Okay, that was kind of cool.

Thinking of how I first commanded the sword when I needed it to listen to me, I said, "Wig, off."

And just like that, my wild bedhead curls were back and the lock of red hair was in the pouch. Magic was some weird shit.

I settled on a straight black bob after trying six different pouches.

The rings changed both the length of my fingers and the color of my nails. The earrings altered the shape of my jaw. I tried one of the clip-on hoops as a nose ring for giggles and gave myself an instant rhinoplasty. Wild.

I joined the others, modeling my new look. Mathias and Geraldine smiled appreciatively. Welsh didn't even look up from his task at hand, hunched over the small kitchen table while he furiously scribbled what I assumed was a spell. I leaned against the counter, arms crossed.

Welsh had a case on the table that looked identical to the one I'd left on the bathroom counter. Inside his, though, were vials of liquids, pots of powders, and pouches of dried herbs. He was crushing something with great vigor with a mortar and pestle. Once done, he dripped a few drops of my blood into it. The contents bubbled a frothy pink.

"Do extensive glamours hurt?" I asked.

"Yes. The goblin transformation will feel quite terrible." He glanced at me then and gave me another head-to-toe scan, taking in my disguise. He flashed his boy band leader smile, and my stupid stomach did a little flip. I wasn't even attracted to the little weasel. "I would like to say, 'Just kidding! You won't feel a thing!' But that would be a lie."

He returned to his work.

An hour later, I was sprawled out on the couch, still waiting on Welsh. Apparently, glamour tonics took a while. There had been a minor explosion in the kitchen half an hour ago and I'd sat up long enough to see Geraldine dart into her bedroom. She came running back out, her eyes wild and her arms full of towels. I decided I didn't want to know any details and lay back down.

I used my time well, thinking deep, philosophical questions. Like, how had Geraldine and Mathias gotten a couch of this size through a door that narrow? Had they hired a company to move the couch in here? Moving Magic Company, run by two air elementals, operated out of uptown Luma. It was the least creative name ever, but I had to admit they were doing God's work. No one enjoyed moving—why not hire magic users to move everything for you, especially since they could do it without breaking much of a sweat themselves? The couch might have been purchased from one of those magic-sealed furniture places where the item in question came in a tight package, like a mattress.

The question was, how would they get it back out when they moved?

A series of beeps sounded from the kitchen. Followed by trills. Chimes. Muttered voices. Then the tinny sound of what might have been sirens. I propped myself up on my good arm and peered into the hallway over my hanging feet. No one stood there. I shot a glance to my right, where their modest-sized TV was perched on a low stand. The screen was dark.

The tinny sounds grew louder. Definitely the wail of sirens.

A moment later, the Stones stood in the hallway, their tiny frames looking even smaller with Welsh standing behind them. They all wore identical expressions—some combination of concern and confusion.

"What?" I asked, sitting up. I winced at the pain that lanced through my arm.

"Is it possible she's an excellent actress?" Welsh asked, staring at me even though he addressed the Stones.

"That arm is definitely broken," Geraldine said. "She couldn't have faked that."

"The video was faked then?" Mathias asked.

"It wouldn't be the first time. But what could be threatening enough about *her*," Welsh said, waving a hand dismissively, "that they'd go through this much trouble?"

They had this entire conversation while they stared at me, yet were talking to each other as if I weren't there.

"Someone want to explain what's going on?" I asked.

Mathias walked over, leaving the other two to watch me apprehensively from the hallway. He had a cell phone in his small gray hand and tapped at the screen while he approached. Once he had it cued up, he handed the device over. I took it, shooting curious glances at the other two before returning my focus to the screen. It was a video posted by a local news station.

Videos, much like cell phones, were prone to magical interference. Even though the news was largely a human-run operation, even in the hubs, trusting anything on TV was foolhardy, since it was a badly kept secret that the Collective had final say in what was released. Most of what was covered were human interest stories, crime in Luma, and news about other magical hubs. But it was impossible to know how much of a spin the Collective put on things to make themselves look good.

The sorcerers held press conferences periodically, too. They were rarely live, and for the past six months, if not longer, it had been a werecat representative on-screen in human form who delivered messages, in lieu of sorcerers. The Collective chose which reporters got to attend the conferences, and the footage of the event was released after the fact. Holding a live press conference with the leading members of the Collective in attendance was too dangerous, they said, since their enemies could figure out where they were in real time. Seeing as the sorcerers were at the top of the food chain, with their trained cats just below them, the safety concerns never rang true for me. They wanted a closed press conference to ensure they could control the message that hit TVs. So I didn't watch the news.

I was a little surprised that the thing that had disconcerted the three of them was a news clip. Especially Welsh. Even more surprising was that the thumbnail showed a woman standing at the mouth of an alley, her unbound black curls wild around her head. I scanned the surrounding frame. The background didn't give away the location, as the brick buildings on either side of her could be anywhere in Luma. The time of day could have been either dusk or dawn—the sliver of sky behind her was a soft blue-gray, clouds painted yellow and orange. My gaze shifted back to the woman in the middle, positioned rather theatrically in front of the alley. There was a hard set to her features and a blood-slick sword in her hand.

My curls, my face, my sword.

I tapped the play button with my thumb, unsure if I was ready to see this. The second the video began, the sound of sirens wailed through the phone's speakers.

A police car sat on the edge of the frame on either side, officers shielding themselves behind open car doors. Over a megaphone off-screen, a voice rang out. "Put down the weapon!"

My head swiveled toward the voice, but otherwise I didn't move. The camera shakily zoomed in. Blood coated my arms, splattered across my jeans and light blue shirt, and dotted a cheek. Every place not coated in blood was smeared with soot. My shirt was ripped across the stomach, and my curls flapped in a slight breeze. I looked like something out of a post-apocalyptic movie.

"Harlow Fletcher," the voice over the megaphone said. "You have five seconds to drop the sword or we will be forced to take you down by any means necessary."

Two pumas stalked into the frame, their massive bodies low to the ground, their muscles rippling below short, sleek fur.

I took off like a shot. Not for the officers, but down the alley behind me. The cats broke into a dead run after me, the camera person doing his or her best to follow. The camera operator reached the alley, recording the dark brick walls, a green dumpster, and a few closed metal doors. When I reached the end of the alley, I expected to see myself turn around to square off against the pumas. Instead, I launched toward the wall to my right, one foot hitting the brick for half a breath before launching toward the left, a little higher up. Back and forth I went, and after a matter of seconds, I had scaled the fifteen-foot-tall brick wall and disappeared over the other side of it, out of sight.

"How is this even possible?" I muttered.

"We were going to ask you the same thing," Mathias said.

The scene changed. Now, a stoic-faced man stood behind a podium, the Collective's logo painted on the black wall behind him in gold paint. It wasn't a werecat this time. This was one of the rarely seen sorcerers. He had light brown skin, dark eyes, and short-cropped black hair. At first glance, I'd guess he was in his mid-forties. But his eyes and cheeks looked sunken, giving him the air of someone much older—or someone fighting a chronic illness.

"As you've just seen, a very dangerous woman by the name of Harlow Fletcher is on the loose. Though Fletcher is a full-blooded human, she has gained abilities through the sword she's wielding. She stole the sword twenty-four hours ago and has already been driven mad by the dragon magic in the blade. With the aid of the sword, she has killed a caracal shifter, as well as three shifters from the Collective's guard.

"The Collective's priority first and foremost is the safety of Luma's residents. This is why magical items such as this dragon sword have been banned. They must be collected and destroyed. They are too dangerous to exist. Because we are determined to fix this problem as quickly as possible and restore order to the best city in this nation, myself and the rest of the Collective are offering a reward of $20,000 to anyone who provides information of Fletcher's whereabouts that directly leads to an arrest."

He turned a couple of inches to the left, staring into a different camera. My pulse quickened, as if he were staring right at me now.

"Harlow Fletcher," he said, "if you are watching this, the Collective understands you are under the power of the sword. We know *your* will is stronger, and that you can fight its intoxicating pull. If you turn yourself in, you will receive the lesser sentence of theft. If you do not, when you're apprehended—and you *will* be apprehended—you will face four counts of aggravated homicide. The punishment will be swift and severe."

I swallowed hard.

A soft, unconvincing smile graced his tired face as he turned back to the first camera. "Citizens of Luma, know that we will not rest until our city is free from this threat. Good evening ... and stay safe."

The video faded to black. I stared blankly at the screen for a long time before passing the phone back to Mathias. I'd gone from horrified, to confused, to numb.

I slowly turned to Geraldine and Welsh, who hadn't moved since they first stepped into the hallway. "Are you going to turn me in?" I asked, voice hoarse, as I looked from goblin to witch. "Twenty thousand is a lot of money."

Welsh walked into the living room and sat on the short stool before the couch again. He rested his forearms on his knees and stared at me for several beats. "No."

I let out a shuddering breath. "Why not?"

"If I hadn't met you first, I wouldn't have hesitated to call in a tip if I spotted you. But Mathias told me himself that he put wards on his doors and windows last night. If you had tried to leave, he and Geraldine would have known. You were here by ten in the evening last night, and your arm was broken. Your arm was not broken in that video."

I'd also awoken around midnight to the sword lying on my chest, but I didn't tell them that.

Geraldine came to stand on Welsh's other side. "Was it illusion magic?" she asked the witch.

Welsh thought about that for a moment. "No. Illusion magic is tricky. Illusion magic affects the viewer, not the person or object being viewed. A glamour, on the other hand, actually changes what someone or something looks like. The more people who view an illusion, the stronger the magic behind the spell needs to be. A weak illusion will break apart if viewed by a crowd. An illusion will hold in a still photograph half the time, but is rarely captured in moving photography. There are too many variables."

"So it *was* a glamour. Someone made to look like Fletch?" Mathias asked, and I smiled softly at the hopeful note in his tone.

"Maybe," Welsh said, cocking his head, as if examining me from another angle would reveal something he hadn't seen before. "But why? When was the last time one of the sorcerers on high deigned to address us peons? This is all very curious. I hate you on principle a lot less now."

"Thanks," I said. "I think …"

He smiled his boy band smile.

Mathias wrung his hands. "I know I said not to tell me details, but … Fletch … what your neighbor saw … the sword?"

Geraldine and Welsh looked at me expectantly, too.

I weighed my options. They didn't think I'd killed all those shifters, but they also thought the entire video had been staged. The video had taken bits of the truth and twisted them into a lie. Yet, the sword *was* dangerous. It *had* killed. And even if I wasn't the one who had wielded the weapon when the shifters had been cut down, the sword had imprinted on me and kept returning to my side. The sword had been MIA when I'd fallen asleep in my apartment but had come back of its own volition. The recorded standoff I'd just watched might have happened exactly as it appeared, tied to yet another facet of the sword's power.

The sorcerer said they would only charge me for theft if I turned myself in, but the Collective's attack cats who had broken down my door hadn't shown up intending to quietly escort me to Collective headquarters. They'd shown up ready to rip me limb from limb. Mathias had been right the first time. The less he knew, the less the sorcerers could pry out of him. If I said nothing, Welsh and the goblins could never inadvertently tell the Collective that I had the dragon sword.

"I don't know what your neighbor saw," I finally said, raising my brows.

Mathias pursed his lips and nodded once, still wringing his hands.

My attention swiveled to Welsh. "You going to turn me into a goblin so I can get out of here or what?"

CHAPTER FIFTEEN

I stood in the middle of the Stones' living room with Welsh in front of me. He studied me intently, like I was a bug trapped under glass.

The glamour did not, in fact, hurt. It tingled at first, like when a limb falls asleep, then gave way to a vibrating hum. Within minutes of drinking the glamour tonic, my entire body buzzed. It was unsettling more than anything—like all my molecules were separating and breaking apart to float away on the wind like so many specks of dust. I was made of TV static.

And then, all at once, I shrunk almost two feet. Welsh and I had been face-to-face, and now we were face-to-belt. I tipped my head back to look up at him.

"Did it work?" I asked. "Oh, why do I sound like a squeaky mouse?"

Geraldine, now the same height as me, walked over to peer in my face. "This is quite impressive, Zander."

I moved to take a step forward and wobbled dangerously. Though I was wider around the middle, my legs were significantly shorter. The hems of my pants pooled around my enormous feet. Thankfully, I hadn't been wearing my boots during the time of my sudden transformation. Unfastening the button of my jeans, I groaned in relief as my rounded belly popped free. My broken arm throbbed, the sling not fitting snugly anymore. As I flapped my unmangled arm, my too-long sleeve fluttering, I said, "This seems like a problem."

"Come with me," Geraldine said with a laugh. "I already picked out some old clothes you can have."

I tried to follow her, but between my new clown feet and the oversized clothes, I pitched forward. Welsh caught me around the middle and settled me on my feet before I face-planted and re-injured my arm.

Geraldine, a hand on her hip, gestured at my lower half with her free hand. "Take those things off."

I shot a glance at Welsh, heat rushing to my cheeks. The blush was no doubt more prominent on my new sickly gray skin than it ever had been on my natural brown.

"Trust me," Welsh said, with barely contained disgust, "you have nothing I want to see." Sighing, he said, "But if it makes you feel better …"

In the blink of an eye, the boy band hottie was gone, and the King of the Zombies had returned. I involuntarily shuddered.

I tried to get the pants off, but with only one hand, it was slow going. Geraldine came over to help, while Mathias stood nearby and fretted. The jeans I wore had been of the skinny variety, so even though my new legs were shorter now, getting my massive feet out of the tiny leg holes was such a struggle that I eventually ended up on my back, squirming around like an overturned turtle, while Geraldine and Welsh each took hold of a pant leg and yanked as hard as they could.

"We should just cut them off!" Welsh said, followed by another great heaving tug.

"No!" I squeaked. "I have a limited wardrobe and these are my favorite pants! You should have warned me this would happen!"

"I've never actually turned a human into a goblin before," Welsh grumbled and yanked hard enough on the pant leg that I scooted across the carpet. Now I'd have a tramp stamp rug burn.

"Ouch, Welsh! Easy!"

"Aha!" Geraldine said, finally getting the foot out of the leg hole.

"Why does my foot feel slimy?" I asked, propped up on a tiny elbow.

Geraldine handed Welsh the jar of mayonnaise.

"Ugh," I said, flopping onto my back.

By the time I was free of my pants, waddling after Geraldine while holding up my very ill-fitting underwear, I smelled like salad dressing. Cool air nipped at my new goblin backside. Zombie Lord Welsh offered me a wolf-whistle as I ran by. I whipped around to glare. He'd added a trail of blood to the corner of his mouth, as well as a few sores around his nose and temples. His dead eyes were going to haunt my nightmares for all of time. His laugh trailed after me, and it somehow echoed, conjuring up an image in my mind of a dilapidated Victorian house backlit by flashes of lightning.

When Geraldine closed the bedroom door behind us, I muttered, "That guy is one creepy sonofabitch."

Geraldine sputtered a surprised laugh and clapped a hand over her mouth. "One day I hope he'll trust us enough to show us his true face."

"Do you know much about him?" I asked, watching as Geraldine ducked into her closet.

"Only as much as he wants us to know," Geraldine said a moment later as she came bustling out with a neatly folded stack of clothes. She placed them on the bed. The shirt had a giant three-dimensional flower on it, the petals of the sunflower sticking up at all angles. "And who knows how much of that's a lie."

I nodded absently as I dressed in a pair of pants first, with her help, and then we got my too-large shirt and bra off and the new smaller shirt on. A goblin's breasts were virtually nonexistent compared to what I was used to as a human, so no need for a bra. I was S.O.L. with my giant underwear. Geraldine also brought me a better-sized sling, and we got my splinted arm into it.

Running a hand across the soft fabric of the sling, my throat unexpectedly tightened. "Thank you for helping me," I choked out, not able to look at her. "I know this was a lot to ask of you, and now the danger of possibly—"

She placed her cool hands on my elbows. "I don't know if you know this, but Mathias was deeply depressed when he first contacted you about finding a goblin artifact."

I glanced up.

"Nyla had been missing for four months by then, and it was the most down he'd ever been. Could hardly get out of bed. His parents didn't say it in so many words, but they implied that her running off was his fault because he was supposed to look after her. He's her brother, not her parent, but his parents are very elderly and Nyla's care had fallen on Mathias in a lot of ways." She sighed softly and then crossed her arms tight across her chest. "I was scared for a while there that I would lose him. That the grief would consume him, and then me. But when he got that crossbow bolt …"

I remembered how emotional Mathias had been when he'd finally held it in his hands.

"I know in a big-picture sense, the bolt is such a trivial thing, but it meant the world to him to feel the magic of our people again," Geraldine said. "It's easy to lose touch with it in a place like this. Every generation gets a little further away from their heritage. He felt lost, and getting that piece of home grounded him again. Some days are still hard, but receiving that bolt brought him back from the brink." She hesitated a moment. "I'm sorry if I was not as welcoming initially as I should have been. We've just dealt with so much flak from the Collective, police, *and* werecat guards already. I don't want anything to take Mathias from his search for Nyla."

I nodded, my throat still tight. "I hope you find her."

"We won't." Geraldine smiled sadly. "But Mathias needs to believe we might."

I blinked. "Why are you sure you won't?"

She cast a glance at the door, then walked farther into the room, motioning for me to follow. We huddled in the doorway of the master bathroom and Geraldine lowered her voice. "I've done some investigating on my own. A few of the girls from the Ghost Lily where Nyla worked seemed like they wanted to talk when we first went by there to ask questions, but not in front of Mathias. I went back to talk to them by myself. Mathias doesn't know that.

"The girls said Nyla and Vian weren't the only girls to go missing from there, just the only goblins. An elfin girl and two griffels went missing over the course of a few months. Gone without a trace."

Naomi and I hadn't worked at the Ghost Lily when Naomi had gone missing, but we'd both been servers at a bar, just like Nyla and Vian had been. They'd been young ladies trying to survive, just like us. Naomi had disappeared and was found dead a week later. Nyla and Vian had been missing for a full *year*. Which was worse? Knowing for a fact that someone you cared about was gone forever, or to be left wondering if, all these months later, they were still alive somewhere?

"The girls said one of the bouncers at the club, a draken man, watches them in a predatory way," Geraldine said. "He doesn't touch them or threaten them or anything, but asks a lot of questions about where they're from, things about their family, stuff like that. The ones he takes an interest in are usually the ones who go missing. The young goblin girl I talked to said she'd never been happier to be homely. She says only the really pretty ones disappear."

I frowned at that. Either the bodies of these missing girls were being disposed of better than Naomi's had been, the girls were alive and being held captive in Luma, or they'd been shuttled out of the city entirely. "What are you thinking ... trafficking?"

Geraldine shrugged. "My gut says yes. But I don't want to put a thought that horrible in Mathias's head. Whatever happened to Nyla, it doesn't sound good, and it doesn't sound like something you come back from."

Poor Mathias ...

"The police and guards' efforts to shut us down at every turn makes me think they know what happened to Nyla, though," Geraldine said. "They aren't acting in the best interest of people here, I know that much. Whatever you've gotten yourself mixed up in is no business of mine. I can't imagine you're guilty of even half of what they're accusing you of. All I know is that you can't trust what the Collective says. Don't turn yourself in, all right? You run and you don't look back. If you go into a precinct, you won't come back out. I'm sure of it."

I hugged her, the sunflower on my shirt crushed between our bodies. I wasn't sure where the impulse had come from. Maybe because I knew I couldn't go to Kayda anytime soon, nor to Jo, and I needed comfort. If these glamours didn't work and my actions resulted in Kayda, Jo, the goblins, or even Welsh landing in hot water with the Collective, I'd never forgive myself. When I left here, I'd be on my own. Just me and my murderous, diabolical sword.

When Geraldine squeezed me back, a sob unexpectedly broke loose. I wept softly on her shoulder. I was homeless, had a bounty on my head, and a countless number of everyday citizens would be on the lookout for me too, ready to throw me to the werecats for the hefty reward. The unknown awaited me beyond the walls of this little apartment, and Geraldine's gentle, warm hug currently felt like a life preserver preventing me from drowning.

I sniffed hard when we pulled away. Embarrassed, I grabbed my human clothes and shuffled back out into the main part of the apartment.

Welsh was now glamoured to look like a haggard old woman with a heavily curved spine and skin so wrinkled, coins could be hidden in the folds. He walked me through the glamours he'd prepared for me. The goblin one would last for three hours tops, and he gave me two more vials of the tonic, labeled "G." The second glamour was of a human male, of which he gave me three vials labeled "H." He also let me take a few more of his glamoured items—I'd taken them all off before downing the goblin tonic. Along with the first three, I picked a long, reddish-brown wig, a pair of earrings, and a hair tie that instantly tied hair into a French braid.

Backpack on, I grabbed the handles of the duffel bag, grateful that it still felt as heavy as the last time I picked it up, which hopefully meant the sword was still in there. I hoped it didn't get bored and slice its way to freedom. I was impressed with it for staying hidden for this long.

I turned to face my hosts. I knew the clinic was on this side of town, but that was it. My question about the clinic's location was interrupted by Welsh.

"I will escort you." He now employed a shaky old-lady voice.

I wrinkled my nose. Partly because it was bizarre not to have any idea what the guy's true form was, and partly because I only trusted him as far as I could throw him, and considering one of my arms was broken ...

But if I was willing to believe that his glamour tonics would keep me safe, I had to at least try to believe that he would walk me to the clinic, and not into a trap.

I hugged the Stones goodbye one last time, and then followed Welsh out of the apartment, up the narrow flight of stairs, and onto the sidewalk.

"Come now, dearie." A walker had materialized in front of Welsh somehow. He jutted it forward on its bright yellow tennis ball feet, then shuffled toward it. The pink bunny ears on his slippers flopped with every step.

Within a couple of blocks, we had reached a busy intersection. It was disorienting being around individuals so much taller than me. Hardly anyone paid me any mind, though. Most of them were annoyed that they had to sidestep the ancient woman who moved slower than a tranquilized sloth. And yet, any human who glanced down at me, gaze skirting over my bound arm, could be a werecat in their other form. It wasn't public knowledge that my arm had been broken, but O'Neill had been in my apartment when Harrison had trampled me. Werecats might have been told to search for anyone with obvious injuries. Every curious glance sent a spike of fear into my gut, sure someone had seen through my glamour.

The light at the crosswalk on our side flipped to green and a stream of people flooded across the street, including Welsh and his walker. No one ran toward us or shouted my name. The glamour was strong and held firm.

On borrowed goblin feet, I trotted after Welsh.

CHAPTER SIXTEEN

It took about twenty minutes to get to the clinic. It would have taken closer to ten if Welsh hadn't been taking his new persona this seriously. Halfway through the agonizingly slow trip, he placed a hand on his lower back and let out a low groan. I stood nearby and sent weak smiles of apology to the pedestrians who had to go around the wailing old lady. He cut me a sidelong glance and when I made eye contact with him, he groaned again, louder this time.

Sighing, I said, "What's wrong, *Granny*?"

"My sciatica is acting up again," he told me, his voice wobbly, as if someone shook him violently by the shoulders. "Can you get the ointment out of my bag and give me a good rub down? If you get into the gluteus, it helps diminish the black spots swimming in my vision. From the pain, you see." With a blink, his blue eyes were larger and droopier. He was using puppy dog eyes against me!

I stalked past him.

The old bat caught up fast enough that I knew the aches and pains hadn't come with the glamour. Welsh just delighted in horrifying me in myriad ways.

A few blocks from our destination, during a brief lull in pedestrian traffic, Welsh said, "The clinic is down a small side street that's only accessible by foot or bike. The road is unnamed. You'd have been hard-pressed to find it on your own."

"Why did you offer to escort me? I thought you hated me on principle."

"Oh, I do, little sprout," Welsh said. "But I owe the Stones a favor, you see, and I'm a woman of my word. I have to see this through till the end before the favor is complete."

"And 'through till the end' equals the front door of the clinic? You need to see me safely inside so you can tell them I made it?"

"When the true healing starts on your arm, the bones will reset and heal at a speed your puny human mind can't comprehend, let alone your body." Welsh's new voice made the insults sting less. "You'll need magical reinforcement to make sure your glamour stays in place, as a shock to the system is the fastest way to knock a glamour loose prematurely. Can't have you sprout twenty inches as soon as the pain gets bad, revealing the most notorious face in Luma, can we? I would pay good money to be a fly on the wall and watch that unfold, though."

I shot him a glare, but I wasn't sure how effective it was on my goblin face. It was hard to feel intimidating at this height, too. The giant yellow sunflower on my chest probably made me look like I was still in elementary school.

"Don't worry your misshapen little head, dearie. I like the idea of helping a fugitive escape—even if you *are* a human."

"Aren't you technically human, too?" I finally snapped. "You have magic, but your DNA is mostly human. It's not like you have fae ancestors the way Mathias and Geraldine do."

Welsh wrinkled his nose. "Technically. We refer to ourselves as Ameliorates. It's a step—several steps—above human. We're on a higher plane of existence."

I rolled my eyes. "Whatever. Sorry I asked."

We walked the remaining few blocks in silence.

Welsh stopped his walker at the entrance of what looked like an alley at first glance. Beside us was a boutique furniture store where nothing was less than $800. The sidewalk dipped, creating what looked like a driveway, though, as he said, it wasn't wide enough to accommodate cars. On the other side of the mini driveway was a dairy-free ice cream shop. Neither store got much business, not even window shoppers. But that had largely been by design, I guessed.

Hydrangea bushes covered in bright pink flowers grew in front of each shop, their thick branch-like trunks growing out of a gap between the wall and sidewalk. The climbing vines met in the middle above the narrow alley, their branches intertwining, as if the plants were trying to pull the two buildings together. The bright flowers drooped halfway down the opening of the unmarked street.

Welsh uttered an incantation and the tingle that raced over my skin told me he'd used an illusion this time, since my goblin body was still in place. Perhaps he'd made us fade out of sight entirely. Or put us in workman uniforms to make it appear as if we had reason to be ducking into this alley. I glanced around, but no one looked our way. Even with Welsh's hunched old-lady form, he still had to duck to get below the hanging flowers. I strolled under them and only felt a slight tickle as a leaf brushed the top of one of my pointed ears.

"The clinic is off the grid," Welsh said as we moved through the narrow space between the two buildings. "They do what they can to accommodate lower-income fae or those who have been denied medical care by the Collective."

The gap was so narrow, we had to walk in a single-file line. The walls were smooth brick aside from occasional inch-long metal protrusions. They looked like the shorn-off ends of pipes. A row lined the wall at ankle height, with another row six feet above that.

With each step, Welsh's appearance changed. By the time we reached the dark glass door at the end of the alleyway, he was still an elderly woman, but now he was in a goblin body. His hair was tied into two long silver braids that hung over his hunched shoulders and he'd swapped out his walker for a cane.

The alley ended in a door that filled the space on either side. I glanced over my shoulder and saw no sign of the street beyond; it was a solid wall of black. A magical space hidden from others with magic. Veils within the veil. I wondered how many places there were like this that I'd passed by dozens of times, not knowing the truths hidden from my mundane eyes. Much like Welsh's true face.

He pulled open the door and shuffled inside. I met him at the reception desk, which was attended by a griffel man. In appearance, he was somewhere between human and an eagle-headed beast. His movements were quick and jerky, like a bird, and the skin on the underside of his forearms was reminiscent of a chicken's yellow legs. His dark hair was literally feathered—a combination of white, brown, and black downy feathers. I wanted to touch his hair, sure it was incredibly soft. But seeing how I wasn't terribly fond of anyone wanting to touch my natural hair, I resisted the urge. The receptionist's eyes were a deep black and spaced a bit too far apart. Shifter magic and avian DNA never seemed to gel. Griffels, like draken, had lost their ability to shift over time. While draken looked mostly human, griffels were often more bird-like, leaving them hovering between human and beast.

As Welsh explained to him that we were referred by Mathias Stone, I examined my surroundings. The clinic was more triage bay than a standard hospital. The huge open space was dotted with cots, and freestanding curtains on wheeled platforms were used to give patients privacy. Toward the back of the room were several wooden room-divider panels lined up in a row to block off whatever went on behind them. Perhaps more involved surgeries took place back there. Nurses of all races, save human, tended to patients and bustled about with supplies.

Once we were checked in, I followed Welsh and a goblin nurse to a back corner and sat on a creaky cot. I placed my backpack and duffel on the bed with me. The nurse got a chair for "my grandmother," assured us a doctor would be by soon, rolled a curtained platform in front of us on wobbly wheels, and then left to attend to someone who had come in just after us.

I wanted to ask Welsh something, but I wasn't sure how to interact with him now that we had this many people within earshot. The place was full of activity and noise—coughs, whimpers, the occasional shout of pain, murmured voices, shuffling feet—but it was subdued. "Uhh ... Grammy?"

Welsh shot me a withering look, yet replied in the tone of a doting guardian. "Yes, scrumptious?"

"I don't see any humans in here. Are shifters allowed in? Non-werecat ones, I mean?"

"No. Hence ..." He gestured to his persona now, silently explaining why he'd shifted from a human-looking glamour to a goblin one. "Patients with human forms, such as shifters, go elsewhere. One can never know who a shifter is allied with. There are spies all over Luma, pet."

"But, Grammy, couldn't a shifter wear a glamour to look like a non-human?" I asked.

"Yes, but the alley has very specific wards on it that are triggered by shifter magic. Even if the shifter was glamoured to look like something else, it doesn't eliminate the shifter's magic. It only masks it. If we had been shifters who had breached the ward, it would have triggered the alarms. A neutralizing gas would pour from the vents in the walls of the alley, giving everyone in here time to escape out the hidden emergency exits. This place would be empty by the time authorities stormed it. It's why nothing is bolted down. And if it's not on wheels, it can be folded up or carried."

I looked around again, though I saw little now that we were behind one of the rolling curtains. "All of this precaution because the people treated here are ones the Collective blacklisted?"

Welsh nodded. "The Collective hopes the undesirables will be so miserable here that they pack up and move to a different hub."

A lithe brunette goblin poked her head around the curtain.

Goblins were typically short and squat, not long and elegant like this one. She was five-five, and her ears were more elfin than goblin. I guessed she was of mixed parentage. I'd lost myself in the visual image of a short round goblin and a tall thin elf going at it, and I missed the doctor's initial question. Welsh kicked me in the shin to snap me out of it.

"S-sorry, what was that?" I asked.

The doctor smiled warmly. "I asked if it was okay to take your arm from the sling and examine the injury." She had a light, lilting voice.

I granted her permission.

The doctor gave me two options. First was to have the arm set in a cast, and I'd need at least two checkups over the next three months. Given the way my life was going right now, a cast would eventually become like an identifying tattoo. I needed my arm healed and back to normal. Which brought me to option two: magical healing. Three months of healing smashed into an hour.

I was only a minute into the hour-long treatment when I deeply regretted my decision. The intense agony made me glad to have creepy-ass Welsh with me. I wouldn't have even minded if he'd been the sore-covered, blood-drooling zombie lord while he sat at my side.

Just when I thought I would pass out from the pain, a jolt of magic from Welsh would tingle all over my body, both reinforcing my glamour and giving me a boost of energy. The healing had to be done in three waves, because even fae with magic baked into their marrow couldn't withstand this rapid-pace healing in one shot.

It was currently between waves two and three, and I was sprawled out on my back on the cot, my duffel bag tucked by my side. When the pain had started during the first wave, and I'd barely bit back a scream, the bag had twitched on the floor in the corner of my eye. Worried the sword was growing restless or agitated by the sound of my discomfort, I had begged for the bag

DIABOLICAL SWORD

to be placed on the cot with me. It had remained there ever since, no signs of movement coming from within.

I reached out to grab Welsh by the arm now. He curled his old-lady lip at the contact. "Thank you," I croaked out.

"You truly are a pathetic sight," he said, but his tone wasn't as venomous as it was before. It almost sounded like he cared. Either he was developing a soft spot for me or he was getting worn out by all the magic he had to keep pouring into me to keep me from losing my glamour. "Are you ... are you doing okay?" he asked in a male voice, violently contrasting with his outer appearance. He cleared his throat and gave his head a quick shake, brow pinched as if he couldn't believe he'd let his real voice slip through.

"More or less. Who knew there were this many tiny bones in the arm and wrist?"

"Everyone," he said, but laughed softly. He still spoke in that smooth-as-butter male voice. Given how much pain I was in, and how tired, it was a soothing sound. I was probably delirious. At least he wasn't wearing the boy band hottie face right now, or the delirium would make me do something stupid.

He looked around, then scooted his chair closer. His eyes went a vibrant green. Eyes that belonged to a human rather than a goblin, especially an elderly one. "I can ask her to slow it down. I know I was making fun of humans earlier, but there's truth in what I said. This might be too much too fast. Mathias won't agree that I paid my favor if this doesn't work." Leaning over me, his face morphed into the hottie, and my insides went all slushy. He tentatively reached up to swipe a lock of sweat-damp hair out of my face. I involuntarily fluttered my lashes. What if this *was* his true form?

"Can I ask you something?" he said, all breathless and sexy.

"Yeah," I replied, just as breathless but not too sexy because I was still rocking a squeaky goblin voice.

"If I were to open the bag you have tucked next to you," he said, running a warm finger along my jaw, making my toes curl, "would I find the dragon sword?"

"Yes," I breathed, then stilled.

Welsh sat back, the elderly goblin persona slamming back into place. "Thought so," he sing-songed, shaky old voice back in place, too.

Sonofabitch seduced information out of me!

Stop making decisions based on how pretty something is! Kayda's voice echoed in my head.

Before I could get a nasty word out of my mouth, the doctor was back for round three. Welsh's magic kept my glamour in place for the last excruciating wave of healing, but it was my fear of what Welsh would do with this information that kept me from passing out. The deal with the Stones was to get me to the clinic, healed, and headed somewhere safe. Nothing in that request said I had to have my dragon sword with me when I did it, seeing as the Stones were unaware that I had it. If Welsh took it from me, who knew what the sword would do. The brute strength of the werecats hadn't been able to subdue the sword, but could Welsh's magic? And, if he *did* plan to steal it from me, where he attempted the heist could cause even more trouble. What would happen if Welsh pissed off the sword in this room full of fae the Collective had blacklisted? It could destroy the Stones' livelihood in seconds.

When the doctor finished and I'd downed a revitalizing tonic she gave me, something occurred to me that should have earlier. "How much is this going to cost me?" I asked blearily.

"Your grandmother already took care of that." The doctor smiled down at me. "If you feel any slippage in your arm, return to us right away and we'll get you patched up, okay?" She patted my shoulder. "You can rest here as long as you need. Take care."

Slippage? I rolled my head along the pillow and eyed Welsh. "Was paying for my treatment also part of your favor?"

He leaned forward, elbows on his knees. The posture was all Welsh. "Can you stand? The revitalizing tonic should have kicked in by now."

It had.

Sighing, I slowly slung my short legs over the side of the cot and shakily got to my feet. My head swam, and I swayed. Welsh caught me by the elbow to steady me. When the world settled around me, I snatched my arm away, remembering how he'd seduced a confession out of me while I was hopped up on pain and magic.

I quickly strapped on my backpack and grabbed my duffel bag off the cot before he could, marveling that my arm didn't hurt at all now. Settling the handles on my shoulder, I twisted and rolled my wrist. No clicking, no soreness.

"Let's go," he said, heading for the door. "We need to talk."

CHAPTER SEVENTEEN

Welsh led the way to a burger joint, of all places. By the time he'd pushed his way inside the hole-in-the-wall Al's Burgers fifteen minutes after leaving the clinic, Welsh was in a human body again, but this one was a bland-looking man with a dad bod. He was of average height, had a receding hairline, brown hair, brown eyes, and a beige shirt tucked into his khakis. I couldn't pinpoint an ethnicity. Some combination of parentage that didn't make him unique so much as homogeneous. The only thing exotic about him were the little tassels on his brown loafers. He was impressively unimpressive.

He raised a hand in greeting to three workers behind the counter. Booth seats ran along the wall to our right, and the lunch counter to the left was lined with stools. Every stool was occupied and most of the booths were too. The place was loud with conversation, the crackle of cooking meat, and the sizzle of large baskets of fries and onion rings being dunked into vats of boiling oil. The place smelled like hot grease and bacon, and my mouth watered, but Welsh kept moving.

A gap in the counter separated the diners on their stools from the little sliver of front-facing space occupied by the cash register.

A soda fountain sat on the longer counter arm behind a female employee with a phone cradled between shoulder and ear as she took a call-in order. Welsh strolled through the gap, with me trailing behind. The employees hardly acknowledged him, save for an "Afternoon, Mr. Brown," from the cook as he flipped five burgers in rapid succession.

I followed "Mr. Brown" through the small kitchen. A stainless steel island sat in the middle of the space, one white-apron-clad woman on either side. One busily chopped produce while the other threw ingredients into a massive steel bowl for a reddish-brown sauce. One lady gave me an elevator scan, then went back to work. Nothing malicious or even curious lingered in her perusal of me. Did that mean Mr. Brown brought goblins through here often, or had she just learned not to ask questions?

The strangest thing about this place was that, as far as I could tell, there was nothing magical about Al's Burgers—the building, the food, or its workers. I was almost positive all the patrons were human, too.

We passed out of the kitchen and into a narrow wood-lined hallway. It was sweltering back here. The wood looked slick, and I wasn't sure if it was because of a film of years-old grease or if someone lacking in both skill and care had painted on cheap shellac. Straight ahead was a break room, evidenced by the microwave on the counter and someone's lunch bag on the round table which was surrounded by mismatched chairs. A bathroom was to the right. Welsh stopped in front of it.

"Your glamour is due to wear off soon," he said in a tone as bland as his appearance. "Strip down in the bathroom. Knock when you're in your birthday suit and I'll restore you to your natural form. Clothe yourself however you wish. I'll wait here."

I did as instructed, reemerging a few minutes later as myself. It was nice being able to glare at Welsh from this height again.

Without a word, he turned on his heel and headed straight down the hallway, past the break room. I hurried past the open doorway that led back toward the kitchen, but no one else was around to see me. A noisy AC unit was wedged into the wall above us, long tendrils of greasy dust blowing from the vent like banners, working overtime to keep the back of the restaurant cool. The bathroom had been no less sweltering and sweat beaded my brow. Every spot on my body that the backpack touched was damp. My arms felt as slick as the walls looked. We stopped at a closed, unmarked door.

He pulled a set of keys out of his pocket and unlocked what turned out to be his office. It was about the same size as Josephine's cluttered workroom, but wasn't stuffed to the gills with boxes. Two five-shelf bookcases stood flush on the far end of the room, packed with binders, notebooks, and what looked like law books. Nearby was a desk with two monitors on it and a stack of papers on the otherwise cleared-off surface. A computer tower hummed softly on the ground under the desk. In the middle of the room, two chairs sat on either side of a low, oval-shaped coffee table. That was it. Nothing decorated the walls. No photographs of him and a zombie lord wife throwing dual peace signs in front of the Eiffel Tower or the Space Needle.

Welsh closed the door behind us and locked the door. I whirled away from my perusal of the bookshelves when I heard the uttered words of a spell leave his lips. The air around me crackled, instead of my person. "Sound-dampening spell. I would like to see the sword."

It wasn't a demand, but it wasn't exactly a friendly request either.

I deposited the duffel bag on the coffee table, but kept the backpack on in case I needed to make a quick escape out the door. Steeling myself, I unzipped the bag. The sword floated out immediately, then moved to hover near my shoulder, the blade's tip pointed in Welsh's direction.

Welsh cocked his head. "Incredible."

The sword hummed.

"Where did it come from?"

I gave him the rundown. "The sword knows Haskins purchased it at an auction, but doesn't know where it came from before that. It's like it woke up after I grabbed it."

The sword quickly flew to the table, inverted itself, and knocked on the wood. I turned to it, staring at it curiously. Did that mean it had been in some kind of hibernation before I'd taken it?

"You never tried to hurt Haskins," I said slowly, working through my theory. "Was that a choice?"

Tap-tap.

No. It would have taken Haskins out if given the chance, then. "Were you in a sort of half-sleep when you were sold? Aware of what was happening around you, but not able to act?" I asked.

The blade glowed a faint blue for a moment, then tapped once on the table. Blue was new. Maybe blue meant it was pleased, as opposed to deep pissed-off red.

I felt Welsh's gaze on me and turned to face him. "I'm going to warn you now that your blood will paint the walls if you try to take the sword from me."

Tap, the sword said in agreement, and offered a brief hum for good measure.

Welsh held up his hands in innocence. "That was never my intention. What's fascinating me the most is that I can't figure out if it's the sword itself that has the Collective freaked out, or if *they* know where it came from and they want to get their hands on you before you figure it out."

I stared. "Why do you hate the Collective so much?"

He smiled what I guessed was a true Welsh smile, and it made the bland persona he wore infinitely more appealing. "Don't think I'm going to play confessional with you because we've gone on a little adventure together. I'm in the business of keeping individuals off the Collective's radar. All you need to know about my motives is that I hate hypocrisy—the Collective itself I could take or leave. The Collective got to where they are because of the service they provide: they keep the veils intact. Everything else came to them through brute strength supplied by their trained cats. They muscled their way into a place of power. They argued that a collective of sorcerers would be the fairest governing body, as they make no decision unless it's unanimous. A collective, they said, eliminated the chance of a single individual making all the decisions. Unanimous decisions made by clones don't inspire faith that things are fair behind closed doors.

"I could get behind the Collective idea if it weren't made up only of sorcerers—especially since there's also a *worldwide* collective. It's bad enough that they run all the individual hubs, but for them to also basically have a UN of sorcerers? It's too much."

"This is some very forward thinking for someone like you, Welsh," I said. "Between that little speech and your headquarters being in a human-run restaurant even though you claim to hate us? I think you're chaotic good rather than chaotic neutral like I first thought."

His lip curled. "Please don't tell me you have nerd tendencies."

"You say that as if it were an STD."

"Might as well be." Turning to the sword, he said, "Can I photograph you? I may have a way to track down where you originated from."

The sword tapped once on the coffee table.

"That means yes," I said.

The sword floated nearer to Welsh and angled itself sideways, giving Welsh a close-up view of the sword's hilt. He snapped a few photos with a cell phone he pulled from his pocket.

Without being asked, the sword glowed a deep red. I was about to explain to Welsh that runes appeared on the blade when it went molten, but Welsh immediately spotted the etchings.

"Which one do you think it is?" I asked, watching him.

"What are you talking about?" he asked, then thanked the sword and pocketed his phone again.

"Is the Collective more interested in the sword or where it came from?"

"My guess is the latter," Welsh said. "You know about Nyla Stone, right?" When I nodded, he said, "For months now, I've had people just like the Stones come to me to ask if I smuggled their son or daughter out of Luma. Parents and siblings and concerned friends who had loved ones up and vanish without a trace. Nine times out of ten, I had nothing to do with it. I'm still in contact with a lot of the families, as I am with the Stones. The police gave them all the same runaround. They looked into it, found nothing, so the individual in question must have left of their own volition. Something doesn't add up there.

"I'm not saying the sword's presence is connected with the disappearances. And even if they're completely unrelated, either thing on its own is unsettling. They've essentially turned the entire city against you—a human who is little threat, even *with* a sword like that. They have the resources to take you down if they truly want to. But I think they're more interested in where you got the sword and what you know. It's partly a safety concern, but I believe the asses they're trying to save are their own."

What in the hell had I gotten myself into?

"I have something for you," he said.

Welsh turned to his desk, where he opened a drawer. When he turned back, he had a necklace hanging from an outstretched pointer finger. The trinket dangling from the end was a flat circle made of a silver-colored metal that looked as flimsy as aluminum foil. A faint hum of magic tickled my palm as I took it, though, and the metal was heavier than I expected.

"It's a one-way travel talisman. You can use it as a backdoor exit through one of the less-traveled sections of a veil, rather than using one meant for tourists. Just in case you need to get out of Luma. Though it's likely our Collective will warn the other hubs that you may try to flee to their city. There's a vortex caught in the middle of the trinket that will absorb the jolt humans get from passing through a veil. It'll be nothing more than a dormant necklace after that."

"Thanks," I said, briefly closing my fist around it before clasping it around my neck and tucking the tiny vortex under my shirt.

"I'll do some research for you. Do you have a private telepost box? That would be safer than cell phones right now."

"Yeah. It's in Ardmore under a different name."

"Good," he said, and handed me a small notebook and pen. "Write the box number down and I'll be in contact in three days. You have somewhere to lie low until then?"

I didn't, but he'd done enough for me already. "I have a couple of ideas."

"Three days, okay?" he said. "The possibility of the Collective losing their collective marbles over this is too great for you to fuck it up by getting yourself killed or captured."

"Yeah, you're definitely chaotic good."

His appearance, for three terrifying seconds, flipped back to the sore-covered zombie lord. My loud screech startled the sword, which then inadvertently embedded itself into the ceiling. It vibrated, the blade going red. I jumped and grabbed the sword by the hilt, pulling it free before something caught fire. Last thing we needed was to give this grease-soaked place unconfined flames while we were trapped in the back.

The hilt pulsed under my palm.

"Calm down!" I said, giving it a shake. "Scaring the bejesus out of me is how Welsh gets his rocks off."

Slowly, the blade cooled, so I let it go. It hovered nearby.

Eyeing the sword warily for a moment, Welsh, back to Mr. Brown, said, "Try the human male glamour I gave you. That tonic will only alter surface appearance, and since you're staying human, this one should last at least twelve hours."

I swung my backpack off one shoulder and rooted around for the carrying case of glamour tonics. The human one was a murky white, while the goblin one was a transparent green. After taking out one of the human ones, I resealed the case, zipped the backpack up, and strapped it onto my shoulder. I swirled the contents of the vial. "When I transform, will I be ... uhh ... anatomically correct?" I asked, motioning to my crotch with an open palm.

Welsh stared blankly. "*That's* your first question?"

"I'm honestly surprised I didn't ask sooner."

Sighing, he said, "The human reproductive system is complicated and since you're not using this glamour to seduce anyone, you'll be male except for the middle bits."

Shrugging, I uncapped the vial. "I guarantee you I could still find someone to seduce with that combination." Plugging my nose, I knocked the concoction back. It tasted like the inside of an old shoe and left an oily film on my tongue, but other than that, it went down smoothly.

"There are glamours that are extensive enough, they can also alter internal plumbing," Welsh said. "But the magic is so potent, it's likely your organs would liquefy."

Well, that sounded unpleasant.

My skin tingled, but my height didn't change. "Did it work?" My eyes widened. "Oh! This voice is amazing. Hello. Helloooo. This is a radio announcer voice. Coming to you live, live, live from the bowels of Al's Burgers ..."

Welsh shot a look at the sword. "If you ever feel the need to impale her, please know I'm interested in an alliance."

The sword hummed.

"Hey!" I said.

The barest hint of a smile graced Mr. Brown's boring face. "Get somewhere safe and we'll be in touch soon," he said, heading for the door.

I ushered the sword back into the duffel and once it was zipped up, I followed Welsh. "If you hate humans so much, why do you conduct your business out of a place full of them?"

Welsh stopped with his hand on the doorknob. "The Collective's spies conduct regular scans of the city. If they detect too much magic seeping out of a place that shouldn't have any, the

Collective's minions show up in one form or another to check things out. I layered this room with dozens of cloaking spells. Everything else in here is as mundane as you can get—burgers and fries, and the menu hasn't changed in years. They overlook this place regularly. The criminal activity that humans get into usually doesn't even register as much more than a blip on the Collective's radar. Especially since if a human gets involved with magic too strong, natural selection takes the idiot out anyway."

I resisted the urge to mention that it was humans who almost single-handedly drove the ancient beasts to extinction. After the Glitch, when it became more and more likely that the portals couldn't be reopened, humans and fae brokered a shaky alliance, knowing they had to coexist. The fae were outnumbered, but the humans also knew the fae would be a formidable force should they decide to band together. The fae were unexpected refugees—they didn't come to Earth on purpose or with evil intent. Hostilities were initially low, all things considered, especially since the fae were unsure if the inhabitants of this new planet might hold the key to reopening the portals. The goal for everyone was to keep fae and humans alike safe until someone could figure out how to get the fae back home.

Fae and humans formed a council with representatives from both worlds. Dragons, at least at the time, had been the most powerful beings from the fae world, and since they could shift forms, they communicated well enough with the humans. For the safety of both species, the fae created a magical hub to house the marooned fae. The location for that first hub, and for all since then, was chosen based on areas with large swaths of available land. As the marooned fae population started to grow, so too did the number of hubs. Luma had only been created seventy-five years ago in Central California, but the first hub, in New York, was just under a century old. Human instinct had driven many to kill the foreign beasts, or to catch and tame them, intending to turn them into work animals, pets, or oddities to put on display in zoos and circuses.

This plan worked for a time, but poachers became obsessed with making the ultimate kill: a dragon. When they took down an injured animal who had been taking refuge in a cave, the thrill-hunters had stolen bits of their kill as proof and souvenirs. They discovered that the magic of the slain animal lived on in scales, talons, and horns. When added to weapons, it gave magic-less humans the ability to wield power they'd never known before. When added to armor and shields, humans withstood forces that would have otherwise killed them instantly.

The stronger humans became, the more the beasts were pushed out of their safe hubs. The larger fae moved to more and more remote locations, specifically the fabled ever-moving island, the waters of which are said to still be guarded by ancient water beasts that the poachers were unable to kill. But eventually, humans found the island too and killed off the last of the ancient beasts. All that remained of them now were charmed items, like the sentient sword in my bag.

How many stories passed from fae elders to fae youth about murderous humans? Humans who had stolen from the fae—beings on Earth who ended up here through no fault of their own—and then were slain with their own magic. How many of the longer-lived ones had seen the images of me on TV last night and were brought back to the time when the fae were hunted down by humans, driven mad by their ill-gotten power?

Maybe some of Welsh's hatred of humans had more to do with the past than anything else. We didn't have the best track record with wielding power beyond our means, and the fae and their descendants were stuck here with us.

But I kept all that to myself.

As Welsh and I strolled back down the hallway, through the bustling kitchen and loud restaurant, none of the employees blinked an eye at us, even though Mr. Brown had walked in with a goblin and now walked out with a dark-skinned man. I couldn't decide then if I was more curious about the humans' stories, or Welsh's.

Once out on the sidewalk, out of earshot of the short line of people waiting to get into Al's, Welsh slipped his hands into his khakis. "I'll talk to you in three days."

I nodded once, thanked him, and walked away with no idea of where I'd end up tonight.

CHAPTER EIGHTEEN

I wandered around for twenty minutes feeling sorry for myself, wishing I could contact Kayda and Jo to at least let them know I was okay. Had they seen the clip of me on the news and believed what they saw? They'd both "met" the sword, and Kayda had gotten a glimpse of what it could do when provoked.

I was debating about getting an ice cream cone for my troubles when I stopped dead in front of an internet café. Something about the news story had been bugging me—aside from all the obvious parts—and I ducked inside. The bank of public-access computers was in the back, and I bought an hour of computer time from the witch barista at the counter with cash. I also got a cupcake piled high with pink frosting and dotted with red heart sprinkles infused with a Level 2 magical energy boost. I liked the idea of this male persona with the sex-operator voice chowing down on a bright pink cupcake.

I parked myself in between two alarmingly sweaty men, and though access to porn sites in public cafés was forbidden, all one needed was a little magical intervention from a witch hacker and one could get past the firewalls. There were privacy partitions in place, but they were made of fabric-wrapped corrugated cardboard. I did not feel safe.

I logged into the café's internet as a guest and pulled up the site for the *Luma City Times*. I searched for "caracal shifter murder." The sorcerer spokesperson had said I was wanted for *four* murders, not the three I had known about before the newscast. Had the sword killed the caracal when it had gone missing, only to return covered in blood to my apartment?

An article popped up with the headline "Fashion Celebrity Slain by Human Wielding an Illegal Sword." Fashion celebrity? I glanced down at the duffel bag by my foot long enough to cock a curious brow at it. The bag didn't move. At least I had further confirmation that the sword hadn't developed the ability to read minds. I returned my focus to the screen.

"*Oliver Randal, 35, was found slain today behind a Fae Lighting Design & Decor building in the Warehouse District. Randal was a beloved member of the fashion community in Luma, and the news of his violent death shocked his friends, fans, and colleagues. Randal made his living as a model and a dancer, as well as being a renowned clothing designer. His admirers describe him as 'otherworldly beautiful.' Randal was a shifter and took the form of a sleek rust-colored caracal when in feline form.*

"*A close friend of the enigmatic dancer said Randal was 'too beautiful for this world. He was striking both as a human and as a cat. I can't believe he's gone.' Despite the outpouring of shock and sadness over his death, very few people seem to know much about him. The consensus is that Randal had moved to Luma recently, or that he'd been on a long vacation here—but no one was sure when he got to town. He doesn't appear to have kin in the area, and no one is sure where Randal laid his head when he wasn't dancing or strutting down the catwalk.*

"*The one witness in this case, who requested anonymity, told the* Luma City Times *that she had been walking home after a night at a club when she saw a dark-skinned human-looking woman with a sword covered in blood walk out onto the sidewalk from behind the Fae Lighting Design & Decor building around 1 a.m. The witness said when she* watched the news later, she recognized the woman on-screen. It was Harlow Fletcher—the same woman seen in the now-viral news clip who eluded police with her inhuman agility.

"The witness claims Fletcher didn't see her because she was crouched behind a trash can. When Fletcher was out of sight, the witness ran behind Fae Lighting Design & Decor and found Randal's mangled body. Cuts and gashes she attributed to a large blade covered Randal's arms, legs, and torso. The witness was so horrified by what she'd found, she retched in the bushes. 'It was the most disturbing thing I'd ever seen. Why would someone do that?'

"That, of course, is the million-dollar question. Why is Harlow Fletcher on a killing spree, and why is she targeting shifters? Is the illegal, highly dangerous dragon sword controlling her? The answers to these questions could save countless shifter lives.

"Several other reports were called in that night about seeing Harlow a little after 1 a.m. People up late saw her from their windows, stalking down the street with her bloody sword.

"Remember that the Collective is offering a reward of $20,000 to anyone who provides information of Fletcher's whereabouts that directly leads to an arrest. You are encouraged to call the Luma City Times or the Luma City Police Department with any information you have. The fate of our city lies in Fletcher's capture."

I fought a grunt of annoyance and clicked out of the article. I wondered how much the Collective had paid—or threatened—the Luma City Times to throw in those last couple of paragraphs. Leading the readership much? Ugh.

Sitting back in my chair, I crossed my arms. What connection could there be between the sword and this model? How had the sword even known how to find the caracal shifter?

How strange it was to not only be accused of a murder I hadn't committed, but to have the murder weapon become the closest thing I had to a friend right now. A friend who couldn't speak and tell me why in the hell it had killed the shifter in the first place. I pressed a fist to my mouth when a yawn seized me, my eyes watering. I needed sleep. Between the shock of learning the Collective had issued a bounty for me—while also giving the general public a monetary incentive to find me—and the intense healing process at the clinic, I was wiped out.

But where could I go?

Almost immediately, an image popped into my head of a run-down, abandoned factory. It sat on the southernmost edge of town. There were rumors that the land was cursed because every business that attempted to sprout up there never lasted longer than a year or two. It was a graveyard of failed projects. The area had once been known as Clemmons, the neighborhood named after one of the founding sorcerers, just as the others were—though the Industrial and Warehouse Districts had lost their original names over time, too. The neighborhood formerly known as Clemmons went by the Necropolis now, at least to locals.

Several rows of stacked train cars sat in what used to be a shipping yard, the rusted and dilapidated boxcars worn down by the blazing sun in summer and the rain in winter. A man-made lake had once been there. Well, water elemental-made. The Necropolis had a failed brick factory, too. The last unsuccessful attempt had been a factory that made construction equipment.

High school parties used to be held out there. Bonfires raged beside the now-filled-in lake, the shore littered with chunks of dull red bricks and concrete blocks shot through with bent rebar. Teens used slingshots and magic to hit glass bottles off the tops of broken-off wooden stakes and concrete columns. Not more than a mile away was the edge of Luma itself, where, if you stood very still and under the right conditions, you could see the protective barrier of the veil shimmering in the moonlight. Human teens in particular would dare each other to touch the veil to see which ones could stand it the longest.

In the Necropolis, the true danger for humans didn't come from the proximity of the veil, but from the proximity of what lay behind it. Twenty miles to the south was Tercla's hub—the West Coast's largest population of vampires. The Pact forbade vampires from killing humans from the hubs, but if a human was reckless enough to get too close to the veil and stick his hand through—well, what recourse did a bunch of teenagers have when that reckless human was snatched through the veil by something unseen, never to return?

The night a game of truth or dare got Jimmy Nance yanked off his feet and through the veil marked the last time kids like me went out to the Necropolis. Werecat guards patrolled the area, searching for misbehaving teenagers and vampires alike. When parents of the rebelling teens started getting hefty fines from the Collective itself, the visits dried up entirely.

The old factory in the Necropolis could be the perfect place for me to get some sleep. No one would expect me to go out there, and if a vampire sniffed me out, I wouldn't shed a tear when my sword shredded their undead carcass to ribbons. Problem was, I didn't have a vehicle, and telepad stations were out since they'd knock my glamour loose. I'd get a cab to take me halfway there, then I'd hoof it the rest of the way. I was looking at a two-hour walk. My stomach rumbled. I should have picked up a burger or seven from Al's.

I walked a couple of blocks to a sandwich place, bought four of them, several bottles of water, two energy drinks, and some chips. Then hailed a cab.

Getting to the Necropolis was uneventful. I silently thanked Welsh dozens of times for the glamour. My insides were a nervous jumble with every person I passed and with every glance I got. This male version of me was evidently hot, though, because I got a couple of appreciative glances from ladies who strolled by. As well as a very large draken man who propositioned me, promising he could throw my back out "in a good way" if I wasn't "too intimidated by adventure." I realized later that shortly after my hour-long cab ride, I'd strolled right through the red-light district.

When I reached the old factory, nothing set off my sixth sense. I didn't sense any magic in the deserted graveyard of lost capitalistic dreams, but I felt the very distant crackle of the veil, almost like static electricity. Or the feeling of a loose hair you know is there but can't locate, brushing against the back of your arm like a phantom finger.

The front doors of the old factory were padlocked shut, the thick metal chains rattling when I gave the handles a jiggle. The latches were gone, hence the chains, and pulling them apart awarded me only a foot of space. Not wide enough to get through. I went around the side of the building and stumbled around in the dark, testing the edges of the plywood attached to many of the windows. Scrubby brush that smelled like sage impeded my clumsy movements. I didn't dare take my fae light out.

A board near the halfway mark of the building's length came free with some minor cajoling. I jumped back when the wood slipped free from the one remaining nail holding it in place, and backed into one of the bushes, the sage smell cloying now.

After a lot of scraping up my arms and cursing, I got through the broken window without slicing off a limb. If a werecat guard did a patrol of the place later, I hoped the bushes lining the building would hide my entry point.

I faced the dark factory interior and gave my eyes a minute to adjust to the low light. Menacing shapes of old machinery squatted haphazardly around the space, but none of them moved, which was a check in the pro column. I scanned the ceiling, searching for the glowing red eyes of wild pixies, but didn't sense any movement up there either.

In addition to the old machinery, the sides of the factory were littered with broken bits of old worktables and tools. A large swatch of the cement floor in the middle of the massive space was empty, though, and I cautiously picked my way toward the unobstructed area. Once I reached it, I placed the duffel on the ground and crouched next to it. Unzipping the bag, I watched as the sword cautiously floated out.

"Wanna do a perimeter check?" I asked, my voice sounding too loud even as a whisper. "Keep the glowing to a minimum, but make sure we're alone here. I'm not going to be able to sleep if this ends up being a vampire nest."

The sword hummed once, very softly, then disappeared into the darkness.

I strapped the duffel back on and cautiously made my way up the middle of the room. An upraised platform—maybe a foreman's tower—loomed in the distance. Weak moonlight poured in from a hole in the roof, cascading over what looked like a metal staircase. By the time I reached it, the sword had returned.

"All clear?" I asked.

It hummed.

"I was thinking we could wait the night out up there."

The sword harpooned upward.

When it didn't shoot back down seconds later, I figured it had cleared that area, too. The ladder creaked as I made my way up, but it felt sturdier than the death trap of a fire escape that had hugged my building. The platform had a hulking metal contraption on it that I guessed had once been part of a crane. Now it would serve as something to sleep behind, keeping me out of sight should anyone come in.

The back of the metal platform had a small glass-sided office on it. The glass was dingy, and there was no door. It would be like sleeping in a phone booth. No thanks. I opted to make camp between the crane and the office. After settling down on the uneven makeshift bed, I ate half a sandwich and chugged a bottle of water before curling up on the ground, a balled-up pair of pants as a pillow.

I stared out into the graveyard of failed dreams through the row of dingy windows that lined the top of the factory. Every once in a while, moonlight winked off the veil out in the distance, or the rune-covered obelisk that the veil's magic emanated from. The obelisks were spaced a mile apart, but I only saw the one from this vantage point. Seconds ticked away in the dark.

I was exhausted, but I didn't fall asleep as fast as I thought I would. My legs and back ached from all the walking, and the hard, unforgiving ground wasn't helping. But the idea that a werecat guard or vampire could be lurking out there somewhere kept me awake. I wondered if I would feel it when the glamour wore off and I returned to my usual form. What disguise would I choose next?

The nostalgia I felt for this place, for the fun times that were had here in my slightly rebellious youth before Jimmy was snatched, wasn't enough to assuage my anxiety. I yawned deeply. I was so tired it hurt, but I felt more vulnerable and alone here than I expected.

The sword laid itself on the ground beside me. I rolled my head toward it and it glowed a faint blue. Its color for a positive emotion, though I wasn't sure which. The color told me it would look over me, that I could close my eyes and it would make sure I would open them again.

I fell asleep.

CHAPTER NINETEEN

Something crunched, and my eyes snapped open in the dark. I told myself it could be a wild animal that had sniffed out the food in my bag. Anything scrounging around way out here would be near starving. Picturing a half-starved dog was far preferable to the idea that a vampire, werecat guard, bounty hunter, or money-hungry Luma resident had already found me. The length of that list unnerved me.

I scarcely breathed as I waited for another sound. A scuffle came next, like that of a boot scraping against concrete. Starving dogs didn't wear shoes.

Shit.

I stood carefully, doing my best not to disturb the sword. It was ludicrous to think of it as something that slept and therefore could be woken up, but it was also impossible to think of it as anything other than a living being at this point.

I needed to get a view around the crane to assess what I was dealing with. A fellow human might not even be a threat. It could be a starving runaway kid instead of a starving dog. I could handle a kid. But if it were a draken?

Crouched low, I tiptoed to the front corner of the crane's base. I was glad I'd slept on the platform. How I'd get down if whoever it was gave chase, though, was something I'd worry about later. I waited, scanning. The yellow or orange eyeshine of a draken would be all the information I'd need to know I had roughly ten seconds to pack up and run before I was spotted and caught.

Another shoe scuffle and I hunched even lower, willing myself to become one with the shadows. A soft beam of blue fae light appeared on the ground below, followed by a figure all in black. It passed by the sagging arm of a piece of construction equipment, obstructing my view. I readjusted my position. When the figure reappeared, I studied the shape, cataloging every detail as I compared it to the list of beings who resided in Luma. Too short to be a draken, too tall to be a goblin. It was definitely a human, but that could mean anything from sorcerer to shifter to magic-less human. My gut told me it was a man.

The man passed under the platform I was on and disappeared underneath. The stairs were to my right and the only way up here. If he checked out the platform, he'd need to double back to make his way up. Unless he was an air elemental, of course, and then he could just float his ass up here.

The familiar notes of an old pop song rang out into the room for a moment, followed by a softly muttered curse as the guy silenced his cell phone. The song dredged up memories with such speed, it was like getting punched in the face. I hadn't heard that song in years.

Below me, I heard a muffled, "Hi. Yeah, sorry. I'm just heading out the door. I had to pick something up first. It'll take me twenty minutes to get there from the Industrial District."

There was something familiar about his voice. Not the voice itself, but the cadence of his words. He must have thought no one was in here if he was answering his phone. And he was lying to whoever he was talking to; he sure as hell wasn't in the Industrial District.

I hunkered down when he walked back into view. He stood at the base of the stairs. Would he come up to do a sweep of the place, or would he leave now to go meet whoever had called him?

The faint glow by his head told me he hadn't ended his call yet. When he glanced up, sweeping his fae light into the dark rafters above me, I scooted back a couple of inches. My pulse pounded in my temples.

Something appeared in my peripheral vision and I glanced over in dread, knowing what I'd see before I looked. The sword was awake and hovering by my head. It vibrated softly.

"Don't," I mouthed, not knowing if it could read lips.

It vibrated a little more intensely, then stilled.

Though I was sure the man was doing what he could to make a quiet ascent, the old metal staircase rattled with every footfall. The sound gave me some serious fire escape PTSD.

"Yeah, man," the guy said, clearly irritated, his voice clear and so close now as he'd reached the halfway point of the stairs. "I'm coming, all right?"

As realization dawned on me, all the blood drained from my body at once, like it had been leached out. I was half surprised I didn't hear it land on the ground below with a great splash, like a bucket of dropped paint. The ringtone. The cadence. The brief glimpse of his face.

"Yep, see you soon." As he presumably slipped his phone back into his pocket, he muttered something to himself. The way he always did when he was annoyed.

The shock gave way to anger, and before I knew what I was doing, I rounded the crane. The man came up short, hands out in a placating gesture. He almost lost his balance and pitched back down the steps, but righted himself quickly and grabbed hold of the railing surrounding the platform.

"Felix fucking *Turner*?" I snapped.

"*Harlow*?" He swung the fae light up and into my face, and I shielded my eyes from the glare.

A warm hand wrapped around my elbow and he yanked me farther back onto the platform behind the crane. He let me go just as quickly, as if my skin had scalded him. His fae light swept over the makeshift bed, food wrappers, and bags. He cursed.

When he focused on me again, his arms were crossed, the beam of the fae light jutting out behind him and shining on the dirty windows of the foreman's office. My wild-haired outline illuminated in the glass gave me further confirmation that my glamour had dissolved while I slept. This was his authoritative stance. His "you better tell me what the hell is going on" stance. As if I owed him an explanation for anything.

"Harlow," he finally said when all we did was stare at each other in the dark for several long seconds.

"How did you find me?"

He worked his clean-shaven jaw. "It was a hunch. It was your—our—go-to place for years. A lot of good times happened here before it went to shit. This was where we ... the first time we ..." He sighed. "It's also where we went to break shit after you, me, and Kayda got kicked out of the ax-throwing bar because you kept drunkenly proposing duels to people just trying to eat their dinner."

My eyes itched with unshed tears, pissed off and touched at the same time that even five years later, he still knew me. I hated him for that.

"What's going on, Low?" he asked, his tone so gentle, so concerned, so much like how it used to be that I almost broke right then and there.

But the tide of grief and heartbreak receded in one fell swoop, replaced by a flood of anger. "Don't call me that. You lost the right to call me that the day you walked out on me."

His anger rose to meet mine. "What am I supposed to call you then, huh? *Fletch*? Isn't that your street name now?"

I clenched my fist, more to redirect my anxious energy than anything violent, but I also wanted to punch him a little bit. "What are you doing here? Need that reward money or something? Is that the only way you'd stoop to be in the same room with me—a stack of cash?"

His head jerked back a fraction, as if I really had punched him. "How can you say that?"

I glared, hand on hip.

He grunted in frustration. "I came here to check on you. All of Luma has gone batshit trying to find the human driven crazy by the dragon sword. Now there's a rumor going around that you aren't human at all, but a dark sorceress. My personal favorite is that you're a long-lost dragon princess, and you stole the sword because it's your birthright and now you'll shift into your true dragon form and burn Luma to the ground."

I snorted humorlessly, shaking my head. My stomach was in knots and my head pounded. Something was off. I wasn't sensing magic, but something niggled at me all the same. "Who were you talking to on the phone?"

"Can't see how that's any of your business."

"You lied to him about where you were. Even though you came here specifically looking for me, you didn't want the person on the other end of the line to know that."

"I wanted to investigate on my own first," he said, and my brow furrowed. "Haskins reported that if werecat guards didn't show up to seize his goods, he would be robbed. Ironic that a thief is worried about robbery, huh? We were all ready to write the guy off, but then your name of all names comes up during his interrogation."

How did Felix have access to reports about Haskins? And who was this "we"?

"He said if he *did* get robbed, Harlow Fletcher would be at the top of his list of suspects. And then who do I see on the news, waving around an illegal sword?"

Something on his person buzzed in reply. It wasn't his phone. This sound was familiar, too. A sound I'd heard the day my parents were killed, and the night I got the tip that Haskins had been apprehended, and dozens of times in between. Three buzzes. Quick, quick, slow.

I stumbled a step, my back hitting a corner of the crane. It was the sound of a buzzing pocket mirror—*two* pocket mirrors. Mine *and* his. Reports. We. Felix Turner. FT. "You're bounty hunter FT97," I said, a statement not a question.

His earlier bravado dried up, and he snapped his mouth shut.

"After everything, you *still* became a bounty hunter?" I asked, my throat constricting. "And now you're here for *me*?"

"Harlow, this isn't what it looks like. I—"

Something red blazed in my peripheral vision and I only got out a shout of "No!" before the sword harpooned toward Felix.

Felix tried to jump back, but he glanced off the office wall behind him. His heel snagged on a piece of my clothing on the ground, and down he went. The sword took advantage of his fall and pinned him in place, its tip hovering right above his heart. The blade's red-hot glow illuminated Felix's shocked face, giving me the first good view of it since he'd gotten here. The whites of his eyes shone in contrast to his dark skin.

"Sword! It's okay. Well, it's not, but—"

The sword vibrated.

Right. Don't give the murder sword mixed messages.

"Let him go, please," I said. "He's a ... friend. Sort of."

The cherry red dimmed to a fainter pink, but it didn't budge.

"They said it drove you mad," Felix said, voice shaky. "That when you're using it, you have powers humans shouldn't have. But you're not even touching it ..."

"Here's a news flash for you," I said, "the Sorcerers Collective lied."

Felix's jaw clenched at that. Bounty hunters were employed by the Collective. Was that where his loyalties lay these days? How much had he changed in five years?

"I don't control the sword," I said, not sure if I was defending it or me. "It does what it wants, but it also protects me. We have a sort of ... alliance. It will listen to me when I ask things of it, but it doesn't always obey. It currently feels like you pose a threat to me, and therefore to it. Convince it you're not a danger to me, and then it'll let you go. Right, sword?"

It hummed.

"That usually means yes."

"Usually?" Felix croaked out.

"It's not a perfect system of communication."

Felix's gaze found mine for a moment, and I knew he was trying to determine if I really had been driven insane. Turning his attention back to the sword hovering above him, he said, "I came here not to apprehend her, but to find out what happened. I wanted to help her get out of Luma if she needed it."

It wasn't lost on me that he had yet to say that he knew I wasn't capable of murder, and therefore, there had to be another explanation for all this.

The sword turned its blade tip to me, and I nodded. The sword backed off, returning to its usual cool steel before switching to an inverted position and floating next to me. Its hilt hovered near waist height and the blade tip angled to the ceiling. I took it to be a neutral position, yet one that showed Felix the sword and I were a united front.

Felix cautiously got to his feet, brushing off his hands on his jeans. After a long pause, in a soft, strained tone, he said, "Talk to me, Harlow. Explain what I saw on the news."

Thing was, I *couldn't* fully explain it. The sword was real, but nothing else shown on-screen had happened—unless I'd been sleepwalking, of course. Sleep murdering?

Something shimmered next to me.

When I turned toward the sword, I expected to see its iridescent hilt doing that pretty glowing thing that had gotten me into trouble initially. What I saw knocked the breath from my lungs. It was like looking in a mirror. The sword still hung in its inverted position, but now dark fingers wrapped around the hilt. "I" wore the same outfit as I had on the news—ripped shirt, dirty jeans. My hair was wild, the look in my eyes even more so.

My brain short-circuited. Did this have something to do with it being imprinted on me? Jo had said imprinting gave the marked pair a way to share a closer bond. "*Sometimes that meant granting permission for telepathic communication. For others, it meant that when they were in proximity, they could share their magic or strength."*

"Did you ... like ... borrow my DNA or something?" I asked the sword, my mind spinning.

The sword dropped hilt-first to the metal platform and gave a single tap in response. The image of me broke apart like dandelion fluff.

I pressed a hand to my forehead, trying to work through this. "You borrowed my DNA so you could go on a killing spree?"

The sword hesitated, then tapped once. Followed by a second tap a couple of seconds later. *Maybe.*

"I just told him we're allies! Are you trying to frame me?" I snapped. "You want me to get arrested and turned over to the Collective? Torn apart by the werecats?"

The blade blazed red and gave the floor two hard taps.

"Don't get mad at me, buddy. You're the one who fucked up." I paced in a tight line. The Collective claimed I'd murdered three werecat guards and Oliver Randal. I needed confirmation. "Did you kill a caracal shifter before the werecats stormed my building?"

Tap.

How I wished I could ask "Why are you doing this?" and get an answer!

"Were you using my form when you did it?"

Tap.

"*Why?*" I groaned. Then remembered I needed yes or no questions. "Was it to give you access to buildings?"

No reply.

"Was it to make you stand out less?" I tried. "Easier to lure someone outside when they have a human body, rather than being just a floating sword?"

The sword hummed, then tapped once quickly on the ground. It liked that question. *See*, it seemed to say, *I had a good reason for wearing your skin and getting you accused of murder!*

The witness, at least according to that article, had claimed to see "me" at 1:00 a.m., sometime well after the debacle at my apartment, and after the sword was in Mathias's apartment with me. I'd woken up at midnight to the sword lying on my chest. Yet the sword just confessed to killing Randal. Who was lying, then? The witness, the reporter, or had the Collective or werecats fed the newspaper false information? Did the anonymous witness even exist?

I whirled on Felix then, who took an involuntary step back. He looked like he was considering running out of here and never looking back. As a bounty-hunting dropout, I knew the Collective had given the team a brief on who I was, and who my victim —*victims*—had been. The more information the bounty hunters had, the better chance they had of finding the person in question. "So, FT97, what are you being told? I know what the Collective said publicly isn't the same thing they're telling their hired hands."

He scoffed. "Hired hands? Did you forget you used to be all about this job?"

"I was *all about it* until it got my dad killed," I snapped. "Or did *you* forget *that* part?"

A muscle flexed in his jaw. "Of course not."

I crossed my arms. "Well?"

He was clearly debating about what to tell me, but he was already here, "investigating" on his own in secret. "There's a missing cache of weapons, all supposedly as powerful as that sword of yours. The Collective has intel that the weapons were part of a larger shipment of illegal goods that someone was trying to smuggle into Luma. Your boy Haskins got his hands on some of it during an auction held here about three weeks ago. The weapons runner was supposed to take the entire cache southeast to a hub in Nevada, but because humans here are known to pay way too much money for dangerous shit, the runner sold a crate of them to a local supplier, then went on his merry way with a fat wad of cash. Now there's an unknown number of weapons loose in the city."

"*Other* sentient weapons?" I asked, directing the question at the sword, rather than Felix.

One quick tap followed by a second hesitant one.

"The sword hasn't come across any other weapons like itself from this supposed shipment," I said.

Felix's gaze flicked between me and the sword. "You're ... really allied with it?"

I didn't dignify that with a response, because mostly I wanted to reply with *duh*. "Do you know where the auction was held? Who ran it?"

"Nah. No one I've talked to is being forthcoming with anything solid. Haskins didn't even know who was running the auction, and he attended it," Felix said. "Truth serums only work if there's a truth to reveal; he couldn't tell us information he doesn't have. Smart on the organizer's part, though. Keeping details from the attendees is saving his ass, too."

"Why are you so sure it's a *he*?"

"All signs, what few there are, point to Caspian Blackthorn. When you check your mirror, you'll see that there's a bounty out for him now, too."

My brows jumped at that. *Caspian*? It felt too obvious. But maybe the Collective had been needing a reason to go after the guy for a while, and now they had an excuse to pour a truth serum down their fellow sorcerer's throat. "Multiple birds, multiple stones, huh?"

Three buzzes cut off Felix's reply. Quick, quick, slow.

Felix pulled his pocket mirror from his back pocket, and I fished mine out of my backpack. The first message on the glass was the one I'd received earlier.

UPTOWN. BLACKTHORN. CODE 154.

An illegal item code? That was like arresting a well-known mafia boss for jaywalking. I waited a moment, knowing the message would dissolve on its own thirty seconds after the mirror had been opened. When that message faded, a new one etched itself on the glass.

Possible Fletcher sighting in Industrial District. Highest priority.

I cast a glance at the sword to make sure it was still here, and that it hadn't teleported to the Industrial District in the blink of an eye to lead authorities on a wild goose chase. Though I didn't hate that idea.

It still hovered where I'd left it.

Felix's phone rang a second later. He held up a finger to me and answered the call. "Hey, man. Yeah, I just saw it. I turned around to head back to the Indie. Nah, I didn't see her. But if the tip says she's there, she couldn't have gone far. Yep. See you there."

By the time he hung up, my arms were folded tight across my chest. "Guess you better get going, huh?"

"I know you don't owe me anything," he said, pocketing both his mirror and phone. "And I know you're pissed off and probably always will be, but I meant it when I said I want to help you. If that means getting you out of Luma to somewhere safer, I'll do it."

I didn't know what to say.

"Can I ask you to stay here?" he asked. "I'll do my rounds tonight, and when that's over, I'll come back. Then we can talk about options. But if I don't go now, Deever is going to get suspicious."

Something occurred to me then that should have registered as a possibility earlier. "Can you be tracked here?"

"Nah. I have a signal scrambler talisman." He pulled a chain out from under his shirt, a finger holding the chain aloft. Three items hung there. Two half-moon-shaped talismans and a ring. It was a simple gold band that very well could have been a wedding ring. Bounty hunters often wore their wedding rings on chains rather than on their fingers when out on jobs. My mom told me it was to keep criminals from figuring out if the hunter had a family who could be exploited.

He'd not only left me, never once making contact in five years, but he'd gone off and started a life with someone new. I shouldn't have cared. It was none of my business. *He* was none of my business.

"If I take too long to meet up with him, Deever will have no problems following me later. I can get him to back off, but it'll take some time," he said.

As much as I hated everything about this, Felix was second on my list of people who could safely get me out of Luma—if I decided I wanted that. He could help keep me one step ahead of the hunters, especially since he had an indirect line of communication open with the Collective. The rest of it didn't matter. "I'll stay here."

He stared for a long beat, then nodded, and turned for the stairs.

"When you come back," I said—my snarky, bitter inner voice wanted to say "if" instead of "when"—"can you bring me something?"

He turned back, a dark brow cocked.

"A signal scrambler and a burner," I said.

"What for?"

"To play Lollipop Jumble. The amenities in this place are awful." He didn't laugh—didn't even crack a smile. "For research."

"Fine. Don't go anywhere. I have a million questions." Then he pointed at the sword. "And you, don't go murdering anyone else."

The sword hummed.

With that, Felix walked down the rattling steps, across the dark lower floor of the factory, and out of view. I wondered if he'd really be back, or if he'd just walked out of my life forever for a second time.

CHAPTER TWENTY

Five years ago

I stood at the open doorway of the kitchen in nothing but my underwear and one of Felix's oversized shirts. I craned my neck to peer through the sliver of space made by the ajar bedroom door. It was still early, and Felix was a fairly heavy sleeper.

After a few long seconds of no movement, I crept to the fridge, gently easing it open to keep it from creaking. I grinned at the half-a-cake still inside, the white cake shot through with swirls of blue, pink, and green. Creamy chocolate frosting coated the tops and sides in messy swipes. Felix had made it for my birthday three days ago and even if it wasn't the prettiest cake I'd ever seen, it was the best I'd ever had.

I carefully grabbed a fork out of a drawer. Not bothering to take the cake out of the fridge, I sliced off a large chunk and popped the piece into my mouth. I chewed slowly, eyes closed. I didn't normally have much of a sweet tooth, but this cake had been a shining light amid very dark days. For the last couple of nights, when I couldn't sleep, I'd steal a piece or two of this cake, and as the rich chocolate frosting melted on my tongue, I got a little jolt of hope along with the sugar rush.

A throat cleared behind me, and I whirled around to find Felix sitting on the counter. He rubbed the heel of his palm against his eye. He only wore a pair of sweatpants. "Babe. It's five-thirty in the morning."

"There are eggs in the batter," I argued. "That's basically breakfast."

He tried not to smile but failed. He hopped off the counter and grabbed me around the middle in one fluid motion, pulling me to him so our stomachs were flush. Hope flared even brighter.

"And chocolate comes from the cocoa plant, which is sort of like a vegetable. It's basically a salad."

I grinned. This was the Felix I knew. The Felix I missed. I draped my arms around his shoulders.

Felix was my best friend, aside from Kayda. Best friends since we were fourteen. Ten years of being each other's first ... everything, and living together for two of them. Him being there for me every moment I was sure I'd be crushed under the grief of losing my dad and being abandoned by my mom. Through all of that, I'd never once questioned anything about our relationship, our bond, our connection—until recently. I had no specific concern, but my sixth sense was trying to tell me something. The constant niggling in the back of my head told me something was wrong. I'd felt it the day my dad died, well before everything had gone to hell. That day had been as normal as any other, aside from the sense of dread that had weighed on my chest like a bowling ball. When I'd gotten the news that he'd been killed on the job, I was somehow blindsided and validated at the same time.

I had that sense of dread again now. A feeling that had lingered for weeks. I didn't think Felix was on the verge of being killed, but he was acting differently. Secretive. My birthday had been a blip in the sea of dread. We'd had the best day: a magic show in downtown Luma, a fancy dinner I knew we couldn't afford, and a cake at home, decorated with twenty-three candles that had taken me five tries to realize were trick candles. I'd gone to bed happier than I had in ages, only to wake up at 5:00 a.m. to find that he'd left for work early again.

In the weeks before and after my twenty-third birthday, he was out at all hours, claiming it was work-related. When I asked for details, he was vague. Yet, the few times I followed him, his car was always in the lot, right where it should be. The dread wouldn't abate, no matter how many times he told me everything was okay.

That was our thing. Our one rule. If one of us asked the other if everything was okay, the other was honor-bound not to lie. Going to bed angry or with a fight unresolved wasn't an option. Saying "nothing" when asked what was wrong, when it was clear something *was* wrong, was a no-no. Leaving for work with things unsaid was especially not allowed.

The day my dad died, I had asked my parents if everything was okay. The crease of my mother's brow, the thinness of my father's lips, and the tingle in the back of my skull had all told me that no, everything was not fine. But Mom had smiled and said, "Yes, of course. We'll see you tonight." Dad had said, "I'll make my famous chicken casserole for dinner." They'd kissed me on the head and left the house with their gear. They'd never come home. Dad was dead and Mom had fled Luma without saying goodbye.

That fateful night, I'd found Dad's pocket mirror in a pile of clothes in the bathroom, and his favorite watch on the counter. Things he never left the house without, but the job he and my mother had gone out on had stressed him out to the point of being forgetful. That feeling of dread had tried to choke me when I'd found his mirror, and I'd almost screamed and thrown it across the room when it buzzed in my hand. Three buzzes. Quick, quick, slow.

NF23 killed in action. **CF24** awol. Ferguson still at large.

Now, every day that Felix came home late and every night that I woke to find him awake and staring at the ceiling, unable to sleep, I knew something was wrong. Something would take Felix from me.

But every time I asked him, "Is everything okay?" he said yes, and I believed him. I believed him because I had to. If he was lying to my face day after day, it would break me in an entirely different way.

"Is the cake the only reason you're up?" Felix asked now, pulling me from my tangle of thoughts. "Is this about Naomi?"

"No. Yes? Maybe. I don't know."

"You can't blame yourself for what happened," he said.

But I'd had a bad feeling when I parted ways with Naomi, watching her walk away with that so-called stepbrother of hers. I should have asked more questions. I should have trusted the feeling in my gut. I hadn't, and now she was dead. Her body had been found on the shore of Luma Creek that ran through the southern end of the Industrial District. She'd been out there long enough that animals had destroyed all evidence of what had happened to her. Her boyfriend had been a top suspect, and I'd been freaked out that we'd invited a murderer into our home for countless game nights. He had an airtight alibi, though. The hunt for her killer was still ongoing.

I absently licked a flake of chocolate off my lip. "I know. But it's hard to not cycle through all the what-ifs."

Her death *had* been eating me up. Nightmares had pulled me awake this morning just as much as my concerns about Felix had. I tried to convince myself that the grief of losing my new friend was making me lash out at Felix. There had been too much death in my life already, and I wasn't handling it well.

Yet, the dread only grew worse each day.

Silence stretched between us.

"What's going on, Low?" he asked, dark brown eyes searching mine. "Talk to me."

I clenched my jaw and looked away. I fiddled with the fork,

DIABOLICAL SWORD

turning the handle over and over in my fingers behind his head. "Could say the same to you. You're not telling me something."

"For the millionth time, there's nothing to tell," he said.

I clenched my jaw. "Don't lie to me."

He gently pushed me back, and a chill swept over me. This was the new Felix. The imposter Felix who wore the skin of the most important person in my life.

"I'm not lying," he said, then stalked back toward the bedroom.

An itchy, panicked feeling clawed its way up my body, from toes to chest, and I blurted, "Is everything okay, Felix?" Desperation made my voice crack on the last word. I squeezed the handle of the fork hard enough to make my fingers ache. I would give him one more chance to tell me the truth.

He turned, his brow creased in that heartbreaking way, his jaw tight. For a moment, I thought he'd lie to me again. I thought he'd stare into my eyes and tell me everything was fine. "I'm handling it."

"Felix ... Felix, what does that *mean*?" I stammered, tossing the chocolate-stained fork in the sink with a clatter before running after him.

He was back in the bedroom now. He'd pulled on a white undershirt and was buttoning his uniform shirt over it. White thread spelled out the name of the casino. He stepped out of his sweats and pulled on a pair of slacks he'd grabbed from the closet.

"Felix," I tried again, near tears. I leaned against the doorframe as I watched him. I was gripping it, really—my fingers held tight to the lip of the jamb, needing something solid to hold on to because I was sure it was only a matter of time before the bottom fell out from underneath me.

By the time he looked up, all warmth had fled his expression. Imposter Felix was firmly in place. "I said I'm handling it. We've had such a nice couple of days. Don't ruin it." He dropped his head in regret the second he said it.

"Don't *ruin* it?" I snapped. "Tell me what you aren't saying!"

"Nothing!"

A disturbing calm washed over me, my shoulders instantly relaxing. It happened that fast. Some instinct-driven defense mechanism working overtime to shut off power to nonessential parts. I was so bone-chillingly pissed now that the fight had left me. I walked out of the room. He called my name, but I didn't slow my pace back into the kitchen. I yanked open the fridge and pulled out the cake. I ungracefully dropped the plate onto the counter, picked my used fork out of the sink, and got myself a nice, huge mouthful.

"Harlow …" he said, exasperated now.

I swallowed the too-large bite. "Don't you have to get to work?"

"Yeah, but I can't leave when you're like this …"

I stuffed another bite in my mouth, chewing slowly as I stared at him, my arms folded on the counter. I was a ticking time bomb, and we both knew it. If he pushed me too far one way, I'd start throwing things. If he pushed me too far in the other, I'd burst into tears.

He collected the rest of his belongings and then stopped on the other side of the counter. "We'll talk later, okay?"

I pointed my fork at him. "Don't come back until you're ready to tell me everything."

"Low …"

"I'm done with the gaslighting, Felix. Either be honest with me or don't come back."

The hurt in his eyes almost made me take the ultimatum back, but I held my ground. I wouldn't lose him by letting him keep me in the dark. I'd been blindsided by my dad's death. By my mom running out on me. By Naomi's murder. I refused to be blindsided again. Not by him.

When I came home later that night from my shift at the Mongoose, all of Felix's stuff was gone. His work clothes no longer hung in the closet, his dirty clothes weren't scattered on the bedroom floor, and his toiletries no longer graced the bathroom counter. I called his cell, a knot of emotions I couldn't untie lodged in my throat. The number had already been disconnected.

The only thing he'd left had been a note on the counter.

I'm sorry.

The moment I'd read the words, the tingling in the base of my skull vanished. This had been the cause of the permeating dread —Felix leaving me without warning, without an explanation.

As I sank to the floor, I wondered if we hadn't been as strongly bound as I thought, and that all he'd needed was a push toward the door to get him to leave—or if the truth of what he was hiding was so bad, leaving me heartbroken had been the lesser of two evils.

CHAPTER TWENTY-ONE

Present Day

It was mid-afternoon before Felix came back. I'd slept a few more hours, but it had come in fits and starts. The sound of scratching had woken me in the middle of the night. Tapping, clawing—something rending metal. When my eyes popped open, I expected to be careening to the ground, the metal legs of my platform severed, or for the roof to be caving in above my head under the weight of an enormous dragon.

But as I lay there frozen, my skin slick with sweat and my chest heaving, no monstrous beasts came crashing through the windows, walls, or roof. Just my dreaming mind playing tricks on me. Worse still, when I fell asleep again, my dreams were populated by Felix's dumb mug. Felix smiling, Felix glowering, Felix hovering over me. I didn't appreciate my traitorous thoughts one bit.

I'd done some exploring of the old factory in the light of day, but found little. As angry as I was with Felix, I was glad for his company. It didn't seem right that I was bored when the whole city was looking for me, but here we were.

Aside from the signal scrambler and burner phone, he also brought a grease-splattered bag. We settled on the platform again, and while he talked me through how to use the signal scrambler, I pulled things out of the bag. Two burgers, an order of fries, and an order of onion rings. One of the white burger wrappers had "xtra pick" written on the top, and I stared down at the scrawled black letters as if they were a complicated math problem.

"What's wrong?" he asked. "You still like extra pickles, right?"

I nodded absently as I unwrapped the burger, unable to look at him. As I took a bite, a tear slipped down my face. I'd gone from being devastated over losing him, to letting rage fuel me for years so I could get out of bed in the morning, and now here he was, casually sitting across from me as if the last five years hadn't happened. I was pissed off, heartbroken, confused. Maybe he didn't have this war of emotions going on inside him—maybe he hardly thought about me at all now. He'd left, made a new life for himself, and was only here out of some sense of charity. I took another bite, then angrily stuffed an onion ring in my mouth.

"Harlow?" he tried, craning his neck to peer into my face, which was angled toward the mesh platform below us. "What's wrong?"

I sniffed hard, looked at him through my tears, and said, "Nothing."

His jaw tightened.

We ate in silence.

By the time he'd balled up his wrapper and tossed it into the bag, I'd finished eating and had gotten myself back under control. "What's changed out there since last night?"

Felix said, "The police are being run ragged trying to chase down the flood of tips pouring in. There are reports that people are on hold for up to half an hour before anyone answers the phone."

"Glad I've given the community something to be excited

about." I sighed. "Has the Collective changed the narrative at all? Any new lies floating around I should know about?"

Felix sat with one leg folded in front of him, flush with the ground, and the other bent at the knee, a forearm thrown over it. The posture was casual enough, but I sensed how tense he was, even from a few feet away. Tense about being here, tense about how I spoke of the Collective, tense about how much he should tell me, since he apparently still thought I might be guilty of murder. His hesitation to speak grated on my nerves.

"I get it, okay?" I said. "Your loyalty is to the Collective. Helping a fugitive like me goes against your morals. Blah blah. But you're either here to help me, or you're not. Make up your mind."

He leveled his intense gaze at me. "More ultimatums?"

Hmm. Maybe the past five years weren't totally behind him.

Sighing, he said, "The latest thing going around is that you and Haskins used to be involved romantically and had been in the charm-collection business together before he dumped you for being too reckless. He got an invite to the auction, and you tried to rekindle your old flame, all as a ploy to get into his basement."

"First, gross. Second, is that a euphemism or …"

The barest hint of a smile flashed. "The theory is that when Haskins wouldn't share his bounty from the auction with you, you called in an anonymous tip that led to his arrest. You were lying in wait for him to be taken in, so you could swoop in and take what you felt was your due."

It was another case of part of the truth being used to craft a sensational lie.

"Let me guess … you got this tip from draken men named Pratt and Igor?"

Felix cocked his head. "And how did you know that?"

I explained how I ended up with the sword in the first place—the actual story behind my "relationship" with Haskins.

"That makes more sense. Those two are doing everything they can to get their hands on that reward money," Felix said.

"They promised to keep their mouths shut if I took the sword with me," I grumbled. "Maybe the sword needs to pay them a visit to let them know what happens to snitches."

The sword lifted itself from the platform beside me, vibrating softly and glowing a dull red. I knew if I gave the sword the word, it would take off to maim the draken.

I lifted a hand. "Chill, sword. They aren't worth it. They're opportunistic assholes, but I can't fault them for that."

The sword hummed and settled beside me on the platform again.

Felix pursed his lips, his gaze flitting between the sword and me. He gave his head a little shake.

"Pump those guys full of truth serum and they'll tell you what happened," I said.

"The Collective currently has no reason to bring them in for that level of questioning."

"Convenient," I muttered. "What about the Caspian angle? I haven't gotten an update from the mirror about his takedown …"

"He bounced. I don't know if he's got a bounty mirror too or what, but a full team raided his place early this morning. When we got there, the gate to the property was open, and the wards were down. He'd known we were coming and took off well before we got there. No one's got any idea where he is. He doesn't use telepads and the three vehicles on the lot that we found were all unregistered—no VINs, no plates. We're guessing there's a fourth one, and he's in it."

The Collective had known where Caspian's lair was all this time—or at least had known where to get said information if needed—yet they'd left him alone until now.

"Do they have a running theory on why I killed the caracal shifter?" I asked.

"That one has them stumped. Was he a client of yours or anything?"

"Nope. Never met the guy. I had to look him up because I didn't even know what he looked like."

Felix hmmed noncommittally. "With all the tips being called in, the Collective is having the hunters investigate the leads that sound the most promising. A couple of hours before I got here, Deever and I were in the Warehouse District talking to a guy who works at a bar near the dump site of Randal's body. His theory is you were one of Randal's scorned lovers—apparently there are a lot of them."

"For someone with no love life, I sure get around."

He ignored that. "This guy's call was flagged as more viable than others, if only because scores of women have been calling in saying if they had a living sword, they'd use it to cut down Randal, too."

"Ouch."

"Yeah, sounds like the guy was a dick. One of his power plays was to tell young ladies—only fae, though; no humans—that he had a career-making gig for them all lined up. He'd gently pressure them into sleeping with him in exchange for said job, and once he got what he wanted, the gig would suddenly fall through."

"Ugh." I gave the sword next to me a little pat. Not so much a "Good job!" pat, since wantonly murdering people who were jackholes wasn't the way of civilized societies, but an "I sort of get why you hated him" pat. The sword vibrated softly under my palm. "Did he drug them or anything?" I asked Felix.

"The bartender we talked to said Randal was addicted to Bliss. It's very popular with the club crowd. The Collective isn't particularly interested in Bliss cases, since it's more of a human problem than a fae one. Hunters can offer their services on those cases—since we're all human too—as long as it doesn't interfere with our bounties. The weirdest thing about Bliss is that no one on the mundane force can figure out what's in the stuff."

"I'm not even sure what it looks like. They're tabs, right?"

"Yeah. Little white tabs, like Tylenol, that have a bat stamped on one side. Every time the cops get their hands on some of it, the labs come back saying it's nothing but sugar and super potent caffeine. Kids love the stuff, swearing it's like ecstasy, yet it's made with over-the-counter ingredients. It being a placebo seems improbable—too many people have a supposedly psychosomatic reaction to it, and they all describe it the same way."

"And it kills humans most of the time. Another alchemist-crafted drug claiming to give humans powers."

Felix nodded. "Yeah, that's what we hear, too. That, or it can open up a portal in your mind to allow you to see the fae world. Not quite ayahuasca-level, but close enough. Yet, one human can take five tabs and just be hyped out of their mind, while another takes only one and is dancing one minute, and dead on the floor the next. I mean, maybe that's a heart attack from the caffeine, but that would be a rare reaction given the age of most victims. And it happens too often for it to just be that. And then tons of others report that it's a mellowing drug that makes them feel good—similar to what the fae report. All the anecdotal information we have about it is wildly inconsistent."

"You said Randal used it a lot?"

"According to that bartender, yeah," he said. "He said Bliss moves through the Ghost Lily nearly every night, and either management can't figure out how it's getting in, or they aren't trying that hard to stop it. In humans, the effects can be anything from mind-numbing euphoria to death. When fae take it, they just get 'blissed out.' Randal supplied it to his entourage when they were partying in one of the private rooms. The bartender said young, pretty fae got invited into Randal's private room a lot—I wouldn't doubt that Bliss played a role in at least some of those girls getting taken advantage of."

The name Ghost Lily rang in my head—the same bar Mathias's sister had worked in. A pretty fae who had gone missing. Had Nyla crossed paths with Randal? Had he promised her a modeling job in this big, busy city she'd grown to love? Had he slipped Bliss into her drink to get her nice and compliant so he could take advantage of her?

None of this explained why the sword had wanted the guy dead, though. Or how it even knew who Randal was.

"Something doesn't add up …" I muttered.

"Only one thing?"

"Randal was killed in the Warehouse District around 1 a.m., if that witness quoted in the paper is to be believed. I know for a fact that the sword killed the caracal before 8 p.m. That was when the werecats were tearing up my apartment looking for a murder weapon, and the sword showed up covered in blood shortly after that. Someone somewhere is lying about the time—maybe even the location."

The sword quickly inverted itself and tapped once on the platform.

I turned toward it. It had reacted to the comment about the murder location. "You *didn't* kill him in the Warehouse District?"

Tap-tap.

"At his house?" I asked.

Tap-tap.

Where the hell had the murder happened, then? My thoughts went into overdrive. If it wasn't in either of the districts, it must have been in the Ardmore or Montclaire neighborhood, where mostly lesser fae and humans lived. The community vibe was stronger there. The lesser fae especially looked out for each other. And since I'd developed a reputation for finding charmed items for the beings whom they rightly belonged to, or supplying them to humans who needed a little extra protection, I'd gotten to know the nooks and crannies of the neighborhoods pretty well—even more so than the bustling Luma Proper.

Pretty fae ladies could no doubt make a killing in tips in a place like the Ghost Lily, frequented by working men who needed to unwind after a backbreaking day in either district. And, at least according to Felix, where one found pretty fae ladies, one found Oliver Randal.

"Did you kill him at the Ghost Lily?" I asked.

Tap.

"And you looked like me when you lured him outside?"

Tap.

Glancing at Felix, I said, "The bartender who called in the tip didn't know that Randal had been killed *at* his bar?"

Felix's dark brows bunched on his forehead. "He said he hasn't been in for two days. He goes back tonight. We talked to the guy at his house while he got ready for work. He said he was too nervous to talk to authorities while at the bar, and he wanted to talk to someone before his shift started because it's always chaotic in there."

"Human guy?" I asked.

"Yeah … why? What are you thinking?"

"I'm not sure yet," I said slowly. "Something's not right at that bar, though. I know that much. I just wonder if the bartender was lying to you, or if he was oblivious to the fact that the murder happened there. You'd think *that* rumor would have reached him by now, especially if Randal was a regular."

"Maybe the owners are trying to keep it hush-hush so it doesn't hurt business."

"That wouldn't explain the bogus account in the paper, though," I said. "Or the showdown on the news of 'me' evading the werecats. It wasn't fully dark in the footage they showed—it could have either been dusk or dawn, but since the sun sets later in summer, what they filmed could have easily been from as late as 7 p.m. They filmed 'me' and the sword in the window after it killed the caracal, and just before the guards came to my apartment at 8 looking for the sword. The werecats must have thought I sprinted back to my place, changed my clothes, and then pretended I'd been asleep the whole time." I chewed on my bottom lip. "Even though the sword showed up shortly after the werecats did … its whereabouts were unaccounted for for a second chunk of time that night—between 9 and 11:30 p.m. But it was back with me by midnight."

Felix eyed the sword. "What was it doing *then*?"

"Your guess is as good as mine. But that means the witness

couldn't have seen me or the sword after 1 a.m. in the Warehouse District because we were both in for the night by then."

"You're saying the witness story is bullshit? The witness, the location of Randal's body, *and* time of death are all made up?" Felix asked.

"Not necessarily. What if the witness account I read was true, and she *really did* find Randal's body behind the Design & Decor building at 1 a.m.? It would just mean someone had found Randal's body at the Ghost Lily, moved it to the new spot in the Warehouse District, and then set up a scenario where there would be a witness. Someone could have easily glamoured themself to look like me. They already had the footage from earlier in the evening, so a skilled glamourer could replicate my appearance based on the video."

"Who is *they*?"

"The Collective. When you live in a hub, the 'collective they' is literal."

Felix sighed. He *used* to think I was funny. "You honestly think there's a conspiracy going on here? Why would they go through this much trouble just to frame a human for murder?"

"Why do you think they wouldn't? You know better than anyone that sometimes secrets are worth keeping even if you ruin lives in the process. Something is happening in Luma that's bigger than me, and bigger than this sword. Your precious Collective is in the middle of it. If I'm going to have any chance of proving I didn't do what they're accusing me of, I have to figure out what they're hiding."

Sounding a touch incredulous, Felix asked, "That's what you want to do then? Instead of getting the hell out of Luma until this all blows over, you want to piss the Collective off even more by poking your nose into their business?"

I hadn't known that was what I wanted until this conversation.

"Yep. I'm not leaving Luma. They've taken everything from me. They're not taking my city away, too," I said. "You have to make a decision now, too, Felix. You came here to help me escape. I'm staying. Are you going to turn me in for that bounty?"

"No," he said, without hesitation. "How could you even ask me that?"

I didn't reply.

The silence stretched on.

Clearing his throat, he checked his watch. "I've got to get going, but I can come back later tonight. If you get antsy and leave, at least give me a warning. I programmed my number into your phone."

We both stood, and he grabbed the bag of trash. After staring at me for a long beat, he shook his head and then headed for the stairs.

"Thanks for the food. And the phone," I said.

He glanced over his shoulder. "No problem. Try not to drain the battery playing Lollipop Jumble all day."

An involuntary smile tugged at my mouth. I watched him descend the steps. When he reached the bottom, I called out, "There's one more thing you have to decide."

He glanced up from the base of the steps. "What's that?"

"Which side you're on. Mine or theirs," I said. "If you don't come back, I'll know which one you chose."

CHAPTER TWENTY-TWO

Being holed up in an abandoned factory all day with nothing but a sentient sword for company was *very* boring. I almost called Kayda half a dozen times, but I had no doubts they'd tapped her landline and cell. Between the Collective throwing all their resources at finding me, the bounty on my head, and reward money on the line, someone somewhere had probably reported that Kayda and I were close. Hell, I wouldn't have been surprised if an old classmate had called it in.

I imagined a pair of intimidating werecat guards strolling into Jo's Apothecary and asking if anyone had seen me in the shop lately. Jo wouldn't rat me out, but her high-strung assistant, Erik, probably would—anything to protect his "Lady Josephine." I just hoped no one was blatantly harassing Kayda—just creepily stalking her from afar.

I did another internet search on Oliver Randal, looking for any new details—fabricated or not—on his murder. No updates since yesterday.

Fearing that I'd drain the battery, I didn't use the phone much. Which left me with my thoughts. I wasn't much better company than the sword. I'd eaten the rest of my soggy sandwiches out of boredom. And had scoured suitable places in the corners of the building or in the bushes outside to relieve myself. I would have killed for a shower. My head itched. Why hadn't I packed dry shampoo? Or leave-in conditioner?

I only had one more night here before I had to make the trek back into Ardmore to check my private telepost box, assuming Welsh kept his word and sent me a message. I had my doubts as to what he'd learned about the sword in three days, but he was my best source of information at the moment. Somehow, I had to retrieve the message without getting caught on the way. But that was a problem for the morning.

As the sun set, the sky outside the row of windows near my platform turning a blue-gray, the sword and I were deeply involved in important matters. The wadded-up ball of paper flew toward my face and I hopped to the side to avoid getting hit, then drew my arm back and whacked the ball back at the sword with my open palm. It dove low and lobbed it back. Its speed wasn't fair. Back and forth we went in an impressive fifteen-second rally before I feinted a hit to the right, causing the sword to zip that direction, before I smacked the ball left, sending it sailing over the edge of the platform.

"Aha!" I called out, fists in the air. "Ten points for me!"

We hadn't crafted rules *or* a point system. The sword burned red, then darted over the side after our toy. When it returned, the wadded-up paper ball was balanced on the tip of the blade. I readied myself, feet shoulder-width apart and body hunched forward a couple of inches, hands out.

The blade tossed the ball into the air, but just before it lobbed it, the blade went cherry red and turned the paper into a puff of blackened ash.

I stood to full height, hands on hips. "Spoilsport! It took hours to find a piece of paper big enough to turn into a ball!"

The sword vibrated.

I was about to tell it that it needed to find more paper for us, when the cell phone buzzed in my back pocket. Seeing as only one person had this number, I knew who the text would be from before I pulled the device free. The trill in my stomach was some combination of giddy anticipation and anxiety.

> **FELIX**
>
> Won't make it tonight. Sorry. This isn't me making a choice. Something urgent came up with work.

I deflated. Even five years later, work came between us.

Before I could reply, the chains on the door to the factory rattled. The sword swiveled toward the sound, and I crouched behind the wide base of the crane. I stuffed the phone back into my pocket, my concerns about Felix shoved in there too. Felix clearly wasn't here, since he'd just texted me. Besides, he came and went through a window, as I had. This was someone or something else. My gut wasn't screaming *danger!* so much as *caution!*

I waited for another sound to offer me clues about my new visitor. The jangle of the door was too loud and aggressive to be the wind on a summer evening as still as this. The chains rattled again, followed by the creak of door hinges. The space made by pulling the two doors as far apart as the chains would allow offered maybe a foot of space. Not enough for a full-grown adult to get through. Which ruled out draken, thankfully.

I closed my eyes, trying to give my sense of hearing a little boost. Faint clicks. Talons or claws tapping an uneven rhythm on the cement floor. Not a goblin. Possibly a smaller shifter. Lord, I hoped the loopy badger shifter hadn't found me.

I heard an unfurling *whoomp* of wings, then the sound of them cutting through the warm air of the factory. My eyes popped open. A large black shape soared straight for my hiding place and in a matter of seconds had alighted on the railing surrounding the platform with a muted thud. Dark talons wrapped around the topmost bar. My gaze traveled from talons, to scaled legs, to a feathered chest, and a dark intelligent eye. A falcon—one twice the size of an average, mundane brown eagle.

The sword hovered by my head, humming slightly. The fact

that it hadn't immediately severed the wings off the intruder spoke to the sword sensing the same thing I did: this bird wasn't a threat, but it wasn't to be underestimated either.

As my eyes adjusted, my pulse thrumming in my temples, I studied the bird. There *were* avian shifters, but most of them had settled in weather-controlled avian-dominated hubs. The biggest one was somewhere in Canada. For whatever reason, most avian shifters were corvids—crows, ravens, magpies.

They were also human-size in bird form, which made it impossible for them to hide in plain sight among Earth birds, and when in their human-like form, they retained too much of their bird qualities to fit in among humans either. I remembered the griffel receptionist from the clinic and tried to imagine an avian shifter who looked even more unsettling in human form. I pitied the sorcerers assigned to maintain the veil in the Canadian hub. Rumor had it that several water elementals had very well-paying jobs there, solely tasked with making it rain periodically to wash away the muck that accumulated when one's society consisted almost entirely of five-foot-tall birds who preferred their avian form.

My gaze returned to the bird's feet. A dark plastic tube, the size of a small shotgun shell casing, lay flush with one of its legs. This was a courier falcon. Had Welsh realized that my private telepost box would be too risky?

Falcon couriers were highly trained and very expensive. Runes adorned their legs and feet, heightening their senses of sight and smell. Locator spells built with blood-painted runes allowed the birds to find a person without the sender knowing where said person was. The blood had to be fresh, though—and Welsh had just taken a vial of mine two days ago.

Since the language of runes could be taught, anyone could buy a courier animal. The buyer just needed to study the accompanying rune manual. One incorrect rune could send your animal courier on a never-ending delivery mission.

Though I'd never been sent a falcon courier before, I knew

they were trained to tolerate being touched by people other than their handler. The bird wouldn't poke my eyes out, but it was still next-level intimidating. It had hardly moved since it had landed on the railing, its head turned slightly so it could stare into my soul with one of its beady black eyes. Then, with great caution, it lifted a taloned foot from its perch, silently urging me to take the message strapped to its leg. I was pretty sure the falcon would have rolled its eyes if it could.

I approached the bird, coming nose to beak with it. Hinging at the waist, I gingerly reached for the black plastic tube. The bird's focus was fixed on me, probably wondering what the holdup was. I pressed the round button on the side of the tube, and the bottom popped open. I caught the small scroll just before it slipped through the mesh holes of the platform. Once I stood to full height with the message in my hand, the bird propelled itself off the railing with such a powerful beat of its wings that warm air swirled around my head. A couple of wayward curls whipped into my face. I watched, heart pounding, as the falcon silently soared back through the factory.

Swallowing, I looked down at the small scroll in my hand. It was just past dusk, so the sky hadn't gone completely dark yet, but the light was dwindling quickly. "A little light, sword?"

It floated by my head and glowed blue. It wasn't as bright as a fae light, but it would do. I unfurled the note.

MEET ME IN THE RAIL YARD PARKING LOT. I'M A FRIEND OF WELSH.

That was the entire message. I turned the paper over just to be sure. Blank. This might have been a trap, but if the Collective had found me, they'd just storm the building. A bounty hunter would have found his or her way in like Felix had, not send a note. Perhaps a draken would try to lure me out, since they were too bulky to gracefully break in, and would fear ambushing me and getting a sentient sword to the gut for their trouble.

As I stared at the note, the words dissolved as if they'd been eaten away by acid. New words bled into the paper.

IF YOU'RE STILL READING THIS, WELSH SAID YOU CALLED HIM "CHAOTIC GOOD." HE BELIEVES I'M NEUTRAL EVIL.

I smiled faintly. No one else had been in the room when Welsh and I'd had that conversation. He'd also put a sound-proofing spell on the room—no one could have been listening in. It said a lot about me that the curiosity of meeting one of Welsh's "neutral evil" friends was currently winning out over something more practical, like personal safety.

I turned to the sword. "We're going to the rail yard. I don't know who's out there, but if this is an ambush, I'm giving you permission to protect us. Just try not to murder them, okay? A light maiming is more than enough. We just have to be able to escape."

It took a moment for the sword to hum in response. I imagined it saying, *But murder is a much more permanent solution*, before its reluctant agreement.

In short order, I packed up my things, strapped on my backpack, grabbed the duffel bag, and started for the stairs. The sword hovered nearby to make sure I got down the rickety steps in one piece, then zipped across the factory floor back toward the entrance. As I made my way to the window I'd crawled in originally, the sword slipped through the small gap of space between the chained doors and disappeared into the evening.

Once I and all my belongings had made it outside, I crouched low and picked my way along the side of the building, the sage-scented bushes to my left hopefully shielding me from anyone who might be out here aside from my new neutral-evil friend. When I got to the end of the bush barrier, I dropped to one knee and peered around. I reached out with my senses, but the only magical crackle I felt was from the veil a mile away. The same veil I had to get closer to in order to reach the rail yard. It would put me even nearer to the spot where Jimmy Nance had been yanked through the magical wall by a vampire. The veil was supposed to keep vampires out entirely, but clearly one could get through if provided with ample motivation. I hoped Welsh wasn't friends with vampires.

The sword found me a moment later. When I asked if the coast was clear, it hummed.

"Let's go," I muttered, and crept out of my hiding place.

My path was an unnervingly wide-open space for most of the way. Cracked asphalt gave way to packed earth, and then coarse sand as the looming stacks of abandoned railcars grew nearer. A few towering fae lampposts dotted the rail yards, their dull blue glow just bright enough to chase away some of the shadows, though it deepened others.

The sword zipped around in my peripheral vision and sometimes backtracked, taking stock of our surroundings. It never strayed far and didn't dart ahead into the unknown. Perhaps it too knew the stories of the rogue sword forcibly subdued in the farmer's market.

Lined up in rows—the longest sides facing me—the cars were stacked three high. Butted against each other, they made a rather substantial wall of metal. Small walkable gaps broke the wall at random intervals. Walking between the cars was the fastest path to the rail yards themselves, where dilapidated buildings and cracked train tracks wasted away under the watchful eye of the veil. After a ten-minute walk, I stopped at the mouth of the closest narrow opening. The stacks were eight cars deep.

I shot a glance over my shoulder, assuring myself I didn't have a pack of bloodthirsty vamps, money-thirsty draken, or revenge-hungry shifters hurtling toward me. The coast was clear, the warm air unmoving. I had no clue where the sword was, though. I glanced up at a nearby fae light, where a swarm of insects swirled around the glass. A bat winged by, scattering the insects for a moment before it snatched up an evening snack and then swooped away.

I stared down the narrow path. The opening ahead suggested a wider pathway. I ducked inside, the scent of iron and dust thick in my nostrils. My heart thrummed hard in my chest. The memory of the only time I went into a hedge maze on Halloween taunted me. A maze not only crafted by magic, but populated by magical beings that lurched out to scare anyone loopy enough to venture into its depths. Fae manipulated the hedges to change the maze's shape and had animated vines and branches to grasp at hair, arms, and legs. I'd had plant-based nightmares for weeks afterward. If one of these cars started groaning and shifting, I was getting the hell out of here.

The temperature dropped several degrees, as if the metal had absorbed the heat and consumed it. My boots crunched lightly over the coarse sand. The sword remained suspiciously absent. I was too nervous to look anywhere other than forward.

Only one car length from the opening, something scratched across metal. Something digging deeply into one of the cars, like a giant can opener ripping metal apart. I stopped dead. It was the same sound that had pulled me out of sleep the night before. The sound I'd discounted as the remnants of a bad dream.

I scanned the dark sky and the tops of the car stacks on either side, half expecting to see a large, reptilian dragon head peering down from thirty feet above my head. All I saw was another bat wing erratically by. Thankfully the whole vampires-shifting-into-bats thing was strictly a human fiction—otherwise I'd have high-tailed it back to the factory.

The rending sound came again, and I shrank back, bumping into one of the walls of the makeshift metal alleyway. The cold metal bit into my arm. I whirled around, gaze frantically scanning the ground I'd already covered. Nothing crept in the opening. I wanted to call out to the sword, but if something threatening *was* out here, I didn't want to give away my location. Running back the way I'd come was out of the question—too much open space. If something was after me, I'd be like target practice out there.

Carefully, I placed the duffel bag at my feet, squatted before it, and quietly unzipped it. Two smaller weapons lay inside, along with a few talismans. I might not have been good with a weapon, but I figured having something on me while I ran wouldn't be a terrible idea. I pulled out the hooded mace. The spell on it remained a mystery, but touching the grip didn't zing me into next week—the magic was centralized in the head. I prayed it was covered in wicked-sharp spikes and infused with something as potent as that Level 4 lightning spell that had knocked me on my ass.

Taking the cell phone out of my back pocket, I put it inside my backpack. I'd text Felix later—assuming I didn't get killed or arrested or worse out here. I zipped everything back up, secured the bags to my person, and gave the mace a couple of practice chops. If I could wield a hammer, I could wield this, right?

I had to get past three more rows of cars, rusted-out engines, and cabooses before I reached the rail yard parking lot. The location of the neutral-evil friend hopefully meant an awaiting getaway vehicle. There were a few roads out here that were in decent enough shape if you had four-wheel drive.

I crept to the end of the alley and slowly poked my head out into the opening. The walkway made between this row of cars and the one across the way was a good six feet wide. To the right, blue fae light periodically illuminated the sandy ground, the path eventually consumed by shadows. To the left, there were fewer rows of cars, and I spotted the front of a rusted-out train still on the tracks. I knew from my days out here in high school that bushes and lichen had overtaken the train, nature reclaiming the hulking machine. The left was also the direction of the veil's edge, the way littered with broken pieces of concrete, the dilapidated foundation of a stone building, and random piles of pale bricks stripped of most of their color by an unrelenting sun.

Still no sign of the sword, which unnerved me more than anything. The rending shriek hadn't sounded again, so maybe what I'd heard had been the cars adjusting. Like the creaks and groans of a house settling.

Screeeeech.

Terror settled over me, and my gaze snapped up. A crouched figure perched on the corner of the topmost car. The curve of a back here, the shape of a head there. Its proximity to the light should have resulted in eye shine—like the orange of a draken, or the bluish-white of an animal. Perhaps the being wore a pulled-up hood.

The figure shifted, and I involuntarily stepped away, my backpack hitting the wall of cars behind me. I faced the right side of the alley now. My gut told me this thing watched me.

Quick as a snake, it launched from its perch across the short opening to the top of the opposite railcar stack. I spun to watch it, pressing my back against the other wall now. I'd only clocked two things when the creature leaped: one, it was definitely human in shape, and two, it had very long claws or fingernails. Those claws *screeched* against the metal when it landed, allowing it to gain purchase on the hard surface. It sent goose bumps up my arms and scratched against my frayed nerves.

"You're going to move when I tell you to."

My heartbeat stuttered to a stop for a moment before it lurched into a gallop at a dead run. That voice hadn't been my own, or even Kayda's. It had been distinctly male. I had yet to take my eyes off the figure on top of the railcars. Were these damn things telepathic on top of being ten kinds of wrong and one hundred kinds of terrifying?

"Don't look, but I'm behind you to your right," the voice said. Now that the initial shock had worn off, it was clear the voice hadn't been *in* my head, but my ear. No breath had accompanied the calmly stated words. A spell to allow words to carry on the wind, like the one Jo had used just a couple of days ago. This was a witch or sorcerer.

"There's a rune circle etched into the sand behind you. You're going to run and the vampire will chase you. Get her within a couple of feet of the rune circle and I'll do the rest."

He wanted me to get chased on purpose? Was he nuts? I readjusted my grip on the mace. Couldn't I just club it to death?

The vampire skittered forward and down the side of the railcar. That was the only word for it. She skittered like a human-sized spider with claws on the end of its legs.

"*Run!*"

I had already whipped around the side of the car stack and was sprinting full-broke into the open. As if I needed to be told to run when something like *that* was after me. The sound of my booted feet hitting the coarse sand sounded like gong beats. The thing—the *vampire*—skittered back up the side of the cars, if the horrible scratching noises were any indication. I sure as shit wouldn't look over my shoulder to get confirmation. That was how damsels in horror movies ended up tripping over roots in the forest and face-planting. I kept plowing ahead, urging my legs to pump faster. I was a runner in a relay race, sprinting to my partner to pass the baton. Amazing how fast you could haul ass when scared out of your gourd.

Scratch, scratch, scratch ... thump.

Scratch, scratch, scratch ... thump.

The vamp was running along the top of the stacks, then leaping to the next one. Two rows up, a figure stood in one of the makeshift alleyways. A decidedly human-looking figure. I was so focused on him, I almost missed it when he said, "Watch out for the circle!"

I skidded to an abrupt stop, rising on my toes at the edge of the circle, arms pinwheeling, before rocking back to my heels. The edge of the circle remained intact. Phew!

Whoomp!

I spun and locked gazes with the vampire who had landed in the middle of the six-foot-wide opening. Crouched low on all fours, she watched me from several feet away with her unblinking, wall-to-wall black eyes. Her fingers were too long, too unnatural, and faded from pale white to the blackest of black. I would have guessed necrosis ate away at her fingers, but they ended in glistening black claws, as if her hands—as if all of her—were slowly morphing into something else. I'd heard stories about the vampires that had gone fully feral in the years after the Glitch, when their dining on magic-tinged fae blood had caused permanent physiological changes, but I'd never seen one.

Even from this distance, I saw the blue veins snaking under her nearly translucent skin. Her long black hair fell around her shoulders, but large patches of her scalp peeked through, as if she'd taken great fistfuls of stringy hair and ripped them free. She had no eyebrows, and her mouth and nose had an almost dog-snout shape. She snarled, revealing not just long front canines, but a mouth full of razor-sharp teeth.

"*I need her closer,*" the sorcerer said. I knew it was a sorcerer now; only they worked with rune circles.

What did he expect me to do? This feral vamp was the last thing I wanted to piss off. If provoking an elemental water witch got me blasted with a fire hose, provoking a feral bloodsucker would get me dead—probably disemboweled for good measure.

Going against my own advice, I shot a glance over my shoulder. "Any bright ideas?"

The way his eyes went wide before he even got a word out was my only warning before something yanked me by the backpack, sent me airborne for a long terrifying second, and body-slammed me to the ground. Stunned, I stared up at the dark sky, the wind knocked from my lungs. I'd kept hold of the mace, at least. Something sharp in my still-strapped-on bag poked me in the kidney.

Everything snapped back into focus when the vamp wrapped one of her disgusting, blackened hands around my ankle and spun me around on my back. She didn't let go. My head jerked up, but I couldn't get out a word of protest, couldn't react at all, before she started sprinting away with me in tow from the rune circle and my sorcerer savior, and toward the veil.

The train cars whipped by at alarming speed. I was so shell-shocked by her agility and how disorienting it was to be yanked away like this that I hardly had time to scream for help, let alone get myself out of her grasp—which I was sure was the point. By the time I figured out a game plan, I'd be pulled through the veil and that would be the end of me.

Yeah, no, fuck that.

My backpack snagged on something and the bottom of the bag's straps slammed into my armpits. The duffel bag was long gone already, but I still had hold of the mace. The ride was so bumpy, it felt like my brain rattled around in my skull. My shirt rode up. Sand, rocks, and who knew what else shredded my lower back. Gritting my teeth, I willed my arms to meet in the middle, and after a couple of tries, I yanked the leather hood off the mace. The mace's head *was* mercifully covered in very pointy spikes, and now free from its confines, it hummed with magic. Level 3 at the bare minimum.

The vampire sensed it too, because she glanced back. And, just like a damsel in distress, her foot connected with a broken piece of concrete and she went down hard. She fell forward, and with blinding speed she threw me over her head. Airborne again, my legs and arms flailed wildly as the ground rose to meet me. I slammed my eyes shut and curled into some semblance of a ball, praying I didn't smash my head open like an overripe melon when I hit asphalt.

My hip hit first, and oil spots floated in my vision. I let the mace tumble from my grip, not wanting the spikes embedded into my face. I rolled like a tumbleweed caught in a windstorm, elbows and knees hitting every hard surface available. When I finally skidded to a stop on my stomach, my chin bounced off the ground, probably scraping the skin raw.

I gave myself two seconds to catch my breath before I used my aching palms to push myself up, scrambling onto wobbly legs. The vampire slowly got to her feet, too, shaking her head like a dog. Shimmering light winked off something metallic a foot away from me from atop a pile of broken bricks. The mace! I darted for it and snatched it up just before the vampire could get her necrotic hand around it. I thrust the mace in her direction and magic crackled in erratic, bright lines between the spikes, like the electric current on a Taser. The vampire hissed, her needle teeth on full display, but she kept her distance. She hunched low, circling me. She splayed her fingers wide, her long black claws even more terrifying this close.

A shriek sounded to my left and the vampire and I both whipped our heads in that direction. If I hadn't known any better, I'd say it was another vampire, but what were the odds that two of them would be on the wrong side of the veil? When the undead lady in front of me let out a shriek of her own that sounded identical to the distant one, I grew very worried very quickly that a swarm of them lurked out here. Was there a proper term for a group of feral vampires?

A couple of human shapes lurched into view from behind the corner of what had once been a brick wall, brandishing weapons above their heads. They weren't far from the rune-covered obelisk I'd seen from the factory's window. Blue, purple, and red light flashed as the humans swung weapons at what was definitely another vampire. The humans crowded it farther and farther toward the veil. The undead woman a few feet from me let loose an agonized wail, as if she'd realized what was happening to her comrade.

I felt the edge of the veil behind me. It was only fifteen feet away, maybe ten. I needed to get farther away from it, but if I ran, the vamp would chase me—and I couldn't outrun her. Neither the sword nor the sorcerer were here to save me. If I kept my vamp occupied for long enough, maybe the pair battling near the obelisk could help me with my problem, too.

With a final great swing from a magic-crackling spear, one human drove the vampire back through the veil. The wall of magic rippled. Goose bumps sprung up on my arms when the humans turned toward me, their arms waving in the air. They weren't saying hello; they were trying to warn me.

A snarl sounded a second later. I whirled. A necrotic hand

thrust through the veil, long claws thrashing blindly. I'm not sure what came over me—maybe seeing the other humans successfully fighting off one of these things—but I sprinted toward it on aching legs. I knew the female vampire was giving chase now too, but if there was a horde of these things outside the veil, I needed this new one to know it wouldn't get an easy snack in here. Not tonight. This was my city, dammit, and if I wasn't willing to let the Collective take it away from me, I sure as hell wouldn't let feral vamps take it either.

When I reached the blindly writhing hand, I grabbed the handle of the mace with both hands and brought it down hard on those black claws. The crackle of magic that shot out of the mace's head smashed every bone in that disgusting hand and flung me backward, straight into the female vamp. We went down in a tangle of limbs, my backside landing with a thud on her chest. I scrambled to my feet a second before the vamp did, and I swung wildly. The mace clipped one of her blackened elbows, sending me backward again, but I stayed upright as the force of the blast rocketed me several feet, the heels of my boots scraping across the asphalt. I'd probably shredded a layer of rubber off the soles.

My chest heaved as I watched the vampire. I clutched the mace with both hands again, just in case I needed to whack her like her head was a baseball and I was going for a home run. She clutched her ruined arm to her chest, hissed, and then sprinted forward. I braced myself, not sure I could take a direct assault and live to tell the tale, but she gave me a wide berth and then bolted through the veil. The wall of magic rippled, like a rock thrown into a pond, and her muted, distant scream told me it hadn't felt good running through it. But at least she was gone.

When several seconds ticked by without another vamp trying to get through, I lowered my hands to my sides, my shoulders sagging. A little zap hit my calf, and I yanked the mace back up. Right. Super magically charged weapon needed to be kept away from all fleshy bits. The dampening hood was … somewhere. Hopefully near the duffel bag that I'd lost along the way.

The sound of footfalls sent my heart into my throat, but when I whirled around, two black-clad humans came my way, not more vamps. They were both women, one tall and one short. They had tan skin, tied-back dark hair, and appeared to be in their late twenties, like me. I guessed they were both Latina—possibly related. The logo on the breast pockets of their shirts told me who they were, even though I'd already guessed as much: members of the Vampire Hunters of America.

"You all right?" the taller one asked. "You were kicking ass and getting your ass kicked at the same time."

I laughed wearily. "Well, I'm alive, so I guess I'm doing okay. How many of them got through?"

"We knocked three of them back in," said the shorter lady. "A couple of our guys are about a mile up and knocked two in." She held out her hand to me. "I'm Marisol, and this is my cousin Daniella."

Realization kicked me in the gut a second later. I had a bounty on my head, and a $20,000 reward was up for grabs should someone offer information that led to my arrest. And here I was, wearing my natural face.

"Harlow, right?" Marisol asked, her hand still out.

These two ladies fought feral vamps regularly. A handshake could result in some kind of martial arts move that landed me on my back with the wind knocked from my lungs—again.

Marisol dropped her hand. "No need to worry about us. We don't exactly play by the Collective's rules, and we don't want their money. What you're doing out here is none of our business."

I stared at her for a beat, then held my hand out. Marisol grinned and shook it. "Is this kind of thing ... normal? Knocking ferals back through the veil, I mean?"

The taller one, Daniella, shrugged. "Pretty light night, actually."

Horrifying.

"Where'd you get that thing? Same place you got that sword

everyone is in a tizzy over?" Marisol asked. "Do you have any more?"

I stared down at the mace, deeply fond of the thing now that it had shattered the limbs of two feral vampires. "Collecting weapons is a hobby. This is the only electrified mace I've got, though."

"Bummer. I'd totally buy one of those from you."

"Where's that sword of yours, by the way?" Daniella asked, gazing this way and that.

"I'm honestly not sure. That thing does what it wants."

They assessed me for several long seconds. Marisol spoke first. "You're not nearly as terrifying as the Collective wants everyone to believe."

"And no offense, but you're a scrappy fighter—someone who's fueled by the instinct to survive, not by skill," Daniella said. "Even if the sword gives you heightened abilities, you don't fight like a hardened killer."

"That's because I'm not."

Marisol slipped a hand into her back pocket and pulled out a business card, handing it to me. The familiar logo took up the right-hand corner. "Your instincts are good, though. If you ever wanna join us for a patrol and bring that badass mace—or the sword—with you, we'd be happy for the help. Call the office line and drop my name. The hunters won't give you hell if they know I sent you."

Given how much my aches and pains were catching up with me after fighting off one vamp, volunteering to do it again sounded ludicrous, but I thanked her for the card all the same.

Daniella asked, "Where you headed? Need help? You're kind of a mess."

"To be fair, I was a mess before the vamp." Normally I'd wave off the offer, but the thought of having my back vulnerable to the veil and what might come creeping through made my stomach twist. "I'm trying to get to the rail yard to meet someone. Maybe you could just walk with me until I'm back on flat land?"

"You bet," Marisol said. "Not every day we get to escort an enemy of the state."

I smiled wryly.

We walked in silence for a minute before I cracked. I needed something to distract me from how much my body hurt. "Do you ever run into the werecats out here?"

Daniella said, "We haven't in a while. We've been out here every night for a couple of months now and hardly ever see the cats. I think they've accepted we're going to protect the veil from vamps, especially since their bosses don't care about the breaches."

"You think the Collective knows about the ferals?" I asked.

Marisol nodded. "No doubt. But between us and the cats, the ferals get taken care of so the Collective doesn't do anything more about it."

"But we're just treating the symptom, not the problem," Daniella said. "We can't get the Collective to care about it. We can't even get the Collective to agree to a meeting. They just sit in that monstrosity of a building of theirs, staring down their noses at us, and do nothing to help. This city is going to come crashing down around their ears and they'll act shocked when it happens even though we've been warning them for years."

"And what do you think the true problem is?" I asked, recalling the standoff I'd seen on the streets of downtown a few days ago. The Vampire Hunters of America were on one side of the street, their leader yelling into a megaphone, while their rivals sat on the other, playing looping videos meant to discredit the organization and present it as one populated by delusional loons. "A vampire uprising?"

"At the very least," Marisol said.

Well, that was unsettling.

A few minutes later, I came up short when the semi-familiar shape of a man materialized atop a small mound of broken bricks. Marisol and Daniella stopped too. One of them gasped softly. I was ninety-nine percent sure this was Welsh's useless sorcerer friend. I hadn't sensed his approach, but I'd also been focused on the ground, trying not to trip and knock out my teeth.

"Is *that* where you got your fancy weapon?" Marisol asked.

"No wonder you were vague," Daniella said.

What the hell were they going on about? Adrenaline was wearing off quickly, and walking was becoming too taxing, let alone skirting and stepping over the debris that littered my path. It was a miracle I hadn't brained myself on any of it.

"Looks like you're in good hands now," Marisol said, though the mysterious guy was still a way off. "Please consider joining us some night, okay? Especially when you're this well-connected."

Before I could ask what the hell they were talking about, the pair waved at the guy, then cut left, walking in a single-file line along a narrow path made beside the rows of stacked train cars.

Baffled, I resumed my trek forward, focused on finding my duffel bag. As I finally made it to the sorcerer and stepped past him, I muttered, "Thanks for nothing." I didn't care who he was friends with. I didn't care that Marisol and Daniella seemed to know who he was. After I found the sword, I'd get to my private telepost box to send Welsh a message. His friend was no friend of mine. Staying safe and clearing my name were my top priorities—getting turned into feral vamp food wasn't on the list.

The sorcerer fell into step beside me. I guessed he was around my age—late twenties or early thirties. Was that Welsh's age range too, then? Impossible to tell with that guy.

After a moment, the sorcerer said, "Welsh didn't tell me you had friends in the Vampire Hunters of America."

"I don't. But clearly, they're better allies than you are." I shot him a side-eye that I hoped conveyed that I'd happily smash the mace into his face if I'd still possessed the energy to swing my arm. "Why did you want the vamp in the rune circle?"

"Powerful sleep incantation," he said casually, as if we were old friends having a chat about the weather. "I wanted to bring her back to my lab to study."

I didn't ask any follow-up questions because I didn't care

about this either. The mace's hood lay on a pile of bricks. After wrapping up the murder spikes, I kept moving. The sorcerer and I remained silent the rest of the way back to where I'd lost my duffel bag. Dropping to my knees in front of it, I got the hooded mace zipped into the bag. I was about to say "Well, see you never!" when what looked like an elongated toolbox *thunk*ed to the ground. I gave a start, stared at the box, and then swung my gaze up to the sorcerer.

The toolbox jumped a fraction to the left, paused, then jumped again. I instinctively placed a hand on the box. The metal grew faintly warm under my palm. "I'm okay," I croaked, knowing my sword was inside. How in the hell had the sorcerer captured it?

Relief that it was safe overwhelmed me, and I flopped onto the sand on my butt. I wasn't sure I'd ever get up again. My head throbbed, my hip ached, and I felt like my body was covered in road rash. My chin itched, and when I swiped at it with the back of my hand, it came away with a streak of wet blood.

I swiveled my attention back to the pair of sorcerers. Whoops. One sorcerer. Back to two. Fuzzy vision probably wasn't a good sign. I swallowed down a wave of nausea. He solidified back into one average-looking guy. "Who are you, anyway?"

"Caspian Blackthorn."

I let out a semi-hysterical laugh. "Of course you are."

And then I passed out.

CHAPTER TWENTY-THREE

I awoke on a couch, and for a moment, I thought I was back in my apartment. Reality kicked me in the teeth a second later: I no longer had an apartment. Everything I owned could fill two bags. The view I had of the ceiling here wasn't the familiar ceiling of Mathias's place, either.

Groaning, I pushed myself up, wincing as I scooted back to rest against the cushions. I lay on the long arm of a sectional couch that ringed an oval-shaped glass coffee table, under which lay a fluffy white rug. The more consciousness took over, the more unease settled in my gut. Where was I?

My chin itched, and I swiped the back of my hand under it, finding my wrists and the lower half of my palms wrapped in stark white bandages. I probed my chin with my unbound fingers and my skin met the soft material of a Band-Aid. I took stock of the rest of my person. My tumble-and-drag across the ground by the feral vampire had ripped one knee of my jeans. Even though someone had patched me up, I still felt sore down to my bones.

Then I remembered something else. The sorcerer sent to help me at the behest of Welsh was Caspian-flipping-Blackthorn. The supervillain himself.

I gave the living room a more thorough appraisal, noting the closed vertical blinds to my left, the large flat-screen mounted on the wall above the fireplace in front of me, and though my neck ached, I turned to the right to take in the open kitchen.

Scooting back a little further against the cushions, I called out, "Hello?" I sounded like an old lady who had smoked too many cigarettes.

Behind me to the right, and just beyond the kitchen, was an open doorway that led to a hallway. To the left of the kitchen stretched a tile-lined walkway that led to what looked like another sitting room, as well as the front door. When a figure appeared, however, it was in the doorway beside the fireplace.

Caspian Blackthorn.

Lightning didn't strike, nor did thunder boom when he entered the room. In my head, he had been crazy hot—like something out of those network TV dramas where teenagers are played by abnormally attractive people in their thirties—and stalked around his mansion while his leather cape flapped behind him. The reality was much blander.

Short dark hair, hazel eyes, average build and height. Sorcerers weren't known for being flashy and dramatic; they were practical and sticklers for detail. The kind of people who could calmly pull off a years-long con without getting antsy. Becoming a full-fledged sorcerer required so much schooling that only the truly even-keeled, disciplined, and unflinchingly focused saw it through until the end. This was even truer of full-blooded humans who dedicated themselves to learning the discipline, as opposed to those who had been born with an innate proclivity toward wielding magic.

I'd called this supervillain useless—to his face—before I'd known who he was. He'd put in little effort to help me against the feral vamp, yet he'd subdued the sword when multiple members of the highly trained werecat guard hadn't come anywhere close.

He stepped into the room and stopped on the other side of the coffee table, tucking his hands behind his back. "I haven't given you any healing tonics yet. I wanted to examine your injuries, as well as let you get some natural sleep before I gave you anything." His voice was even and matter-of-fact. "How are you feeling?"

I tried to imagine him teaching one of the introductory sorcery classes. Maybe that was how Marisol and Daniella knew who he was—they'd attended one of the rare ones taught by the rogue himself.

"I feel like I've been dragged by my ankle for nearly a mile by a feral vampire," I said.

He cracked the faintest of smiles. "Before we get into everything and figure out a healing regimen for you, would you like to take a shower? When I was tending to your visible wounds, I detected an ... aroma."

Heat flooded my cheeks. I hadn't showered in three days, and had just been pulled across sand, gravel, and dirt. When I stood from his pristine leather couch, there'd likely be an outline of filth marking where my body had been.

"*Please.*"

The hint of the smile returned. "It's through here," he said, and angled his head toward the doorway closest to him. "There are towels and a change of clothes. I only have men's clothing; you're on your own for undergarments. If you leave your soiled clothes outside the bathroom door, I would be happy to launder them for you."

I stared blankly at him. *This* was the supervillain? The neutral-evil friend of Zander Welsh?

I would figure the guy out later. For now, I needed to shower.

Once I was off the couch, I followed Caspian into a small den, and then made an immediate right into a spacious bathroom. He stepped to the side and gestured for me to enter. A large shower took up one side of the room, and a freestanding tub sat on the opposite side if I wanted to indulge. A pile of fluffy beige towels waited on the white marble counter, the surface shot through with swirling veins of brown, black, and gray. My dirty, beaten-up backpack and duffel bag slouched against each other on the floor like the exhausted travelers they were.

With my dusty black boots positioned in the middle of a fluffy white bath mat, I turned to Caspian, who stood placidly in the doorway. "My sword?"

"It's in its case. I imagine it will be furious when it's released. I wanted you to be in peak condition before we do that."

I had so many questions.

"Take as long as you like," Caspian said, then reached into the bathroom to pull the door closed.

I plopped down on the closed toilet lid and untied my boots. What seemed like a pound of sand poured out of them when I wrenched them off my sweaty feet. Wincing, I hoped he had runes that would magic away the destruction I was about to unleash in here. I wasted no time stripping out of my disgusting clothes. I rooted around in my backpack and pulled free my other dirty clothes—including the skinny jeans that had crusted mayonnaise on the hems. Balling up all the offensive items, I discreetly tossed them out the door, hoping Caspian wasn't a perv waiting out there to catch a glimpse. He wasn't. Of course, he could plan to magic his way through a wall once I was all sudsed up with nowhere to go.

I peeled off the gauze wrapped around my wrists, but left the Band-Aid on my chin. Small scratches marred the heels of my palms, the spots shiny with an ointment Caspian had implemented. I decided in that moment that if Caspian *was* a perv, I didn't care. I let myself into the glass-walled shower, turning the water to scalding. The shower was mercifully stocked with both shampoo *and* conditioner and not that 2-in-1 nonsense Felix always used. I froze, water beating my shoulders and the top of my head. I'd forgotten to text him that I'd left. How long had I been passed out on Caspian's couch? How long had it taken to get here?

Sighing, I vowed to worry about that later.

After shampooing my hair twice, I used nearly half the bottle of conditioner and finger-combed the knots out of my curls. My scalp felt raw by the time I finished, but my hair fell around my shoulders in healthy spirals again. I'd keep it braided or in a bun until I got my hands on some decent product, but at least it was clean now.

As I scrubbed my body with a bar of soap, I cataloged my cuts and bruises to report to Caspian. I wondered if sorcerers dabbled in potion work. If he had a healing tonic that worked even half as well as Geraldine's burnt-cherry-tasting one, I'd happily take it.

In addition to the fluffy towels, Caspian had laid out a T-shirt and a pair of basketball shorts for me. His pajamas, maybe. They smelled clean, so I put them on over a pair of underwear and a bra I'd been wise enough to store in their own zippered bag. That was a trick I'd learned from Mom. *Always keep the underwear fresh*, she'd say. *You can figure out the rest later.*

This advice had come after she and Dad had been chasing an earth elemental bounty who, to escape, had opened a muddy hole beneath my parents. Even though bounty hunters rarely went after witches— especially hot-headed elementals—they'd been assigned this case because the guy's powers only extended as far as making giant mud puddles when he was upset. His threat level was low. Mom had plunged in to her neck before she'd realized what had happened. Dad had leaped over the puddle and tackled the elemental. Later, when they'd returned to headquarters, Mom covered nearly head to toe in mud, she'd taken a shower at the facility, washing mud out of places where mud shouldn't have been. Her pack had gone into the mud with her, too, but her clothes had been in air-sealed bags. Pulling on clean underwear after a night like that, she said, had been like wrapping a warm blanket around her shoulders on a cold night.

I fought down the lump in my throat as I finished dressing. The glamoured hair tie I'd taken from Welsh fixed my damp hair into a perfect French braid in seconds. I tried not to think about Mom too often. Losing Dad had been hard, of course, but I knew where he was—six feet under in a graveyard specifically for bounty hunters killed on the job. Dad hadn't left me on purpose. Mom had made a choice, and that choice hadn't been me.

I rooted around in the backpack for the cell phone. I had three missed calls and two messages from Felix. According to the time in the screen's corner, it was almost noon. I'd been out of commission for nearly twelve hours.

He'd called at midnight last night and seven forty-five this morning.

At eight, he'd texted with:

> Are you awake? I'm heading your way now. How do you feel about donuts and coffee?

At nine-fifteen, he'd sent:

> At least let me know if you're ok.

Another call had come in at ten-thirty.
Shit.
I fired off a quick text.

> Ran into some vamp trouble, but okay. Honestly not sure where I am. Will give you details later if I can. Can't talk now.

It took him ten minutes to reply with a simple OK.

Knowing Felix, he had uttered several variations of *"What the hell, Harlow? What kind of vamp trouble!"* to himself, realized we were a long way from owing each other details about anything, and had settled on the most neutral answer he could muster.

Collecting my things, I pulled open the bathroom door, a billow of steam wafting out first. My pile of dirty clothes was gone. "Caspian? What should I do with the towels?"

No answer.

I stared guiltily over my shoulder at the pair of soiled towels heaped on the floor next to the small mound of boot sand. A pair of male voices sounded from the living-room-slash-kitchen area, and I crept out to see who had joined us in Caspian's house. An unfamiliar man stood at the large kitchen island, manning the electric stovetop. On the counter beside him was a tub of butter, a bag of bread, and a packet of cheese slices. He slathered butter on two slices of bread and then dropped them onto a hot pan, issuing a satisfying sizzle.

When he realized I stood there, he looked up and grinned. "Grilled cheese sandwich?"

Two high-backed chairs were positioned in front of the island, one of which was occupied by Caspian. My gaze flicked between the man and the back of Caspian's head.

"Uh ... sure?" I said.

The mystery man's appearance changed in a blink of an eye into the boy band hottie.

My shoulders sagged. "Oh. Hi, Welsh."

"Nice to see you, too," he said with just as much enthusiasm.

Caspian turned in his seat and gave me an elevator scan. "Feel better?"

"You have no idea."

"Good," he said, then patted the seat beside him.

I deposited my bags on the ground and climbed into the chair. I propped my bare feet on the bottom rung. The silence lasted for all of five seconds, save for the sizzling bread in the pan, before I turned in my seat to address the side of Caspian's head. "Why is the Collective after you? I mean, aside from the Frankenweapon thing where your creations keep killing humans ..."

He cocked a brow, then swung his attention to Welsh, who currently only had eyes for his grilled cheese sandwich.

"Told you that's what the unwashed masses think," Welsh said, expertly flipping each slice of bread with a practiced flick of his wrist.

"Rude," I said. "Also, I'm no longer unwashed."

Welsh pointed his spatula at me and flashed his one-dimpled grin.

"All those ... Frankenweapons, as you call them," Caspian said, addressing me now, "were weapons I made while under contract with the Collective *for* the Collective."

I blinked. "Wait, what?"

"I've held high-level auctions and private sales in Luma for years. At first, it was items like the ones you've made a career of finding and re-homing. After a while, I got curious about creating my own—nothing over Level 3, though. My wares drew the attention of the Collective, but not for the reason I expected. They told me they would allow me to keep doing what I was doing, with no restrictions, if I also worked for them. They gave me the specs of what they wanted, provided the materials I needed—no matter what I asked for—and paid me a lot of money to do it."

"Weapons with higher than Level 3 magic, then?" I asked, but already knew the answer.

"Oh yeah," he said. "We're talking Level 7 and 8—magic that tipped the scales. They paid me to craft weapons that gave off so much magic, it made *my* teeth rattle. It was clear they were preparing for something. I kept telling myself that it was all part of some top-secret military Collective project. Something they were doing to better protect the city. But then full-blooded humans who had no business being anywhere near this stuff began dying in truly horrible ways. When I confronted them, they started a low-grade smear campaign to convince people I made the weapons for fun, selling them directly to humans just to see what would happen. They sent their minions out into the city to ruin my name."

I winced slightly, since I'd believed all those rumors. I tried so hard not to be manipulated by the curated messages coming out of the Collective, but if they had spies scattered among the population planting little untruths in unsuspecting people's minds ...

"There's a bounty out for you because you refused to work for them anymore?" I asked.

Caspian's head tottered back and forth. "Yes and no. My contract with them ended a year ago and when I met with them to renew the contract, I instead said that I wanted out. They tried to get me to sign a Soul NDA, but I refused. We parted ways with the promise that we'd keep each other's secrets and leave each other alone—both of us knowing that their ability to destroy me far outweighed my chances of destroying them. I knew it was too easy, though ... the way they let me go without a fuss."

Welsh chimed in. "They wanted to end things on good terms, keep the door open in case they needed your services again."

Caspian nodded. "This cutlass has them spooked. My guess is, they're hoping it's one of mine. If it's mine, they can track down all the other weapons they hope I have—after injecting me with their truth serum, that is. But if it's not ..."

I glanced around the room, searching for any sign of the toolbox containing my sword. Caspian referred to it as a cutlass—a more accurate name for it than the generic "sword." How very sorcerer of him. My attention refocused when a plate topped with a perfectly browned grilled cheese sandwich slid in front of me.

"Your cutlass is safe," Caspian said, just as his sandwich was placed in front of him. "Eat."

My stomach rumbled at the scents of toasty bread and melted cheese and I took a healthy bite, realizing how hungry I was. I cleaned my plate in record time.

"What's your grand plan?" I asked, wiping my greasy fingers on a napkin. "You said yourself that ruining the Collective won't be as easy as them ruining you."

"You and that cutlass are my grand plan," Caspian said.

I cocked my head. "A magic-less human and a sword with no impulse control? *We're* your plan?"

"We're going to find out where that thing came from," Caspian said. "The Collective, in its heart of hearts, knows it isn't one of mine. They just need me crossed off their list before they move on to their next possibility. I'm certain they already know what that possibility is, but they're keeping it close to the vest so they don't show their hand. While they're running around looking for me, you and I are going to unearth whatever their secrets are."

My own desires, the ones I'd voiced to Felix just last night, lined up with those of a supervillain. As I watched him carefully chew his grilled cheese sandwich, the label lost some of its adhesive.

I eyed Welsh. "And what about you? You just in it for the chance to upset the ruling party in Luma?"

"Pretty much. Curiosity is a powerful motivator for me, too. I get bored easily."

Maybe that was why he changed his appearance so often. Not to protect the secrecy of his true form, but to keep things fresh. Every time he walked out the door with a new face, he had a completely different experience than the day before it.

"I'll get your cutlass," Caspian said once he finished eating.

By the time he'd returned, I was on my feet. The sword bucked and flailed, if the thwacks and twangs issuing from inside the toolbox were any indication. Caspian placed the box on the opposite end of the island where we'd been eating. Welsh put the sandwich supplies away.

"You're not going to eat?" I asked Welsh.

"He had four of them while you were in the shower," Caspian said. "Glamourers burn up a lot of calories. It's also why he's always grouchy. He gets very irritable when his blood sugar drops. Why do you think one of his offices is in the back of one of the best burger joints in Luma?"

"Al's was a good find," Welsh agreed, shutting the fridge. "Second only to Pie in the Sky."

"R.I.P.," Caspian said solemnly.

At my curious expression, Welsh said, "I had a back room in a pizza place downtown a couple of years ago. A disgruntled orc who'd been fired for stealing pies on a daily basis came back one night and smashed the interior to pieces with a war hammer. Every time they tried to rebuild, the orc came back to destroy it."

"What hub did you get the owners set up in again?" Caspian asked.

"One in Michigan," Welsh said, a distant look in his eye.

"Those lucky Michigander bastards."

Welsh grunted in agreement.

These two were even closer friends than I thought. For guys who seemed to thrive on their anonymity, they seemed to know a lot about each other. How had *this* friendship started?

I cupped a hand around my mouth so Welsh couldn't read my lips when I asked Caspian, "Do you know what his true form is?"

"Not sure," Caspian said. "I always seem to know it's him, though. When you get to know someone well enough, you recognize things unique to them. Those things sneak in no matter what glamour he wears. I always recognize that part of him, even if my eyes don't."

There was something decidedly Welsh about Welsh, I'd give Caspian that much. And hadn't some deep instinctual part of me recognized Felix, even when he'd been nothing more than a dark shape in the factory? The way he moved, the timbre of his voice—things I knew deep in my bones even if my eyes hadn't had confirmation yet.

Perhaps they were more than friends. Welsh stood opposite us, on the other side of the counter. Glancing first at Caspian, and then at Welsh, I asked, "Have you two been … together long?"

For a split, horrifying second, Welsh's appearance flipped back to the zombie lord covered in sores. I shrieked, clapping a hand over my chest.

Caspian laughed—the first true sign I'd seen that he had a personality under all that composure. "Lucky you. He's already found a glamour to scare the piss out of you when you annoy him."

"To answer your question," Welsh said, back to his pretty-boy persona, "we're friends. Men are allowed to have a close bond and care about each other without it being romantic. Women can be sister-level close without anyone making assumptions—why can't that be true of men, too?"

Shrugging, I said, "Fair enough." Turning to Caspian beside

me, I asked. "How'd you even capture the sword? Everyone else who tried got stabbed."

Caspian produced a small white pouch from his pocket and handed it to me. It looked like one of Welsh's magic hair pouches. Maybe they put in a bulk order of the things and split the cost. I imagined one of the many bedrooms in this place filled with wall-to-wall boxes of little fabric pouches. I pulled open the cinched-closed top and peered in. What looked like metal shavings mixed with glitter lay in the bottom.

"That's a silver and iron alloy powder," Caspian said.

"The metal used in dragon hunting," I said.

"Right. When you and the cutlass headed for the rail yard lot, I was actually behind you." Caspian's lips started to move rapidly, though no sound came out, and his hands flitted through the air as if he'd just been possessed with the desire to conduct an invisible orchestra. But it was a spell he was conducting, his fingers quickly etching runes in the air.

A few seconds later, Caspian popped out of view.

"Whoa …"

I reached out and patted the air where he'd been. Even freakier than seeing him disappear from view was that when my hand landed on the hard curve of a shoulder, my *hand* disappeared.

"What the …"

I yanked my hand back toward myself, and back into existence. Brow furrowed, I touched his shoulder again, then slowly pulled my hand away. It was like I had dunked my hand into camouflaging paint, and as I drew my hand away, the "paint" rolled off my solidly brown skin.

"It's a kind of glamour," Welsh said. "He's glamouring himself to blend into his surroundings, rather than making himself invisible. The camouflage glamour is a much easier spell, and as long as too many people aren't around to lay eyes on him, it will hold for a lot longer than an invisibility spell."

Caspian reappeared. "The spell is low-level enough that a full-blooded human wouldn't be able to detect it, but I knew the cutlass would. When it flew back toward the factory to investigate, I sent a cloud of the alloy powder at it."

The sword *thunk*ed loudly inside the box. My stomach twinged at the idea of it being hurt.

"What happened when the cloud hit it?" I asked.

"The hilt went black and the whole thing dropped to the ground like a stone. I used way more than I needed, but I wasn't in the mood for getting impaled. There's a layer of the alloy powder in a false bottom of the box—enough to weaken the cutlass's magic to keep it from breaking free, but not enough to incapacitate it completely."

"And you think letting it out in your kitchen is a good idea?" I asked.

Caspian shrugged. "Those runes on the blade could be the key to figuring out where it came from. I need a close-up look. The pictures Welsh took aren't clear enough."

"It's your funeral …" I sighed. "I'll do what I can to talk it down, but when my friend only lightly insulted it, it slashed up her apartment. I don't even think it'll be most pissed about *me* being in danger, but that you dared to capture it. When I say this thing has a mind of its own, that's not an expression."

Caspian nodded with the calm poise of a sorcerer, but he also gently took the pouch of alloy powder from me and then several steps back. Welsh hurried across the kitchen and ducked into the front entry hall, peeking around the corner at us.

"Chicken," Caspian muttered.

Welsh's head was suddenly covered with a rubber chicken mask. He gave his arms a flap for good measure.

Squaring my shoulders, I stood in front of the toolbox and flipped open the latch. Instead of lifting the lid all the way, I leaned close to the top seam and put my mouth near it. "Sword. It's me. I know you're mad, but these two people are here to help us, okay? Remember my no murder rule? No maiming these guys either. I promise I'm okay. Understood?"

It took a few seconds, but I got a single tap from inside the box as a reply.

I glanced over my shoulder at Caspian to make sure he was ready, and watched as he dumped a handful of the alloy powder into his hand.

Swallowing, I lifted the lid.

CHAPTER TWENTY-FOUR

Before I'd gotten the lid on the toolbox all the way open, the sword shot out with such force, I stumbled back into Caspian. The sword darted around the ceiling of the kitchen and living room in frantic circles, like an agitated trapped bird.

"Hey! Calm down!" I said, head tipped back and hands out.

The sword stilled in the air and then zipped toward me. It came to a quick halt in the inverted pose, the curve of its blade level with my nose. Caspian stumbled away from us. Then the blade glowed a bright blue—brighter than I'd ever seen it—and spun around me in dizzying circles. I held stock-still.

After a moment, the sword flew a few feet away from me, where the air shimmered. My form materialized, wearing the same outfit from the viral news clip. Maybe the sword could only work with the information it had been given the last time I'd touched the hilt. That or it preferred that version of me over my current one, dressed in Caspian's pajamas. My apocalyptic self stared at me intently, then jabbed a finger in my direction before mouthing, "Oh-kay?"

I smiled softly. "Yes, I'm okay."

The image of me dissolved as the sword glowed blue once

more and spun around me in another excited series of circles. Huh. The sword had an excited puppy mode.

I laughed, unable to help myself. "I missed you too." After stopping before me again, I asked, "Do you promise not to hurt either of them? Caspian Blackthorn is the one behind me, and Zander Welsh is cowering in the hallway. You met Welsh already, but he wore a different glamour then."

The sword's tip swiveled toward each man in turn, and then it floated to the counter and tapped the butt of its hilt on the counter once.

"All right, you guys are safe."

Caspian came up behind me. "I apologize for the drastic measures, cutlass, but I assure you it was solely because I was concerned about Harlow's safety and yours."

"About that," I said, turning to face Caspian. I leaned against the counter and crossed my arms. The sword hovered near my shoulder in the inverted position. "Why did you want to capture the vamp? That wasn't an impulsive request. You needed time to draw that rune circle—was it there before or after you sent in your falcon?"

I wondered where that giant bird was now.

"Before." Caspian carefully dumped his handful of alloy powder into the pouch and put said pouch into his pocket before he elaborated. "Because the ferals are in a state that's somewhere between human and animal—but too warped to be either—they're able to withstand crossing the veil. Mundane animals can pass through, though most instinctively avoid the veil's magic."

"I recently helped a witch couple get out of Luma," Welsh said, coming to stand beside Caspian. His rubber chicken mask was gone. "They had been out to a late dinner with friends uptown and were ambushed a few blocks away from a telepad station. The wall-to-wall black eyes gave their attacker away as a vampire, but he also had long black claws and translucent skin. The witches used what magic they could, but it was quick enough on its feet to dodge any defensive spell they threw at it. The vamp knocked the man to the ground and ran off with him. Before the woman could call out for help, werecat guards came out of nowhere and attacked the vamp. Once the witch had been freed, the werecats chased the vamp away."

"Was it a case of right time, right place for those guards, or had they known a feral vamp was in the city?" I asked, thinking out loud. "And in uptown, of all places …"

It was like hearing rabid grizzly bears were running down the streets of Beverly Hills.

Welsh nodded. "My question exactly. The witches said they needed out because Luma had grown too unsafe, that they 'couldn't take much more of this'—which makes me think that attack was the last straw rather than it being their first time dealing with dangerous circumstances here."

"Welsh has heard a few stories like that over the last year and we started staking out a few spots on the veil's edge rumored to have high feral activity. The rail yard is one of them—we're guessing because of its proximity to Tercla," Caspian said. "The Vampire Hunters of America, as you saw, are out there a lot, knocking the ferals back like they're playing a game of whack-a-mole."

"How long have the ferals been slipping through?" I asked. "Marisol and Daniella said five in a night wasn't uncommon. Even one is way too many if you ask me."

"It started getting bad about eight or nine months ago," Caspian said. "Not long after the infamous auction where your friend came from." He jutted his chin at the sword. "I set up containment rune circles out there often—like a rabbit trap. If the trap gets sprung, I'd feel it. But I've been leaving those circles out there for months, never catching one. The last two had been crossed out with a very deliberate X drawn in the sand. The vampires might be too much like wild animals now, but they're highly intelligent wild animals. I hoped if I caught one, I could figure out what makes them tick. Blood composition, brain activity, reaction to stimuli—that kind of thing. Since the vamp was very interested in you, I used you as bait. Of all the times I've been out there, I've yet to find anything to entice one."

I frowned, shaking off the feeling of phantom, necrotic fingers wrapped around my ankle.

"I think she left you alone while you were in the factory because of the cutlass. I didn't realize that until later. Once the cutlass was no longer on you, you were just another tasty human snack far away from anyone who could save you. That mace you used to bash her elbow to bits likely would have kept her away, too, had it not been dampened by the hood when she grabbed you initially."

I cocked a brow, considering most of what he'd described had happened after the vamp had dragged me away from him. "And how did you figure all that out?"

Caspian shrugged. "Observation."

"And he snooped in your bags while you were sleeping," Welsh added.

Caspian jabbed a thumb in his direction. "And that."

I didn't even have the energy to be mad about it. And we'd gotten off course. "You said you need to see the runes on the sword up close?"

Caspian nodded. "I'll be right back." He strolled through the open doorway behind the couch and disappeared to the left. He returned a minute later with a black sketchbook and a pen. Sitting in the same chair he'd sat in earlier, he pushed his plate aside and laid out the book. He flipped to an open page and then cast a glance at me. "Ready when you are."

Without me needing to say anything, the sword floated in front of Caspian, then went molten. The runes appeared along the curved edge of the blade's inner seam. Caspian's mouth dropped open, pure appreciation shining in his eyes even brighter than the sword itself. His pen worked quickly across the page, drawing without taking his focus off the glowing runes.

A good twenty minutes passed before Caspian spoke again.

Welsh and I had played a heated game of Go Fish while we waited.

"Thank you, cutlass. I have what I need."

The sword floated back to my side.

Welsh shoved our half-finished game out of the way and rested his arms on the counter. "What are we dealing with here?"

"This is very curious," Caspian muttered, idly tapping his capped pen on the page of sketched runes. "These are all battle runes, which makes sense, since swords are meant for that. None of them are particularly surprising—speed, agility, perception. But they're meant to bestow these attributes on the *wielder* of the cutlass."

He climbed off the chair and ducked into the den-like room beside the bathroom I'd showered in. The brief glimpse I'd gotten of the room boasted nothing but a cleared-off desk. A muted thud sounded, and a moment later, Caspian was back, a leather-bound tome in his hands. He flipped the pages as he walked.

"When I had to flee my house, I packed a few essential books," he said as he returned to his seat. "I only had a few minutes, so I grabbed half a dozen."

"You had a few minutes' notice and 'very heavy books' made it to the top of your emergency supply list?" I asked.

"He's a nerd," Welsh said.

To Welsh, I said, "You said my nerd tendencies were as bad as sexually transmitted diseases."

"Oh, they are. Both of you disgust me."

Since Caspian didn't acknowledge the slight, I didn't either. "Okay, you see here?" he said, tapping on a page with "Cerulean Clan" written at the top in looping cursive. "The dragons' word for their clan was complicated enough that Earthlings had to refer to the clans by their dominant scale color instead."

I remembered what Jo had said about the schooling sorcerers received, and how it included deep dives into the ancient beasts that had only graced Earth for a short time after the Glitch.

I sidled up on one side of Caspian, while Welsh rounded the

counter and took up the other spot. A detailed drawing of a blue —*cerulean*—dragon filled most of the page. I wasn't sure what kind of magic had been used to ink the gorgeous rendering—a spell or the natural magic of an artist—but the scales on the beast seemed to glow with the same iridescence as the sword's hilt. The sword hovered on my other side.

"The dragon scales on the cutlass, if I'm not mistaken, came from a dragon of this clan—a powerful leading family on the fae home world."

The sword hummed.

"It says you're right," I translated.

"Excellent. My knowledge of dragon lore is rusty, but according to this, they were fair rulers, though they exacted swift punishment when necessary. Strong personalities with strong moral compasses. The power of those scales matched with these specific runes gave the cutlass sentience, as well as giving it these specific attributes, as opposed to giving those powers to the one who held the cutlass."

The sword glowed blue in my peripheral vision. It liked this information.

I mulled all this over. "Does any of this explain why it's able to take on my form? Is that solely because of the imprint?"

"It *has* imprinted on you then?" Caspian asked, sitting up a little straighter so he could look over my head and acknowledge the sword directly.

The sword hummed.

"Yep," I echoed.

Caspian returned his focus to the books on the counter. "The creator of the cutlass truly didn't know what they were making. I believe when you made physical contact with the cutlass, the imprint and the perception runes allowed the cutlass to not only share a bond with you, but transfer information."

"What, like telepathy?" I asked.

"More like osmosis. The intention of the perception runes is to give the wielder of the cutlass a heightened ability to sense things about their enemies during battle. Being able to intuit what direction the enemy will move next during a fight, for example. The magic in the cutlass is supposed to flow *into* the one holding it."

"But since the runes gave all those abilities to the sword itself," I said, catching on, "information from the wielder of the sword flows the other way—giving the *sword* details about its possible enemies."

The sword glowed a bright blue and hummed.

"Correct," Caspian confirmed.

An odd thought occurred to me, and I turned to the sword. "Did the caracal—Oliver Randal—ever come in physical contact with you? Before you murdered him, I mean ..."

It zipped to the counter and knocked its hilt on the counter once.

I blinked. "When?" Then I shook my head. Only yes or no questions.

Welsh chimed in for the first time in a while. "At the auction."

Tap.

Admittedly, I knew very little about Randal, but a black-market auction where all the items cost hundreds of thousands of dollars didn't seem like the right scene for a guy who was a regular at the Ghost Lily. It wasn't the right scene for me either, but I'd been to a handful of auctions on my clients' dimes. The Ghost Lily was a nice enough bar, but it was also a rough bar. Ghost Lily patrons and black-tie attendees of the auctions were on opposite ends of the socioeconomic spectrum. Maybe Randal had lived dual lives. He was a renowned fashion icon while also harboring an addiction to Bliss and young pretty girls, after all.

"Did Randal attend as a buyer?" I ventured.

Tap-tap.

No? Why else would Randal have been there?

I cycled through what little else I knew about Randal. He had a clothing line and was a model and dancer. "A performer?"

Tap.

Caspian hmmed. "Interesting. My auctions are more straightforward. I prefer non-flashy silent auctions. Only serious buyers attend. Anyone who wins a bid on an item and doesn't pay within twenty-four hours is banned from attending another one. I require black-tie and don't allow alcohol."

"In other words," I said, "yours are for the boring high rollers."

Laughing, Welsh said, "Exactly. The ones run by others are a show as much as they are about making sales."

That sounded exactly like the one I'd attended with Kayda a year ago. "Did Randal display you to the crowd?" I asked the sword.

Tap.

Caspian hmmed again. "Something the cutlass sensed from that contact allowed it to pick up information about Randal and deemed him an enemy."

Tap.

I said, "And you were able to track him down because of what the runes showed you?"

Tap.

Welsh gusted a sigh. "Too bad Randal is dead. It would be a lot easier to interrogate him if he wasn't."

"I wouldn't shed too many tears for the guy." I relayed to them what Felix had told me about Randal—that he lured young, impressionable fae girls into his private room at the Ghost Lily, convinced them either through beautifully crafted lies or inhibition-numbing drugs to sleep with him, and then dropped them once he'd gotten what he wanted.

Both men wore identical frowns.

"I take that back," Welsh said. "Good riddance."

After a moment of silence, I voiced the thing that had been weighing on me ever since the Collective had put out the bounty for me. "So … uhh … I know neither of you owes me anything. But I—"

Caspian held up a hand to quiet me and I snapped my mouth shut. "If we didn't want to help you, you wouldn't be here."

I eyed Welsh.

He shrugged. "Yeah. You're growing on me even if you're not an Ameliorate."

Caspian chuckled. "You're such a snob."

I said, "Okay. Well … I know your priority is government upheaval and general anarchy, but if I'm going to have any chance of not living the rest of my life like a fugitive, I need to clear my name. I'm obviously not turning the sword over to the Collective. But there's something sketchy happening at the Ghost Lily. Randal was caught up in some kind of fae trafficking scheme. He was killed there, but his body was left somewhere else, and then *I* was framed for the murder. Someone is working very hard to both cover up what happened to Randal, and to take me down. Two birds, one stone. If I can find proof of what Randal was up to, and who glamoured themself to look like me, it might be enough to shift the focus."

"And," Welsh added, "if this person glamoured themself to look like you, why couldn't we argue that the sword had been part of the glamour, too? After all, whoever supposedly saw you stalking out from behind the building didn't have *this* sword, right? It was in Mathias's apartment with you by then. You're both being framed in a way."

I thought about the attacks I'd seen the sword conduct on the werecats. Its kills had been quick and efficient. Yet, in the report from the witness, the destruction to Randal's body had been brutal enough that the witness had lost her dinner in the bushes. I hadn't thought much about that part of the story before. I figured the sword hadn't wasted precious seconds with time-consuming slicing and dicing with the werecat guards because we'd been under a time crunch. But with the caracal, the sword might have taken its time with the kill, since it had happened in a remote location. But now I questioned my previous thinking.

"Hey, sword? Did you *maim* Randal?"

The blade burned red. Tap-tap.

"One clean stab to the gut?"

Tap.

Had whoever moved the caracal's body been the one who went overkill on him?

"There might be two murder weapons," I said to the guys. "If we can find the second one, we could get Randal's murder blamed fully on someone else."

Welsh tapped his nose and pointed at me. "I like it."

I had no idea how to go about any of this, though. Whoever had done that to Randal was a magic wielder—a witch like Welsh, or possibly a sorcerer. It was also possible that *that* murder weapon had been incinerated by now. Magical beings could get rid of evidence a lot more efficiently than humans could.

Caspian suddenly turned in his chair and draped an arm over the back of it. I instinctively took a step back as he scrutinized me. He started at the tips of my bare toes and slowly traveled up to my arched brows. My cheeks heated. Finally, he spoke. "How do you feel about an undercover mission?"

Welsh, standing behind Caspian now, grinned and rubbed his hands together. "Ooh! I like the sound of this!"

"I'm not sure I do," I said.

"As you said, something is off at the Ghost Lily. Where did the girls like Nyla Stone disappear to? Was Randal killing some of them?" Caspian asked, though he seemed to be talking to himself more than to me or Welsh. "Or did Randal shuttle some of those girls out of the bar? He was either just a creep who took advantage of impressionable young girls, or he was working for someone—maybe whoever was keeping him in constant supply of Bliss."

I pursed my lips.

"We're going to glamour you and Welsh to look like the prettiest fae the patrons of the Ghost Lily have ever seen," Caspian said, "and you're going to do reconnaissance."

In a matter of seconds, Welsh had morphed into a willowy fae with pointed ears and large, angelic doe eyes. She looked a bit like the doctor who had healed me at the clinic. Welsh sauntered toward me and batted her long lashes. In a sultry purr, she said, "We're going to have so much fun."

I sighed. "I'm not sure anymore if you're neutral or good, but you're definitely chaotic."

Welsh grinned.

CHAPTER TWENTY-FIVE

Four days later, I was fully healed thanks to a series of tonics and salves the guys had whipped up for me. We also had a plan in place. Since Caspian and I were both fugitives, we had been stuck in his house during the entire planning phase. His *second* house, I should say. His mega-mansion in uptown Luma had been his main home base, but after the bounty hunters raided it, he'd brought us to this little cabin that I'd since learned was tucked away behind an abandoned orange orchard—which he also owned—in the western corner of the Necropolis neighborhood. I hadn't been off the property other than to stand on the back porch and stare out at the scrubby, barren landscape. The cabin was layered in the same heavy-duty cloaking spells that had kept Caspian off everyone's radar for so long. The Collective had broken through some of his cloaking spells before, so he knew they could do it again eventually.

I'd also learned that Caspian was wealthier than God because of, as he put it, "Smart investments, day trading, and a few purchases of business shares in a fae light mega-company that recently bought out another one." No extortion, no grand larceny, no hefty blackmail payments. Nothing about this guy lined up with the image I'd had of him in my head.

Welsh, being the non-fugitive in the group, came and went, bringing with him news from the outside. And, even better, I'd somehow convinced him to buy me a few essentials: hair products. I assumed he'd been horrified the whole time, as if he'd been tasked with purchasing tampons. An Ameliorate degrading himself by buying curl creams and oils for a human puny of mind and spirit? Perish the thought!

But I had styling milk now. I could face anything.

He sent a telepost letter to Kayda for me as well, set to disintegrate five minutes after arrival. I'd written a short and sweet note letting her know I was okay.

Hi, Kay. I'm safe with a new pretty friend. Miss you.

Welsh took the note with him to a telepost station, copied the message onto telepost paper, and sent it to her a few minutes before she left for work. I hoped the timing had been right and that it would lessen some of her worries. I couldn't risk calling her. An in-person meeting, no matter how brief, and no matter how good the disguise, was out of the question.

Caspian made for a good roommate, if a quiet one. He spent most of his time poring over his books and scribbling spells. I watched a lot of TV while my body healed. I texted Felix nightly, just to let him know I was okay. Last night, our messages had been brief, as always, but had strayed from the usual pattern.

ME

Just checking in …

FELIX

Do you need anything?

ME

No, I'm okay.

A reply had come ten minutes later, my eyes heavy and the living room dark. Caspian had set up a guest bedroom for me, but I felt safer in the spacious living room.

FELIX
What level are you on in Lollipop Jumble?

ME
965.

FELIX
Slacker. I'm on 1403.

ME
That is alarming, Felix. I'm on the lam with nothing to do. What's your excuse?

FELIX
I've developed a bad case of insomnia since the night of your "vamp trouble."

I didn't know what to make of the confession. I pictured the furrow of his brow as he stared at the screen, waiting for my reply, his face awash in the blue glow. It would frustrate him that he'd admitted that. Maybe I wasn't just a passing thought for him after all. But then I'd remembered the gold ring he wore around his neck.

ME
How does your wife feel about you being awake at all hours?

This time, it took almost fifteen minutes to get a response.

FELIX
I wouldn't know. We've been divorced for two years.

I *really* didn't know what to do with that information, so I'd powered the phone off entirely. I didn't even know how to qualify my feelings—betrayed, shocked, confused. Maybe all three. I'd developed my own case of insomnia after that and had a breakfast feast fit for a king ready for Caspian by six in the morning. When he'd crept out of his bedroom, probably lured out by the scent of bacon, his expression told me he knew I'd had a rough night. But, because he was a good roommate, he asked no questions.

Instead, when Welsh showed up around noon, the only thing we discussed were the finishing touches on our Ghost Lily recon mission. We'd decided that Welsh and I would show up to the Ghost Lily that night as twins to help maximize the chance of enticing one of Randal's friends or associates. We would each be five-foot-five, willowy thin, pale-skinned with bright green eyes, and our pointed ears would stand tall on either side of our heads of stick-straight black hair. While Welsh's disguise was another of his many glamour spells that would hold for hours with no problem, I had to rely on glamour tonics. Welsh and I would stick together as much as possible while in the Ghost Lily, allowing him to reinforce my glamour should I need it. The sword was coming with us too, even though I'd argued against it.

We had two objectives we would try to carry out while there, in addition to soaking up any information we could about Bliss or the missing girls. One, flirt with anyone who showed an interest in us and try to get an invite to one of the private rooms. Two, try to smuggle a tab of Bliss out of the bar and back to the house so Welsh and Caspian could determine what was in it. According to Felix, law enforcement didn't know what was in the stuff. Welsh and I would flirt our little fae asses off to change that.

Last night, before that upsetting text conversation with Felix, but after dinner, while Welsh and I were loading the dishwasher, Caspian said, "I've been thinking … there's no reason why the cutlass can't do recon, too."

The sword, which had been floating listlessly around the kitchen like a drowsy fly, had hummed. It flew to the counter, inverted itself, and tapped once.

I pointed a soapy wooden spoon at it. "It's almost two feet

long. Where am I going to hide it while wearing that slinky dress?"

"It has cloaking magic," Caspian said. "And Welsh can glamour it with camouflage."

The sword flew to the other side of the counter, closer to where Welsh stood, and tapped on the counter once before laying itself on the granite. It did a little shimmy on the surface as if to say, *Yes, yes, this is a good idea. Let's show Harlow how good this idea is.*

Welsh laughed, wiping his hands on a dishtowel. He tossed it over his shoulder and then approached the sword, his palms hovering over the blade. The quick words of a spell left his lips, and a few moments later, the sword vanished from view. I knew it wasn't gone-gone, yet my heart lurched anyway. "The sword could hang out by the ceiling in the Ghost Lily and watch the goings-on from up there. If it's glamoured to blend in and it stays in remote areas, the glamour should hold."

The sword lifted itself from the counter and darted around the kitchen. I clocked its movements by way of a shimmer in the air; the sword moved too quickly for the glamour to keep up. After two dizzying loops around the kitchen, the glamour fell away, and the sword winked into view.

"You're going to have to move at a snail's pace, my friend," Caspian said. "Remember ... you're a fugitive, too. If you're spotted, that puts Harlow in danger."

The sword hummed.

Currently, the guys were still going over every detail of tonight's plan, but I only half listened. I kept imagining being in the middle of the dance floor and my glamour falling away, like the sword's had. It would be like those dreams where you're back in school, only to realize you're stark naked. The lights would go up, people would gasp and point, and then I'd be mobbed by the crowd before being turned over to the Collective.

Geraldine's warning echoed in my head. *"If you go into a precinct, you won't come back out. I'm sure of it."*

I was sure of it, too.

Caspian, glamoured to look like a human chauffeur, drove Welsh, me, and the sword to the Ghost Lily in one of his many unregistered vehicles. Welsh and I rode in the back, the sword lying camouflaged on the seat between us. By the time Caspian pulled into the lot behind the Ghost Lily, I half wanted to tell him we should turn back, that our plan wasn't solid enough yet, that I needed more time. Welsh placed a cool hand on my arm and I looked into a face now identical to my own.

"I'll be with you every step of the way, okay?" he said in his high, light voice.

"Thank you for helping me," I blurted, in a voice just as lilting as his, though mine shook. "You don't have to. And I know how much you hate humans—"

"We've been through this, Harlow. None of this would be happening if I didn't want to be part of it. I hate you *so* much less than I did when I first met you."

I snorted, recognizing Welsh's weird sense of humor for what it was. I had no doubt he still harbored a deep disdain for humans in general, but he was civil with me now. Any biting verbal jabs he threw at me were similar to the ones he tossed Caspian's way, and those two were best pals. We'd formed a friendship of sorts, and I was immensely relieved he was with me tonight.

"I got your back, all right?" he asked.

I nodded.

"And me," said Caspian.

The sword hummed.

With a hand on the handle of the door, Welsh said, "I bet $50 I can snag more phone numbers tonight than you, though."

I scoffed. "We have the same face."

"Yes, but we look better in blue," he said, motioning to his slinky navy-blue dress. I was in forest green. "And you're as charming as a snapping turtle."

I glared. "Oh, you're on."

"Remember the mission, you two!" Caspian chastised like an exasperated parent, but we'd already climbed out.

The sword hummed softly as it floated past me and through the open car door, letting me know it was there, preventing me from slamming the door on it.

"If I need help, sword, I'll call for you, okay?" I asked the empty air. I was fairly confident the sword had gotten itself out of the car. Something hummed by my head and I flinched. I shut the car door, then turned toward the sound. "Please stay as far out of sight as you can. I don't want anything to happen to you."

A brief sword-shaped flash of blue. Its happy color.

The Ghost Lily sat on one of the longer sides of a cul-de-sac, and the parking lot, shaped like a long rectangle, stretched out behind it, running flush with one of the building's walls. The lot was half full now, as it was still early, relatively speaking, but it would be packed within the hour. Hopefully Caspian wouldn't get too antsy out here by himself. Then I spotted a stack of books on the passenger seat and figured being alone in the car with his tomes sounded infinitely more appealing to him than being surrounded by sweaty, Blissed-out bar patrons.

Caspian rolled down his window. "Be safe in there."

I squeezed his shoulder, then met Welsh, who stood behind the car waiting for me. We strolled around the side of the building and onto the sidewalk. A tall sign at the corner of the lot proclaimed that the bar had the best cocktails in town. The bar's logo, a giant white lily, flashed twice and then held steady. The pattern—quick, quick, slow—conjured memories of Dad's pocket mirror tucked away in the front pouch of my backpack back at the cabin. Caspian and I had monitored the mirror during the past four days, ready to flee the hideout should a tip about our location materialize on the glass. The only update on the bounties was that Caspian's had gone up to $40,000, while mine had only gone up to $25,000. Caspian's "paltry sum" offended him.

The Ghost Lily's walls had been fashioned out of vertically positioned logs. Fae lights shaped like lilies ringed the thatched roof, and benches made entirely of logs sat below the windows of the front room. We got into line behind a pair of men who had eyed us appreciatively as we walked by. It was a well-known fact that if the bouncer at the door thought a lady was attractive enough, he'd let her in for free. Confident that we'd be ushered in with little fuss, neither one of us reached for our identical over-the-shoulder, gold-beaded clutch purses as we reached him.

The bouncer gave us both an evaluating scan. He was a draken man and had to be at least eight and a half feet tall. His bright orange eyes seemed to crackle and spark like flames as he took us in. Then he smiled, revealing yellowed teeth.

"Have a nice time, ladies," he said, and gestured us inside.

"Thanks, sugar," Welsh said, trailing gentle fingertips over the draken's bulging bicep as we stepped inside.

The man grunted in pleasure, then asked the ladies behind us for their IDs and the $10 fee. I glanced back at them and found two perfectly normal-human-looking women standing there. Did the draken not find human women attractive, or was he unmoved by anyone who looked normal? The glamour we had settled on was most assuredly *not* normal. We were preternaturally beautiful —a beauty that could only result from winning the genetic lottery, or magic.

"The girls said one of the bouncers at the club, a draken man, watches them in a predatory way," Geraldine had said. *"The ones he takes an interest in are usually the ones who go missing."*

I whispered this to Welsh. "Talking to the giant sleazeball at the door might have to be added to our agenda."

Welsh shot a look behind us. "If we need to chat him up, I'll take one for the team, all right? That guy is bad news. I don't want him anywhere near you if we can help it."

"Aw, you do like me," I said, grinning.

He did his best not to smile back. "Don't be gross."

For the next hour, we made our rounds, batting our eyes at ogling men when appropriate and acting demure with others. We accepted every drink that men—and some women—bought for us, but we didn't drink any of them. We kept an eye on each other and discreetly disappeared glasses when no one was looking. Welsh could also glamour a glass to look empty in a pinch.

I tried not to glance up at the ceiling too often, but I caught what I thought was a faint shimmer near the slowly whirling ceiling fans a few times. Perhaps the sword had gotten bored and was taking a spin.

The only time we'd fully lost sight of each other was when one needed to use the restroom. One would go in, and the other would stand guard at the door. Just after my facilities break, about two hours after our arrival, the clock struck midnight. A cheer went up from the dance floor just as I stepped into the dimly lit hallway.

"What's going on?" I asked Welsh, finding him where I left him leaning against the wall.

"Dancing starts in earnest at midnight," Welsh said, and as if on cue, the music's volume jumped. "Let's go, sister dear," he said, then grabbed me by the hand, pulled me down the hall, and into the crowd.

I was nothing short of creeped out when he started dancing suggestively with me, seeing as we were twin sisters on the outside. He grabbed me by the hand, swung me out, and then back in, my back flush with his chest. He wrapped his arms around me.

"There's a guy at the bar to our left who has been watching us all night," he said in my ear as we swayed to the frenetic pop music blasting through the speakers. The beat was fire, but I could have done without the goblin rap. There aren't words to describe how bad goblin rap is, so I won't even try. "Getting a shifter vibe off him. While you were in the bathroom, he chatted me up, then asked if we liked Bliss. I said I did nothing without my sister and had to talk to you first. He said we'd have a good time upstairs if we were interested."

"That sounds promising in the worst way possible." I kept swaying with Welsh while I casually scanned the crowd. Being shorter than I was used to made it difficult to see over the bouncing heads of surrounding dancers.

The Ghost Lily had two floors. On the back wall, which I faced now, a set of stairs hugged either side wall. A short balcony overlooked the dance floor. Tables, chairs, and booths took up most of the second story, as well as an additional bar. I'd been up there a few times in the past, but only because the bathrooms were usually less crowded.

My sixth sense suddenly tingled and my gaze snapped to the staircase on the left side of the room. A medium-set man in a dark suit slowly ascended the steps, then turned toward the dance floor when he was halfway up. His steely focus landed on me—on both of us—like a homing beacon.

"That's him on the stairs. What do you want to do?" Welsh whispered in my ear.

Fae lights of soft pink, blue, and purple waved lazily from the ceiling. I put on my best coy smile. Swirls of pastel lights danced over my pale, borrowed skin as I waved shyly at the man.

His white teeth flashed in the dim lighting, and he crooked a finger at us.

"Let's go," Welsh said, then slipped his hand into mine and pulled me along behind him, cutting a path through the twisting, undulating bodies on the dance floor.

I hadn't been offered Bliss tonight like Welsh had, nor had I seen any signs of it being palmed to anyone or dropped in drinks. Yet all night long, and now as we made our way off the dance floor, dancers angled their faces up, shimmering lights cascading over noses, cheeks, closed eyelids, and raised palms. The euphoria clearly on their faces came from more than an alcohol buzz. Whoever supplied the drug had perfected discreet to an art form.

By the time we'd broken free of the mass of bodies, my skin was slick with sweat. It seemed to glitter under the lights. Perhaps it was another preternatural characteristic Welsh had bestowed on the otherworldly, beautiful twins.

The man rested his forearms against the railing that overlooked the dance floor below, watching our ascent with unnerving, predatory stillness. The tips of his ears were round, which ruled out elf. Magic crackled off him, though, and set my senses buzzing. My gut said shifter, just as Welsh's had, which likely meant the man had shifted into this form recently if my human senses were picking up on his magical aura this easily.

When we reached him, standing side by side, he rested his back against the railing. His tongue flicked across his bottom lip. "Hello, ladies." His focus turned to Welsh. "Did you talk to your sister?"

"Sorry?" Welsh asked, taking a tentative step closer and cupping his pointed ear. "It's hard to hear you. What did you say?"

Another flash of white teeth. He jutted his chin to some spot behind him. "Come with me."

We trailed after him, walking farther into the darker upper floor. I cast a glance up and caught a dark ripple moving in time with us. I willed the sword to slow down. Welsh and I skirted occupied tables surrounded by talking, laughing, and drinking fae and humans. The man led us to a burgundy-colored booth in a back corner. Two draken guards stood against the back wall, keeping a watchful eye on Ghost Lily's patrons. But then a slight breeze rustled the wall, revealing that it was actually curtains they stood in front of. They weren't there to watch what went on in front of them; they were there to prevent drunken, clueless guests from wandering into the area behind them.

The draken men gave me a cursory scan as I slipped into the booth. Our new companion headed for the spot across from me, then changed his mind and scooched in beside me, grabbing Welsh by the wrist and dragging him in on his other side.

The man placed either hand on our thighs. "Isn't this cozy?"

I resisted the urge to pull my lock picks out of my purse and jab them into the back of his wandering hand.

Welsh leaned forward, turning in his seat to face the man a little more head-on. He shot a glance over his shoulder at the draken guards who had lost all interest in us already, and then back at the man. "I don't even know your name …" Welsh said.

"Leon. And yours?"

"Peony. And my sister is Paisley."

A waitress walked up to the table then, a circular black tray balanced on her open palm. Her nametag announced her name was Holly. "Can I get you folks anything?"

She pursed her lips as her gaze flicked between Welsh and me. She'd probably seen young women here with men like Leon all the time. Had she seen Nyla here with Randal, or someone like him?

"Water for me," I said.

"Scotch," said Leon.

"Same!" Welsh chirped, and Leon grinned.

Holly nodded tightly. "Coming right up."

When she left, Welsh refocused on Leon. Welsh's eyes went a little bigger, full of teenage innocence. I detected the slight change as a glamour, as Welsh had used the puppy dog trick on me once, but Leon was too ensnared in Welsh's charm to notice. "You said you had Bliss? Our parents are out of town in Kensey and we wanted to make the most of our freedom before they get back."

"Oh, Peony, I don't know if we should …" I said, eyes downcast, slipping into the role we'd discussed several times over the last couple of days.

"Paisley!" Welsh hissed. "You said you'd try it. Ugh. You *always* do this. You can't chicken out now."

I looked up and glared fiercely at him across the man's chest. "I'm not … *chickening out*. I just don't want Mom and Dad to find out."

Welsh rolled his eyes. "They won't. They don't get back until tomorrow night. Plenty of time to recover."

"It's true," Leon said to me, and the deep bass of his voice vibrated through the booth seat. "It will be out of your system by morning. Won't even come up on a drug test."

"Really?" I asked, staring at him with what I hoped looked

like wide-open trust. When all he did was leer as if I were a three-course meal, I grabbed my purse, preparing to open it. "I don't know how much Bliss costs, but we brought all—"

Leon placed a warm hand on my shaking fingers. "No charge, ladies. No charge. I'm happy to share with you. The only thing I want in payment is to see your faces when you try it for the first time." His focus lingered on the plunging neckline of my dress for a long moment before he dragged his gaze back up to my face. "And maybe a dance or two. I was watching you two dance out there. Maybe I can be in the middle next time."

Welsh giggled, then slowly walked his fingers up Leon's arm. "You're already in the middle, silly."

An involuntary groan escaped Leon's throat. Shifters were notoriously sex-crazed, especially if they hadn't been back in their human form for very long, like a cat in heat. Or whatever the equivalent was for feline males. I didn't get the appeal of shifters. I'd almost made an exception for the badger, but he'd been too certifiable for his own good. Shifter pheromones were too intense for me, their "passion" too borderline violent. Welsh better have extra tricks up his sleeve for putting Leon down if he couldn't control himself.

The waitress reappeared with our drinks. After placing them on the table, Leon told her to put them on his tab, and then she was off again.

"So ... *Paisley*," Leon said, focused on me again, drawing my fake name out like taffy. He reached a hand into the pocket of his black slacks and produced a small baggie with four white tabs in it. A black bat graced the face of each one. My mouth fell open at the sight. He took the expression to mean I was overly eager, but it was due to shock at finally seeing Bliss in person. He waved the little bag in the air between us. "What do you say? Want to have one of the best nights of your life?"

I took a sip of my water. "It's safe, right?"

"Yes," he said, taking an even longer pull of his scotch, while Welsh only took a dainty sip. "And don't worry. I'll be right here.

You'll have a great time, we'll dance, and you'll be home safe and sound before your parents even know you were gone."

I hesitated for a long moment, then nodded. "Okay."

"Yes!" Welsh said, beaming at Leon, then held his palm out. Leon fished one out of the baggie and placed it in Welsh's awaiting palm, then handed one to me.

To me, Leon said, "Now, my dear, you'll feel the effects more if you place it under your tongue and let it dissolve."

"Leon …" Welsh said, thankfully getting Leon's attention back to him. He reached up and ran a delicate finger along Leon's jaw. "Oh, wow. I like the way your face feels. The boys at school don't have stubble like this."

Even though the man's back was turned toward me, I heard him gulp. "Have you spent time with many men? Real men, I mean."

Welsh fluttered his lashes. "Not really."

"We can change that tonight, too," Leon said.

With another giggle, Welsh held the tab between pointer finger and thumb. "Can you tell me what to expect?"

While Leon gave Welsh details, his voice all sultry and smooth, I carefully opened my clutch purse and wiggled my finger against the lining of the bag where I'd stored a mundane tab of Tylenol. Once it was in my hand, I slipped the bat-stamped Bliss into the place where the Tylenol had been. After re-securing my bag, I leaned over slightly to nod at Welsh.

On cue, he said, "Oh, I'm so excited about this!" and thrust out his arms, knocking over Leon's glass of scotch. "Oh crap! I'm sorry!"

Leon waved away the apology. "Not to worry, my dear," he said, and craned his neck behind us to flag down our waitress.

Welsh climbed out of the booth while the woman hurried over to mop up the mess with a towel. As she did, Welsh cast a quick glamour spell, and a small black bat appeared in the middle of the Tylenol tab in my hand. Since taking Bliss meant I'd lose my glamour—and, you know, maybe die—we'd agreed that my task

DIABOLICAL SWORD

was smuggling the drug out. If Welsh could get his out too, we'd really be in business.

"Oh, I'm such a klutz!" Welsh said, head bowed and shoulders slumped.

"No, my dear, not at all," Leon said, rubbing his hands up and down Welsh's arms.

I climbed out of the booth, too, and stood on Welsh's other side. "I think we're both just nervous … about all of this. It's so new. There are so many people around."

"Would you like to get a private room?" Leon asked, still rubbing Welsh's arms.

Welsh sniffed and looked up. "You have a private room here?"

Leon grinned at Welsh's awed tone. "I do. We can relax in there until your nerves settle. Does that sound good?"

"That would be wonderful," I said.

Welsh grabbed his nearly full glass of scotch and handed it to Leon. "You can have the rest of mine since I knocked yours over. I want you to have a good time, too."

Leon stared at Welsh as if he wanted to ravish the fae girl right there in the middle of the floor. Without breaking eye contact, he took the glass from Welsh's delicate fingers and gulped the rest of it down. Welsh held the stare, which seemed to arouse Leon even more. But, since the two were busy screwing each other with their eyes, Leon missed how quickly Welsh had slipped the tab of Bliss into the man's glass before Leon guzzled it down. The tab had fizzed and dissolved into the amber liquid so quickly, I would have missed it had I not been watching for it. The ease of it made me clench my jaw. How many girls had Leon drugged this way?

"I know I'll have a good time with you two." Leon thunked the empty glass on the table and said, "Right this way," before angling his head toward the draken guards.

I followed Welsh and Leon, my heart thrumming. Glancing over my shoulder, I'd intended to search the ceiling for the sword, but my attention snagged on Holly the waitress a few tables away.

When we made eye contact, something like determination washed over her and she hurried to close the distance.

"Do you know him?" Holly whispered urgently.

I glanced over my shoulder, finding Welsh and Leon in a quiet conversation with the draken guards.

Looking back at Holly, I said, "We just met him tonight, but he seems nice."

Holly's lips thinned. "My friend Bonnie thought the high-roller guys were nice, too. She left with one of them one night and I haven't seen her since." She reached into her back pocket and produced her cell phone. Frantically tapping on the screen and swiping her finger across it a few times, she angled the phone toward me. An impossibly beautiful fae girl who was some exotic mix of elf and possibly even faun, smiled on the screen. "She's gorgeous, just like you. Gorgeous girls disappear when they get involved with guys like that. Don't go back there."

I wanted to hug her for trying to help me. This was what any person should do when they thought someone was in trouble. I just couldn't tell her that what she'd just told me was even more confirmation that Welsh and I *needed* to follow Leon.

"Paisley!"

I turned to find Welsh and Leon eyeing me expectantly.

I smiled softly at Holly, told her I'd be okay, and squeezed her arm. As I turned away from her, I discreetly scanned the ceiling, searching out the sword's shimmer, but I didn't spot it.

Steeling myself, I walked away from the concerned waitress and slipped through the dark curtains the draken held open. Welsh and Leon had already disappeared inside. As the curtains swished closed behind me, and I found myself in a dimly lit hallway lined with closed doors, I hoped we hadn't just made a terrible mistake.

CHAPTER TWENTY-SIX

The hallway's walls were black, the floor a dark wood, and all five doors—two on each side and one straight ahead—were black, too. The only light came from the glass-enclosed fae lights dotting the walls, casting wide blue circles.

Leon led the way, looking over his shoulder periodically to make sure we still followed. Every time he looked back, his features had slackened a little more. He stopped at the last door on the right, which bore no markings on the wall beside it or on the door itself. "Right in here, ladies," he drawled, producing a locking talisman from his pocket. Once the mechanism in the door clicked, Leon pushed it open and gestured us inside.

I followed Welsh, offering Leon a shy smile as I walked past him into the room. The way he peered down the hall again before closing the door didn't sit well with me in the slightest. The soft shimmer that passed over his head as he closed and locked the door did, though. The sword had found us.

Burgundy-colored leather couches lined two walls, and a small circular glass table sat in the middle of the floor. A mini-fridge hummed softly in a corner, the glass door revealing rows of sodas, wine, and small bottles of hard liquor. Welsh slid onto one of the couches, running his hands over the supple material. I remained standing.

To the left of the door was a small screen that lit up when Leon tapped it. A few seconds later, music filtered in through speakers embedded in the ceiling. A thumping beat pulsed through the room, and Leon tossed his hands into the air. "*Here* we go ..."

The Bliss had kicked in.

Leon swayed, eyes closed, as he peeled off his jacket, tossing it in Welsh's direction. It hit him square in the face, but Welsh giggled as he pulled it off his head and deposited it onto the seat beside him. Leon uncuffed his long sleeves and rolled them up his arms, doing a little shimmy. He unfastened the top two buttons on his shirt, then flopped onto the couch, his long legs splayed, one arm thrown over the back of the couch. His eyes were still closed.

Welsh crawled toward Leon on hands and knees, like a sultry cat. Leon's hooded eyes finally opened, and he slowly licked his bottom lip as he watched Welsh's approach. "You feeling okay?" Welsh purred.

Leon crooked his finger at Welsh. "I feel incredible, but I'll feel better when you're closer. Have you taken the Bliss yet?"

Welsh dipped his fingers into the front of his dress to produce the pill hiding in his cleavage. Leon nearly came undone. Welsh held the bat-stamped tab out between finger and thumb again and asked, "Count of three?"

Leon didn't take his eyes off Welsh as he reached into his pocket and produced the small baggie with two tabs still in it. He fished one out. "Under your tongue."

Welsh slowly slid out his tongue, then flicked it up to brush gently against his upper lip. Leon groaned. Welsh's fingers hovered just under his tongue when he shot me a look. I still loitered by the door. "You have to take yours too, Paisley."

Oh, right. The unnerving display made me momentarily forget why we were here. With two tabs of Bliss coursing through his bloodstream, Leon's tongue would loosen. Loosen in the sense that he'd give us information, and not in the sense of whatever foul things he thought while ogling the high-school-aged fae girl on the couch a foot away from him.

The glamoured Tylenol was still in my hand, and I held it up. "Ready?" But I might as well have not been there. Leon only had eyes for Welsh. "One, two, three ..."

We all took the pills, though it was only Leon who had taken the drug. Welsh's Bliss was hopefully slipped into his clutch purse by now.

Leon's hyper-focused predatory stare took in Welsh's every movement, waiting for the sign that the drug had taken hold and relaxed him, waiting for the sign to pounce. But that focus slowly eased off his chiseled features, his limbs slumping.

"Feeling even better now?" Welsh asked, on hands and knees once more as he eyed the slouching Leon.

Leon reached out to touch Welsh's face, but got distracted by a new song piping in through the ceiling's speakers. "Oh, yeah. That's what I'm talking about. This. Is. *It.*" He placed a hand on the couch cushion to push himself into a more upright position and got distracted once again, this time by the feel of the material under his palms. With a hand on either side of his thighs, he rubbed his splayed fingers along the leather, moaning in such intense pleasure that Welsh and I recoiled.

Welsh scrambled off the couch to stand beside me and we watched with curled lips as Leon flopped onto his side, pulling his feet up onto the couch. With his face on the leather, he then scooted along the cushions, like a dog after a bath. We had no way of knowing what two tabs would do to a fae, only that it wouldn't kill him.

"Did we overdo it?" Welsh whispered, arms crossed.

"Maybe?" I asked, head cocked.

"I want this couch all over my *fur*," Leon groaned.

"What the hell does that even mean?" I asked.

"Leon!" Welsh called out in his natural voice—well, one of them.

Leon abruptly stopped molesting the couch and sat up, head whipping toward one corner of the ceiling and then the other. "Did ... did you hear that?" He hopped onto the cushions in one fluid motion and smashed his face against the wall, trying to peer behind the couch. "Who was that? Is someone in here?" he shouted into the thin crevice made between the couch and the wall. He galloped across the cushions on all fours, flopped onto his stomach, and slid halfway off the couch, peering underneath it. The space below the couch was perhaps an inch tall, and pitch-black.

"Relax, Leon," Welsh said, and Leon flung himself upright, knocking over the glass coffee table, the edge of which hit the wooden floor. A spiderweb of cracks skittered across the surface.

Leon clapped his hands to the sides of his head. "Oh no." He reached out one hand toward the table, then yanked it back as if the air had scalded him. His chin quivered violently, and I wasn't sure if he was on the verge of bursting into tears. "Oh *no*," he hissed. "I'm going to get fired. I just started this gig. I can't get fired!" His wide eyes snapped up to us and Welsh and I instinctively huddled closer together. "Did you *see* me knock over the table? Like with your eyes? Can we blame it on a ghost? I think it was a ghost." In a tight little voice, all ten of his fingers pressed against his lips, he added, "I don't like ghosts."

Welp. Now I knew that two tabs of Bliss didn't make a shifter very chill. It did the opposite. Leon had completely *lost* his chill.

Something rippled above me and I glanced up just as the sword shimmered into view. I clutched Welsh's arm, needing something solid to hold on to while I watched the sword slowly lower itself from the ceiling. I didn't want to tip Leon off that the dragon sword was just above his head. The sword could take the shifter down—but who knew how Bliss would affect the shifter's powers? If the shifter felt threatened, he could easily go berserk on us and tear us to shreds before the sword could intervene.

I held stock-still as the sword hovered a few inches above the shifter's head for several long seconds.

A blink later, the sword was beside me in the inverted position, and the surrounding air rippled. Welsh and I stumbled back when a man materialized, his hand wrapped around the sword's hilt.

Leon's attention shifted to the man, too. Slowly his eyes widened and his head tilted back little by little, the panic mounting in tiny increments. And then he shrieked as if he really *had* seen a ghost. He scrambled into a corner of the couch and flung his arms over his head. "No, no, no," he moaned, but in despair this time, not pleasure. "You're supposed to be dead!" Gasping with some great revelation, his back went ramrod straight, though he still crouched on the cushions. "Did you break the table because you're mad I took your job? I didn't have a choice, man! You died!"

The figure holding the sword turned toward Welsh and me. I recognized him from the picture in the newspaper about his death. And, I realized with some shock, the auction from a year ago. Somehow, Oliver Randal's ghost stood in a private room of the Ghost Lily, the bar where he'd been murdered.

I lightly shook my head. That wasn't right. I scanned Randal's face. He wore the same murderous expression that my image had worn in that news clip. In that instance, the sword had projected an image of me holding the sword so observers would focus on the wielder of the sword instead of the sword itself. The sword had taken a piece of my essence, my DNA, through osmosis when I'd held the sword's hilt.

This was further proof that Randal had handled the sword as well. Just as Randal had participated in a demonstration with the chimera-hide shield at the auction I'd attended a year ago, Randal must have done something similar with the sword during the auction at which Haskins had purchased it. The sword had created Randal's image just as it had created mine.

Thinking quickly, I turned to the crouching, ashen Leon. "Randal's ghost haunts these rooms because he has unfinished business here."

Leon's wide gaze swiveled to me. "You ... you see him, too?"

"I do. He has manifested before you for a reason. Are you his killer, Leon?"

"Wh-what?" he sputtered.

Randal lunged toward Leon, his arms outstretched. He halted a foot away, arms up and shoulders hunched. His free hand was curled into a claw. He looked like a taxidermied bear, forever trapped in mid-attack. Randal bared his teeth in what I suspected was a growl, but looked more like a toothy grimace. Welsh choked back a snorting laugh. Nothing about Randal was terrifying at that moment, but the display had scared the bejesus out of Leon.

"Please, no! I'm sorry! I didn't kill you, I swear. I was assigned the job after you kicked the bucket, man!"

Randal turned his head toward me without dropping his menacing stance. I shrugged. Randal took a few steps back and stood in a more neutral position, the sword's hilt held at chest height. I knew the sword hovered in its comfortable inverted position, but while using Randal's form as part of its disguise, Randal looked as relaxed as a statue awaiting the call of battle.

"Who assigned you the job?" I asked Leon.

He swallowed hard. "Wh-who are you? Why aren't you scared of the ghost?"

"We knew he would be here. We can speak to the dead," I intoned with a dramatic air.

Welsh stiffened beside me for only a second, then nodded. "We sensed Randal's energy clinging to you. We apologize for tricking you up here, but when spirits want to be heard, we are but a vessel."

Randal, as if on cue, took on his scary bear pose again. Leon shrieked.

"What do I have to do to make him go away?" Leon asked, swallowing hard. He unfastened another button on his shirt. "Is it hot in here? Why am I so hot? Oh Goddess. Is he roasting me with his ghost vision?"

Good grief.

Welsh grabbed a soda out of the mini-fridge and handed it to Leon, who popped the top and guzzled the drink down. I wasn't sure how sugar would help Leon's current state, but it was too late for that now. Leon grunted, crushed the empty can in his fist, and tossed it to the ground. He belched loudly.

"We don't know specifically what Randal's ghost needs, so please answer all our questions to the best of your ability," I said. "Be honest and thorough, so that we can arrive at the information he needs. When he has what he's come for, he will cross over."

Randal returned to his neutral posture, and Leon sagged in relief.

Leon's legs must have been tired from being in a squat for that long, but it wasn't unlike the way a cat sits on its haunches. Maybe it was a natural position for him, even if it looked awkward when a human did it. Especially a very sweaty, well-toned, macho adult male. "All right. Okay. Yeah. Information. Got it. Go."

"Who assigned you this job?" I asked again.

"I don't know his name ..."

Randal glowered.

Leon squeaked. "Honest! I don't know his name. He's not in Luma, but he's got guys who work here. The boss gives Bliss to his runners, and his runners get it to the people assigned to the club, bar, casino, whatever."

"And what is your assignment?" I asked.

Leon swallowed hard, Adam's apple bobbing in his throat. "To ... uhh ... to uhh find pretty fae ladies, give them Bliss, and when they're doped up, we call one of the runners to take them away."

The blade burned red in my peripheral vision.

Leon hunkered into his shoulders, as if he were a turtle trying to pull his head into his shell.

"Easy, Randal," I said, a hand in the air. "Easy."

The blade slowly cooled.

"You ... you really *can* talk to the dead," Leon muttered.

Welsh spoke up. "Where do the runners take the girls?"

"I don't know. I swear. All I know is that they get taken out of Luma. I don't know what happens to them when they leave the hub. It isn't my job to know. Things go smoother if I don't ask questions. My job is to choose the ones I think the boss would like."

"You don't care what happens to them?" Welsh asked, arms crossed. "Was that your plan for us? Get us high on Bliss and then call up some anonymous runner to whisk us out of here?"

Leon froze, the whites of his eyes prominent. Perhaps he thought one of the skills of the ethereal twins before him was to wield the might of pissed-off ghosts.

"Who killed Randal?" I asked.

Leon started vigorously shaking his head before I even finished the question. "Don't know. I got the call that it was my turn to take over at the Lily, and to get over here ASAP. I was told to meet Travis and Wallace in the back corner of the parking lot for a debriefing. When I got here, Randal was already dead—dumped in the parking lot with a gash in his gut." Leon sucked in a dramatic gasp, wide eyes homed in on Randal.

I peered over at Randal and watched as blood, wet and bright red, seeped into the fabric of Randal's white shirt. I had to hand it to the sword for thinking on its borrowed feet.

Leon muttered what might have been a prayer.

"Who are Travis and Wallace?" I asked.

"Head of security. Travis works the front door."

The sleazeball bouncer.

Leon hurried to continue. "Travis and Wallace are the cleanup crew, too. When shit gets messy here, I mean. Stuff that could lead back to the boss if the cops start snooping around. Dead bodies are real messy. They told me the boss said my first task on the job was to make sure Randal's body got off the property so the murder couldn't be tied back to the Lily."

"Why the Warehouse District?" I asked.

Swallowing, Leon said, "My boss said someone would show up in a van. When the van got there, I was to help the guy get

Randal's body inside, and then the guy would drive us to the Warehouse District where we'd throw the body in the dumpsters behind the Design & Decor building. I don't know who the guy was, only that he was a sorcerer. They're the only ones who fuck with runes.

"After we threw the body in a dumpster, he got in the driver's seat, but instead of driving away, he took off his shirt and started drawing runes on himself. I asked him what he was doing, if we were going to drive back to the Lily or what, and he didn't answer me. Ten minutes later, after all the runes were drawn on him, he turned into that Harlow Fletcher chick. You know, the lady on the news who killed all those werecat guards?"

My mouth had gone dry. When I didn't respond, Welsh spoke for me. "Yeah, we know who that is."

"Glamours are freaky. Like ... how can you just wear someone else's face?" Leon bobbed his head, agreeing with himself. "I asked the sorcerer what the hell he was doing, and that's when I blacked out. I woke up in the passenger seat around one in the morning. The sorcerer was gone, but I heard sirens in the distance. Randal's body was lying in the middle of the parking lot and I got out of the van, trying to figure out what the hell was happening. Like maybe he wasn't dead? But he was *super* dead. He was ... his face and arms and stomach ... ruined. Just ... slashed to hell."

"Did the sorcerer come back?" I asked.

"Nah. Not right away. Some chick was there, though. I was screaming my head off ... like 'Sorcerer! You out here?' Then his lady comes out of the bushes, wiping her mouth. I think she was throwing up or something. Then she, like, wigged and said she'd call the police on me. She was like, 'Where's the murder weapon? Where's the murder weapon? You're going to prison for the rest of your life, you monster!' Shit like that. I tried telling her I didn't do it. She pulls out her cell phone, and I was like, 'Fuck this, I'm out of here.'

"Behind us, we hear someone go, 'If you call the cops, you'll get even worse than he got.' And that Harlow chick—or the sorcerer glamoured to look like her—was standing a few feet away. Blood dripping off the sword and this crazy look in her eyes. She pointed the sword at me and said, 'Get back to the Lily and keep your mouth shut.' So that's what I did. Harlow walked back toward the street, I got my ass back in the van, and drove back."

That account had been left out of the article.

"You left the lady there with Randal's body?" Welsh asked.

"Hell yeah, I did! I'm not stupid. Like I said, you get an order from the boss, even if it's indirectly, you listen. You don't ask questions. If you don't ask questions, you don't end up dead."

If one of the Collective's sorcerers had not only framed me, but made sure an eyewitness was there to find Randal's ruined body miles from the original location of his murder, it was no wonder Leon's involvement in the incident had been left out. Leon had been recruited by his boss to drive the getaway vehicle, since the sorcerer setting me up had been instructed to flee the scene on foot, making sure that several people saw "me" that night, stalking down the street while holding a bloody sword. How much had that reporter been paid to keep the full truth out of the paper?

When the silence ticked on for longer than Leon's Blissed-out nerves could handle, he said, "That's everything I know. Look, I'm sorry for what I was going to do to you ladies, all right? It's a job. I get Bliss, girls, and a fuck-ton of cash when one of the runners delivers a pretty girl to my boss. It's nothing personal."

I wanted to punch him in the face. The sword didn't hesitate and beelined for Leon.

Randal's image dissolved like ink wafting through water, leaving only the sword hurtling for Leon's face. The shifter's mouth dropped open, but before he could get a word out, the sword abruptly flipped itself around and slammed its hilt into Leon's temple.

Leon's eyes rolled back in his head and he toppled off the couch, crashing into the overturned glass coffee table that completely shattered under his dead weight. Welsh darted forward, rooted around in the pockets of Leon's black slacks, and produced the locking talisman. I stood there gaping.

Welsh unlocked the door and wrenched it open. He peeked out to make sure the coast was clear. He ducked back into the room to grab Leon's discarded jacket off the couch and handed it to me. "All right. Give me a second."

What the hell was he doing now? I figured it out a moment later when his beautiful fae features began to morph. His skin went from pale to tanned, his pointed ears rounded, and he sprouted almost a full foot taller. My lip involuntarily curled when Leon stood before me. I knew it was Welsh, but my instincts told me to knee the guy in the balls and make a run for it.

"I need you to look drugged up and dopey," Welsh said, and without further explanation, scooped me into his arms. I instinctively threw one arm around his shoulder to keep from tumbling to the ground, my other hand still holding the jacket. "Sword. Get in her lap."

The sword complied. Knowing what the jacket was for now, I draped it over the blade.

Welsh started for the exit, and I let my head loll on his shoulder, my eyes droopy. "Good girl." As we approached the curtained wall, Welsh called out, "Coming through!"

The curtains parted and Welsh ducked his head as he stepped out into the seating area of the second floor. Even though my eyes were half-closed, I still squinted slightly at how much brighter it was here than in the creepy mood lighting of the back hallway.

Welsh stepped between the two draken guards, then turned back to address them. His tone implied his expression was mischievous. "I'll be back for the other one, but if either of you wants to have a go before I get back, the door is unlocked."

The draken men grinned.

Welsh turned back around and stalked away from the men. In a low tone meant only for me, he said, "Disgusting. I knew the guards were at the very least turning a blind eye to what was happening here, but they're clearly more complicit than that."

"When we figure out what happened to the girls here," I said softly as Welsh practically jogged down the stairs, "can we add draken slaughter to the list of mission objectives?"

The sword hummed beneath the jacket draped over my lap.

"Absolutely," Welsh said, pushing his way through the crowd of Blissed-out dancers.

No one stopped the man carrying an unconscious girl out the door, partly because by now, the partiers who remained were too drugged up to notice. And the ones who weren't, like Travis standing guard at the door, didn't care.

"You lucky dog," Travis drawled as Welsh strolled past him and out the door of the Ghost Lily.

We had just rounded the side of the building when shouts sounded from behind us. Shouts that sounded a lot like Travis's deep baritone.

"Shit," Welsh said. Then, louder, he called out, "Start the car!"

"Hey!" someone shouted behind us, followed by the pounding of footsteps.

The parking lot was packed to the gills.

I peered over Welsh's bouncing shoulder. Travis was most definitely in hot pursuit. A second draken was on his heels. "Put me down. You can run faster if you aren't carrying me."

In one fluid motion, Welsh let go of my legs and my feet swung to asphalt. I hit the ground running. The sword had flown upward, still draped in the jacket, just as Welsh had let me go. We booked it for Caspian's car, which he'd inexplicably moved to a far corner of the lot.

"Start the car!" Welsh called out again, then cast a spell to send the words on the wind.

"Did he fall asleep!" I glanced behind us. The draken were gaining on us. The fact that they hadn't caught us yet spoke to either alcohol or Bliss in their systems slowing them down—if not both.

Caspian's SUV flared to life and zipped out of its parking spot, slamming into the car parked directly behind it. Tires screeched as Caspian threw the car into drive and barreled forward. We parted so the car wouldn't mow us down. The doors flew open on their own and I dove into the back seat while Welsh flung himself into the passenger seat.

"Stay down!" Caspian said, and I knew he meant me.

My still-open door cracked into the charging body of one of the draken men, knocking him flat, and the door slammed shut. The SUV lifted off the ground for a moment, followed by a sickening thump, and I knew the back tires had just run over the draken who'd been creamed by the open door.

Caspian gunned the gas. Travis loudly cursed. He must have dived out of the way though, because the SUV flew out of the lot without further resistance. I sprung up and grabbed hold of the headrest, peering out the back window. Travis was getting to his feet. He bolted for us, only to come up short so quickly that he pitched backward, down on the asphalt again. It looked as if he'd hit a glass wall and bounced off it onto his ass. But the glint of metal told me what had happened.

I hit the window button on the door and stuck my head out, my curls whipping around my face. "Sword! Not yet!"

Caspian whipped around a corner and I almost pitched out the window, but Welsh had grabbed me by the back of my shirt and yanked me back. Curls. Shirt. No dress. I sat up and quickly fastened my seat belt. My glamour had dissolved.

A minute later, the sword zipped through the open window and landed on the back seat. Not a drop of blood on it.

"You'll get your chance," I said.

The sword hummed softly.

"What were you doing in here, sleeping?" Welsh asked, echoing my question, back in his boy band hottie form.

"I was reading and lost track of the time. I got sucked into a really interesting passage about how the rystel swirling pattern of a quicksaw rune—"

Welsh issued a fake snore.

Caspian grunted. "How'd it go in there? You get it?"

Welsh held up a hand, and between two fingers was a dime-sized white tablet with a black bat stamped in the middle. "We got it."

CHAPTER TWENTY-SEVEN

It was two days later, and we were no closer to figuring out the secret ingredient in Bliss. I said "we" as if I had anything to contribute.

As a witch, Welsh had some proficiency in tonics, potions, and tinctures—I didn't know the difference between the three, but he assured me there was one. Yet, Welsh's proficiency only went so far as following recipes. One could be a proficient cook by following recipes someone else created, but the true chefs were the ones who could *create* the recipes—who could deconstruct a dish and understand the science behind cooking temperatures, the properties of ingredients, and why certain ones paired well with others. Welsh was not a chef. I barely qualified as an assistant.

Caspian's forte was spells and runes, and given enough time, he could probably craft something to deconstruct Bliss, but it could take weeks or months and I couldn't hole up with them indefinitely.

Knowing what was in Bliss could lead us to its source, which could lead us to Leon's boss and the reason fae girls were being trafficked out of Luma. The Collective knew more about it than they were telling the public. Between the mundane police making it difficult for Mathias and Geraldine Stone to find out what had happened to Nyla, a sorcerer on Leon's boss's payroll helping Leon move Oliver Randal's body to help take the heat off the Ghost Lily, and the Collective working damn hard to get both Caspian and me in custody, this had all had snowballed into so much more than me clearing my name. It wasn't like clearing my name would work now anyway—if the sorcerer was part of the Collective or at least hired by it, I couldn't stroll into a Collective-loyal precinct with evidence of the Collective's guilt and expect them to drop all charges and pat me on the back for being a good little detective. It was impossible to know where the Collective's spies were hiding. Like Geraldine said, if I went into a law enforcement office of any kind, even with evidence proving I was innocent, I wouldn't walk back out. Yet, if I did nothing, I'd be a fugitive forever. Win-win for them, lose-lose for me.

The way things were going, my old life was gone with no chance of returning.

I eyed the small white pills lying innocently in a plastic bag beside Caspian's stack of books. One of the pills had been split into four pieces using a pill cutter. Two of the pieces had already fallen victim to the guys' experimentations, and one had been shuttled off to Mathias and Geraldine to examine, though Welsh hadn't told them about the possible connection between these pills and the disappearance of Mathias's sister.

It was just after lunchtime and Caspian was ten minutes deep into a long-winded monologue about rune construction. I sat beside him and I honestly tried to follow along, but it was just so tedious. Caspian's teacher voice lacked even a hint of inflection. I tried to imagine what sorcery school must have been like—day in and day out, for *years*—and almost fell asleep instantly. And I'd thought this guy was a supervillain! He didn't even get rich in an interesting way. He wasn't neutral evil—he was just neutral … neutral.

Welsh had an elbow propped up on the counter, his face on his fist, listening to Caspian with more intensity than usual. Across from him, Caspian drew a demonstration rune on a piece of paper. The sword spun in slow circles on the other side of the counter.

I couldn't take it anymore. I blurted, "I might have someone who can help us."

Caspian trailed off. The sword came to a stop.

Welsh issued a snorting inhale and stood bolt upright, rubbing his bleary eyes. That bastard hadn't been listening at all. He'd been sleeping and had just glamoured his eyes to appear alert and open. "What? Who? Do you have a secret alchemist friend you forgot to mention?" He yawned loudly.

This was something I'd been thinking about since last night. "He's … uh … a bounty hunter."

The men stared blankly at me. The sword floated to hover beside Welsh across from us. A Welsh meltdown was imminent. I waited him out.

Three, two—

"You're serious?" Welsh cocked his head. "You want to contact a *bounty hunter*—one of the Collective's hand-selected human lackeys—about the composition of one of Luma's most notorious street drugs? While you're a fugitive hiding out in the house of another fugitive, because you're both trying to *avoid* bounty hunters … *that* kind of bounty hunter?"

"Yep."

He flung his arms into the air and gestured vaguely at Caspian. "Tell her why that's a bad idea. She apparently doesn't understand logic and you're much better at breaking things down into pieces digestible enough for humans."

I glared. "Is your blood sugar low? You're crankier than usual."

He grumbled something to himself, but then stalked toward Caspian's fridge and yanked it open.

Caspian turned in his seat, resting his arm on the back of it. "How do you know this bounty hunter?"

"We used to date."

Welsh snorted derisively, his back still turned to us as he perused the fridge's shelves.

I ignored him, then gave Caspian a brief history of my parents, the profession I'd almost had, and the rise and fall of my relationship with Felix Turner. "When Felix saw me on the news, he tracked me down intending to get me out of Luma despite the bounty on my head. Bliss came up in conversation and he told me the hunters and the mundane police have been working closely on trying to figure out where Bliss is coming from and what's in it. The Collective doesn't seem super interested in finding the suppliers or distributors of Bliss themselves, but they've allowed the hunters to work on Bliss-related cases with the police as long as it doesn't interfere with Collective-assigned bounties."

Halfway through my monologue, Welsh closed the fridge and returned to the counter, arms crossed.

"He told me that every time they analyze what they *think* is the drug, the results show it contains nothing more than common over-the-counter stimulants like caffeine."

"What, like placebos?" Caspian asked.

I shrugged. "My theory is that they've never actually gotten their hands on the real thing." I pointed to the remaining full tab we had. "He might have someone in the mundane police who can analyze it for us."

Welsh asked, "And you're sure you can trust him?"

Was I sure of that? I wanted to be. I didn't know Felix well anymore. Not after five years with no contact. But I knew he still cared about me, even if the nature of our relationship had changed. His concern about me had overridden everything else, otherwise he wouldn't have shown up at that factory, ready to get me out of the city instead of turning me over to his bosses.

"Your hesitation isn't exactly comforting," Welsh said.

"I can trust him," I said. "But I'd have to meet him as me, not glamoured. And I should go alone. If he thinks for a second that I'm in trouble, he'll try to do something noble and selfless that's well-intentioned, yet results in me sobbing my eyes out on the kitchen floor."

Welsh said, "Well, *that's* weirdly specific. I'd ask details, but I don't care."

Caspian sighed. "Go make yourself a sandwich already!"

Welsh scowled, then stomped back to the fridge.

To me, Caspian said, "Counteroffer: If you talk to him and still think this is a good idea—I trust your judgment—I'm willing to let him take *half* a tablet, not the whole thing. Welsh and I will go with you, but we'll arrive separately, as well as stay glamoured and out of sight. Even if you trust him, and he meets you with the best of intentions, as you say, he may show up with backup as well. If something goes awry, we'll get you out of there."

"Sword? What do you think? You met Felix."

It still hovered on Welsh's side of the counter. After a few moments, it glowed a faint blue and hummed.

"This plan is sword-approved," I said.

"Call him and see what he says," Caspian said. I was just about to climb off the high-backed chair when he lightly grabbed me by the arm to get my attention. When I cocked a brow, he asked, "Are you still in love with Felix?"

I stilled. It wasn't an invasive question, but an assessing one. Despite saying that he trusted my judgment, Caspian wanted to know if my feelings for Felix would influence my decision-making. After a moment, I said, "I don't know."

Caspian let me go and nodded. With a brief smile, he said, "Let us know how it goes."

Welsh was biting into a turkey sandwich just as I pulled the signal-scrambling talisman Felix had given me out of my backpack. I grabbed the burner cell phone and stepped onto the back patio. Before closing the door behind me, I heard Welsh say to Caspian, *"This is going to be a disaster."*

With that lovely vote of confidence, I dialed Felix. My hands trembled slightly as the phone rang, and I shoved my free one into my jeans pocket.

The phone rang five times, and I was sure it would click over to voicemail, but Felix finally answered a bit breathlessly. "Harlow? Hi."

I swallowed. "Hi."

He blew out a long sigh. "It's good to hear your voice. To know you're okay, I mean."

"Good to hear yours too," I said, cheeks heating.

"Where are you? Are you safe?"

"I'm fine. Still not going to tell you where I am, though."

"Because you don't trust me. Even after I risked my job to help you."

"*Wow*," I said, drawing the word out. "Laying on the guilt extra thick this early into the game, huh?"

There was a hint of a smile in his tone. "It used to work."

"I trust you, but the people I'm staying with don't."

"People who know about the sword and the whole running-from-the-law thing? I would think it would be hard to find people willing to risk the possibility of that much heat landing on their doorstep."

I lightly kicked a pebble off the back porch, where it bounced twice on the dry lawn in desperate need of water and a mow, before disappearing. "They took me in because of that, not in spite of it."

"Ah," he said, in that sage-like way that meant he'd just figured something out and found it disappointing. "Other criminal types."

He'd gotten very judgy in the last five years. Maybe he'd always been that way. Maybe whatever had made him abandon me had turned him bitter, while it had made me untrusting and paranoid.

He cursed softly. "Sorry, Harlow. I didn't mean …"

I thought about what he'd told me a couple of nights ago. Both that his worry about me had given him insomnia, and that he was divorced now. There was too much to unpack in all of that, so I zipped that suitcase of "shit I don't want to deal with right now" closed.

"I don't know why I keep doing that," he said. "It's just that ... look, ever since—"

"I wanted to ask you something," I said, cutting him off.

His rambling sputtered to a stop. "Okay ..."

"Do you have anyone on the mundane police force who you trust implicitly? Or someone who works in a crime lab?"

He was silent for a long beat. "Why?"

"I may have gotten hold of Bliss. Like, the real thing. I want to know what the secret sauce is."

"I'm scared to ask how you got your hands on it."

"So don't ask. Can you get it analyzed for me without red flags going up everywhere? I don't want you to end up in hot water over this. If you can't do it, I can figure something else out."

"Did the people you're with get it?" he asked.

"It doesn't matter how I got it, Felix."

"Yeah, it does. If you want my help, I have to know what I'm agreeing to. My ass is on the line already. I've caught Deever following me twice. I don't know how he found out, but he knows that you and I used to be together. He keeps asking me if I'd give you up if I knew where you were. If I'm going to do this, I need to know if the people you're with are dangerous. You were already in over your head, Harlow. How much worse has it gotten?"

"I'm not some petty criminal," I snapped. "I'm safer here than I would be in police custody, I can tell you that much."

Felix scoffed. And when he finally spoke, he said something I hadn't seen coming. "Do you know what the running theory was —still is—about your dad and why that particular job made your mom take off before the dust even settled?"

Why did he sound so ... cold?

"The theory was that your parents weren't just busting those guys for dealing Bliss to human kids," Felix said. "It was that your parents were caught up in selling and distributing too, and the perp they went to go collect was actually their supplier. Something bad went down on that job—and not your normal kind of bad. Whatever happened was bad enough that your mom left without even telling you goodbye. The theory goes, she was up to her eyeballs in trouble and she fled town to keep the dealers from tracing any of this back to you. Why else would she leave like that?"

I clenched my jaw so tight my teeth hurt. The pain kept the tears at bay—tears of anger, not sadness. I wasn't sure if I was more upset about the old wounds Felix had just torn open, or at how callously he'd ripped off the scabs.

I *had* heard this theory, of course. It wasn't true. My parents might have kept that last job a secret, they may have lied to my face when they said everything was fine, but I didn't believe for a second that they'd gotten caught up in a Bliss trafficking scheme. They'd seen firsthand how easily Bliss could kill a human. When I was old enough to handle it, they forced me to watch videos of human kids dying while under the influence of it, took me to morgues to show how sunken and hollow the faces of those young kids had become after abusing Bliss for too long. They wouldn't have been using it themselves, nor selling it to the very people they were trying to protect. I would have known.

"Why are you bringing any of this up, Felix?"

"I'm not saying I believe that theory," he said, "but it makes me wonder how deep you've gotten. I don't want to lose you the same way you lost them."

How dare he. He lost me because he *chose* to leave.

"Even if they hadn't been selling or distributing Bliss," Felix said, oblivious, "they took countless Bliss-related cases. They *volunteered* to take them. Put themselves in really dangerous situations with really dangerous people. All because of Bliss. So … I ask again … how did you get it?"

I worked my jaw. If I wanted his help, I'd have to give him at least part of the truth. "A guy gave me some at the Ghost Lily. When he was distracted, I swapped it for a Tylenol, pocketed it, and only pretended to take the Bliss."

"How were you at the Ghost Lily, of all places, when half the city is looking for you?"

"Glamour spell." After a brief hesitation, I told him about Oliver Randal, his murder, and the frame job that had come after. "I know this all sounds like conspiracy theories, but it's the truth. Your bosses are trying to set me up for murder. I need to find out why. Several shady things in Luma keep getting tied back to the Ghost Lily. The secret ingredient in Bliss could help me figure out why the Collective has it out for me and the sword."

Silence.

"I know you're loyal to the Collective. They sign your paychecks. I get that. Selling your soul to the devil so you can afford a luxury apartment. But they're hiding something, and they're using me to cover it up, or deflect the attention from themselves," I said. "Even if you think I'm mostly out of my mind, doesn't some little part of you wonder if maybe I'm not?"

Felix grunted.

This time I waited him out. I paced the short length of the back patio three times before he replied.

"Fine. Yeah, I got a guy."

I came to an abrupt stop. "Really?"

"Yeah. I can meet you tonight. You choose the place. Text me the address."

"Thanks."

"Don't thank me yet." In a flat, borderline pissed-off tone, he added, "And, for the record, I'm not blindly loyal to the Collective. If you're *in* the pit of vipers, you're in a better position to chop off their heads. Don't assume you have me all figured out, Harlow. I guarantee you don't know the half of it."

I blinked.

"Text me the address," he repeated, then the call disconnected.

It took me several minutes to get my legs working again. When I stepped back into the house, Welsh was gobbling down last night's leftover spaghetti.

"How'd it go?" Caspian asked, still perched on the high-backed chair in front of the counter, surrounded by his books.

"We're meeting him tonight."

Caspian cocked his head as he assessed me, calculating gaze roaming my face. "Everything all right?"

I plastered on a bright smile. "Yep."

Everyone in that room knew I was lying.

CHAPTER TWENTY-EIGHT

The guys and I arrived at the meeting location first, though in separate cars. The spot was an abandoned playground in the Industrial District—some short-lived attempt to give the workers here a chance at having on-site childcare. But during the day, the Industrial District was loud, busy, and not at all kid-friendly, so the playground had been in bad shape for a while. I knew of the place because it was a favorite meeting spot of a client of mine who lived nearby. A derelict playground was about as creepy as it got, but my client was a weird dude.

The Industrial District took up most of the western side of the city. On the upper western edge of the district, the veil sat close to a highway on the mundane side. The veil got a lot of action during the day as trucks shipped in construction supplies, and the district shipped out goods destined for other hubs. The telepads couldn't handle the frequent transfer of larger vehicles and shipments without the whole system wigging out—especially if said shipment had to travel a long distance. To maintain the integrity of the veil at heavily trafficked spots, a Collective sorcerer was stationed there during the day, while werecat guards patrolled the area at night. The playground was a good five miles from the werecats' roaming grounds.

Even though the playground was secluded, and it was well past sunset, I felt exposed being out here while wearing my true face. Welsh and Caspian parked on the other side of the playground behind a storage shed. I knew if Felix staged some well-meaning kidnapping attempt, the guys—and the sword riding on the dashboard—wouldn't let me go without a fight. I parked Caspian's unregistered truck in the lot, then slowly made my way over to the wood-chip-filled pit frequented most often by stray cats, evidenced by the periodic whiff of ammonia. Cement ringed the play area, dotted with benches. I gingerly sat on one.

The pair of swings on the swing set were nothing more than hanging chains, and they creaked on their hinges as they swayed in the slight breeze. I sat facing the parking lot, the guys' hideout spot behind me where they'd literally watch my back.

When Felix finally pulled into a spot across the playground, his headlights shone in my eyes for a moment from across a weather-worn seesaw. I popped off the bench as if someone had hit an eject button. With the way our last conversation had ended, I didn't know what to expect now.

He strolled over, hands in the pockets of his jeans. He wore a black long-sleeved shirt and tennis shoes. The picture of casual. The blue light of a nearby fae lamppost winked off the trinkets he wore around his neck—two half-moon-shaped talismans and the ring. The wedding band he'd once worn on his finger while married to some unknown woman. Yet he still wore it, even if it was around his neck.

"Hey," he said as he approached me, keeping his hands in his pockets.

"Hey."

His assessing dark eyes scanned the area behind me—checking for any sign of movement in the shadowy alcoves of the quiet lot. When his attention flicked back to me, he cocked a brow in question.

I dug into my pocket to pull out the little baggie holding the pill. The bat's body had been cut clear down the middle, its wing stretched wide and gracing the curved edge of the tablet.

Felix took it and angled the bag to examine it through the plastic. "Only half?" he asked as he placed it in his own pocket.

"We could only get two of them, so we're in limited supply."

"We ..." he said, gaze scanning the area behind me again, as if he were sure monsters would come stalking from around the corners of buildings and storage sheds if he just waited long enough. "You look good."

"Uhh ... thanks?"

"I just mean ..." he said, dropping his head for a moment. "You look healthy. Well taken care of."

"I told you I was safe."

"Safer than you'd be with me."

It wasn't a question, but I answered as if it were. "Yeah."

We stared at each other for a long moment before he said, "Can you at least tell me what kind of 'vamp trouble' you got into? Were you bitten or anything? Do I have to worry about you turning?"

"No. I'm fine. Let me know if your crime lab guys get anything interesting out of that, yeah?" I jerked my head toward his pocket, then started back toward the truck. The air between us felt charged already. I needed to get out of here before we ended up in another argument. What if he got so pissed, he refused to get the tablet analyzed? Or he called on his backup waiting for the signal that it was time to throw a bag over my head and toss me in the back of a van?

"Wait," he said, and I turned back to him. He dropped the hand that had been reaching for me. "I know a lot has changed, but you can still talk to me. I can be an ally even if we aren't together anymore. But I can't help you if you keep me in the dark."

A laugh, sharp and bitter, rumbled out of me. Felix wisely took a step back.

"Are you *kidding* me?" I asked, rubbing at a brow, eyes closed as I tried to center myself. If I got too riled up, the sword would sense it, and I didn't need that complication right now. I stared him dead in the eye when I said, "Let me address the elephant in the room because you won't. You want me to talk to you, but you *left* me, Felix. I got nothing from you but a fucking note saying you were sorry. You changed your phone number before the door had slammed shut behind you. I haven't seen you in five goddamn years after we'd been nearly inseparable for a decade. And you want me to *talk* to you? Why would I tell you *any*-fucking-thing when you never even bothered to tell me why you ghosted me in the cowardliest way possible?"

His jaw clenched, a muscle ticking just below the day-old stubble. "Because they killed Naomi."

Now it was my turn to take a step back, as if he'd struck me. "What? Who killed her?"

Felix gusted out a sigh, glancing behind him on either side as if he expected someone to be listening in. Hell, maybe someone was. "After your dad died, I was investigating what happened to him. I was doing it on my own time—often telling you I was at the casino when I was actually tracking down information. I got too close to it—the Bliss cartel, I mean. I'd made contact with a guy online who I was pretty sure worked for the cartel, and I was trying to get in with him by agreeing to distribute the stuff. He and I had a good rapport going, and I thought we'd bonded, but I must have asked the wrong question or made the guy nervous or something, because the day after I was sure I'd been accepted into the ranks, I got accosted at work."

"What do you mean, accosted?"

"Jumped in the bathroom. They hit me—with tire irons—where no one could see the bruises. It was why I came home late so often and left before you got up during that week before your birthday. The less time I was at the apartment, the less likely you were to see what had happened to me."

Something in my chest twinged. "Why didn't you tell me?"

"Because they said if I didn't back off on my little investigation, they'd go after you," he said. "Naomi went missing the next day. I didn't think it was connected, since they'd threatened you, not her. She was just a girl I knew through you."

I worried at the inside of my cheek.

"I called their bluff and kept nosing around. Met with a couple of retired mundane cops who had worked the drug beat and had a lot of experience with Bliss-related cases. There had to be a reason your parents were obsessed with those cases specifically, and I found it very hard to believe they were secretly using. Not just because Bliss is deadly to humans, but it just didn't fit with who they were."

Relieved to finally hear him say that after his insinuations on the phone, I asked, "What about your parents?" He hadn't once brought them up, so I'd been avoiding the topic just in case something terrible had happened to them over the last five years. I'd lose it if they were gone too.

When Felix didn't flinch at the question, I relaxed. "They didn't get as involved with the Bliss cases as yours did, and when they retired last year, they completely gave up everything about the life. Dad is deep into gardening now and Mom makes quilts. They went from a rough-and-tumble life to a very quiet one."

It felt bittersweet to imagine the Turners like that. Funny to think of them slowing down and embracing the retired life, but heartbreaking all over again that my parents would never get that.

"When I went to see them the week Naomi went missing, they asked if I knew Naomi used to work with your parents. They'd seen an article about her disappearance. Your parents had supposedly started running raids on distributors of Bliss, and Naomi was working undercover for them."

I cocked my head. That didn't make any sense. Naomi had been like me—a twenty-something trying to make ends meet by working as a server in a bar. She'd never once mentioned that she'd known my parents.

But then I remembered something from our last conversation

—something she'd said that I'd taken as a friend showing sympathy, but meant something entirely different in light of this.

"Did you ever hear from your mom again?" Naomi had asked.

"Nope. When she left, she left for good. I don't even know if she's still alive."

"I hope she is," Naomi had said, *a little hitch in her voice.*

It hadn't just been sympathy that had caused that hitch—it had been Naomi's grief over someone she cared about. Why hadn't she told me?

"How did she even end up working for them?" I asked.

Felix started to say something, then stopped, his eyes glazed over. He just stood there like a statue for three solid seconds, and I was honestly worried I'd been talking to a cyborg this whole time. Then he shook his head, blinking rapidly. "Do you have theories about what's going on at the Ghost Lily?"

The question—the whole last five seconds—threw me off. Guess we were changing topics, then. "Uh ... yeah. I think fae women are being trafficked out of there after being drugged with Bliss."

Felix nodded. "Naomi and your parents had similar theories. Naomi was half-fae. That's why she was undercover."

"How do you even know all this?"

"I learned it."

I blew out a slow breath and tried to center my chi. "After your little speech about us talking more, you go cryptic on me?"

"I don't have a choice."

"What the hell does that mean?"

"I mean there are certain things I can't tell you."

"Withholding information doesn't make you more mysterious, Felix. It makes you annoying."

He smiled softly at that, and he mulled over his next words. "The day Naomi's body was found, I got cornered in the parking lot of our old apartment complex. Same pair of guys who'd jumped me in the bathroom at work. They said Naomi's death was a message and that I needed to drop my investigation, or you were next. They handed me a stack of photos—they'd been watching you for weeks. According to them, Naomi was a spy who'd been sent to befriend you to uncover what your parents told you, and to find out if your mom was in contact."

"But I thought she was working undercover for my parents. Who was she reporting to after my dad died?"

Felix's expression went blank, one eye twitching. "Naomi got removed from the situation before she told you who she really was. The goons believed you truly knew nothing and that it needed to stay that way. The only way they wouldn't hurt you was if I cut you out of my life. They'd be watching us both, and if I didn't leave you, they'd kill you."

I searched every inch of his face, looking for some hint of a lie. He'd skipped over the question about who Naomi had been working for. "Why are you telling me this now? Won't this mysterious 'they' come after me now that you're back in contact?"

"I don't know," he said, and I wasn't sure which question he was answering. "When I left, I honestly believed it was the best option. You could live a life free of all this bullshit your parents, Naomi, and I got caught up in. Your moral compass always pointed true north. I knew you'd be okay, even if you hated me for the rest of your life. But then I saw you on the news and it was like everything I gave up was for nothing because you'd gone completely off the rails. It was like I didn't even recognize you anymore."

My face heated. "Sorry being abandoned by two of the three most important people in my life didn't turn me into a saint."

"Dammit," he huffed. "I never say the right thing anymore."

After a beat, I said, "Why did you say you don't have a choice about being cryptic?"

"Exactly what I said."

I clenched my teeth. "You always have a choice. You chose to be here, didn't you?"

"*Bounty hunters* don't always have a choice," he said. "When

Naomi was killed and I ... I walked out on you, I went to headquarters and requested a meeting with one of the higher-ups."

"With one of the sorcerers themselves?"

"Yeah. I knew they'd see me since both of us dropping out of the program was a sore spot for the Collective. My parents had told me as much. When I met with the sorceress, I asked her straight up what I was supposed to do. How was I supposed to make losing you worth it? She told me they'd still take me as a hunter if I passed my exam, even though it had been a year since I'd bailed. When I—"

"Felix?" I asked, concerned that his eyes had glazed over again.

He shook his head. "Sorry. Uhh ... I was told I'd have a better chance of taking down the cartel if I was a hunter because I'd have their resources, plus the resources of the mundane police. I joined that day. Now I have resources and knowledge, but I can't tell you any of it." He worked his jaw, then said the next words as if they tasted foul. "Contractual obligation."

"You're cryptic because of hunter-Collective confidentiality?" I asked, rolling my eyes. "Glad you're upholding your promises even when no one is here to witness you breaking them."

He eyed me pointedly and in a slow, measured tone, as if he thought I was very simple, said, "The consequences are the same regardless of who's in attendance."

I was about to snap at him again for being mysterious when several things clicked into place. The glazed-over eyes, the detailed answers that were cut off and then became cryptic, the careful way he was speaking. *Contractual obligation.*

A conversation I'd had with Jo what felt like a million years ago floated to the surface. *"When she hit a topic she was soul-bound not to speak about, her eyes glazed over, as if the words she'd been about to say had been plucked right out of her head."*

My mouth dropped open. "You have to sign a Soul NDA to join the hunters."

"Which is why your parents couldn't always tell you the

nature of their jobs. Not everything falls under the contract, but enough of it does that it can make conversations with non-hunters ... tedious. They weren't trying to keep things from you. They had to. *I* have to."

Shaking my head, I said, "They left *that* out of the brochure." I took in his furrowed brow and his clenched fist by his side, and then my shoulders slumped. "*Why* did you sign something like that, Felix?"

He smiled sadly, shrugging once. "I had nothing left to lose."

I bit down on my bottom lip to keep it from trembling.

"I should get going," he said, taking a step back. "I'll be in touch about this, okay?" He patted a pocket, then turned away from me. He only made it two steps before he turned around, walking backward. "Low?"

"Yeah?"

"Just know that as much as you hate me," he said, "I hate myself ten times more."

I was still standing there, listening to the creak of the swing's chains, numb and heartbroken all over again, well after he'd driven away.

CHAPTER TWENTY-NINE

When we all got back to Caspian's place, I didn't go into anything Felix had told me. The vast majority of it was personal, and as Welsh had already made *very* clear—he didn't care about my boring mundane problems. All they needed to know was that Felix would be in contact if his buddy at the crime lab came up with anything.

An hour later, after Welsh had gone home, Caspian had gone to bed, and even the sword had retired to the duffel bag, I settled onto the couch with my phone, determined to get past level 965 on Lollipop Jumble. But as those brightly colored lollipops stared back, I only thought of Felix. *"Just know that as much as you hate me, I hate myself ten times more."*

I tossed my phone to the other side of the couch, turned my back on it, and tried to sleep. Instead of Felix, my head filled not just with memories of my parents, but of Naomi. I desperately wanted to call Kayda. I wanted to sit across from her at our favorite ramen place, eat noodles until we couldn't button our pants, and talk about normal stuff—job nonsense, the infuriating men in our lives, plans for the weekend.

Something else was crowding out all my other thoughts, no matter how hard I tried to stamp it down. Being pissed at the

Collective was futile—even more futile now than when I'd been holed up in the factory. Yet, the thing I wanted most right now was to knock them off their pedestals. Yes, they kept the veils up, allowing the small, contained worlds of the hubs to exist without interference from the majority of Earth's population. But should they be this revered because of it? Should they be able to control everything solely because they kept us hidden? Their priority had always been keeping Luma as-is: the city that never slept, the city where humans and fae could coexist in relative safety, where humans had opportunities beyond what was offered in the mundane world. And yet, they had taken everything from me: my parents, Naomi, Felix, and now my home—the only city I'd ever lived in. Naomi was dead. Nyla, Vian, Holly's friend Bonnie, and countless others had gone missing. Bliss took out humans left and right. Feral vampires were slipping through the veil. The Sorcerers Collective may have provided the only way to keep us undetected in Luma, but were the veils protecting our way of life, or were they keeping us locked inside it? I sounded like the megaphone-waving leader of the Vampire Hunters of America.

There needed to be an upheaval, a change in priorities, something ... but what recourse did a nobody like me have?

———

Twenty-four hours passed with no updates from Felix or the Stones about what was in Bliss. I didn't have any ideas about how to overthrow the government either.

The night after my conversation with Felix, I tossed and turned on Caspian's couch. I couldn't get comfortable. It was too hot, so I kicked off the blanket, but then it was too cold, and I pulled it back over me. My thoughts spun in a million directions without settling on anything in particular. I picked up my phone to check my messages. Still nothing. Just like there'd been nothing an hour ago, or six hours ago, or twelve hours ago. I started and stopped half a dozen messages to Felix. I played Lollipop Jumble until my eyes crossed.

I eventually gave up on sleeping altogether and crept into the kitchen. As I quietly poked around in Caspian's fridge and pantry, I recalled the late nights where I'd snuck into the kitchen to steal bites of my birthday cake. My little sugar-infused oasis when I worried—when I *knew*—my world was about to crumble around me.

That was what I needed. I needed cake.

Caspian's pantry was well stocked—mostly thanks to Welsh. I looked up recipes on my phone and pieced together ones for both batter and frosting. After the dubious concoction had been in the oven for about half an hour, the kitchen and living room filled with the warm scent of sugar and baking cake, Caspian came wandering out. I heard the shuffle of his bare feet and turned to glance over the back of the couch. He wore basketball shorts, an oversized white T-shirt, and his usually tidy dark hair was mussed, but only on one side. He'd let his locks grow too long while in captivity.

"What are you doing?" he whispered, though we were the only ones in the house. He rubbed the heel of a palm against his eye.

"Baking therapy," I whispered back.

He eyed the disaster I'd left in his kitchen, wrinkled his nose, and plopped down on the other side of the couch. He crossed his arms and assessed me. "I tried to give you your space yesterday, since you were dealing with complex emotions. You've been uncharacteristically quiet for almost a full day. I like the peace and quiet just as much as the next guy, but it's a little *too* quiet. So, uhh ... did you want to, like, talk about what happened with your ... ex?"

I laughed, an abrupt, sharp sound that startled us both. "You couldn't have sounded more uncomfortable if you'd tried."

He sighed. "Sorry. I'm not good at this kind of thing. My last breakup was uneventful, and yours seems ... involved. I haven't even attempted dating since I got out of the academy, which was over three years ago."

"You dated another sorcerer, I'm guessing? Sorceress?"

"Sorceress, yes. It was a relationship of convenience. It helped expel energy when the coursework became too taxing and we needed an outlet. When she got her certification, she left for her home hub in North Carolina."

His "reminiscing about an old flame—or rather, an old lukewarm ember" voice was as lacking in emotion as his teacher voice.

"You didn't want to go with her?"

Cocking his head as if I'd just asked the strangest thing he'd ever heard, he said, "Never considered it."

"Do you two keep in contact?"

"We send each other cards on our birthdays."

They'd clearly had an unbridled passion for each other.

I imagined him and Lady Caspian growing weary after studying for eight straight hours. *My, I am quite exhausted mentally, but physically I am abuzz with restless energy. What do you say, Lady Caspian, would you like to perform coitus to wear ourselves out?*

Why, yes, Sir Caspian, she would say. *Coitus sounds like an excellent use of our time. Please keep the activity to no more than fifteen minutes to ensure I have time to shower and lay out my clothes for the morning.*

Fifteen minutes will be more than sufficient, Lady Caspian. Let us away to partake in coitus.

I snorted to myself.

"What?" he asked.

I shook my head. "Nothing."

The egg timer mercifully dinged a minute later. The cake *looked* like a cake. Smelled like one, too. I'd had to get creative with a few substitutions. The frosting looked more ... chocolate-adjacent than actual chocolate, and was somehow lumpy and runny at the same time. Undeterred, once the cake was cool enough, I slathered on the entire contents of the bowl.

Caspian had perched himself on a high-backed stool to watch. The slight curl to his lip told me he found my baking skills even less palatable than discussing my dating history.

"Want a piece?"

He craned his neck to look past me at the glowing green numbers on the oven. "It's four in the morning."

"If you give me some speech about how it's too early for cake, I will slap you with this spatula."

Tamping down a soft smile, he nodded. "Yes, I would like some cake."

Steam wafted up as I sliced into it. The inside looked decent. I slid the spatula between the crispy edge of the cake and the baking dish, then transferred the chocolate-covered square onto an awaiting plate. Once the concoction was on the ceramic, it just sort of … crumbled. As if the secret ingredient had been sawdust.

"Oh dear," Caspian amended. "I do not want any cake."

"Maybe it tastes great and looks horrible," I said, cutting a slice for myself.

We clinked forks across the counter in a toast, and then each took a bite. It was a toss-up between which was worse—the cake itself, or the gelatinous frosting. I chewed valiantly for a solid three seconds before dry heaving and spitting the cake into the sink.

Caspian was so shocked by the unladylike sight that he sputtered a laugh that sprayed crumbly cake bits all over the counter, the top of the still-cooling cake, and me.

"Caspian!" I said, wiping the crumbs off my shirt and a very wet glob of frosting off my cheek.

"I'm sorry!" he said, then coughed. "Oh my God, it's so dry. What the hell did you put in this?" He coughed a second time, spewing even more cake onto the counter.

We stared at each other for a second, then burst into raucous laughter. I laughed so hard I cried, forehead resting on the counter. I would try to get myself under control, then he'd start up again, and I'd lose it. We were making such a racket that the sword freed itself from the duffel bag and zipped into the kitchen, vibrating up a storm, ready to lop off the head of our intruder. When it figured out that we were just delirious, it hummed *very* loudly, glowed a deep red, and then retreated to its bag.

I snorted softly, wiping at my eyes. "Sorry. For … oh gosh, all of it."

He shook his head, smiling and holding his side. "Nothing to apologize for. I haven't been sleeping that well lately. This was way better than tossing and turning. That's the hardest I've laughed in a *long* time …"

"Do you miss your home—your primary home, I mean?" I asked, realizing I'd never once asked him how he felt about being trapped here for over a week. Even if his home hadn't burned to a crisp, he was still homeless in a way—as much of a fugitive as I was.

"A little bit," he said. "I'm mostly worried, like you, that the Collective is determined not to let me get back to my old life. My options are to remain even more hidden than I was before, or start over somewhere else. The Collective wins either way."

"What they're doing to us isn't fair," I said.

"No, but they're also too powerful at this point—even for someone like me who's been trained in their ways. They're too protected. They've built a system where they can stay sequestered, rarely show their faces, and yet get to call all the shots. They have spies all over the city, and when they need muscle, they have trained shifters *and* humans to do their bidding.

"We don't even know the true nature of the enemy. Does anyone even know how many sorcerers make up the Collective? There were six when Luma was founded, but how many are there now? They didn't even divulge that during my schooling. There could be five, there could be five hundred. We're not flashy like the elementals; the nature of our magic use doesn't lend itself to quick battle magic. Elementals are the hand-to-hand fighters; sorcerers are the siege weapons. A trebuchet is big and clunky and could easily be destroyed by ground troops. But if it's well protected and is given time to do what it does best—those fortified castle walls don't stand a chance."

Perhaps passion raged in Caspian after all. Passionate hatred for the Collective.

"You didn't want to join the illustrious ranks of veil maintenance?" I asked.

He smiled ruefully. "At first I did. My parents are sorcerers, and my little brother joined the academy a year after I did. Luma has one of the best sorcery academies in the country, mostly because the Collective is always looking to increase their numbers —whatever that number is—to accommodate how much power is needed to keep the veil maintained in a city this big. In smaller hubs, sorcerers can work to maintain the veil while also having a life beyond that. Here, that's all they can do. That's why they outsource the heavy lifting to their minions. I saw what I was heading toward if I went down that path, so I decided I would finish my training but pursue other things."

"What about your parents and brother?"

"Parents are in Alaska. Veil maintenance is minimal. My brother couldn't handle the academy and dropped out after a year. He lives in the mundane world with his very human wife and their very human kids."

"Why'd you stay in Luma when your schooling ended?"

He shrugged. "I like it here. I've felt more at home here than anywhere else I've been. Some cities just grab hold of you and don't let go."

He was more in love with Luma than he ever had been with Lady Caspian. That much was clear.

He stifled a yawn. "I should probably get back to bed ... I think I'll be able to sleep now."

"I'll clean this up," I said. "Promise. And I'll hang up my baker's cap because ... holy shit."

He laughed easily this time. When he relaxed, it shaved a good five years off his usual stuffy demeanor. "Good idea. Night, Harlow."

"Night."

After brushing my teeth thoroughly, washing my face, and changing my shirt, I settled back on the couch for the night, vowing to clean up the horrible mess of a kitchen in the morning. It felt like I'd only been asleep for a few seconds when I was startled awake again.

I blinked slowly, trying to orient myself.

Then the sound came again. A cell phone. *My* cell phone.

I lurched for the device on the coffee table and answered the call after the fourth ring. "Hi!" I breathed.

Felix hesitated. "Did I wake you? Sorry. I figured you'd be awake by now since it's almost ten …"

"I was up late," I said, then yawned deeply. "When you're on the lam, you don't have to conform to society's rules."

"You're on the lam *because* you don't conform to society's rules," he countered.

"Don't come at me with semantics this early in the morning."

He huffed a laugh. "Anyway … results are in. And the results are weird."

I sat up, wide awake now. "How weird?"

The sword must have heard that I was awake because it emerged from the duffel bag and hovered above the coffee table. Maybe it realized too that only one person had this number.

"Vampire venom weird," Felix said.

"Uhhh …"

"Exactly," Felix said. "The hunters and the mundane police both have a pretty extensive record of various toxins and poisons that are fae-based, since those things tend to do bad things to humans. There's all kinds of stuff already in the system—even from fae who are extinct on Earth now. Chimera ichor, werewolf saliva, vampire venom. The concentration levels of the venom are insanely high in Bliss. When a match popped up in the system for the venom, my buddy ran a sample of Bliss we had on hand, and the stuff we usually can get a hold of has the venom in it, too, but a tiny quantity. So small that it doesn't even register as present during a standard analysis. He had to specifically search for it. No one even thought to look for venom before this."

"Okay … give me a second …" My mind whirled. "Vampire venom is like a neurotoxin, right?"

"Yeah, like what's in spider venom. It's meant to numb and subdue their victim. When a vamp bites a human for too long, it kills them. Not from being drained of blood, but because the venom floods the bloodstream and short-circuits the heart. That's why they only take a sip at a time if they want to keep their source of warm human blood around for a while."

"Any idea why there's caffeine in Bliss?" I asked.

"My buddy guesses that since in humans, the venom subdues them, the caffeine counteracts that effect. It's made it harder to figure out what's going on in the human cases since the side effects of it have been all over the board," Felix said. "Even in these super small quantities, the venom has a psychotropic effect too—making the victim feel good, and with enough small doses of the venom, it creates a sort of symbiotic bond. The victim craves the euphoric feeling the venom gives them, and the vamp gets blood."

"Does the bond happen between vamp and fae too?"

"Yeah. The fae has to have high quantities of it in their bloodstream for the bond to take hold, but it works the same way it does in humans," Felix said.

Did the girls at the Ghost Lily get exposed to the venom over a long enough period that they'd eventually leave willingly with someone like Randal or Leon? Was that why more of these missing cases hadn't been reported? If the ladies were seen walking out with these so-called runners, maybe no one thought anything of it. Strangers going home together after meeting in a bar wasn't uncommon.

In these cases, the reality was like a supernatural version of Stockholm syndrome brought on by concentrated doses of mind-altering venom coursing through the girls' veins.

Was there some kind of Bliss-making empire hidden inside

Luma? My parents had been trying to track down the leaders of the cartel. The only vampires inside Luma's veil were the occasional feral ones, and domesticated vamps—like the cabbie I'd met.

"Bliss has to be coming from outside Luma, right? Either someone is milking vamps for their venom to use it in the manufacturing of Bliss or—"

"Vampires are making the stuff themselves and trafficking it in," Felix said. "Which means someone in Luma is in contact with the vamps on the outside. Vamps can't bring it in themselves. If they could get into Luma, they wouldn't need Bliss. The vamps provide the drug in exchange for the girls. The street value of this stuff is off the charts. We've been assuming all this time that the Bliss cartel was headquartered in Luma since the clubs and casinos here are flooded with it. But it must not be made here; someone is bringing it in. It would explain why the real stuff is impossible for law enforcement to find. The potent tabs are brought in in much smaller quantities."

"*Who* is bringing it in, though?" I asked. "Sorcerers on the outside who can manipulate the runes on the obelisks so people can move across the veil with it? Shipments of it hidden in cargo that comes through the Industrial District, and our sorcerers are letting the drugs in without knowing?"

"Maybe both. Maybe ten other possibilities we haven't thought of yet."

Something clicked for me then, and I cursed.

"What?"

"Leon's boss is a vampire."

"Who the hell is Leon?"

I launched into the whole sordid thing—Mathias's missing sister Nyla, rumors about fae ladies going missing, my run-in with Leon at the Ghost Lily, and his confession about what had ultimately happened to Oliver Randal. I left Welsh and Caspian out of it, letting Felix think I'd done all this on my own. I trusted

Felix well enough, but it wasn't my place to give up the identity of the guys.

Was there a chance Nyla was still alive? A vampire wouldn't go through this much trouble to get their undead hands on beautiful fae girls just for fun. The girls were needed for something. If they were needed, they weren't mere throwaways.

"Geez, Low," Felix said, cutting into my thoughts. "*Please* back away from this. This shit—Bliss—is what got your dad killed. What got Naomi killed. Dealing with a drug cartel is dangerous enough, but you're a human, and these guys all have magic on their side. There's millions of dollars in Bliss. These people would kill over a lot less. Unraveling this isn't worth dying over."

I felt someone watching me and I glanced over the back of the couch. Caspian stood in the doorway, his hair damp from a shower.

Felix grumbled in my ear. "I didn't want to tell you this yet …"

I looked away from Caspian, my focus back on Felix even though I couldn't see him. "Tell me what?"

"This morning, the Collective announced they're going to start doing door-to-door sweeps for you and Caspian Blackthorn. They're outfitting hunters and werecat guards with what's basically a magical version of a Taser that we're supposed to use on anyone who we think is wearing a glamour."

That wasn't good. "Do you know where the raids are starting?"

"Yes, but I can't tell you."

I tamped down my irritation, knowing that he'd tell me if he could. The information was locked behind the parameters of his Soul NDA. Stupid Collective.

"I'm assuming you're well hidden, since no one has come close to finding you yet, but it's only a matter of time, Low." Softer, he said, "And it'll happen a lot faster if you piss them off. Stay wherever you are until this blows over. Please."

This would never blow over, though. The Collective had to find Caspian and me if they wanted to save face. First, they'd turned the town against me, then the bounty hunters after us both, and now they were going to turn over every stone in Luma to find our hiding place.

I glanced over the couch again. Caspian still stood there, brow cocked in question. He wouldn't even be in this predicament if I'd never stolen Haskins's sword. Caspian and I were on the same page as far as the Collective went—we wanted to knock them down a peg. Our window of time to do that, however, was shrinking by the second. I wouldn't make any decisions until I talked to him. I appreciated Felix's concern for me, but he didn't understand the position we were in. Not really.

"You're right," I told Felix. "Thank you for the information."

"Harlow ... you don't give in this easy. Are you thinking of doing something stupid even after everything I've just told you?"

"Who, me?"

I hung up on him calling my name.

CHAPTER THIRTY

As I tossed the phone onto the couch, Caspian lifted his brows in question. "What's going on?"

I told him what Felix said about the upcoming raids. Would they start in Luma Proper, thinking that we'd choose to hide in the most population-dense part of the city, or would they start in the outskirts? They also had no idea that Caspian and I were together. Would they spread their hunters and cats wide, covering as much territory as possible in one grand sweep, or would their searches be more concentrated, swarming entire neighborhoods at once?

"I'm surprised they hadn't started that already, honestly," Caspian said. "I knew we couldn't hide here forever."

If I were smart, I'd pack up, take the travel talisman Welsh had given me, and get the heck out of Dodge. And yet, that wasn't what my gut told me to do.

After a beat, Caspian said, "You looked distressed even before he dropped that last bit of information on you. What did he tell you before that?"

"I know what's in Bliss," I said. "Vampire venom."

His brows hiked toward his hairline. "Interesting …"

Several seconds ticked by in silence. He still stood in the entrance to the hallway.

"That's it? Just … 'interesting'?" I finally asked him.

"I'm thinking …" he said, his eyes glassy as that brain of his went into overdrive.

I didn't have proof yet, but my gut told me that Nyla Stone and her friend Vian had befallen the same fate that had awaited Peony and Paisley. Oliver Randal, more than likely, had gotten the girls doped up on vamp venom, the neurotoxin overriding their defenses, and called an anonymous runner to come pick them up. The runner took the girls out of the Ghost Lily, out of Luma, and into the waiting clutches of a vampire on the other side of the veil for who knew what.

I recalled my conversation with Mathias about the disappearance of his sister and the efforts he and Geraldine had gone through to find her. *"Human cops get the fae cases that are considered low priority. After a few months, the police told us they'd concluded their search and had ample evidence to suggest the girls had left Luma."*

I clenched my jaw. The girls *had* left Luma, just not willingly. Which begged the question: did the Collective know the girls were missing and had turned a blind eye, or were they somehow complicit in the disappearances? Were the mundane police in on it too, or were they coerced into making sure these investigations went cold and grieving families' questions left unanswered?

The couch cushion beside me dipped, and I jumped at Caspian's sudden appearance. I'd gotten so lost in my head, I'd forgotten he'd been loitering in the doorway.

"What are you thinking?" he asked.

"I'm thinking that the missing girls are in the hands of vampires. But, even if the Collective wasn't currently sending out their minions to tear apart the city looking for us, we couldn't present this to anyone in authority here. The Collective doesn't even want families investigating the disappearances." Felix would hate this next idea; I was glad it was Caspian beside me right now.

"I think our best bet for finding them is the Vampire Hunters of America."

"I agree. I must also state that our best bet for not getting caught in this city-wide search is to leave Luma immediately. The girls' disappearances are tragic, and I know you and Welsh are fond of Mathias and his wife, but this is ultimately not our fight. We could leave right now, regroup somewhere far from Luma, and leave the mystery of the disappearances to someone else to solve."

My first instinct was to be offended by his callous tone. But I also knew Caspian well enough now to know he was presenting the neutral position. No emotion, just facts. He wanted me to decide which side of that position I fell on.

I didn't feel a connection to Nyla—I'd never met her—but I felt one with Mathias. I knew what it felt like to have someone abruptly disappear from your life, to forever be stuck in limbo, always wondering.

Finally, I said, "I want to find them."

Caspian nodded once. "Me too."

The night the feral vampire had tried to run off with me, I'd tucked Marisol's business card into a pocket of my jeans—jeans Caspian had laundered for me that same night. Thankfully, because he was a stickler for detail and also very nosy, he'd checked all my pockets before throwing my dirty clothes in the washer. He told me now that he'd affixed the card to the side of the fridge.

I grabbed my phone and strolled into the kitchen, then plucked the card free from its spot between a flyer from a local Chinese place and a magnet for a plumber. "And you're sure you're good with me calling them?" I asked, heading back across the kitchen.

He had moved from the couch to his preferred spot in front of the island counter. "Are you?"

I stared at the vampire hunter logo. Marisol had assured me that the hunters wouldn't be interested in handing me over to the

Collective, but I hardly knew Marisol and I didn't have any reason to trust her. Of course, she and Daniella could have easily hidden in the rail yard and followed Caspian back here that night, their fellow vamp hunters in tow. Since there had yet to be an ambush here, it was unlikely Marisol had lied to me, but being paranoid was one of my favorite pastimes, and I was good at it, dammit.

Instead of replying, I dialed the number, then pressed the cell phone to my ear.

"This is Irving," a gruff male voice answered. "Which neighborhood is your top choice for the evening?"

I blinked. "Uhh ... Marisol gave me this number? I met her and her cousin Daniella near the old factory in the Necropolis."

Irving was quiet for a long moment. "This Fletch?"

I swallowed. "Yeah."

"Dammit. I'm out thirty bucks now! I didn't believe you'd ever call."

"Sorry to disappoint."

He chuckled. "One sec. She's around here somewhere. Mari? You in here? Marisol!" Long pause. "Hey, you seen Mari? Fletch actually called. Ha. You're out thirty, too?"

What felt like half a century later, Marisol was on the line. "Hey! How are you?"

Was this number a landline? A community cell phone?

"I'm all right," I said. "I just came across some information I thought you all might be interested in. And ... I ... sorry, but are you sure this line is secure?"

Marisol said, "Yep. We have a couple of tech guys on the team who are constantly checking for that stuff. We would have been raided by the werecats a long time ago otherwise."

Deciding once again to trust her, I told her about Bliss, how it was trafficked into the Ghost Lily, and drugged-up girls were ferreted out. "I'm sure this is happening in other clubs and bars. I just know for a fact it's happening at the Lily."

"Damn," came a tinny male voice, and I suspected that during my explanation, Marisol had put me on speaker. I did the same so Caspian could hear, then placed the phone on the counter between us.

The guy continued, "There's a contingent of VHoA stationed about twenty miles outside of Luma, and Tercla is a mile beyond them." My brain tripped over the odd-sounding word after "contingent." It sounded like "voe-ah." I guessed it was the acronym for Vampire Hunters of America. "We can ask if they've heard or seen anything about fae girls popping up in mundane areas. Bliss is a problem everywhere, though—trouble and odd instances follow that stuff like a stinking fog. Fae get addicted to the garbage just as much as anyone else. An influx of young fat girls might not be enough to stand out to anyone as particularly strange."

I wondered if this was knowledge the Luma chapter of VHoA had gathered through reports from members beyond the veil, or if this was information they'd collected themselves.

"No one knows vamps are making this crap, though," Marisol said. "That's new. And explains … a lot."

"They're making it or they have someone who's making it for them. They're supplying the key ingredient if nothing else," I said. "Do you all travel outside Luma often?"

"As much as we can. In addition to the tech guys, we have a couple of witches on the team who keep us supplied with travel talismans. We won't win the war against vampires hiding in Luma, but by fighting outside it. As sorcerers, all the Collective knows is defensive magic. Strengthen the veil, fortify the walls—but it's not enough. The vamps are coming. Their attack dogs being sent out to hunt and scout is a pretty good sign that we're already in deep shit here."

The phrase "attack dogs" made my mind jump to werewolves. Last I heard, the werewolves had all died out. While fae blood had caused changes in vampires, it had made the wolves so sick it had decimated them. For whatever reason, it hadn't affected the other shifters. "Attack dogs?" I asked.

"Okay. Vamp 101. There are three tiers," Marisol said. "Tier-one vamps are the old-school ones, like those who live in Tercla. They believe in keeping things pure and don't drink fae blood—human only. They mostly stay out of everyone's way. A lot of old-school vamps have actual contracts with their humans. Some humans dig the euphoria they get from being bitten, and willingly agree to be blood-bound to a vampire. Humans who want to get turned go there, and if a human and a vamp get involved romantically, they usually hole up in Tercla, too. It's the biggest hub on the West Coast of 'pure' vampires. Out of all of them, tier-one vamps are the sanest of the bunch."

This was all news to me. Even Caspian appeared perplexed by this information. My thoughts about the bloodsuckers had been much simpler: all vamps were the same and that the West Coast ones lived in Tercla, the vamp-only hub. But like most citizens of Luma, I hadn't worried much about vamps. The Pact and the veil kept them out and unable to attack humans in the hubs. Out of sight, out of mind. Except this had led to many people being very ignorant—myself included. The Vampires Hunters of America were the only ones who seemed to know the truth about them, and most everyone thought they were nuts.

"Tier two are hybrid vamps," Marisol continued. "They mostly sustain themselves on human blood, but they drink fae blood, too. They're all a little unhinged because of the fae blood, but if they limit how much they drink, they keep their wits about them—like functioning alcoholics. Once they get a taste for it, it can completely overtake them. There doesn't seem to be any rhyme or reason why fae blood drastically alters the DNA of some vamps. That's the biggest reason a lot of the old-school vamps don't even want to try it. Slippery slope into madness." After a slight pause, Marisol said, "You can probably guess which ones are tier three."

"Ferals," I said.

"Yep. Those are the ones who gave into the temptation of fae blood and are junkies for it now. They don't organize into societies the way the other vamps do and don't even form nests.

They'll come to each other's aid if one is cornered, though, and they're smarter than anything that animalistic has any right to be," Marisol said. "The weird thing with ferals is that they seem to listen to the hybrid vamps. The hybrids sic them on enemies."

"Like attack dogs," I said, understanding what she meant now. "Is there a hub of hybrids like there is for the tier-one vamps?"

A male voice chimed in. "No. The hybrids form nests—somewhere between ten to twenty vamps each—with one leader they answer to. They typically have hierarchies. Head honcho on top who calls the shots, couple of right-hand men or women who make sure the honcho's orders are carried out, etcetera. Nests are scattered all over the country. There are at least a dozen of them in California alone. But now that we know vamps are making Bliss, it seems likely that areas with high concentrations of drug activity could be where these nests are. It's been assumed for a while that the headquarters for the Bliss cartel is here in California, too."

Marisol said, "There have been a ton of overlapping cases of Bliss overdoses, battles over drug territory, and humans killed by vampires lately, but we just assumed that the vampires were taking advantage of the chaos that comes with the drug scene. Disappearances from dangerous areas aren't uncommon; authorities have a hard time proving—or in a lot of cases, caring—what's happening to the victims from drug hot spots. When we investigate possible vampire attacks, we usually find our cases are tangled up in the mundane police's Bliss cases where humans get sick or die in droves."

The VHoA was so much more than a fringe group of weirdos shouting that the sky was falling—in this case, the sky *was* falling. But no one was listening or looking up. Well, I was looking now, and what I saw was slowly scaring the crap out of me. I wanted to take the Collective down, but they might also be the only ones with enough power to save the city from this threat.

We could save the city first and *then* think about bucking the system.

"I know you said the Collective doesn't care about the vamp

problem, just that the symptoms are treated," I said, "but what if we can *force* them to care?"

A faint series of mutters sounded on the other end of the line.

"What do you have in mind?" Marisol finally asked.

"I first heard about the fae disappearances when a friend's sister went missing. She's a goblin teen named Nyla Stone; her friend Vian went missing at the same time. If we can find her, or any of the missing girls, they could be the proof we need to show the veils are far more porous than anyone thought. The girls could give firsthand accounts of what happened to them—they could let the public know. If the public is up in arms about this, the Collective will have to listen to that, right? They care about appearances and saving face. Maybe they'd crackdown on the vampire problem if their reputation as our ultimate protectors was on the line."

"While I like this idea," Marisol said, "VHoA's got a serious reputation problem of its own. We've been trying to tell folks for years about this and no one will listen. And knowing the Collective, even if we got some of the girls back, they'd change the narrative and get all the credit."

"Maybe, but now you have us," Caspian said, speaking up for the first time. He eyed me across the counter. He didn't look away from me when he said, "This is Caspian Blackthorn."

I swore I heard the stunned silence on the other side.

"I *told* you that was him, Dani!" Marisol yelped into the phone.

"With my resources, I can get the Collective's attention," Caspian said, unfazed by the reactions reverberating from the other line. "If that means informing the general public on our own of what's going on in Luma, and tarnishing the Collective's reputation as they've tarnished yours, then that's what we'll do."

"They'll come down harder on you than they already are," a woman said. "They've driven you both underground already. Did you hear they're starting door-to-door searches for you? They don't seem to suspect you're together though."

"We heard. We've already discussed it. We want to try to find these girls. If we want to kick the Collective where it hurts, we're going to need a lot of feet. Finding the girls could help with that."

"Well, you've got VHoA on your side," a guy said. There were several murmurs of agreement.

I asked, "Where do we start? Based on what you've said, it seems unlikely that the girls are ending up in Tercla since old-school vamps aren't interested in fae blood. It's probably the hybrids, right? Vamps who want a supply of fae blood?"

"That's my best guess, yes," Marisol said. "There's too much planning involved for it to be the ferals. The hybrids want the girls for something specific; they're not collecting ones who match a certain criterion just to turn around and feed them to their pets—the ferals aren't that picky."

"You say the vampires in Tercla are the sanest of the bunch, yes?" Caspian asked. When he got confirmation, he asked, "Have any of you been *in* Tercla? Are they sane enough that we could talk to someone in charge there? Vampires would be more clued in to what their fellow bloodsuckers are up to, wouldn't they?"

A few chuckles rippled through the phone's small speakers.

"Sorry," said Marisol, clearing her throat. "They're sane, but the bar is low. That place is anarchy. It's every vampire for themself in there. There aren't riots in the street or anything. Vamps just keep to themselves and stay out of each other's business. They've only got two rules as far as anyone can figure out. One, Bliss is banned. If someone gets caught with it in there, they're exiled or worse. Two, no hybrids or ferals. There's a process to help vamps kick Bliss, and it involves getting covered in runes just like the vamps who get vetted to live in hubs. Magical rehab. But even if they get 'clean,' Tercla won't let them in. Their veil has similar properties to ours, except theirs keep out Bliss-tainted vamps. They don't trust the runes on a rehabbed vamp to hold. The last thing they need is for the runes to fail and then they have a feral inside their barrier. Ferals can kill a vampire without any special tools or killing techniques. There's a toxin in a feral's claws that causes necrosis in a pure vampire. One scratch can be enough to kill a pure vamp in an hour flat."

My mouth dropped open. I looked up at Caspian, eyebrows raised in question. He shrugged and shook his head—he hadn't known this either.

"Give us a day or two to ask around about an increase in fae women popping up in areas around known hybrid nest locations," a man on Marisol's side said. "I've got a couple of ideas already. If you've got a picture of Nyla, that could help with the search. We'll be in touch soon."

I tapped the end call button and stared at the device long after the screen had gone dark.

"You can still change your mind. We can leave here right now and not look back," Caspian said.

Leon's words echoed in my head. *I'm sorry for what I was going to do to you ladies, all right? It's a job. I get Bliss, girls, and a fuck-ton of cash when one of the runners delivers a pretty girl to my boss. It's nothing personal.*

"We're in too deep now," I said.

Later, as I lay in Caspian's dark living room, staring at the ceiling, I willed Nyla to hear me. *If you're still alive, hold on a little longer. We're coming.*

CHAPTER THIRTY-ONE

Over the next forty-eight hours, a plan took shape. Welsh had been MIA for almost a full day, helping a faun get out of Luma because of an abusive relationship. When Welsh returned to our little hideout, we filled him in on everything he'd missed. As I expected, he had no reservations about the plan to track down the missing girls. He probably would have been down for the plan anyway, but after spending time as Peony and experiencing the ultimate creep factor of a guy like Leon firsthand, he was as committed to the cause as Caspian and I were.

He took on his gofer assignment with little fuss, too. From Mathias, he got a photo of Nyla and Vian, though Welsh didn't tell the Stones why he needed it. No point getting the goblins' hopes up. From the VHoA, he picked up a few pieces of tactical gear for us. Neither Caspian nor I were skilled fighters, but Marisol had assured us that if they got intel that suggested they found a promising vampire nest, the VHoA had our backs. Caspian would be armed with one of his Frankenweapons, Welsh would have the daggers I'd taken from Haskins—one of which had that nasty lightning spell infused in the blade—and I'd have my electrified mace. The guys also had their magic. The sword was its own weapon and didn't need me slowing it down by trying to wield it.

I'd asked Marisol point-blank why we were tagging along at all. I was a liability. The way the vampire had knocked me on my ass and dragged me off like the clubbed mate of a caveman was proof enough of that.

"We need the numbers," she said plainly. "The Luma chapter has twenty members, and the Fresno chapter who we've been in contact with is down to ten. If we come across a nest of twenty, we're going to need all the help we can get. That sword will do everything in its power to keep you safe. It's almost a good thing that you're untrained. You'll be in danger a lot. The sword will swoop in to make sure nothing happens to you."

Nothing like being told your utter uselessness was an asset.

"Glad to be of service," I deadpanned.

Marisol had merely laughed.

The sheer number of healing tonics Welsh had cooked up in Caspian's kitchen over the past two days didn't bode well for this whole thing either—especially since I was pretty sure they were mostly for me.

I had yet to tell Felix what we were planning. Hadn't heard from him much anyway. I knew it was because he was neck-deep in doing a city-wide search for the elusive Harlow Fletcher and Caspian Blackthorn, but I assumed he was also quiet because he was pissed. Couldn't do much about that. Our lives had diverged in too many ways for either of us to think that being reunited would solve five years of distance, secrets, and broken trust. Picking up where we'd left off wasn't an option. Maybe it would be someday, but not now.

Three days after I first called Marisol, we got the call we'd been waiting for.

"There's a vampire nest to the east of Luma that might fit the bill," Marisol said when I answered. "For the past month, VHoA members from the Fresno chapter have been staking out a club known for Bliss activity. It sounds a lot like what's happening at the Ghost Lily."

"Is it a mundane bar?" I asked, confused.

"Yes," Marisol said. "But a pair of fae women have been showing up with a guy who we know is a hybrid."

"And how do you know that? Do hybrids look different?" I asked.

"Hybrids often have black-tipped fingers—the necrosis you've seen on the ferals. The necrosis affects feet, ears, and noses sometimes, too. A few of them have thickened blood that looks black under their translucent skin."

Gross. "Doesn't that make it hard for hybrids to blend in? I mean, vamps usually have charismatic magic on their side that can turn a human to goo with the right amount of eye contact, but if the dude's nose is rotting off …"

Marisol laughed. "Depending on how often they're drinking fae blood, it may get harder for them to navigate the human world. In most hybrids, the whites of their eyes are swirled with black, too. Only ferals and rehabbed vamps have the wall-to-wall black eyes. This guy isn't that bad on the rotting-flesh scale, but when he's on the hunt, the veins at his temples go very dark. He also wears gloves regardless of the season—we're guessing to hide the necrosis—and sunglasses no matter where he is."

The dude sounded like a hot mess.

Marisol said, "Anyway, VHoA has a couple of members who are in the hybrid's favorite club regularly, keeping an eye on things—glamoured like you and Welsh were. VHoA has a better relationship with mundane police than they do inside Luma—but that's not saying much. Most mundane law enforcement outside the hubs know about the fae, but that doesn't always mean they want to deal with any of it.

"Six or seven months ago, the hybrid was caught attacking a man on his way home from that same club. He didn't bite the guy because a cop happened to be in the area and saw the attack. He shot the vamp and then informed VHoA, gave a description, and we've been tailing the hybrid ever since."

Humans in the mundane world dealing with supernatural creatures sounded absolutely terrifying. But then I remembered all over again that my parents had met that way.

"And you said he's been seen with two fae?" I asked.

"Right, but not always the same two. The average human just catalogs these women as otherworldly beautiful—like the type who ends up in show business. The hybrid's behavior completely changed about six months ago when he started showing up with the girls. The hybrid sits in dark corners of the club with these two gorgeous women. The ladies work the club while he stays seated. Every VHoA member who tails these girls say they flirt, dance, and drink with anyone who shows any interest in them. We've just assumed the girls and the hybrid were in one of those contracted relationships where they both get their rocks off with the blood bond. The fae usually ends up with an interested human, and they leave the club together. Once both girls leave with someone else, the hybrid leaves. It's weird, but we're not in the business of policing anyone's sex life. It all seems consensual on the surface."

"And VHoA has followed the hybrid once he leaves the club?" I asked.

"Yep," Marisol said. "The humans the girls leave the bar with drive the girls back to the hybrid's house. He or she walks in willingly with the fae. Hybrids usually have large houses in the middle of nowhere—they need the space for the several hybrids who live in the nest, plus whatever human and/or fae living food they've got inside. Windows are always tinted or the blinds are closed so we can't see in.

"If the human appears to be of sound mind and walks up that driveway, hand in hand with the fae, we can't do anything, even if we know there are hybrids inside. We're bound to mundane laws

—if there's no actual proof of a crime, we can't raid the place, guns blazing. The police can't get a search warrant solely because the weird guy in the biggest house in town keeps backward hours and has beautiful houseguests. Without concrete proof, VHoA is stuck."

I never would have thought there'd be a time when I wished we had the Collective and their werecats at our disposal.

Marisol continued. "But now that we know the vampires are making Bliss to drug fae girls and get them out of Luma, we've got reason to believe that it's the hybrid's companions who are the prisoners even more than the unsuspecting humans who end up in the hybrid's house. We've compiled a list of missing fae women from across the Pacific Northwest. There are over thirty of them who have disappeared in the last year. We got our cop buddies from Fresno to drop that list on the desk of a superior who is a believer and we've been given the go-ahead to raid a house of this particular hybrid."

My heart tapped out a frantic rhythm. "When?"

"Tomorrow night," she said. "Meet us at headquarters at six."

The headquarters for Luma's chapter of VHoA was in the Necropolis neighborhood—the same area as the factory where I'd holed up for a few days. The factory was on the west side of the neighborhood, and their hideout was on the east, near the border with Montclaire, where my old apartment had been. It was a half-hour drive from Caspian's house, and we took back roads to get there. I'd taken all my stuff with me, planning for the eventuality that this plan would go haywire and I'd need to book it. All my clothes were freshly washed. I was prepared to take on anything. Welsh, the sword, and I rode to the headquarters in one of Caspian's cars, and Caspian drove in separately. Best not to keep the fugitives in one place, I supposed.

I had taken the human male glamour tonic before we'd left, and even though I had donned the tactical clothing VHoA had provided, I'd been glamoured to look like I was wearing jeans and a T-shirt. I amused myself on the drive over by narrating everything we saw, using my newly acquired voice. Welsh threatened to murder me if I didn't stop. I deepened my voice and read every passing street sign. When the sword vibrated *very* loudly in the duffel bag beside me, I shut up.

VHoA's headquarters was positioned in the middle of a residential street lined with small ramshackle houses. Parked cars packed the street on both sides, as none of these houses had garages and their driveways were only large enough to fit a single car. Chain-link fences surrounded dead lawns, many of them patrolled by a snarling or yapping dog. Some of those dead lawns had cars, bikes, or scooters parked on them. Occasional three- or four-story apartment buildings jutted between the squat houses, wrought iron balconies looking over the crowded street below. People stood on the balconies, the glow of their cigarettes like fireflies hovering in the growing dark.

Welsh wedged Caspian's truck into a spot and, as we climbed out, I wondered if the vehicle would still be here when we got back. It was one of the nicer ones on the street. Standing on the sidewalk for a moment, weeds poking between the broken slabs of the concrete, I listened to the sounds of the neighborhood. Cars whizzing past on the street a dozen houses away, screaming babies, people shouting, doors slamming, dogs barking. There was no magic here. Just a bunch of humans living on the fringes.

Standing here in a location that might have been the most human-feeling place I'd ever been in Luma, it struck me that this was exactly the kind of place the Collective cared the least about.

My sixth sense pinged a moment later, and I spun around. I instantly relaxed when I spotted Caspian strolling up the street toward us. He was dressed in casual blue jeans, a semi-ratty T-shirt, and old tennis shoes, and his usually perfectly styled hair was a little disheveled. Welsh wore a glamour to match us—a run-of-the-mill human out to meet up with friends, or at least to find some trouble. The residents of this neighborhood had their own shit to deal with. With its bustling people and noise, we'd go unnoticed. Just another set of faces in the crowd.

Caspian and I followed Welsh since he'd been here before. We casually strolled up the sidewalk. I tucked the duffel bag close to my side. Welsh slid open a rolling chain-link fence and the three of us slipped through. This property differed from the ones on either side of it or across the street. A small house sat a few feet from a wild lawn. We walked past it and up the length of a long driveway with three cars parked bumper-to-bumper. A second house sat at the end of the driveway, the garage closed. The front door to the second house swung open, and Marisol stuck her head out. She waved us over.

The front room of the house looked normal enough. A sad-looking brown couch slouched along one wall, and a TV stand sat against the other, a small flat-screen perched on top. Above the couch, a generic poster of a meadow filled with purple flowers hung on the wall. Worn paperbacks crowded a bookshelf in the corner, a potted plant on top, its leaves browning at the edges and hanging limp.

Marisol closed and locked the door behind us, then used a locking talisman for extra security. "Through here," she said, and headed straight back to a closed door.

As she swung it open, voices flooded out. We stepped into the main part of the house, which had been gutted. There were no room-dividing walls, no windows, and the only doors aside from the one we'd just come through presumably led to a bathroom and either a kitchen or an exit out the back. Electronic equipment cluttered tables pushed end to end, taking up the middle of the room. Large monitors sat on the surfaces, their humming computer boxes below. There were open laptops, black boxes of varying sizes dotted with flashing lights, and wires snaking in dozens of directions.

VHoA members sat and stood around the tables, chatting about whatever graced their screens. I could only see two monitors—the rest of them faced the other wall. It looked like security footage. One showed the street that the guys and I had just been on.

It felt like we'd just walked into a war room. Maybe we had, in a way.

Against one wall stood two massive storage containers. They looked like heavy-duty freestanding pantries, but I doubted nonperishable goods waited behind their closed, shiny metal doors.

"The guests of the evening have arrived," Marisol said loudly, and the chatter in the room tapered off.

After we introduced ourselves—the sword was the most popular—we got debriefed on the plan. Welsh already knew everyone by now. Part of the team would stake out the club, and when they received confirmation the hybrid and his fae companions were inside, the rest of the team would storm the hybrid's house.

Caspian, Welsh, the sword, and I were heading for the club. We'd only be used as backup at the house if the team couldn't handle the vampires inside. We'd be the eyes and ears of the VHoA members stationed in a surveillance van down the street from the club in question, who'd be watching the footage from our hidden body cams. My electrified mace was strapped to my hip and layered in a camouflaging glamour. The magic would hold a lot longer when in the presence of humans, who were unlikely to sense the magic of my glamour or weapon.

Once outfitted, we headed back out—the section of the veil near the rail yard in the Necropolis our destination. Travel talismans would get us through the veil, where the Fresno chapter of VHoA waited for us on the other side.

As anxious as I was about possibly having a run-in with a hybrid vampire, a little trill of excitement buzzed in my veins when I thought about stepping out of the bubble of the only world I've ever known and into the mundane world. A world devoid of magic, and dotted with nests of bloodthirsty vampires driven mad by fae blood. And maybe, in some part of the expansive unknown, my mother.

CHAPTER THIRTY-TWO

Being outside Luma wasn't nearly as life changing as I anticipated. Other than the obvious lack of magical buzz in the air, the city of Fresno didn't look all that different from the world behind the veil. There were more cars on the roads, and there was a grayness to the place—the air, the buildings, the shrubby vegetation. But it wasn't as if it were a war-torn wasteland or anything. Its normalness made the reality of the hubs even more incredible. Whole cities teeming with magic and magical beings brought to Earth by the Glitch had been successfully shoved behind walls, shielding their uniqueness from the majority of the planet's population. I wasn't sure if I felt pity for them for not knowing places like Luma existed, or grateful that I was part of a small percentage let in on the secret.

Getting to our destination took half an hour, with me situated between Welsh and Caspian in the back of a van, the sword in my lap. My stomach fluttered wildly with nerves by the time the van pulled into the parking lot of the bar.

As Caspian, Welsh, two VHoA members—Beth and Jacob—and I strolled through the front doors of the Steel Drum Bar & Grill, I tried to channel my best dude energy. I hoped my swagger looked natural, and that my male persona didn't just seem drunk as hell. Welsh would stick close to me as usual, ready to reinforce my glamour should something knock it loose. Shrouded in a camouflaging glamour, the sword would cruise around the ceiling again, keeping a watchful eye—blade?—on things.

My first impression of the place was how dark it was. Easier for the vampire to hide his slowly rotting face from his easily scared-off food. Music blared—a fast-paced country song from the sound of it. It wasn't my favorite genre, but since no goblin rap played in the middle, I didn't have any complaints.

As Welsh and I slowly made our way through the room, I used Welsh's body to shield the mace from anyone who might bump into me and knock the glamour loose. All five of us had earpieces, keeping us connected to the VHoA members holed up in the van a block away. I kept my eyes peeled for any sign of the vampire or his two fae companions. Since the girls rotated, we didn't know which two would be in here tonight.

We passed a circular bar to our left, three rows of people surrounding it. Dollar bills and plastic cards caught between fingers waved in the air like flags, their owners trying to catch the attention of one of the six harried bartenders trapped in the center. To the right, booths and tables were tucked against the wall, lit only by a handful of glass-enclosed sconces spaced at random intervals. A group of women talked and laughed at a table covered in empty shot glasses. A couple made out in the next booth over, taking advantage of the shadows. Small groups of men huddled together, nursing sweating brown bottles while scoping out the women strutting by in low-slung dresses. No vampires.

Once we'd broken out of the crush of people around the bar and navigated the narrow walkway, the space opened up to a dance floor jam-packed with people. I could hardly make out the wooden floor beneath them. Arms flailed, bodies writhed, lights swirled. The fae women might have been in there, but it was impossible to pick out faces from this vantage point.

On the other side of the dance floor was yet another bar that took up the back wall, flanked by restrooms. Another alcove of seating took up the space to the right of the women's room. We headed into the seating area, scanning the crowd for any sign of our undead mark.

I stopped beside a pillar and rested a shoulder against it, pretending to be taking in the crowd. Welsh stopped nearby, doing the same, facing the way we'd just come. I discreetly peered over his shoulder. Only halfway through my scan of the back wall, my senses flared. A dark-haired man sat in a U-shaped booth, his back against the curve of the U and his arms stretched out wide to rest on the backrest. A young pretty girl sat on either side, each one perched in front of his crooked arms. He wore sunglasses and gloves. Even without those odd accessories in a warm, dark club, the guy oozed a "stay away from me if you don't want to die" vibe. No wonder he needed help finding food.

The trio looked casual enough, but the longer I watched, the more I was struck by how preternaturally still they all were. The ice melting and shifting minutely in the tumbler in front of the man moved more than these three did.

I scratched my nose to briefly shield my mouth as I whispered, "I see them. Different girls than the ones from the footage."

Welsh stiffened for a moment, probably startled by the sound of my voice coming through his earpiece. He didn't turn around to confirm that I'd found the vamp. Instead, we faked small talk. We were five minutes deep into a conversation about the weather when the guy moved slightly, leaning close to the girl on his left. She bobbed her head periodically, listening intently to whatever he whispered in her ear, though she never took her gaze off the dance floor across from the alcove of seating they were in.

When the man leaned back, reclaiming his previous position, the girl scooted along one arm of the U-shaped booth, stood, adjusted her skintight dress that hit her mid-thigh, and then strolled forward. I watched as her flat expression morphed the more she walked. Her shoulders relaxed, her chin hiked a little higher to the ceiling, and a small smile graced her face. It wasn't until she was a few feet from us that I recognized her. Bonnie. The friend of Holly, the waitress at the Ghost Lily, who had tried to get Paisley to go back down the stairs, away from Leon and the private rooms, and had shown me a picture of Bonnie. Holly, who was still kicking herself for not doing more to stop her friend from getting too caught up in the pretty lies coming out of Oliver Randal's mouth.

I squinted into the dark, willing the shape of the other girl to become clearer, but she was too far away. Even if she wasn't Nyla Stone or her friend Vian, Bonnie's presence at least proved that this was where Luma fae girls ended up—at least for a little while. I figured fae traffickers were like human ones, constantly moving girls around so they could never feel fully grounded anywhere, always moving them farther and farther from their homes. Nyla had been gone long enough now that they could have moved her clear across the country, assuming she was still alive.

"Spotted a Luma girl," I said into my hidden mic, watching as Bonnie strolled past me and headed toward the circular bar.

When I pushed off the column to follow her, Welsh's arm snaked out, his hand around my forearm. "There's a big guy beside the dance floor who's been watching us. My gut says draken."

A draken? Here?

"You try to talk to the Luma girl," Welsh said. "I'll watch the draken. If he follows you, back off."

Heart hammering in my ears in time to the thrumming beat of the music, I clapped Welsh on the shoulder—that was a "wish me luck with the hot girl" bro-gesture, right?—and headed after Bonnie. I stuck one hand in my pocket and kept the other one hovering near my leg, protecting the glamoured mace. I slipped into the throng of people in the crowded walkway, feeling bodies closing in behind me and swallowing me up. Bonnie's head of dark curls moved slowly through the crowd. Dozens of heads turned her way. Men watched her in open appreciation, but no one approached her, alcohol not yet prominent enough in their veins to convince them they were actually in her league.

I quickened my pace, pushing my way through the crowd until I was right behind her. Leaning forward, I said, "Is that you, Bonnie?"

She whirled so quickly that to anyone watching, it probably looked like I'd just said something offensive. "How do you know my name?"

"I'm a friend of Holly's."

Bonnie swayed on her feet and I reached out to grab her by the elbow. When she didn't shake me off, I said, "This way," and dragged her to the left, into the dark seating area. The group of women had abandoned their table, empty shot glasses and lipstick-blotted napkins the only evidence they'd been there. They were probably on the packed dance floor. The couple in the next booth over was still going at it. I backed Bonnie into a corner and stood in front of her, hopefully looking like a guy chatting up a girl in a bar. Nothing to see here, folks, keep moving.

Bonnie stared up at me, her features neutral, though her large doe-like eyes scanned every inch of my unfamiliar face. She was cute in an almost kitschy way—like those personified animals created by the likes of Richard Scarry or Lisa Frank. Cute in the way that you inherently wanted to protect her, but striking in the way all fae were. When I'd seen her picture on Holly's phone, I'd pegged her as half-elf and half-faun. The faun part still rang true, but now I guessed that one of her parents had been human.

"How do you know Holly?" she asked.

"I met her at the Ghost Lily. She's been worried sick about you. I have friends here tonight. Friends who can get you back to Luma."

Her eyes widened, scanning the area behind me. "He won't let me leave."

"There are more of us than there are of him. We can get you out. What's the other girl's name? Are there more of them here with you? Fae, I mean?"

Her wide gaze snapped to my face. "You know ... what I am?"

"Yes. And I know what *he* is, too."

A tinny voice sounded in my ear. "I think the vamp is heading your way, Harlow. He seems to be looking for Bonnie—maybe their bond is allowing him to feel her distress." It sounded like Welsh. "Shit. Another draken is in here and following him now, too. Back off Bonnie until we get a sense of what he's going to do."

Bonnie suddenly stiffened in front of me, her face going slack. Robotically, she said, "I do not want to return home. I am happy here. Please tell Holly that I hope she has a happy life. I must get back to Stan."

"Stan?" I blurted. "The vampire's name is *Stan*?"

She sidestepped me, intending to move around me. I grabbed her by the arm before she could.

"I know you're under the influence of Bliss," I hissed. "We can get that crap out of your system and *then* you can decide if you want to stay."

She stared, those doe eyes wide and unblinking. I couldn't be sure if it was a trick of the light, but for a moment it looked like a slit of black ran horizontally through her light brown iris, like a goat's eye. Some deep protective instinct made me want to toss her over my shoulder and bolt for the door.

And then, that adorable-faced young woman, with her features flat and her posture relaxed, screamed bloody murder.

"Help!" she shrieked, flailing in my grasp even though I had a gentle hold on her arm. "He won't leave me alone! Help!"

I let go, hands up.

"No means no, you creep!" She had only taken two steps away from me when she stumbled back. Something shimmered in front of her, about chest height. The sword. The shimmer darted toward her and she skittered back, her cries for help extinguished.

"Harlow! What the hell is happening over there?" That was Caspian in my ear now. "Welsh and a draken are in a full-on fistfight. Beth is heading that way to help. Jacob and I are headed for you. The vamp and the draken will get there first, though. Get out of there."

"Sword!" I hissed, people hemming me in as they tried to assess if the young, innocent girl was in any danger. "Let's go!"

Instead of listening to me, the sword shook its glamour loose. The crowd gasped. What was it doing now?

The sword got itself into an inverted position, hovering between me and Bonnie, and then it tossed itself at her. Instinctively, Bonnie reached toward the sword, whether to shove it away or grab it, I couldn't be sure. Her hand wrapped around the hilt, and then her doe eyes went glassy for several long moments. Everyone crowded around me seemed to hold their breath, waiting. The music kept thumping in the background, clubbers talking and laughing in the distance, oblivious to the altercation happening in the shadows.

"Incoming!" someone shouted in my ear and my head whipped to the side, watching in horror as a force barreling toward me parted the crowd.

I stumbled away from the sword and Bonnie, then started shoving my way to the left, back toward the entrance. Caspian was apparently heading my way, but from which direction?

"Move!" I shouted as I pushed my way through the tangle of bodies. "Out of the way!"

"I'm coming, Harlow!" Caspian shouted, and I wasn't sure then if that had been in my earpiece or not. "Keep running!"

"I'm trying!" I said, putting weight behind my wide shoulders and using those to get people out of my way, like a linebacker. But after three hard hits, my vantage point changed suddenly. Curls bounced in my peripheral vision. "Shit! I lost the glamour!"

Something grabbed me by those curls and yanked me back with such force, I was sure I'd have a bald spot. I screamed, stumbling over my own feet as the draken man dragged me across the ground I'd just fought to cover.

Though my vision blurred with tears, I spotted a man stalking toward me, his hands whipping furiously through the air as he conducted an invisible orchestra. Caspian! His lips moved quickly, but I couldn't hear anything he said, which was probably the fault of the relentlessly thumping music.

"I suggest you get out of the way," a voice said in my ear. That one was Beth. "He's cooking up one hell of an air spell."

I kept stumbling backward as the jackass pulled me by my hair. I dropped one hand to my belt and yanked the mace out from its hiding place. After pulling the hood free, I shouted, "Watch out!" to no one in particular. Swinging blindly up and over my head, I made contact with something hard. Bright sparks of blue light flashed in my peripheral vision.

The draken screamed, and we were flung apart. He most definitely took a chunk of hair with him. Bastard. I avoided slamming into Caspian, but my landing was not graceful. People were finally screaming and running away from us, but their hasty, panicked retreat made it harder for Caspian to get through his incantation. The draken was on his feet again in an instant and coming at us fast. Even in the low light, it was clear he was pissed as hell.

Caspian slowly stalked forward, gaze trained on the draken, hands and fingers whipping through the air at a blurry pace, the spell words silent. I geared myself up for another attack, the electricity in the mace's head sparking.

I had just swung my arm back when a concussive blast of air boomed out of Caspian's splayed palms. The brunt of the blast hit the draken, but anyone in the radius of where he'd stood was tossed aside like debris in a windstorm. The music still piping through the speakers at a deafening volume overpowered the screams from onlookers. At least half of the club's patrons had flooded out the open front doors already.

The draken got up too quickly. Why wouldn't he stay *down*? Caspian and I got into what I hoped was a fighting stance. "Where are you, Welsh?" I asked into the earpiece.

"Taking a long route back with the sword," he said, his breathing labored. "It just materialized a second ago and knifed the draken who'd been trying damn hard to kill me with his fists. He would have succeeded if the sword hadn't shown up. Let's just say that the folks over here who witnessed a seven-foot-tall man get stabbed to death by a sentient sword had the holy bejesus traumatized out of them. Much therapy will be needed."

Another voice joined in my head. "Could use some help from the sword over here!" Jacob's tone was just a hair over frazzled. "Two more of Stan's draken on the south end of the club are trying to drag the other fae girl out a back door. She's desperately trying to get to the vamp even though the draken are trying to protect her from *us*."

I was about to ask where Stan had run off to when I caught movement in the corner of my eye. The vampire, with Bonnie in tow, approached our little group. He had a necrotic hand wrapped around Bonnie's thin throat, and her body positioned in front of him like a meat shield.

I backed away from the hybrid and bumped into Caspian. We crept toward the circular bar. When Caspian's back hit it, he gasped and placed a hand on my hip to keep me from bumping into him. His breaths were ragged. That spell had worn him out, and it had merely slowed the draken down. Caspian wouldn't be able to use another spell like that for at least an hour.

We stood in a triangle now—me and Caspian in one corner, the furious draken in another, and Bonnie in Stan's clutches in the third. A few terrified onlookers peeked out at us from under tables, and I was almost positive a few huddled behind the cherrywood wall of the circular bar behind us, but otherwise, this section of the club was deserted. The sounds of Jacob, Beth, Welsh, and the sword battling it out with the pair of draken on the other end of the club clashed with a rowdy pop song.

Stan the hybrid cocked his head as he regarded us. "I see the Vampire Hunters of America have picked up a couple of new members. A sorcerer and a human playing with toys she's not strong enough to use. Say, Doug, doesn't this human look a lot like the one the Collective is looking for?"

Doug's chest still heaved. Several red welts marred his temple, and I guessed those were from my mace. My palm was sweaty around the hilt. It was nothing short of disconcerting that Caspian's air blast and my electrified mace hadn't flattened the guy.

"Twenty-five thousand is a lot of money," Doug finally panted. "Aren't they looking for a sorcerer, too?"

Stan, his eyes hidden behind a pair of sunglasses, smiled a slow smile. His white teeth gleamed like polished marble. He turned his head this way and that, making a dramatic show of scanning the room. "I don't see the human's magical sword. I bet we could get a lot more than twenty-five thousand for that."

Did the hybrid know about the goings-on in Luma because of the people in his supply chain?

"I'll tell you what's going to happen," Stan said, then used his free hand to push his glasses up into his wavy black hair. Even in the low light of the club, I saw the swirls of black dancing in the whites of his eyes. "My girls and I will leave, you walk out of here and never return, and I won't let the Collective know where you are. If you think you're safe from them in the mundane world, you're quite mistaken."

I found it very hard to believe this guy had a direct line to the Collective. He was no doubt getting information from the inside, though; someone from Luma was helping him.

Stan's head suddenly whipped to his right, black-swirled gaze homed in on something across the club.

In my ear, I heard Welsh say, "We got the girl. It's not Nyla. Knocked her out because she was desperate to get back to the vamp. Draken are dead thanks to the sword. Jacob and Beth are getting her to the van, then they'll double back to see if we need anything. Sword and I are coming to you."

Stan growled, his canines elongating. To someone beyond us, he said, "Get the girl."

I shot a look over my shoulder just as two more draken men I hadn't seen before took off at a dizzying pace across the entryway and out the doors.

"Two are headed outside!" I called into my earpiece just as Stan tossed Bonnie aside like a discarded coat, and he and the draken lunged for us. Bonnie hit the ground, but she didn't make a move to escape, merely cowered on the floor.

Caspian and I jumped apart and I readied my mace, electricity crackling between the spikes on its head. Caspian pulled free a polearm from where it hung on his hip. This was one of his Frankenweapons. I had no clue what it did.

The hybrid came at me with such speed, I froze. He was so much faster than the feral had been. The black in his eyes looked like wind-whipped thunderclouds. I swung wildly with the mace, like a baseball bat. He lunged to the side at the last second, his shoulder slamming into me. We went down, the air knocked from my lungs. Stan landed on top of me, pinning me to the hardwood floor. His necrotic hands squeezed my arms with such force, I was sure he'd crush my bones. He bared his teeth and dove for my neck.

Something bright blue zipped by in my peripheral vision and slammed into the trunk of the vamp's body. A split second later, the pressure of his weight disappeared, followed by a crackle of blindingly bright electricity. Bonnie screamed, flattening herself to the floor just as the vamp sailed overhead and crashed into the wall. I winced. A blink later, Welsh's pretty face swam into view.

"That lightning dagger is my new favorite toy," Welsh said, yanking me to my feet.

I didn't have time to thank him. A familiar snarling sounded behind me and I whirled around just as three ferals loped through the front door on all fours, their necrotic black claws clacking an uneven rhythm on the floor.

The sword darted around the draken who was squaring off against Caspian. The draken had his own weapon, though—a massive broadsword. I felt the magic coming off it, but the weapon moved at such a wildly fast pace, I couldn't clock any details about it. The draken was good—warding off Caspian's polearm and my sword at the same time.

Time seemed to slow as the ferals galloped toward me, black blood fanning out beneath their paper-thin skin, like the rotting roots of a tree. One of them was the female vamp I'd gone toe to toe with mere days ago. I recognized her face, her patchy black hair. One arm was bent at an unnatural angle; it clearly hadn't healed right after I'd smashed her elbow with the mace. Her wall-to-wall black eyes focused squarely on me. She wanted a rematch.

She launched off her back legs, springing toward me like a cat, claws out and swiping the air. I swung the mace like a tennis racket in a backhand swing. The jolt of the blast of electricity reverberated up my arm and I swore my teeth vibrated. The force rocketed me back and I barely kept my feet under me. Then another vamp was there, swiping with its blackened claws. I ducked, feeling wind pass over my head. I thrust out the mace, aiming for the vamp's kneecaps, but he jumped away.

I yelped when someone yanked me off the ground, my feet dangling a few inches above the floor. Something had me by the back of my tactical jacket, the top of the zipper pressing painfully against my throat. My feet flailed, looking for purchase, searching for something to kick. The mace was ripped from my hand.

"Want to see how bad this hurts, little girl?" a gruff voice hissed in my ear.

"Sword!" I called out, thinking nothing other than the reality that if the electrified mace head touched me anywhere near my very human heart, it would stop. That would be it. Lights out. Good night.

The draken holding me gurgled and something hot and wet splashed onto the back of my neck. I hit the ground, one of my ankles rolling, but I was on stable enough footing that I darted out of the way just as the giant draken, the side of his neck sliced clean open, tumbled forward, massive hand over the wound as he tried to hold the blood in. It dribbled through his sausage fingers.

I whirled around, taking stock of how the others were faring. The sword veered off, slamming into the side of a feral just as he made a snarling dive at Caspian's middle. One of the VHoA members, Jacob, had returned, but he was on his back, dead eyes focused upward as a feral tore into his neck with claws and teeth. The feral lapped up blood and tore off chunks of flesh. My stomach roiled as the sword beheaded the feasting feral. Caspian, getting his bearings back, rejoined Welsh, who squared off against a draken and the feral female.

Bonnie crouched beside the fallen Stan, sobbing over his body as she tapped his cheek. "Master! Master, you must wake up!" She frantically scanned the surrounding area, then darted a few feet away and snatched up a shard of a broken glass tumbler. I realized what she was going to do a moment before she did it.

"Bonnie, no!"

She glared, as fierce as any feral, and sliced the shard across her wrist. She pressed it to Stan's mouth. "Please!" she begged.

I ran for her, intending to knock her away from the vampire. Stan already looked one step too close to going feral himself. He was crazy-strong as a hybrid—how much worse would he get if he tipped too far in the wrong direction? Well, okay, all the directions were bad—I meant the *extra* bad direction. Stan came to with a snort, then hungrily grabbed hold of Bonnie's wrist with both hands, guzzling down the blood, his black-tipped tongue lapping up any of the fae blood that threatened to hit the floor. The blood glowed a faint blue. Bonnie moaned as the vampire's venom seeped into her skin, his teeth sinking in. The two writhed on the floor, both getting a euphoric jolt from the experience. I grimaced.

Changing tactics, I scanned the ground for my fallen mace. Maybe I could smash creepy Stan's face in while he was distracted. I spotted the crackling electricity of the mace under a table.

Stan had not only been revived, but had realized what I was up to. With unnatural speed, he got to his feet and sprinted toward me, snatching the mace off the ground seconds before I could.

I stumbled back as he gave the mace a few practice swings, the bouncing lines of electricity as blue as the blood dripping down his chin. He swiped the blood away with the back of his free hand and then assessed me with his unnatural eyes. The black in them seemed even more prominent now. I felt a pang of betrayal at seeing the mace in his hand, but had to remind myself that the mace wasn't alive like the sword was. It held no allegiance. It was just a weapon.

He smiled, his teeth stained blue. And then he sprang for me.

I scrambled away, tripping over a fallen body behind me and crashing to the ground. The hybrid was on me in an instant, the mace held above his head in a killing blow. It would smash me through the wooden floor and into the concrete foundation.

A loud humming sounded, and I glanced to my right just in time to see the sword careening for us. But it didn't aim for the vamp; it changed position as it flew, and some instinct made me reach out a hand to grab it. The hilt slammed into my palm. As I wrapped my fingers around it, a voice, a sensation, told me to *thrust up*.

So I did.

The sword clanged against the descending mace. My shoulder blade collided with the floor and spots bloomed in my vision, but the sword absorbed most of the impact, as well as the blast of electricity. The mace's power ricocheted off the sword and back at the hybrid, sending him off me in a powerful blast that flung him into another wall. With all the fresh fae blood in his body, though, he didn't stay down long.

Up.

I shakily got to my feet. The hybrid snarled, his black-tipped hand opening and closing. He charged. Heart hammering in my ears, I readied myself. I hoped the guys cut down their foes soon because I was going to need help.

Pivot left.

I did.

Other left!

I whirled the other direction, the vampire and the mace whizzing past me. The scent of burnt hair hit my nostrils a second before a severed corkscrew curl fluttered to the ground. If that wasn't a stab-worthy offense, I wasn't sure what was.

The hilt of the sword grew warm in my palm and a pulse of magic flowed into my hand, up my arm, and into my chest, filling it with warmth, like hot chocolate consumed on a chilly day. All at once, my vision sharpened, and I detected specific sounds rather than just a jumbled cacophony. I twirled right, the sword coming up in a sweeping arc that sliced the hybrid's hand clean off his arm. A spray of warm blood cascaded across my chest, but before I could recoil, I darted away and forward, preparing for the approach of the feral female, furious with me for wounding her master. Stan writhed on the floor, his severed hand twitching nearby like a dying insect.

Was this what the sword had been created to do? To give the wielder of the sword this much information all at once?

The words in my head weren't a distinctive voice, but a feeling—a deep-seated urge impossible to ignore. As the female feral came at me, I gave in to the magic. It was like I'd slipped into an in-between pocket in time, existing in a place two seconds into the future. I deflected every attack, surprised the feral at nearly every turn, and always avoided getting hit. I spun and ducked and parried and stabbed. I was vaguely aware of what these calculated moves were doing, but I was too far into the future to grasp what those things were. I had only one goal: defeat them all. I wouldn't stop—couldn't stop—until I neutralized the threat.

Sweat coated my skin, pooled at my lower back, dotted my hairline. Blood and gore coated my front, splashed across my face. My limbs ached, my chest tight from exertion, but I couldn't stop. I was caught in this graceful dance of destruction.

What felt like centuries or mere moments later, I slowed. The sword pulled itself from my hand and I swayed as the magic leached out of me. The warmth that had filled me retreated, and I shivered. I collapsed to a knee, then both hands. I sucked air into my lungs in great, gasping pulls then deeply expelled it, my chest on fire. Someone crouched beside me, and I knew they spoke to me, but I heard nothing beyond my ragged breaths.

My regular human senses snapped back into place a second later, the sounds of the chaotic club scene flooding back in like a typhoon. I screamed, hands on my ears, sure my eardrums would rupture.

A warm hand on my back. "Harlow! Harlow, can you hear me?"

Slowly, I unfurled from the fetal position I was in, the hard floor biting into my knees. I turned my bleary eyes on the man beside me. Caspian. "I can hear you," I croaked out.

"Holy hell, that was some freaky shit," came another voice. I didn't have to look up to know it was Welsh.

As I blinked away the haze, I saw what the sword and I had done. All three ferals lay dead or bleeding out on the floor. There were five dead draken—I hadn't even registered the arrival of the other three. Stan the hybrid was still alive but looked even more undead than he had when this all started. His stump wasn't actively gushing blood—because vampire—and the wound had closed, but his papery skin looked shiny, puffy, and black tendrils snaked across it. I felt itchy just looking at it. He sat propped up against the side of the circular bar, his feet stuck out in front of him. Bonnie had been subdued by Welsh, but she wasn't happy about it, and she flailed around in his grasp even though her hands were bound behind her back.

I glanced up at Caspian. He had the mace in one hand, the hood back on. "Has there been any word from the rest of the team? Did they find the girls at the house?"

Beth approached, limping badly. A gash on her forehead was bleeding profusely down the side of her face. "They got on the property and killed a handful of hybrids. A few others took off. They suspect the girls are in the house but haven't found them yet. They're inside now."

I rounded, albeit slowly, on the hybrid. The only way to truly kill a vampire was to cut off the head, but Stan was slashed up good enough that his healing magic would have a hell of a time patching him back up, fresh fae blood or not. The sword hovered in front of the wounded vamp, the blade's tip an inch from his neck.

I hobbled forward. "Where are the other girls?"

Stan snarled. "Might as well kill me because I'll never tell you. They're mine. Property of our nest. If you kill me, ownership will transfer to my second-in-command."

"Been in communication with *your nest* recently?" I asked. "Because VHoA raided the place while you've been busy here. There's a pretty good chance your second-in-command is already dead. A few members of your undead family—the ones who didn't run off—still have their heads attached. If you want them to keep theirs, I suggest you give up the girls. That's all we want."

Though it was hard to read the emotion swimming around in his eyes amidst all the undulating black tendrils of his fae-blood poisoning, the news had flustered him.

I squatted before him, even though my aching legs protested. "Where are the girls?"

"I need your word that once your people get them out, you'll leave the rest of my nest alone," Stan said. "We can always get more girls."

Bonnie screamed behind me, and Welsh cursed as she almost twisted away from him. "No, master! I don't want to leave with these people. I'm yours, not theirs!"

"I know, pet, but my nest is more important."

With an agonized wail, Bonnie burst into tears.

"I cannot live without him!" Bonnie said. "Kill me now! Stab me in the heart! Tear out my throat! No world is worth living in if I can't be with him. I need to feel his teeth in my skin. I need to feel his long, cold—"

"That's quite enough of *that*," Welsh said.

I glanced over my shoulder to find he'd placed a hand firmly over Bonnie's mouth. Her muffled sobs mingled with her impassioned plea for Stan to keep her by his side. Snot seeped out of her nose and Welsh struggled to keep her upright, her grief weakening her knees.

When I cocked a brow at Stan, he merely shrugged, as if this display was perfectly normal.

"I can call my second-in-command to tell him we've worked something out," Stan told me.

"Any funny business and you're not walking out of here," I said.

He held up his hands in a placating gesture, then frowned at his ruined, blackened stump. "I'll keep the phone call on speaker. You'll hear everything I say."

I nodded, then turned back to Beth. "Can you call Marisol and tell her what's happening?"

She pulled her phone out of her back pocket and tapped at the screen.

"Boss!" came a man's voice through the speakers of Stan's phone and I turned back to him. "Those vampire-hunting sonsofbitches raided the house. I've been calling you for the past half hour. Are you all right?"

"The girls and I are alive," Stan said, his tone calm when compared to the vamp on the other line. "We ran into trouble here. Those vampire-hunting sonsofbitches, as you call them, have us backed into a corner. How many are left in the nest?"

"There are five of us still here, master."

Stan's fist squeezed the phone in his hand. His jaw tightened, and he shot me a death glare. I shot one right back. "We have reached a compromise with the hunters. They're here now at the club and are listening in. I am in a very precarious position and if I do not give up the girls in the basement, I will be killed, as will the rest of the nest. We must protect the nest. Let the girls go."

The silence on the other end of the line was deafening.

Behind me, I heard Beth say, "We're just waiting for confirmation from the vamp that the remaining ones are going to stand down. The girls are in the basement."

"I understand, master," the man finally said. "The nest comes first. We will release the girls."

"We got it," Beth said. "Go."

"Excellent," Stan said to the man on the other end. Bonnie wailed behind Welsh's hand.

Caspian helped me back to my feet. I motioned to Beth, who still had the phone pressed to her ear. "Can I talk to Marisol? Maybe she can describe the girls and confirm Nyla is there."

She handed the phone over.

"Hey, Marisol."

"Hey, Harlow. Wait one sec," she said, then addressed someone with her. "Yeah, in the basement, they said. Go on. Just waiting on Paul. He's taking a leak in the bushes. Tiniest bladder ever on that guy. Excitement makes it worse. Sorry, Harlow. It's a bit nuts over here."

Bonnie shrieked, Welsh yelped, and then she was running across the room toward Stan to throw herself on him.

"Yeah!" Marisol called out in my ear. "The basement! Ugh, Paul, hurry up."

"I am sorry, my old friend," Stan said to the man still on the phone with him.

Bonnie let out a hysterical cry, doubling over in his lap even with her arms still bound behind her back. Where had Welsh gotten zip ties?

"It is my fault we were compromised. Perhaps I will do better in the next life," Stan said, his tone solemn.

My heart skipped a beat, my sixth sense flaring. "Marisol! Marisol, something is wrong. Can you get them—"

BOOM!

I flinched so hard, I almost dropped the phone. "Marisol! Marisol, what happened?"

"Oh shit. Oh shit," she muttered. "The back half of the house —the part VHoA was in—it just ... holy shit, it just exploded. They were in there ... they're all ... oh my God." The line went dead.

I rounded on Stan. "You sonofabitch! What did you do?"

He grinned.

"Did you just kill all those girls?" I asked in horror. "Is that why you said you can get more?"

Now he was laughing.

I was still staring into those unnatural eyes when the sword blazed red, swung back, and cut clean through Stan's neck. His head slid off his body and rolled several feet before bumping into Caspian's boot. Black bile-like blood oozed out of the wound.

My knees hit the ground before I realized my legs had given out. Had we come all this way only to condemn all those girls to death? I hoped it had been quick, even if it had been violent.

I expected Bonnie's grief to hit a fever pitch—something bad enough that we'd have to knock her out. But her cries cut off, as if someone had pulled a plug on her. She sniffed once, twice, then pushed herself up. She took one look at the headless body she was curled up on and screamed, scooting back as best she could while still bound.

"What the hell? Who …" She looked around the club. "Who are you?"

Pushing down my guilt, I crawled tentatively toward her. "Bonnie?"

She stared, eyes wide. "You … you know who I am?"

"I know you're best friends with Holly and that you're from Luma," I said.

Bonnie stifled a gasp. "You came to bring me home?"

Welsh hurried over. "Don't freak out. I'm coming up behind you to cut you free."

When she'd been unbound and had scrambled to her feet, idly rubbing her wrists, I said, "Yes, we came to bring you home." I eyed the headless body of the hybrid. "Do you know how many other girls were in the basement? Stan had his second-in-command blow up the house with our extraction team and the girls still inside."

Bonnie had been near tears, but a sudden realization chased them away. "They aren't kept at the house."

I rocked back on my knees as if she'd just shoved me. "They aren't? They weren't in the basement?"

"No," Bonnie said, shaking her head. "We were always drugged up. I don't remember much. But I know it wasn't at a house." Her brow furrowed deeply as she eyed the body. She gave his lifeless leg a sharp kick. "I just remember that it was a small space in a remote area and there were maybe ten of us?"

I frowned, wondering how we were going to find them now that Stan and all his minions were dead or on the run.

The air behind Bonnie shimmered, and I stood, watching in confusion as a copy of Bonnie holding the sword formed behind the young woman herself. I remembered then that the sword had forced Bonnie to grab it by the hilt earlier. Had it done its osmosis trick to pull out information about where the girls were being held?

The copy of Bonnie strode across the blood-soaked lobby, littered as it was with bodies, broken furniture, and smashed glass. The copy made it to the standing-open doors and turned to me, her expression hard and determined.

Welsh sidled up next to me. "We're going to follow the murder sword to some unknown location possibly filled with even more vampires and ferals, aren't we?"

I sighed. "Yep."

"Life is sure a lot more interesting with you around, Harlow Fletcher," Caspian said, coming up on my other side.

Groaning, I trudged after my sword, hoping this night didn't get any worse.

CHAPTER THIRTY-THREE

Battered, broken, and bleeding, we piled into one of the VHoA SUVs in the parking lot. Welsh drove, peeling out of the lot after the sword who, still using Bonnie's form, took off down the road on foot. Well, not really on foot because not even her cloned legs could move that fast. It was more of a very fast floating. I felt bad for anyone on the road tonight who might see this. The real Bonnie was in the back seat wedged between me and Caspian, but it sure as hell looked like a woman was hauling ass down the side of the road holding a sword aloft, like the wind-whipped maiden on the bow of a ship. If this didn't inspire roadside ghost stories in this town, nothing would.

While Welsh drove, Beth got back on the phone with Marisol, trying to determine how many casualties they'd sustained. And I called Felix.

"Harlow!" he answered almost immediately. "Are you okay? I—"

"I need you to listen," I said, and then told him everything that had happened tonight, including the dead VHoA member, Jacob, still lying on the floor of the club, surrounded by dead draken, ferals, and a hybrid vampire. "I assume the Collective is going to want to get a containment team over there ASAP to get rid of all evidence of magic. Lord knows how many of the humans in there took video of the mayhem and have posted it online already."

"Good God, Low ..."

"I know. Can you get Jacob out of there before all hell breaks loose in that club when a bunch of mundane folk find the carnage? We couldn't take him with us and his family deserves the chance to bury him."

"All right. I'm on it. Don't know how I'm going to explain how I know any of this, but I'll figure it out. Where are you headed now?"

I stared at the spectral form of Bonnie zipping down the dark, two-lane road. "No idea."

"Wonderful," Felix deadpanned. "Well, if you survive wherever you're going, call me."

"Will do!" I hung up.

It was silent for a moment before I heard Bonnie's soft voice. "You really know Holly?"

"I know her well enough to know she's been worried sick about you since you disappeared," I said.

Her quiet sobs filled the car, mingling with Beth's voice coming from the shotgun seat, talking softly to Marisol. It sounded like she was crying, too.

Twenty minutes later, the Bonnie clone veered off to the right. Welsh followed, driving down a paved road, then a dirt one, bouncing along past signs that said KEEP OUT and NO TRESPASSING. When he approached the closed gate of a chain-link fence surrounding a field of dead grasses, he hit the gas.

Bonnie and I linked arms as Welsh smashed through the gate, barreling down the dirt road that snaked off into the distance. There was nothing out here but an open field. Perhaps it was destined to become farmland, or was waiting for someone to buy it and cover it with a sprawling shopping mall, or cookie-cutter homes.

Abruptly, the Bonnie clone zipped to the right and stopped a few hundred feet from the road. She jutted the sword out to her side, pointing. I glanced over at the real Bonnie, wanting to ask her if this area looked familiar, but assumed it would be like asking someone if a white wall looked familiar.

Welsh stopped the SUV and the five of us piled out. A slight breeze whispered past, bringing with it the scent of dirt and dry grass. Except for the occasional skittering of small creatures rustling in the ankle-high weeds, it was silent out here. No movement.

I eyed the Bonnie clone and the sword in her hand, wondering what it expected us to do. Stepping a little closer, leaving Caspian and Bonnie behind me, I approached the area where the sword pointed. If I squinted just right, the air near the sword seemed to ripple, like the surface of a lake disturbed by a thrown rock.

"A veil," I said.

"Give me a second," Caspian said, and then his hands and fingers were a blur as he worked through crafting runes in the air. We all backed away from him, giving him space. He thrust his hands forward, palms out, and a familiar concussive blast of air hit the veil. The wind gust had kicked up dirt and bits of grass, spraying it across the surface of the shield, revealing the edge of what might have been a metal storage shed beyond the shimmering magic.

A moment later, something snarled. A feral vampire leaped through the veil, appearing before me in a blink. I scrambled back.

Thud, thud, thud.

Three more. All feral. All pissed.

I held out a hand, and the sword flew into it, as if drawn there by a magnet. I was ready for the flood of magic this time, though I'd come nowhere close to healing from the last time I'd done this. Senses heightened, perception crisp, I went after the ferals with the sword leading the way. I spun and sliced and stabbed, keeping the beasts good and distracted so the others could figure out how to get us through the veil.

By the time the sword released me, Caspian had burned a rune circle into the ground in front of the veil. I collapsed to my knees in the dry grass. Black, poisoned blood leaked from the ferals' bodies, soaking the earth. My stomach lurched, and I swallowed down bile. All I knew was that if more vampires of any stripe came at us, my companions were on their own. I couldn't handle any more of the sword's magic. My legs trembled beneath me even though I wasn't standing.

I watched as Caspian cast a spell with his rune circle, brilliant golden light shooting from the individual runes and creating an identical glowing rune circle in the air, like a projector. Magic pulsed out of the ground—I felt it in my knees and under my palms. It glowed brighter and brighter, and then Caspian thrust his hands out, palms first, just as he had with the wind spell. The golden light collided with the veil and it instantly dropped. The metal storage container went from not there to there.

"That's it!" Bonnie cried. "I remember. They're in there!"

I tried to get to my feet, but got the spins. I watched the group surge forward. Between the sword, the electrified mace, and Caspian's polearm, they got the padlock and its chains off the swinging steel doors, and the doors open. Beth clicked on a fae light, shining it into the dark interior. Ten mattresses lined the ground. Eight sets of eyes stared back at us.

I staggered to my feet, stumbling toward the swell of confused female voices.

"How did you find us?"

"Why can't I feel the vampire's connection anymore?"

"Where are we?"

"Can we go home?"

I reached the open doors, but listed to the side. Caspian hooked an arm around my waist to hold me up. I scanned the faces of the young women packed inside, their eyes lucid, expressions grim and hopeful.

"Nyla Stone?" I called out.

I got no reaction at first other than a faint murmuring among the women, and then the group parted, and a young goblin girl with long, elegant features, pointed ears, and dark hair stepped into view. I let out a shaky laugh, shocked to see her. I instantly recognized her resemblance to Mathias.

"Your brother has been looking for you for a long time," I said, smiling softly. Then my eyes rolled back in my head and everything went black.

CHAPTER THIRTY-FOUR

I woke on Caspian's couch. For a moment, I feared it had all been a dream—that we hadn't traveled outside Luma, that the hybrid vampire still had dozens of fae girls drugged and hidden away in the middle of nowhere, that Nyla Stone remained missing. But then I tried to sit up and the pain that rocketed through every inch of my body slammed me right back into reality. It had all happened.

"Caspian?" I rasped, my throat raw.

He was at my side in an instant, helping me sit up. A few seconds later, Welsh was there, too, forcing me to drink something that tasted like burnt cherries. I swallowed the concoction down and scanned the room, trying to get to my feet, but Caspian gently pushed me back down.

"Come say hi," he called out, "otherwise she's going to get up too soon and pass out."

My mouth fell open as three goblins walked in from the room to the right of the fireplace. Mathias, Geraldine, and Nyla. I burst into tears. The goblins ran over and threw their arms around me, which was awkward since I was still seated, but I didn't care. They all kept thanking me over and over and I was caught in an exhausting loop of crying and laughing, never settling on either for long.

When we'd calmed down, I said, "Vian's parents aren't in Luma, right? Are they on their way here to see—"

My stomach sank when I noticed the tears sliding down Nyla's pretty face.

"Oh no …"

"They …" Nyla sniffed. "The Bliss didn't take in Vian's system the same way it did with the rest of us. She fought the control too hard. They … they killed her." She hiccupped. "A month after they kidnapped us … they …"

Mathias wrapped his arms around his little sister and hugged her close to his side.

"I'm so sorry, Nyla," I said, the good cheer I'd felt just a minute before leaching out of me.

When she composed herself, Mathias let her go, but stayed close to her side. She looked from me, to Caspian, to Welsh, and back again, resolve sharpening her pretty features. "I heard a little of what the guys were talking about and I'm in. Whatever you need from me, I'll do it."

Caspian eyed Welsh for a moment, then said, "You've been through so much already, Nyla. We don't want you to feel pressured to do something like this after—"

"It's for Vian," she said, voice steady even as her eyes were lined in silver again. "I'll find a counselor or whatever later. Right now, I want to help. I know most of the other girls do, too."

Over the next twenty-four hours, as I slowly regained strength, thanks in large part to Geraldine's healing tonics, Caspian and Welsh interviewed the rescued Luma girls. There were five of them, and they'd all disappeared over the last two years. I recognized two of them from the posters stuck to lampposts in downtown Luma, their smiling faces obscured by flyers for restaurants and posters of lost pets. The other three girls—the ones brought here from Washington and Oregon—were in the hands of the vampire hunters. They were in communication with VHoA chapters in the Pacific Northwest, comparing notes and getting the girls back to their hubs in safe, discreet ways. It would be up to the families what they wanted to do once their girls returned.

I wasn't sure what exactly it was that the guys were planning to do, since I couldn't stay awake longer than a couple of hours at a time. The magic pumped into me by the sword had wreaked havoc on my body. It was like I'd run ten marathons in a row. The more I slept, the better I felt, but I missed out on the planning sessions.

Two days after our rescue mission, I was on the couch—as usual—and feeling better than I had in a while. I was on level 1087 of Lollipop Jumble and the sword lounged beside me. Welsh had assured me that he'd gotten word to Kayda I was okay, but it was killing me that it still didn't feel safe enough to talk to her.

Caspian plopped down on the couch next to me with a bowl of popcorn. Welsh sat on his other side. It was just before six in the evening. The smirks on their faces were enough to make any lady uneasy.

Before I could ask what they were up to, Caspian hit the power button on the TV remote and the large flat-screen on the wall across from the couch flared to life. It was the tail end of a sitcom.

"*Breaking News!*" flashed on the screen.

I glanced over at the guys and their grins only grew wider. I put down my phone and grabbed a handful of popcorn out of the bowl in Caspian's lap.

"Tonight, we're coming to you with breaking news. Forty-eight hours ago, the Collective put a plan into motion that would take their bounty hunters and werecat guards beyond the safety of Luma's veil and into the mundane world. For years now, the Collective has been working to track down the location of several of Luma's missing fae girls. Five young ladies in total have gone missing over the past two years, and we're delighted to report that all five have returned home thanks to—"

The picture of the smiling human woman behind an anchor's desk glitched, shuddered, and then was replaced by Nyla Stone.

She sat before a slate-gray wall in a chair, her legs crossed. Her back was straight and her expression determined.

"My name is Nyla Stone, and I was kidnapped a year ago." In a calm, straightforward tone, she told the citizens of Luma about her ordeal. She told everyone what was in Bliss, and about the network of people in Luma working with those outside. A network that got young fae women out of the hub and into the mundane world to be subjected to the whims of vampires being driven slowly mad by fae blood. Nyla made sure everyone knew there had been *six* girls from Luma, not allowing the Collective to sweep Vian's death under the rug.

Two other girls told their stories, too. Their family members told their audience that they'd tried for months to find their daughter, only to have the police shut them down at every turn. A mother tearfully told the camera that a werecat guard had bullied her into dropping the investigation.

A message popped up on-screen—white letters emblazoned on a dark background. *Whose side is the Collective on? What aren't they telling us?*

After ten solid seconds, the image of the message glitched, and then the openly shocked face of the female news anchor was back.

She coughed awkwardly. "We'll be right back after this commercial break." She yanked off her mic and darted off-screen before the promised commercials materialized.

I blinked several times in dumb silence, then turned abruptly and slugged Caspian in the arm. "Holy shit, man! How in the hell did you pull that off?"

"Money might not be able to buy you happiness, but it can buy you a premium TV slot. Especially when the media here is bought off so often, they hardly blink when you make outlandish requests," Caspian said.

"It's true," Welsh said, leaning forward to look at me. "We went into the office of the news station—glamoured, of course—and requested to speak to the showrunner. The guy balked at the request at first and we thought we'd misjudged the whole thing.

Then Caspian tacked another zero onto the end of the proposed figure and the guy instantly relaxed and said, 'Do you want six or seven in the evening?' If a chaotic neutral guy ever existed, it was that dude."

The Collective had to be next-level furious.

I jumped when my phone rang. "Hi, Felix," I said in greeting. When I'd gotten back into Luma—which I still couldn't remember —I'd texted him to let him know I was still alive. We hadn't talked at all since then.

"I can't believe you pulled this off," Felix said, his voice subdued but awed. "Between this and several videos going viral of you and ... *Caspian Blackthorn* ... involved in a very magical-looking battle in a mundane club, well, let's just say the Collective is a bit preoccupied right now. I'm not saying the threat of them coming after you is gone, but they'll be distracted until they can scrub this from the mundane media."

Unsure of how to tackle any of that, I said, "Thanks for making sure Jacob got brought back to Luma."

"I don't know how much I did other than make myself look suspicious," Felix said.

I'd talked to Marisol once after I'd been back and knew Jacob's body had been returned to his family. The chapter lost seventy-five percent of their group that night in the blast. Her cousin had been in the surveillance van, watching the cameras and monitoring the feed coming through the earpieces. But people Marisol had been friends with for years were gone. If she hadn't been waiting for her team member to relieve himself in the bushes, she would have been in that blast, too. Her survivor's guilt was eating away at her. My own guilt at being the reason any of them were out there ate away at me.

"You didn't hold a gun to any of our heads," Marisol had said, her voice devoid of emotion. "We were out there that night because we believed in the cause, too. We're all glad that nest is destroyed and that the girls are home. It's a dangerous job. We all know that. I'm still glad to have met you."

I'd cried for an hour after that call.

"I know I can't make you do anything," Felix said now, redirecting my attention back to the present. "But leaving Luma while they're distracted can only help you. Public sympathy isn't on their side and there's already chatter among citizens here that maybe you're not that dangerous after all. That you knew what was happening with those missing girls and you stole the sword to help them escape. The Collective might eventually decide that treating you like a hero will turn citizens back to their favor, but that's less likely to happen if they catch you while they're at the height of being royally pissed and needing someone to pin that anger on."

I chewed on my bottom lip.

"I genuinely believe they'll eventually change their tune about you," he said, taking my silence as acceptance. "But you have to give them time to cool off. They have to tear this city apart and not find you."

The thing was, I'd already thought of all this. I was sick of looking over my shoulder every second. I was sick of being cooped up in this house. If I left Luma, I could breathe. I could find some mundane city to get lost in for a while.

"Thanks, Felix."

He sighed. "Let me know what you decide."

Public opinion continued to swing out of the Collective's favor over the next few days. People protested in the streets on my behalf because I'd helped bring the girls home. They didn't think I should get off scot-free since I *had* killed four shifters, but maybe a reduced sentence. Still, I knew if I went directly to the Collective, that would be it for me.

As much as it pained me, the best thing to do was to leave Luma.

I looked down at the sword by my side, the sword that had made it possible for people as untrained in combat as Caspian, Welsh, and I were to still be alive and on this couch now. A sword that had asked me once, in its own way, to figure out where it had come from.

It had helped me. It was only fair that I helped it now. I didn't know how I'd do this all on my own, but I'd figure out a way.

Later that night, after Welsh had gone home, Caspian and I ate directly out of an ice cream carton that Welsh had brought us. Caspian sat on one side of the counter and I stood on the other, arms leaning on the surface as we alternated scooping out large spoonfuls of vanilla shot through with swirls of caramel.

"You're planning to leave, aren't you?" Caspian asked, his focus on scraping caramel off the side of the container.

"Yeah. I need to lie low for a while, and I made a promise to the sword. I figure I'll head up to Washington. Maybe that sunken pirate ship found off the shore there a year ago was where the sword came from. Sounds like a bunch of people involved in that whole mess had to sign Soul NDAs to be part of the cover-up, but it's the only lead I've got right now." I dunked my spoon into the container, since Caspian had finally extracted his.

"Want company?"

I glanced up, the spoon caught between my lips. I slowly pulled it free. "Really?"

He shrugged. "I'm sick of being in this house, too. Sure, Welsh could keep glamouring me to give me a chance at a life here, but I can't do that forever. A little adventure will do us both some good. I feel like I owe the cutlass, too. We'd all be very dead if it hadn't been with us."

I shot a look across the room, where the sword was tucked inside the duffel bag. "It *would* be convenient to travel with someone with gobs of cash."

"Oh, so you only want me around for my money?" he asked before stuffing an ice cream-laden spoon in his mouth, his brows arched.

"Well, it's not for your personality."

He snorted a laugh. "I think you've been spending too much time with Welsh."

"Probably," I said, then studied him. Not an iota of doubt clouded his expression. "Company sounds great. When do we leave?"

"First thing in the morning?"

My stomach flipped. "Perfect."

When Welsh returned in the morning, he wasn't at all surprised to find us packing. Maybe Caspian had already talked to him about it. Maybe he figured, just as we had, that Luma wasn't the best place for us right now. He didn't offer to come with us. He loaded us up with glamour potions and gave us a full box of glamoured accessories.

"I'll be your eyes and ears here," Welsh said. "I'll let you know when I think it's a good time to come back."

Caspian gave him a bro hug goodbye, and they stared at each other meaningfully for a few long seconds, having a silent conversation. When Welsh hugged me goodbye, my eyes widened, unsure of how to react. After a moment, I wrapped my arms around his middle.

When he pulled back, he stared at me meaningfully, too, then said, "Don't do anything too stupid and get him killed, okay?"

"I'll do my best."

He flashed me his worst zombie-warlord-covered-in-sores smile, and I screamed bloody murder. He flipped back to the boy band hottie a second later. "You're going to miss me. Admit it."

"Chaotic evil monster," I muttered, hand over my racing heart. "Can I ask you a favor, though?"

He cocked a brow.

"Keep an eye on my friend Kayda? Let me know periodically that she's okay?"

Welsh nodded. "I can do that."

"Tell the Stones we say goodbye, too," I added.

"Will do."

On our way out of town, each of us wearing a glamour, we stopped by the rookery on the edge of Caspian's property. Welsh would make sure Caspian's birds were fed and taken care of, but Caspian wanted to check on the falcon before we left. I hadn't seen the bird since the night it had arrived at the factory with a note from Caspian, telling me to meet him in the rail yard. That felt like a million years ago.

The rookery had half a dozen birds in it, all of them a little larger than their mundane counterparts. They came and went as they pleased, but on the rightmost wall was a row of whistles, each one labeled with the name of a different bird. The only birds inside at the moment were a pair of dozing barn owls, their eyes closed and heads pulled into their fluffy necks. They hardly stirred when we stepped inside.

After Caspian blew the whistle for Rory, he turned to me. "Would you like to use one of them to deliver a message to Kayda?"

I blinked. "Really?"

"Sure. A songbird would be less conspicuous than the massive falcon. I know you've wanted to talk to her. A bird courier is slightly more personal than a teleposted note written in Welsh's terrible scrawl."

I laughed. "That would be great. Thanks."

He directed me to the small writing desk in the corner, magically not covered in bird poop, as he plucked another whistle from the wall.

I grabbed a small slip of paper and a pen and thought long and hard about what I wanted to say to Kayda. We hadn't gone this long without talking since elementary school.

I wish we could eat ramen until we burst. I hate that I haven't been able to call you. I promise I'm safe, but I've been scared to draw too much attention to you. I'm leaving the city, but not forever.

Stabby, Mr. Supervillain (yes, really!), and I are going on an adventure. Grayson will be jealous. I miss you.

I rolled the note into a tiny scroll, then headed back to Caspian. A scrub jay the size of a house cat sat perched on Caspian's arm. He held a hand out for the scroll. Once the note was tucked inside the tube attached to the bird's leg, I gave Caspian the address, as well as the best time for delivery. The bird waited patiently while Caspian drew intricate runes on its legs and feet.

Once done, he said, "Fly true, my friend."

With a squawk, the bird took to the air, flying up and out the open skylight in the ceiling of the dome-shaped rookery.

Rory the falcon arrived shortly afterward, alighting on a waist-high perch. The small tuft of fur attached to his hooked beak suggested that Caspian's call had interrupted his breakfast. Caspian ran the back of his forefinger along the bird's beak, and given how the bird's eyelids closed contentedly, I figured he wasn't too upset about missing a meal.

"I'm going away for a while," Caspian said. "Can you watch the place for me? Welsh will be around, but you know how he is …"

The massive bird clicked his beak and flapped his wings, presumably in agreement.

"If you see anything that makes you think we need to return, or you think there's something vitally important that I need to know, come find me. I trust your judgment." He laughed. "No, Welsh throwing a house party doesn't count."

One of the bird's beady eyes swiveled to me.

"Yes, the same applies to her," Caspian said, then wrinkled his nose. "I'll ask."

"Uhh … Harlow? Can I ink a rune on Rory using your blood? It will allow him to find you better should he need to," Caspian said.

I cocked my head. Did Caspian speak to animals in general? Or just to Rory? "Sure …"

A minute later—my pricked finger wedged between my teeth—Rory had a new blood rune painted on his leg. The bird took off to finish his breakfast.

"Ready?" Caspian asked as he locked up the rookery and reset the ward on the doors.

"Ready," I said, eyeing my new companion with curiosity as we walked back to his car and climbed in.

As we pulled out onto the dirt road behind his property, I rolled down my window and let the warm summer air tousle my curls. We had two one-way travel talismans to get us out of Luma. If—*when*—we came back, we'd need to get new ones to get us back through the veil.

He chose a section of the veil in the northern part of town in the Warehouse District, though it wasn't an official exit. We clutched the talismans as Caspian gunned it through the veil, the magic washing over us like a bucket of ice water. I shook off the chill and glanced down at the talisman in my hand, now looking like nothing more than a flat circle, the magic inside it spent.

I turned in my seat and watched the slight ripple in the magic wall settle. All I saw now was a desolate field dotted with the occasional scrubby brush. Luma was gone.

Turning back in my seat, I closed my eyes, letting the knot of tension that I'd been holding onto since the day the sword came into my life unfurl. We were free for now. I already felt lighter. It was strange to feel such relief at leaving my beloved city, but the relief told me this was the best choice, even if homesickness kicked me in the stomach later.

I grabbed my cell phone and texted Felix.

ME
Took your advice. I left the city.

He started and stopped typing three different times. Finally, he replied with:

FELIX
Stay safe.

We hit the highway soon enough, zipping farther and farther from home. I tapped a few buttons on the radio, an upbeat song filling the car. I kicked off my shoes and propped my feet up on the dash. Caspian's thumb tapped in time to the beat of the music.

I glanced over and he offered me a small, brief smile before refocusing on the road. I knew so little about this rogue sorcerer, and even less about the sword in the duffel bag lying next to my thigh.

I had plenty of time to unravel both mysteries.

For now, I would revel in this new adventure stretching out before me like a highway.

Want to see what's up next for Harlow and her friends? Find out now in Wicked Treasure!

ALSO BY MELISSA ERIN JACKSON

Thank you for reading *Diabolical Sword*! If you enjoyed this story, please consider leaving a review. Reviews mean the world to authors. Reviews often mean more sales, and more sales means more freedom to write more books.

If you'd like to read a **free** short story starring Harlow's parents before they get to Luma, you can find *Veiled Threats* at https://melissajackson-books.com/the-charm-collector/veiled-threats

Next up in Harlow's adventure is *Wicked Treasure*. If you'd like to be notified when the book is released, you can join my newsletter at melissajacksonbooks.com.

If you're interested in a lighter story, try *A Mythical Case of Arson*, the first book in a fantasy cozy mystery series set in the same universe as the Charm Collector series!

MELISSA ERIN JACKSON

A Mythical Case of Arson

A MYTHICAL PET SITTING MYSTERY

Just when she thinks her day can't get any weirder, she finds a baby dragon ...

Deandra Hendricks works her fingers to the bone at two jobs to keep her Los Angeles apartment. With a rapidly dwindling savings account, the prospects for her future are bleak. So when her cousin invites her to visit Axia—the hidden, magical hub their grandparents retired to—she agrees. Deandra doesn't possess a stitch of magic herself, but a long weekend vacation in a strange new town might be just what she needs.

Her first day in Axia is so bizarre, though, she wonders if her bleak life in Los Angeles hasn't been so bad after all. And, just when she thinks her day can't get any stranger, she finds a baby dragon trapped in a dumpster. At a loss, she takes a trip to the vet, hoping they can help find the little guy's owner.

The dragon, it turns out, only appears in its true form to her, while everyone else sees a dire wolf puppy. She and the vet discover that as long as the dragon wears his bespelled collar, his true identity is hidden. Someone went to great lengths to keep this supposed-to-be-extinct animal a secret.

Then the "dog" is accused of arson and is seized by authorities.

Determined to help him, Deandra searches for the real arsonist. She catches wind of a thriving black market that's populated by those who would stop at nothing to claim an animal this rare. She must work quickly to clear her dragon's name, because if he falls into the wrong hands, she could lose him forever.

Also available as an audiobook!

If you're looking for a ghost-filled paranormal tale, consider *The Forgotten Child*, a haunting mystery starring a reluctant medium.

The dead can speak. They need her to listen.

Ever since Riley Thomas, reluctant medium extraordinaire, accidentally released a malevolent spirit from a Ouija board when she was thirteen, she's taken a hard pass on scary movies, haunted houses, and cemeteries.

Twelve years later, when her best friend pressures her into spending a paranormal investigation weekend at the infamous Jordanville Ranch—former home of deceased serial killer Orin Jacobs—Riley's *still* not ready to accept the fact that she can communicate with ghosts.

Shortly after their arrival at the ranch, the spirit of a little boy contacts Riley; a child who went missing—and was never found—in 1973.

In order to put the young boy's spirit to rest, she has to come to grips with her ability. But how can she solve a mystery that happened a decade before she was born? Especially when someone who knows Orin's secrets wants to keep the truth buried—no matter the cost.

Also available as an audiobook!

ACKNOWLEDGMENTS

I always thank my early readers first, as you all help keep me sane. Some of you have just joined my army of readers, and some of you brave souls have been with me from the beginning. I appreciate each of you.

Thank you, Mom, Jennifer Laam, Lauren Sprang, Margarita Martinez, Garrett Lemons, Cecilie Schulze, Cynthia Sandusky, Emilie Vecera, Taylor Boykins, Holly Starkey, Asa Ortiz, and John Parker.

Thank you, Danielle Fine, for these covers. I'm so glad they're finally out in the world for people to see. Thank you to the artists at Etheric Tales for the drawings of the sword and the travel talisman that graced the pages of the book.

Thank you, once again, to Justin Cohen for being my go-to proofreader.

To my Sunday accountability group, I'm glad we're keeping this thing going even though only half of us are writing something at any given time. Rebecca, Michelle, Cecilie, and Lauren, you ladies help keep me focused.

Sam, thank you as always for putting up with me, and for the long plotting sessions. I can't imagine living with a writer is easy. We're a weird lot. I love you to bits.

Finally, I want to thank my readers. Whether you've only read Harlow's story, or if you're a fan of Riley Thomas or Amber Blackwood, I'm glad you're here. I hope you'll give *Wicked Treasure* a try, too.

Onto the next!

ABOUT THE AUTHOR

Melissa has had a love of stories for as long as she can remember, but only started penning her own during her freshman year of college. She majored in Wildlife, Fish, and Conservation Biology at UC Davis. Yet, while she was neck-deep in organic chemistry and physics, she kept finding herself writing stories in the back of the classroom about fairies and trolls and magic. She finished her degree, but it never captured her heart the way writing did.

Now she owns her own dog walking business (that's sort of wildlife related, right?) by day ... and afternoon and night ... and writes whenever she gets a spare moment. She alternates mostly between fantasy and mystery (often with a paranormal twist). All her books have some element of "other" to them ... witches, ghosts, UFOs. There's no better way to escape the real world than getting lost in a fictional one.

She lives in Northern California with her very patient boyfriend and way too many pets.

You can find out more about her upcoming books and join her newsletter at: https://melissajacksonbooks.com